An UNDETECTABLES Mystery

The Unfathomable Curse

COURTNEY SMYTH

TITAN BOOKS

The Unfathomable Curse
Print edition ISBN: 9781835412213
E-book edition ISBN: 9781835412220

Published by Titan Books
A division of Titan Publishing Group Ltd
144 Southwark Street, London SE1 0UP
www.titanbooks.com

First edition: September 2025
10 9 8 7 6 5 4 3 2 1

This is a work of fiction. All of the characters, organizations, and events portrayed in this novel are either products of the author's imagination or are used fictitiously. Any resemblance to actual persons, living or dead (except for satirical purposes), is entirely coincidental.

A CIP catalogue record for this title is available from the British Library.

EU RP (for authorities only)
eucomply OÜ, Pärnu mnt. 139b-14, 11317 Tallinn, Estonia
hello@eucompliancepartner.com, +3375690241

Printed by CPI Group (UK) Ltd, Croydon, CR0 4YY

Praise for

THE UNDETECTABLES SERIES

"A compulsively readable race against the clock to stop a supernatural killer – downright delightful and unapologetically queer."

Polygon.com

"Unputdownable. Grim and caring, twisted and witty, *The Undetectables* is gripping and charming in equal measure. You won't want to leave Wrackton, while also being really glad you don't live there."

Deirdre Sullivan

"If you aren't already deep into spooky season then here is the perfect book to get you in the mood."

Irish Examiner

"A fun and breezy urban fantasy novel that has an interesting take on using magical forensics"

SFBook Reviews

"If you're looking for a mystery that makes you think, mixed with a healthy dose of supernatural, diverse representation and some of the best dialogue I've seen in a long time then [...] *The Undetectables* is the book for you."

Geeking By

"I got so invested in these characters and by the last page I simply did not want to leave them behind. I'll take a hundred more cases that need to be solved by the Wrackton gang, even if I need to commit them myself."

Read By Ross

Also by Courtney Smyth
and available from Titan Books

The Undetectables

The Undead Complex

For every trans and nonbinary person,
present and future

Even when it feels like the end, it isn't.

Get up. Live. Thrive.

ONE

14 years ago (approximately to the day)

Agatha and Ethel Broadwick had wished death upon their youngest sibling from the moment she burst into the world screaming. Though this story is not entirely about them, it is important to know this.

The world – Occult and Apparent alike – holds a certain fascination with twins. Some believe they are a single soul split in half, resulting in an inherent *oneness* that must be upheld. That to *be* a twin, both members of this unwitting partnership must telepathically think the other's thoughts. That it is a necessity akin to breathing. That a biological event – a division of cells – plants *twins* firmly alongside *other* and *strange* and, occasionally, *ethereal* and, in the extremes, *evil*.

Agatha and Ethel loved to meet expectations, and so they were all of the above, though they were none. They understood their place in Occulture and the power their family held, and that they had roles to play. Agatha enjoyed baking and floral dresses. Ethel enjoyed botanical ventures and green velvet. By the tender age of twelve, they were vaguely aware they were meant to present a united front – be pretty, be particular, be marriage material.

Perhaps this is why their thoughts turned to murder so early in their lives.

The twins were in the back garden of Broadwick Mansion one soggy summer morning. Grey storm clouds covered Wrackton, though patches of sunlight broke through long enough to illuminate Agatha, perched primly on the swing hanging from a willow tree so old it had probably seen the beginnings of Wrackton, and Ethel, pushing her gently one-handed, absorbed in a botany book. Both were trying to ignore the shadow of their little sibling as she ran around the garden in a pair of dark denim dungarees, a notebook clutched in her grass-stained hands, her adventure bag slung over her shoulder.

The twins were waiting, as they had been from the second their grandfather, Cornelius Broadwick III, was pronounced dead some weeks ago.

Usually the Broadwicks had a strict yearly routine: autumn through late spring spent in Wrackton to host balls and attend meetings with the Unified Magical Liaison and the Night Mayor – a man called Vincent Van Doren, of whom Agatha and Ethel were very fond. This also allowed the Broadwick children to attend Apparent schools in the next town over – 'Mother always said Occult schools aren't worth their salt,' Agatha would say any time she was asked, which wasn't often – until the school holidays, when they would pack up their things, climb inside one of the family's SUVs, and drive to the Lake District.

To Wickermere.

To Rowan House.

To home.

This year was different. School wasn't out yet, wouldn't be for some weeks, but Agatha and Ethel heard things and sensed things and knew something had changed. Their parents, Imogen and Ezra, kept talking about *hauntings*, or *haunts*, in hushed tones, and the air was filled with a sense of anticipation.

The twins knew it would be today.

And that meant they had to act now.

'Look at Cornelia,' Ethel grumbled, throwing her book down, but Agatha already was.

In their beautifully manicured garden, Cornelia was the picture of defiant disharmony. She was lifting the backs of leaves and examining whatever insects she found there, oblivious to the general mood of the household as she loudly exclaimed in triumph whenever she found a particularly pleasing snail. Or whatever.

'I think it's time,' Agatha said, stopping the swing to speak softly in Ethel's ear.

Ethel, naturally, knew exactly what her sister meant.

'It's like we always say: this is the rest of our lives.'

'Besides, we aren't far off eighteen. In six years' time do we *still* want to be making excuses for her, instead of preparing for our roles inside the Ghoul Council?' Agatha asked.

They had been promised just that for their entire lives; they'd bent their entire existence around Wickermere and their parents' work on the Ghoul Council there.

'You're right, as always,' Ethel said, watching Cornelia roll underneath a shrub. 'I have not forgiven her for the Worm Incident last year.'

'Imagine how much happier Mother and Father will be without her in the car.'

'No one eating the best snacks,' Ethel – who was particularly fond of cheese and took it personally when someone ate the last piece – said.

Agatha bit her lip; she rarely hesitated. 'Will they take it the way we intended? Mother's highly strung at the moment. Father's not much better. I know they weren't close with Grandad Cornelius' – an understatement, as Cornelius Broadwick III had not particularly liked his son, or his daughter-in-law, and had had next to no time for his grandchildren even before he took ill – 'but it has to be weighing on them. There's the funeral, and then they'll be taking his place on the Ghoul Council.'

'What does that mean?' Ethel asked, and Agatha got a split second of smugness at knowing something her sister didn't.

'It means they'll be important to Occulture, like Grandad Cornelius and Great-Grandfather were. They're taking over the Council and everyone will have to listen to them properly. The Broadwicks will once again define things at the top,' Agatha said, though she was mostly quoting snippets of conversations she'd overheard and it was not, strictly, her own opinion on the matter.

'Hang on, how do you know all that?'

'I had to go down for water the other night and heard them talking. Mother's most direct competition is Uncle Harry' – who was not actually their uncle, and frowned at the concept of being regarded as such – 'because he's "much better positioned" for the role. I think she'll win, though. She has to. Grandad Cornelius wouldn't have left the management of

Rowan House to Father if he thought they'd just sign it over to someone who isn't a real Broadwick,' Agatha said, shuddering.

Neither she nor Ethel had ever had cause to consider the ethical dilemma of one family owning the base of operations of the only Council more powerful than the Unified Magical Liaison of Magical Municipalities, largely owing to them being twelve.

Ethel tilted her head in consideration. 'But what if Auntie Dot won?' It will come as no surprise to learn that this was not a real aunt, though she was softer on the idea of the title. The Broadwick line had thinned when Grandad Cornelius was born, and Agatha and Ethel had populated their family tree with semi-suitable stand-ins.

'What about her?'

'She'd hardly kick us out if she got Grandad Cornelius's job, would she? Great-Grandfather let the Ghoul Council stay in Wickermere as a *gift*, and Grandad Cornelius kept up the tradition. We can't have tradition if someone changes it!'

'Uncle Harry would probably make her kick us out. Or Mother and Father would allow it to happen – you know how they all are about following the rules. There's no point in worrying about it, Ettie.' Agatha smiled up at her sister. 'It'll never happen. Mother and Father are going to take over Grandad Cornelius's job, as Broadwicks should, and everything's going to stay exactly the same. Except for all the parts that will change. Besides, I heard Dorothy and Father have been working hard to bring in "fresh-faced rule followers" for the Council cabinet. To deal with the hauntings,' she suggested, hoping Ethel wouldn't push too hard on that last point.

'What's a cabinet?'

'I think it's just what they call the Ghoul Council Headquarters,' Agatha ventured.

'So it's like a special kind of cupboard,' Ethel said thoughtfully. 'Are you sure about this, though? They've been so short-tempered…'

'Ethel, we'd be doing *ourselves* a favour. Think of all the times they've had to shout at Cornelia to go away, especially in the last few weeks. All the ruined dinners. The fact she took the last piece of cheese,' Agatha added, neglecting to mention she was the one who consumed the other nine pieces before Ethel noticed. 'We could make everything much better. For all of us. For our family.'

'We *have* heard them say how difficult she is,' Ethel said slowly.

Cornelia, meanwhile, was lying on her stomach, nose in a notebook filled with her childish scrawl detailing the genus and colours and walking behaviours and whatever else she felt like recording about the bugs she'd uncovered, a thick pencil gripped in her muddy little hand.

She was utterly oblivious to the plot against her.

'You find the snacks and grab a shovel,' Agatha said, jumping to her feet. 'I'll check the coast is clear.'

Ethel complied, a lingering worry gnawing at her – there was a chance, however small, that the Broadwicks would *not*, actually, be happy with their decision.

The twins prepared the garden bunker.

Why there was a bunker in their garden, the twins had never thought to ask. It was a fixture of Broadwick Mansion, and that was as far as it went.

'If we drag the sundial in front of it, nobody would ever know it had been opened,' Ethel said, scraping soil and leaves away from the entrance. 'We can dig her back up when we return.'

'They'll be so pleased with all their free time, they won't want to bother,' Agatha said dismissively. 'If we're going to be going to Wickermere earlier and earlier every year—'

'Are we? I thought that was to avoid bringing Cornelia's beastly little friends away with us like she keeps asking.'

'Oh, Ethel.' Agatha tilted her head. 'Sometimes I wonder if we really are twins at all, or if I got the brains and you got… nothing.'

'I *will* tell Mother you said that,' Ethel said seriously.

'You won't. You'd have to tell her why I said it, and you won't want me to take credit for this plan.'

She was right, and Ethel wasn't happy about it. Their parents were mercurial at the best of times, and she didn't want to risk delaying going to Rowan House. Ethel missed her other bedroom there. One of the best parts of being a Broadwick, in her not-so-humble opinion, was that she and Agatha could be different versions of themselves. Wickermere meant solitude, and Rowan House was perfectly placed within the centre of that solitude for landscape paintings and propagation experiments in the greenhouse. It meant casual friends a few towns over – family friends, really – who they could go for ice cream with. Pissing Mother off right before what was set to be the best summer ever would start things off *terribly*.

'Father did always say secrets were best kept buried,' Ethel mused. 'It still doesn't excuse you being rude to me, though. Or for not telling me what you overheard right away.'

'You're right.' There was no apology. 'In that case, I also overheard them talking about some kind of Ghoul Council project. A really big, really important one.'

'What kind of project?' Ethel dropped the shovel and her sister shook her hair back so they could commence prising the bunker door open.

'It's something to do with the Witches of Bonemarrow Lake,' Cornelia said.

The twins jumped and Cornelia looked up at them, her glasses frames bent and speckled with dirt. It was unclear how much she'd heard, but the lack of annoyingly righteous indignation suggested she'd just wandered over.

'I heard them talk about it when I got sent home from school,' Cornelia said.

Against her better judgement, Ethel asked, 'What did they say?'

Cornelia shrugged. 'Something about drowning in red tape. They were talking to the Night Mayor. He seemed angry.'

That was not unusual for Van Doren, so it was not of particular interest to either twin.

'What are you doing with the bunker?' Cornelia asked suddenly.

'Nothing.' Ethel cast her sibling a disdainful look. It *was* typical of Cornelia to ruin everything at pivotal moments. 'Just enjoying the garden before we go up north.'

'Cornelia,' Agatha said, in that particular tone of voice both twins employed when they were about to do something dastardly. 'I think I saw a beetle down there, in the bunker. A big one. Very shiny. Why don't you go look?'

Cornelia paused, and Agatha waited with bated breath. She was, after all, smarter than Ethel when it came to getting people to do what she wanted. And Cornelia was only eight; she didn't know enough to distrust her.

Much to both their surprise, Cornelia climbed into the bunker. Agatha started slowly inching the bunker door closed while Cornelia combed around the floor.

'It's down there, you should curl yourself up really small,' Ethel said, tossing the snacks and a bottle of water in after her. The door was almost closed when the worst possible interruption occurred.

'Agatha? Ethel? Get Cornelia and come inside, we need you to pack. We're leaving this afternoon.' Ezra Broadwick's powerful-yet-measured voice boomed over the garden.

Ethel and Agatha exchanged glances. Agatha wanted to continue. Ethel wanted to cut their losses.

Ethel won.

They left Cornelia bewildered and stalked towards the house. Unusually, their father was wearing the sort of suit he normally reserved for the most important meetings. Even more unusually, he was wearing an expression normally reserved for Cornelia when she'd done something to upset the delicate balance in their household.

'Why are you both dirty?'

Agatha and Ethel clasped hands, bowed their heads, and whispered a spell to make the dirt disappear.

Ezra appeared briefly mollified. 'Today is very important. From the moment we arrive at Rowan House, I want you on your best behaviour. The funeral is tomorrow, and then a lot of changes are to happen. You keep Cornelia in line, you keep yourselves in line. For your mother and me. Won't you?'

'What kind of changes, Father?' Agatha asked sweetly.

'If everything goes well, tomorrow will mark the first day of the rest of our lives. Come, now.' He held his arm out to shepherd his children inside, then the soured expression returned.

'*Cornelia*,' he said, in the tone he reserved only for her.

Cornelia was covered in muck and had a shiny, horn-headed beetle in her hands. Ethel eyed it with particular disgust. The worst part of enjoying plant life meant dealing with the creatures who insisted on living in it.

'Agatha and Ethel tried to bury me alive,' Cornelia said, but Ezra was already casting a spell to clean her up, holding his hand out for the beetle that she refused to relinquish.

He never did hear what his twins did to his youngest child, even when told directly.

'Inside. Change into nice clothes, *no* dungarees,' he said, sweeping back into the house instead of commenting on the assassination attempt.

Cornelia turned on the twins before they could say anything else.

'You tried to kill me. You… you… arseholes!'

'Ooh, what a big insult,' Agatha said. 'What horrible little friend did you learn that one off?'

'My friends aren't horrible,' Cornelia said defiantly.

'I beg to differ,' Ethel said. 'And anyway, we didn't try to kill you. We just wanted you to disappear for a while.'

'Yeah, well…' Cornelia visibly struggled to find something, *anything*, to retort. 'I hope you disappear someday!'

Agatha and Ethel raised an eyebrow in unison, mirrors of each other.

'Good one,' Ethel said.

Cornelia's face twisted up into a frown as they walked around her, leaving her cupping the beetle in her hands.

'I do!' she shouted. 'I do hope you disappear! And nobody will try to find you cause you're so HORRIBLE. And me and my friends won't try to find you because you said *they* were horrible, and you'll be lost forever!'

The twins ignored her, climbing the stairs to their respective bedrooms, Cornelia's words hanging in the air like a hex.

PERIMORTEM I

Their targets were acquired.

A shovel hit the earth and parted it, soil falling away. The hardest bit was over, and the shovel had found a rhythm now they'd breached the soggy topsoil.

Soon they'd be through to their final resting place. The place the bodies would stare up from, unseeing, unhearing, unfeeling. Lying in suspended animation until the digger was ready for them again.

They won't have been seen for some time, and will not be seen for some time yet. Not until the decay becomes too much to bear and the ground must be disturbed once again.

They were digging, digging, digging, each mechanical movement a step towards what's to come next.

TWO

NOW

If the phrase 'be careful what you wish for' was a person, it would've taken Cornelia Broadwick tenderly by the chin and whispered, 'I told you so.'

Her card had been declined again, putting her purchase of a beautifully pinned *Chrysochroa castelnaudi* at risk, which led her to check her bank account for the first time in months, only to find that the available funds were £0.00.

A few frantic clicks later showed that she no longer had access to the family accounts, or her savings accounts (not that she was in the habit of topping those up). In fact, the only money she could see was in the Undetectables' joint account, and that looked scarily low.

'Mallory,' she hissed, but was promptly shushed by both Mallory and Diana, the latter of whom elbowed her sharply in the ribs to make her pay attention.

The fact they were at a funeral was irrelevant. Cornelia was broke.

'Mallory,' Cornelia said again, and Mallory leaned closer so she could whisper directly in her ear. 'We don't have any money.'

Mallory turned her head just enough for Cornelia to see her frowning as she took her phone, prompting Cornelia to remember where they were.

Observer Johnson stood over the open plot next to Vincent Van Doren's grave, droning on and on about Occulture and the Ternion – inappropriate, in Cornelia's humble opinion – to an audience of six.

Cornelia, Mallory, Diana, Night Mayor Dr Ray – the current Night Mayor/Medical Examiner of Wrackton, who had amassed more titles in the eighteen-ish months since she came to power – Detective Inspector Alyssa 'Sully' O'Sullivan, and the coffin being lowered into the ground, containing Jacob Gabbott's recovered remains. Or most of them.

Though his body had been recovered over a year ago, right as the Undetectables were taking down the Dollhouse Murderers, a significant amount of red tape and dithering had left Jacob's body in a freezer. Cornelia had seen many cadavers while she was studying entomology, and many more in the course of her work with the Undetectables, but she didn't want to think about what state his body must've been in.

It was a closed casket. Dr Ray had assured her he was definitely dead.

Mallory tapped Cornelia's wrist and handed her phone back, the notes app open.

> Parents cut you off almost eight months ago because you won't speak to them

Cornelia looked at her quizzically, and Mallory nudged her to keep reading.

They sent you an email at the time

Cornelia should've known it would come to this. She'd spent the best part of a year dodging their calls and making excuses not to be in the same room as them. It wasn't a surprise they thought money was her main motivation in life, and yet she found herself feeling mildly outraged they'd cut her off before attempting to confront her in person.

It wasn't her fault she couldn't – and indeed *wouldn't* – speak to her family. There was no question of her being in the wrong given that her parents were, very likely, murderers. It was especially grievous that they were the likely murderers of her friend and un-live-in ghost, as it recast the Broadwicks' enthusiastic hospitality towards almost-doctor-of-forensic-para-anthropology Theodore Wyatt (who had died at a Samhain ball in their home) into something a lot more guilt-ridden and nefarious. It was made all the more a particular sort of pickle by the fact she was co-founder of a PI agency that specialised in murders, and that the ghost in question had resulted in the agency making a collective home in the basement of Broadwick Mansion – though that was a problem she hoped to deal with at another, more convenient time.

'Morrigan and Hecate, your witch is our command. We return him to you, to the earth, to nourish the land. Jacob Gabbott will rest and his bones will feed the magic you guide us in,' Observer Johnson said, cutting through Cornelia's haze of fury.

While he was saying the words, it did not feel as though he meant them in the slightest. She knew he felt as the rest of them did: good riddance to the Whistler.

If she was being honest, her family had unusually good timing, giving her the gift of something else to funnel her worry into. It made what was happening in front of her much less of an issue.

Much less of anything.

Cornelia took a deep breath, feeling a familiar numbness flood over her limbs, leaving her light-headed and able to float above the scene with a detached indifference as Jacob's coffin was slowly lowered into the ground. She'd been allowing herself to, for want of a better word, *disengage* with her surroundings whenever she'd had to leave the house since the Whistler had abducted her eighteen months prior. It took the edge off the jangling, insistent fear that whispered she was in danger every minute she was outside the safety of her front door, so she'd come to almost welcome it whenever it happened. It was preferable to running screaming back to the relative safety of Broadwick Mansion, largely because she was sure that if she started screaming, she'd never stop.

Observer Johnson glanced at them over the rows of gravestones – they were standing several sombre yards away, which the Undetectables had thought would both be respectful, and would also stop Cornelia spitting on Jacob's grave, even if this was something she was sure she wouldn't stoop to doing.

She felt too far away to seriously contemplate it.

Above the scene, she saw herself and her best friends in their most appropriate attire – Diana had bullied Cornelia into wearing smart trousers and a jumper that was only two sizes too big. It was a muggy, cloudy day in Wrackton, and nobody wanted to be in the witch cemetery.

Cornelia had expected many unexpected things would befall them upon starting the Undetectables, Private Investigators – helping you detect the undetectable! – that fateful October eighteen months prior, but standing over the burial of their first serial killer to ensure he really went into the ground wasn't one of them.

Nor was anything else that had happened in that case, or any case they'd taken on since.

'What was all that?' Diana hissed, holding out her hand for Cornelia's phone. Cornelia shook her head even as Diana tried to prise her fingers off it, unlocking the screen in the process and opening apps at random.

'*—Ghoul Council member and acting spokesperson for the Unified Magical Liaison, Nova Khan, has issued the statement "do not fear". This comes in response to calls for the UML to increase security in the weeks following the recovery of the body of the most recent victim of what has been locally dubbed "The Wickermere Reaper"—*'

Cornelia fumbled until the news podcast stopped playing. Nobody else appeared to notice and the proceedings continued uninterrupted as she ignored the burning, curious looks from both Diana and Mallory.

A further complication in not talking to the Broadwicks since Katherine the ghost had shown Cornelia the horrifying truth: no matter how high-profile the Undetectables had become since the Whistler, any case the Ghoul Council stuck their oar into was off-limits. The risk of Cornelia having to *talk* to the Broadwicks was too high. Her reticence to go near the Wickermere Reaper case had created something in the realm of friction between her and the rest of the Undetectables, even if they understood her refusal.

But it didn't stop her following media developments in said case. Principles be damned.

Mallory opened her mouth to say something, when a shadow moving to her left caught Cornelia's eye.

'Oh, shit,' Cornelia whispered.

Observer Johnson stopped speaking, but for once it wasn't her fault.

The others pivoted owlishly to see a woman walking slowly towards them, leaning heavily on a cane as she moved over the soft grass. Rain beaded on her trench coat, her curly hair pinned neatly under what Cornelia could only describe as a 'widow's hat'.

Her face was drawn, but the resemblance was unmistakeable.

The same gait, the same bone structure, though her lips and eyes were somewhat sunken. There was a radiance to her that should've been expected, given her history with Van Doren. Any Apparent who caught his eye would need to be pretty exceptional.

'That's her,' Diana said softly. 'That's Delilah Gabbott.'

Jacob's mother. The catalyst to his actions. Where everything had started, even if that was never her intention.

Observer Johnson's expression was markedly neutral as she approached, particularly given that nobody had expected anyone to turn up, hence Dr Ray inviting the Undetectables.

Sully grabbed the stool Observer Johnson had been using earlier and placed it close to the grave. Delilah sank onto it gratefully.

Observer Johnson had been about to ask if the gathered members wanted to come and flame a handful of earth to toss into the grave, and Cornelia categorically did not want to do that.

'Let's move back,' she said, and they did, adding inches of distance between them and Delilah Gabbott. There was hardly any point. This particular part of this particular witch cemetery – of which there were several, all over Wrackton – was small, the gesture meaningless.

Their presence, disrupting her mourning her son.

That was another thing Cornelia hadn't expected: no matter how badly someone behaved, how murderous or depraved they were, someone, somewhere, probably loved that person. She'd turned a phrase Jacob had said to them over and over in her head, had chewed on it since the Dollhouse Murderers had echoed it – that they always make monsters of the mavericks. Loath as she was to ever agree with him, he was right. They made monsters of killers because it felt safer.

Monsters were, ultimately, people. They could be Occult or Apparent. They could live under your roof, or be your friend or someone you loved very much.

They were just people. And that made them scarier.

Dr Ray stepped up and shook Delilah's hand, which was remarkably gallant of her given that Jacob had caused her many a sleepless night, and was partially responsible for a considerable amount of destruction in Wrackton.

Not to mention the murders.

Delilah Gabbott, Dr Ray and Sully each threw a flaming handful of dirt into the grave, and then it was done. A funeral they'd waited more than a year to witness, over in minutes.

Delilah dropped something into the grave just as Observer Johnson beckoned over two young Apparent-looking men who started up a machine covered in ceremonial runes to finish the burial. That, too, was over in moments.

'Should we say something?' Mallory asked quietly, an anxious furrow appearing on her forehead.

Cornelia almost reached out to smooth it, but stopped herself.

'"Sorry for your loss, he was an awful bastard?"' she said instead.

'Or something sensible.'

'I think we just leave her be,' Diana said decisively. 'I can't imagine anything good would come from talking to her.'

'And we'd be doing it for the wrong reasons,' Mallory conceded. 'To make ourselves feel better.'

'As if that's not what we were doing by being here in the first place,' Diana scoffed.

Cornelia ignored her, both because what she said was true, and because Diana had been the one who'd eagerly agreed to attend the funeral.

'Let's just go,' Cornelia said, her phone still clutched in her hand. She pushed Diana forwards gently.

'Ouch,' Diana hissed, stumbling. She hopped on one leg, her shoe covered in soil. Cornelia stepped around her to see a pile of it behind a particularly ornate gravestone.

It had been dug up recently, the coffin beneath it exposed.

Mallory spotted it before anyone else did. 'This is Mr Blackburn's grave.'

'I had just forgotten all about that case,' Cornelia said, squinting at the epitaph through her rain-spattered glasses.

There had been many, *many* emails from his wife, Mrs Blackburn, who had hired them to look into the circumstances of his death last year, and Cornelia had hoped to never again have to hear the name. He'd died right before they took on the Dollhouse Murderer case; it had been yet another murder-that-wasn't in a long string of them. Cornelia missed the days when their cases were frivolous.

Mallory's expression as she stared at the grave told Cornelia the cogs were turning, though not with the sparkle she got where something piqued her interest. This was a look of careful consideration.

'We got an email from Mrs Blackburn yesterday,' Mallory said. 'Saying she thought his grave had been disturbed, and asking us to look into it. Even though it was originally my directorial decision not to do this anymore, I made a small mistake in reading it aloud to Theodore—'

'Oh, come *on*,' Diana groaned.

Cornelia closed her eyes briefly. 'Is he still trying to get us to take the pointless small cases?'

Mallory bit her lip. 'I think he feels left out, when we travel for bigger ones. He was so enthusiastic about this one. I offered to let him take it himself, but he said cemeteries—'

'Give him the Samhain squirrels, yeah. We were all there when he first workshopped that particular phrasing,' Diana said, scowling.

'I was going to give it a cursory glance as we were leaving.' Mallory met Cornelia's eye as she reached into her pocket and pulled out a roll of crime scene tape and a pair of gloves. 'See if there was anything of interest to report back to him. I expect it to be nothing, so I came underprepared.'

Cornelia sighed. Their latent success since they'd caught the Dollhouse Murderers – preventing them from completing a ghoulish necromantic ritual involving what Cornelia called *Chilopoda titanica*, and everyone else called 'massive horrible centipedes' – particularly after actor and former suspect Sandi Clementine had not been able to stop talking about the 'private investeeegators' she'd met at Oakpass Manor, had made them shed their habit of taking on any and every case that entered their agency inbox. They could afford to be more discerning, even if Theodore didn't seem to *quite* grasp that. He was forever angling to be lead on literally any case.

Mallory wasn't usually so willing to listen.

She was also aware this was probably a consequence of not being able to investigate what seemed to be one of the biggest scandals the Occult world had seen since the Vampire Wars, and nobody even remembered what happened in those. So she tried not to judge.

'What's your cursory glance telling you now?' Diana asked, brushing a clod of dirt off her shoe.

Cornelia *had* tried to tell her that heels in a cemetery were not the best idea.

'I don't think this was opened legitimately, and I can't tell if his body is still in here,' Mallory said.

'Want to talk to Dr Ray about it?' Cornelia pivoted on the spot, realising they were now alone in the cemetery. 'Then we can tell Theodore it's nothing to worry about, and we can all agree not to share anything we don't want to work on with him ever again.'

'Too late,' Diana said, pointing. They watched Dr Ray's

and Sully's slowly retreating forms, in step with Delilah as they shuffled towards Dr Ray's car. Observer Johnson and the gravedigger boys were gone.

'Ah well,' Mallory said.

Cornelia felt a stab of terror, like she'd re-entered her body suddenly. Mallory and Diana had a habit of making her forget her fear, but it always found a way to creep back in.

Shrugging it off as best she could, Cornelia reluctantly accepted the proffered end of the tape roll and got to work securing the area around the grave.

'The machines do most of the digging' – Mallory gestured at the now-abandoned machine standing sentry over Jacob's grave – 'but this looks like someone dug him up with a shovel, or some other non-mechanical means.'

'Magically?' Cornelia asked, tapping her pockets before swearing loudly. 'I don't have any beetles with me.'

Mallory tilted her head. 'Possibly? I'd expect a slightly neater job in that case. If Theodore wants this, he'll have to call in to Dr Ray himself later, and we know he won't like—'

As Mallory said the word 'call', Cornelia's phone buzzed.

MOTHER (DO NOT ANSWER)

She frowned at it, anger rising up in her throat, and she stabbed the reject button more aggressively than was strictly necessary.

If cutting her off was her parents' (six-month-old) last-ditch attempt to get her to speak to them, she wasn't going to fall for it.

'Let's go home,' Cornelia said. 'One of you needs to help me apply for Universal Basic Income.'

THREE

'Mallory!' Theodore exclaimed, bursting through the door of the research room just in time to save Cornelia another round of 'no I can't just suck it up and ask my parents to let us on the Reaper case and you know full well why, Diana'.

The room warmed with his crackling presence as Mallory greeted him with a hug. Diana stomped up the basement stairs, intermittently heaving loud sighs that she was amplifying with a spell to make sure they could all hear. Cornelia refused to rise to the bait.

'I wasn't expecting to see you here, I thought you'd still be— Never mind. Did you look into our case?'

'It isn't our case,' Mallory reminded him. 'It may not even be a case at all. There was a disturbance at Mr Blackburn's grave. Cornelia and I cordoned it off—'

'Cornelia, I know you're stoically resisting the bait,' Diana shouted, her magically amplified voice echoing around the basement. 'I can make all this stop if you'd just go to the Broadwicks, even if they're—'

Cornelia and Mallory shot a look towards the basement stairs as Diana hissed, 'Shit!' and the amplifying spell ended. They'd agreed they wouldn't gripe about the Broadwicks in front of Theodore, lest he realise they were keeping something from them. Mallory didn't want to tell him anything until they were sure, but they couldn't be if Cornelia continued to refuse to talk to the Broadwicks.

'Excellent! Oh, wonderful,' Theodore said, cat ears quivering as he rummaged around on his desk. He triumphantly held up a notebook with a lavender cover. 'I was just dashing back to grab this, but you have made my *morning*. My *decade*. My… unlife! So what's the case? Do we have any complications, any leads? No! Don't tell me. A twisted tree that claims the bodies of all who tended to it, and a mangled corpse has been found in its roots. A flying vampire, impaled on the roof of the Observatory!'

'I think instead of working on any cases, you should take up writing fiction,' Cornelia said. 'I'd read those stories.'

'There're no complications. We've left it for you to look into, it's all ready. We don't know how much the grave was disturbed, or how, but you are case lead—'

'And as case lead, I insist you all work with me on this case,' Theodore said swiftly. 'I believe that's how it works, case lead gets to designate roles.'

'I think I'll go help Diana,' Cornelia said, smiling at Mallory, whose face was betraying several emotions at once.

'Those were the rules, yes,' she said slowly, imploring Cornelia with her eyes not to abandon her.

Cornelia settled for leaning against the doorway into the research room.

'And rules are important,' Theodore said. 'So, tell me. Mr Blackburn. He's a zombie now, I suspect?'

Mallory filled him in.

Theodore nodded seriously. 'Just as well I'm here, then. Not many cases require the specialities of a forensic anthropologist, you know, but it's just as well you have me.'

'Para-anthropologist, I thought?' Cornelia said.

'*Para* does a lot of heavy lifting. They call me the Bone Doctor, you know. I have to dash off, but – as case lead. Can you call Night Mayor Dr Ray, set up an official meeting for, oh…' He looked at his wrist, which was watchless. 'Two hours from now. No! Ninety minutes! Fantastic. Case lead!' he said, before barrelling out the way he'd come.

Mallory stared after him, a fond smile on her lips.

'We don't have to do it,' Cornelia said.

'Don't we?' Mallory asked lightly. 'We've got a significant lead on his first murder that we can't follow, and we're keeping it from him. He had a… strange time, last year' – Cornelia felt that was a generous description of Theodore's borderline terrifying behaviour during the Dollhouse Murderers case, up to and including the time he tried to possess Mallory – 'and he's come back from that. His job at the Mayoral Offices isn't *quite* as fulfilling now they've bricked up a large portion of the section that was producing giant creatures and spectral disturbances, not to mention Katherine the ghost—'

'Who he specifically has never mentioned,' Cornelia said.

'Yes. Nonetheless, he's been working away like nothing happened last year. I still think them almost taking his job away was the reason he was so…'

'Strange,' Cornelia supplied.

'So, I think we can do this. Let him take the case, and support him where he needs – it likely won't even matter, but it'll make him happy. Let him get some practice at dealing with the organisational side of things. I'd rather we did it from a place of wanting it for his benefit than, say, guilt.'

Cornelia felt a stab of it shoot through her, right on cue. It hadn't occurred to her that Mallory would know she felt… she wasn't sure how she felt. Angry, at her family. Betrayed. But she thought she'd done a good job of burying the guilt. Before she had to respond, Diana clattered back down the stairs with a tray of tea and biscuits.

'What did I miss?'

The Mayoral Square had been to hell and back, but nothing was more hellish than the restoration of the oversized neon light in the shape of former Night Mayor Vincent Van Doren's face in the window of the Mayoral Offices.

Cornelia looked at it with disgust, grateful once again for the distraction from focusing on how being outside made her feel like she was being flayed alive. 'Do you think Dr Ray did this as a joke?'

'I think her mind works in mysterious ways, so I wouldn't put it past her,' Diana said. 'Do we have our passes?'

'At reception,' Cornelia said. 'Theodore and I need one, so they're reissuing the lot.'

Part of the Undetectables' recent success had meant the Unified Magical Liaison – the Occulture governing body, known as UML for short – were more keen to work with them, while taking simultaneous pains to bury them under reams of utterly pointless paperwork at every opportunity. The Undetectables had been officially hired more than once to investigate smaller crimes and non-serial murders.

Diana had carefully scrubbed the internet to try to preserve *some* sense of anonymity when it came to stakeouts and following suspects, and so far it was working out nicely. Mallory had confirmed they'd even turned a modest profit, whatever that meant.

'Are you sure we can't just take a quick trip over to Dublin, leave this case to Theodore? Taylor's mum was absolutely adamant there was a banshee in her garden she wanted us to take a look at,' Diana said hopefully.

'We can't all go with you to meet your girlfriend's mum for the first time,' Mallory said, more kindly than Cornelia would've put it. 'The red tape involved in taking a case in Ireland is too much to think about.'

'Thanks, Brexit,' Cornelia said, scuffing the step with her boot.

Anything to prolong having to go back into the Offices.

'You mean thanks meddling of the UML,' Diana said bitterly. 'You'd think they'd have found it in their hearts to let us roam free, solving cases wherever we're needed without needing to have *meetings* about it. Ones like the Wickermere Reaper, for instance, given that we're a handful of hours from the Lake District and could *easily* lend our expertise to a case where someone is *burying victims alive* and it's *overshadowing the entirety of the Occult world now that they've started taking*

Occult victims after a string of Apparent tragedies, if the article I read about it is to be believed.'

'Oh, don't worry, we can just use my family's considerable wealth to— *Oh no wait*,' Cornelia said, both determined to out-bitter Diana, and having just remembered that she didn't have any money. She'd worry about it properly later.

Mallory was focusing on walking up the stairs and didn't say anything. Cornelia watched after her, her pale denim jacket with the little *Undetectables* patch sewn into the sleeve sitting nicely over the black dress that swayed around her legs as she moved, which she'd reluctantly donned for the funeral.

Diana cleared her throat and Cornelia realised she'd been staring, then took the stairs two at a time until she was in step with Mallory.

Diana and Mallory hesitated at the doors of the Mayoral Offices, but Cornelia strode in, her shoulders back, allowing herself to float away out of her head until she could've been walking through a dream. It meant she was waving at passing Office staff without looking to see if they were glaring at her first, but that didn't matter.

The place where Jacob had died had been bricked up, and with it went Katherine the ghost. There was nothing specific to fear, or so Cornelia kept trying to tell herself.

'We're here to see Dr Ray. Dr Night Mayor. Night Mayor Ray,' Cornelia said, slapping a hand down on the reception desk.

'The UML have actually awarded her the title of Honourable after she successfully oversaw the restoration of the Offices, though none of the signs have been updated yet,' the receptionist – an unusually owlish-looking demon who couldn't have been older than nineteen – said, then snapped her mouth shut and handed over four visitor passes.

'That's my cue,' Theodore said grandly, the air instantly warming.

Cornelia held up his visitor badge. '*Can* you wear this? Is it not going to be staticky and illegible?'

'Adds to our mystique. Helping you detect the undetectable… by *being* undetectable,' he said, plucking it from Cornelia's hand.

Mallory fixed it to the front of his cardigan where it immediately crackled and fuzzed, and the four of them began the long walk to Dr Ray's office.

Cornelia inhaled shakily, ignoring all of this as they walked down the corridor with the perennially faulty witchlights. Even post-rebuild, they refused to reliably turn on, suggesting it was a feature of the Offices and not a bug.

She didn't look at the others, refusing to give them an opportunity to ask what was wrong. It wasn't a question she could answer.

Instead, she focused on the facts: Jacob was dead.

Jacob couldn't hurt her.

But the Jacob in her head…

She shook away the thought.

No matter that she'd skilfully managed to avoid setting foot inside the Offices in over a year – she'd always been busy with emails, or in the bug room, or doing a half-arsed job of cleaning the lab. Whether Mallory or Diana had noticed was up for debate, but they'd had the sense not to comment on it.

She could do this.

Dr Ray's office door was open a crack, and after a brief round of rock paper scissors (Cornelia lost) she did the old knock-and-enter.

'There you are,' Dr Ray said, her voice muffled behind a stack of papers on her desk. There was a pretty strawberry-blonde woman beside her trying to sort the papers into piles, but she took one look at the Undetectables and mumbled an excuse to leave.

Cornelia knew her: Hayley Eason. Ex-girlfriend of the last Night Mayor of Wrackton. Last she'd heard, Hayley had been in the hotel business.

'To what do I owe this pleasure, being as I saw most of you a mere ninety minutes ago?' Dr Ray asked.

'Bodies,' Theodore said before anyone could stop him. 'Bodies, and those who would contrive to steal them.'

Mallory held up a hand so Diana wouldn't interject, but when Theodore offered no more detail, Mallory settled herself into the chair in front of Dr Ray.

'We're following a lead regarding a former client – or rather, a decedent related to a former client,' she said smoothly. 'While we were at the cemetery earlier, we noticed he'd been – and there really isn't a more technical way to put this – dug up.'

'Dug... up?'

'Yes. We were notified by our former client that the grave appeared, quote, "disturbed", but on inspection we believe he's been partially to maybe fully exhumed. In a sort of illegitimate, body-snatchers kind of way.'

'Hmm.'

Mallory gave Theodore an encouraging nudge, inviting him

to speak up, but he gestured for her to continue.

'We were just wondering if you, in your capacity as Medical Examiner, had any idea what that was about, given that you examined this decedent,' she finished.

'Remind me of the decedent's name?' Dr Ray pressed a hand to her beautiful forehead and Cornelia felt the familiar swoop of her all-out crush on the most brilliant woman in all of Wrackton, bar one notable exception.

'Paul Blackburn.'

'He's a zombie now,' Theodore said knowingly.

'For the love of Blair.' Dr Ray dropped down into her chair and pulled a file towards her. 'You're certain it's his grave?'

'Absolutely. We saw it less than two hours ago after the funeral, but you'd already departed,' Mallory said. 'Mrs Blackburn contacted me to say it had been meddled with. While the earth over the grave had been lifted and piled elsewhere, I couldn't tell at a glance if it had been fully exhumed—'

'It has,' Dr Ray said grimly. 'I'd bet my life on it. And that is not a bet I make without the intention of winning.'

'It's good to not throw your life away,' Theodore said bitterly. 'Wouldn't want to end up like me. The Cautionary Tale of the Samhain Ghost.'

'Are you *quite* done?' Dr Ray asked him, and for once Theodore's mouth snapped shut. 'This is not the first. There was another last week – different cemetery, but same principle. Mound of dirt beside disturbed grave, and I haven't the faintest clue why. The first victim, though I hesitate to call them victims, was an Apparent named Freya Evans. She was laid to rest last year.'

'Do you have a burial date?' Mallory asked. Cornelia looked at her curiously; Mallory was already establishing a pattern, despite her earlier insistence that this was Theodore's harmless case.

'I'd say about a week or so before Paul Blackburn, if my memory serves me,' Dr Ray said. She handed Mallory a case file. 'Autopsy report's in there. Do you want the case?'

'Officially?'

'Hayley will do up the contracts – usual terms?'

'Do we normally get paid for these?' Cornelia whispered to Diana.

Dr Ray's eyelids fluttered for a fraction of a second. Had Cornelia not been gazing adoringly into her face, she would've missed it.

'Cornelia is impoverished now,' Diana said. 'Hence her suddenly caring.'

'Yes, usual terms,' Mallory said.

This felt reassuring, so Cornelia didn't press further. She had no idea what a reasonable amount was. She'd seen the figures before, but they hadn't made sense to her out of context.

'As long as I am included in these terms, so say I!' Theodore said.

'Okay. Hayley will be in touch.' Dr Ray gestured at the door. 'By which I mean, leave, before I perish beneath this avalanche of papers.'

Theodore exhaled excitedly once they were out on the steps of the Mayoral Offices in the muggy May air.

'Can I say it?' Theodore asked solemnly. 'I think my— Our! *Our* case will go well if I get to say it.'

Mallory nodded before anyone else could ask what the fuck he meant, a smile crossing her lips.

Although Cornelia had not been able to fully forgive Theodore for what he did to Mallory last year, Mallory seemed to have. Theodore had behaved utterly normally – which was a strange baseline to begin with – since he'd helped them escape Wrackton during the emergency lockdown. Back to his wholly usual dramatic self. Until Mallory had said it earlier, it hadn't occurred to Cornelia that being rehired in the Offices might've contributed to Theodore's miraculous recovery. She'd always love Theodore, but she currently loved him like one might love a shark: from a distance, with eyes wide open.

Theodore pulled himself up to his full height, cat ears quivering with delight.

'Undetectables, it's time,' he said grandly. 'To the murder board!'

FOUR

There really was nothing like the smell of a clean murder board in the morning to make you glad to be alive.

'Right. Two "victims",' Mallory started.

'I've got this,' Cornelia said, taking up a whiteboard marker. 'Multitasking.'

'Never mind that you have both the worst attention span and also the agency's least-legible handwriting,' Diana said. Cornelia snapped her fingers and Diana shrieked as the words 'FUCK' and 'OFF!' appeared on her knuckles in whiteboard marker.

'Careful you don't die like that,' Theodore said, stroking his marker-drawn whiskers.

'Freya Evans and Paul Blackburn. Both already deceased,' Cornelia said. 'Paul Blackburn was married to a previous client of ours.'

'Though our conclusions from that case were that he died of natural causes, not from poisoning like our former client insisted,' Mallory said.

'Really didn't think we'd ever have to say that poor man's name again,' Cornelia said.

'Funny how life is full of macro and micro coincidences,' Theodore said. 'That was a time when you were dealing with a poisoning of sorts, and she brought you a poisoning case. What a world.'

'It very specifically *wasn't* a poisoning case. He was, like Mallory said, a hundred and three,' Diana said. 'And Dr Ray agreed.'

'As Dr Ray said, Freya Evans died last February from—oh,' Mallory said, her brow furrowing. Cornelia once again fought the urge to smooth it out with her thumb. 'Cancer. Complications associated with her treatment.'

Cornelia felt a pang of recognition. 'Was that the Evans family that live over on Aster Lane? I had no idea, we should've put in a donation to—'

The words died on Cornelia's lips as an unsettling sense of horror rained down on her.

'Don't worry, you'll come to terms with it soon,' Diana said cheerfully, patting her on the shoulder.

Diana was being much nicer than she probably wanted to be, given that she had every right to be standing on a table shouting *I told you so!* for every time she'd reminded Cornelia that the Undetectables as an entity were in serious trouble if she ever somehow lost her family's money.

It had, truthfully, been unconscionable. The Broadwicks were rich in a way that made other people's eyes widen, which made Cornelia determined to spend it as fast as she could. She'd taken a few minutes while Diana set up the murder board to call the family financial advisor – at Mallory's behest – but whatever he said washed over her because she'd never really had to *think* about money before.

She didn't know where it came from – investments, probably, or stocks, or maybe there were just piles of money sitting somewhere in a vault that had now been shut in her face. The idea that there were people who felt this clawing panic *every single day* was sickening. She'd always tried to be as generous as possible. Scrolling social media at night when she couldn't sleep – in between web searches for a whole day's worth of random thoughts and questions – she'd randomly donate to fundraisers of all sorts, from bugs to debt to escaping war. But she hadn't been certain it was doing anything to help anyone. Money was just a number on a screen.

'Maybe, when we've looked into this case and you've got your UBI set up, you can send them some flowers or something,' Mallory suggested gently.

Cornelia nodded, her tongue sticking to the roof of her mouth.

'It's going to be okay,' Mallory continued, lowering her voice so only Cornelia could hear. 'I promise.'

Theodore cleared his throat. 'So they're unrelated deaths! Buried within a couple of weeks of each other last year, and grave-robbed just over a year later.'

'That could be the linking factor – maybe someone is stealing organs?' Diana asked, but both Mallory and Cornelia shook their heads.

'You take this one,' Mallory offered.

'Putrefaction,' Cornelia said shortly. 'Even with the

embalming process, it'll set in within a couple of weeks. Organs are best kept fresh. There'd be no reason to take the whole corpse if they were after something specific. Besides, I doubt there's a market for centenarian eyeballs. I don't know what the protocol is for harvesting organs from someone who died of cancer, though.'

'She was an organ donor,' Mallory said, examining the file. 'So even if there had been organs safe to take, they'd have done so when she died.'

'This is a horrible conversation, I hope you know,' Theodore said. 'I was to be an organ donor, but alas.'

'Alas?' Cornelia asked.

'They couldn't bear to part me from my kidneys when the time came. Thought I might start appearing in the body of whoever got them. Patient privacy disaster, you'd have all kinds of lawsuits. Haunted by the Ghost of the Guy Who Previously Owned my Kidneys. I think I should take up writing. That's a great book title *and* a hooky concept.'

'You should,' Diana said. 'Not like you sleep, it could occupy your latter hours.'

'Would you even be able to haunt the person, if they weren't in Wrackton?'

Theodore drifted to his desk, muttering and rummaging around in a stack of notebooks identical to the one he'd picked up earlier until he found a clean one. He curled up on his iron chair and started scrawling feverishly across the pages, his hand a static blur. Diana had insisted on 'homogenising the Undetectables branding', and at her behest Mallory had ordered stationery. They were, admittedly, very nice notebooks – soft, smooth lavender covers, each with the agency logo embossed on the lower corner and exactly the right weight paper inside. He closed it with a snap.

'Let us continue! Cornelia, you were saying?'

'Neither in a condition to donate, or have their organs forcibly donated. Different ages, different assigned sexes. Different causes of death. Are there any obvious links between the victims? Where did Blackburn live? And how far away from each other were they buried?'

It felt like playing a mystery board game, simulating a real case. As much as Cornelia agreed with Mallory – that this was good for Theodore – it was hard not to blurt out all the answers.

'I have something that might help Theodore there. A visual aid,' Diana said somewhat mysteriously as she ran off upstairs, returning with a diorama so big that she could barely hold it. 'We're going to need a permanent display place for this.'

Cornelia jumped up to help her before Mallory could. Over the last year they had renovated the lab and the research room to both maximise the space and minimise the ghostly interference Theodore ran on the machines. They were now kept behind a permanent iron partition, so Theodore could pass freely through the lab and not need to stand on the iron plate – apparently this was a grievous indignity he could no longer bear to suffer, much less think about, though he managed to bring up the former existence of said iron plate on a daily basis.

The research room was now wider, with a proper seating area to greet clients, and the windowed partition wall was fitted with a sliding door that meant they could shout back and forth to each other through the doorway without having to get up – but also meant they could hold meetings and not disturb Mallory and Theodore's lab work. They'd requisitioned the long-defunct Broadwick ballroom for filing cabinets and digital backups, which made the research room both less cluttered and less of a privacy threat with visitors coming and going. There hadn't been a sniff of the concept of a Broadwick ball since Theodore had died in the basement, and it was even less likely now that they'd permanently relocated to Wickermere.

Cornelia and Diana hovered in the centre of the lab, each gripping one end of the diorama while Diana looked at her expectantly.

'We'll just lose a lab bench,' Cornelia said, helping Diana place the diorama.

'Surely we'd consult me, the case lead, about that,' Theodore said loudly.

'Majority rules, my friend.'

'Oh, it's Wrackton!' Mallory said, crouching to look at it. 'This is incredible, Diana.'

'It's a smaller scale than I'm used to working with, but Taylor and I wanted a project we could work on together, so. Here it is.'

'Incredible work. There's our agency sign!' Mallory pointed delightedly. 'And my house, and Diana's old house, and the Mayoral Offices, and the Observatory, and the Larix. Hexana, look at the *detail* in the Redwoods. This is your best work yet.'

'Just wait,' Diana said, waving her hand over the miniature cemetery plots as she consulted the sketches in Dr Ray's file. Two tiny red witchlights lit up over the approximate locations of the graves. Cornelia tried not to say, 'Wow!' out loud and failed miserably in the process. 'Here's where they both lived,' Diana continued. Blue witchlights blinked on at the Blackburns' house and at the Evanses'.

'The Blackburns are on the other side of town to the Evanses,' Mallory said. 'And they were buried in totally different cemeteries, so it's not a proximity link. Both were ill, so perhaps worth seeing if there was a hospital link?'

'Diana, do you have any contacts?' Theodore asked hopefully.

'I don't think we need to—' She stopped at the look on his face. 'Fine.'

She pulled out her phone – no doubt an ex or two were on staff. She'd had a brief thing for trainee doctors before moving to Vancouver, if Cornelia recalled correctly.

'I'll check to see if they were on the same wards, or if there were staff rotated between them.' She moved to the corner to place some calls.

'As for times, Mrs Blackburn emailed us around midnight last night, said she'd noticed "a disturbance" about ten minutes prior – it's possible it was too dark to see how badly disturbed the grave was, but I'd expect stronger wording if she thought he'd been exhumed. According to the file, the disturbance to Freya Evans's grave was discovered at seven a.m., Monday last week.'

'So we could be talking overnight body snatching, then,' Cornelia said. She was getting into the case, despite herself. Perhaps it was the random wash of guilt she felt whenever she looked at Theodore. A year ago they'd have been giving this case their all, but now it felt, for want of a better phrase, beneath them. It wasn't murder. It wasn't making headlines. It wasn't a big enough distraction from the terror that had rooted itself inside her and was refusing to let go. 'Are there any cameras around the area? Traffic or otherwise?'

Mallory shook her head. 'We had this in the Loren case a few months ago, remember? Dr Ray told us it was because the Mayoral Office creatures kept escaping and breaking everything. They just nixed any kind of budget for on-street surveillance.'

The creatures that were occasionally giant centipedes and that may or may not be two human souls in a trench coat. Cornelia wasn't fully clear on what Theodore did for work, but he'd made it clear – or as clear as Theodore could – that part of it was to find out what they were and why they happened, but they'd all been afraid to ask too many questions about his findings. Diana had killed one of those creatures; the implications were unthinkable.

'And also because of me. I became an expensive liability,' Theodore said happily.

'Right. I suppose the possibility of witchlight travel likely makes all this moot, anyway,' Cornelia said. 'Anyone could travel anywhere at any time, and it's unlikely anyone would notice unless they were watching for it.'

'Except they'd have a semi-decomposed corpse with them, hard to miss that,' Mallory said.

'A valid point, though some of those gravestones *are* tall enough to hide yourself and a corpse behind,' Theodore said.

'No luck with the hospital,' Diana said, coming back over. 'Freya was referred on to a specialist oncologist in a hospital in London some years ago, and Mr Blackburn never made it past A&E. What were you talking about?'

It had taken Diana some getting used to not being able to

hear everything out of her left ear – largely because she had previously been able to hear everything going on around her – but after she'd had an actual breakdown in front of Cornelia, she'd had conversations with Mallory that eventually led to her making an audiologist appointment, which led to a hearing aid, which led to a period of adjustment that had been deeply frustrating for Diana and Theodore in particular. One of the more unfortunate downsides of having a resident ghost was his propensity to interfere with electronics through proximity – Diana had described the interference as a static crackle, like a radio tuning. Once, Theodore had actually destroyed the hearing aid by getting excited about a fragment of bone Diana had recovered during a case, and they had both taken great pains to ensure that never happened again – largely by coordinating on which was more important on a given day: Diana being able to hear fully, or Theodore being able to be in close proximity. Theodore's lack of further complaining and Diana's lack of further electrocution concerns, coupled with the Undetectables adding "unending supply of batteries" – that were stored all around Broadwick Mansion – to their expenditure list, suggested to Cornelia that it was, effectively, ghost problem managed.

'We were talking about the possibility of eyewitnesses,' Theodore said, and filled her in. 'Who called in the Freya Evans disturbance?'

Cornelia handed him the file. 'It's all yours – that would be a good place to start on interviews.'

'Ah, yes. Interviews. Diana, I am going to delegate this task to you.'

Diana snatched the file from him and all but stomped back to her corner.

'Mallory, Cornelia – seeing as you cordoned off the scene earlier, you can do the leg work. I'll stay here, oversee the interviewee list. Too many PIs spoil the crime scene, and so forth. And!' Theodore added, as Mallory moved to get her kitbag. 'Perhaps you could take a soil sample kit, too?'

Cornelia bit the inside of her cheek to stop herself retorting, already opening the *Sonata lutumae* tank mounted on the wall to scoop up the sound beetles she thought looked happiest, and slotting them lovingly into little matchboxes. They were living litmus tests; in the presence of magic they glowed green and emitted a chirpy little sound that gave them their nickname. Cornelia had written her undergrad dissertation on their potential forensic applications for magical crimes – oddly prescient, given her job now.

'I'll bring the footprint casting kit as well, just in case – Diana already stepped in it, but we can eliminate her easily.'

Diana, evidently having caught that, pulled the phone away from her ear to say, 'If I was going to commit a crime, I'd do something a lot sexier than corpses,' before fumbling to put it back to her ear. 'Sorry, Dr Ray, Hayley put me on hold.'

Cornelia grinned at her as she pulled on her coveralls and a hat, ignoring the prickle of sweat that immediately appeared at the idea of going outside again.

'Walk or taxi?' she asked Mallory, who was fixing her hair into a ponytail.

And just like that, they were on a case.

FIVE

Cornelia and Mallory stood at the entrance of the biggest witch cemetery and exhaled soggily.

The ground was wet, worse than you'd expect for late spring in England, even in Wrackton, and urgent rain had started to fall the moment they'd stepped out of the taxi. Mallory shivered under their umbrella, the air filled with the scent of petrichor, which did not bode well for two people looking at an open grave. The smell and the silence reminded Cornelia of summers in Wickermere, the magical Lake District town – or what was left of it – where her family had fully relocated in recent years.

Former family.

If the Broadwicks were going to try to disown her over something they'd done – whether or not they realised it – she was going to disown them harder.

'Not too late to turn back,' Cornelia said casually, hoping Mallory would take it up as a semi-serious joke and not a plea. She'd already had to leave the house once today, twice was pushing it.

'Freya Evans's grave is down here, in one of the Apparent sections,' Mallory said, a small smile brushing her lips as she consulted her phone.

There wasn't that much of a height difference between them, but the tines of the umbrella brushed the top of Mallory's head as they walked as close together as they could manage, and Cornelia's shoulder kept being exposed to the elements until she gave up, pulling her hat down firmer over her hair and leaving Mallory to the umbrella. The side of her body that had been pressed to Mallory's tingled with something akin to disappointment.

Freya Evans's grave had been left cordoned off with a grey tarp over it, which felt disrespectful at best and evidence-destroying at worst, but it meant the grave had been spared the worst of the elements over the last week. With gloves on, Cornelia carefully peeled back the tarp to reveal the open grave. The coffin hadn't been removed, though the lid wasn't fully closed. It looked brand new, the nails on the lid removed carefully to open it.

'Take these booties,' Mallory said.

'Sure thing, sweetie,' Cornelia said, and Mallory shot her a look, holding up a pair of shoe covers.

'I know this isn't very exciting, and, quite frankly, opens us up to nuisance cases again if clients get wind that we take on the smaller stuff, but we're doing it for Theodore. Right? That's why I'm here, in this goddess-forsaken place. I am here for Theodore's sake. Please help me remember this is why I'm here.'

Cornelia laughed and slipped the covers over her boots. It likely didn't matter, as the Wrackton police had already trampled on it – as much as they were fond of Sully, her team left a lot to be desired – but Mallory cared about protocol and

Cornelia cared about Mallory and figured that, at the end of it all, that was all that mattered.

Mallory opened one of the kit bags and held a powder tub and brush out to Cornelia.

'Can you jump down there, *carefully*, and see if you can lift any prints from around the latches? It's likely utterly futile, given Sully's lot didn't find anything, but we should at least try.'

'Do I have to?'

'No,' Mallory said lightly. 'But if you don't, I'll have to.'

Cornelia obliged, to no avail. The coffin had mercifully stayed dry, but there were clear signs of prints lifted, powder traces telling her there was nothing left to take.

'While I think we'd have done a much more thorough job – they've done sloppy work – I will admit that Sully's lot will have anything worth looking at already. And the body is definitely gone, that is one empty coffin.'

'To be expected. Okay, soil samples and let the beetles do their magic,' Mallory said. 'Literally speaking.'

Cornelia let Lawrence VII (this generation were all Lawrence VII) and Selene IX (ditto) out of their boxes on opposite sides of the grave. Seeing the differences in her colonies of *Sonata lutumae* was second nature to her – Lawrence VII had maintained Lawrence I's saffron-hued elytra with an orange starburst across their heads, while Selene IX had started to develop a rose-gold sheen when you held them in a certain light. She had tried to explain the subtle differences between the two colonies even after they'd merged to Diana and Mallory, but neither had been particularly enthusiastic, though Mallory had tried to appear interested.

'No reaction,' Cornelia said, frowning, the beetles resolutely orange. 'I've one more.'

This time she thought she caught a flicker of *something*, but couldn't be sure it wasn't a reflection on her glasses.

Selene and Lawrence had made it clear: this wasn't an act of magic.

'Never a good sign,' Mallory said grimly. 'But grab a soil sample.'

She handed over a jar as Cornelia examined the gravestone. Freya had only been thirty-eight when she died.

'There's a little shred of paper there,' Mallory said, pointing.

Cornelia looked but didn't see it, and Mallory abandoned the umbrella to crouch beside her, pulling the paper free with her tweezers and slipping it into an evidence bag. She stood up and took a few steps back.

'Hardly worth taking with us?' Cornelia asked, wiping a raindrop off her nose with the back of her arm.

Mallory didn't appear to have heard her, looking around with that look on her face she got when she was thinking of something particularly smart.

'Where would you go? If you'd taken a heavily decomposed body out of your grave, where would you go next?'

Home, Cornelia wanted to say. *I'd go straight home.* But that wasn't what Mallory was looking for, and the question had been rhetorical.

'I thought we were just going to get in and out, and leave this for Theodore?'

'The better the information we bring back to him, the more we can leave him to it,' Mallory said, staring off into the distance. 'Walk down that way and you come out into a residential area – and that's a cul-de-sac. There's a path down the bottom that'll take you around to Main Street, but you'd come out right across from that tapas restaurant and that basement wine bar you and Diana went to that time with Kingston.'

'And there's a smoking area outside,' Cornelia pointed out.

'Right, so even on a Sunday night to Monday morning, that place always has someone outside it until sunrise. No matter the weather.'

She closed her eyes and Cornelia said nothing, just watched her friend think. She could visualise everything in miniature thanks to Diana's latest diorama.

'Walk up the way we came and you're back towards my parents' house. That street is well-lit. Go the other way, or even towards the outskirts of town, you're still going to come into contact with all the supermarkets and that car park. It's not *impossible* that someone could avoid detection twice...'

'But unlikely,' Cornelia said. 'Unless they used some sort of glamour?'

'Here we go again with the glamours,' Mallory said unhappily.

'It might not be. Think about it – a body is heavy. One person struggling with a body would take forever to get wherever they were going, and it can't be close by, because the other cemetery is too far away. Two people are going to immediately be seen as suspicious. If they walked through a residential area you'd probably smell it, same by the restaurant.'

'You're right. It's improbable,' Mallory said.

'Maybe our initial hypothesis will light the way,' Cornelia

said, taking off her glasses dramatically. 'It all comes back to witchlights.'

They called another taxi and were at the second cemetery in record time. Cornelia reached into her pocket to leave a tip and froze. She'd used the last of her cash on the first taxi.

Without looking at her, Mallory did the honours.

'It'll get easier. Your UBI will kick in a couple days after you apply,' she said, leading the way to Paul Blackburn's grave.

They worked quickly in an effort to preserve any evidence that might be imminently washed away. Cornelia could feel boredom seeping in with every step. No matter how much she enjoyed doing fieldwork with Mallory – really *anything* that involved Mallory was instantly made better – she couldn't shake the feeling that, no matter how arrogant Diana would say she was being if she voiced it, the Undetectables were above all of this.

'No beetle response by three, no prints, no footprints save for the one Diana made. One collected soil sample, and one empty grave, same as Freya Evans's,' Cornelia said.

'Shredded paper. Two pieces,' Mallory said, pointing. 'These are bigger than the last ones.'

They were small, round pieces, like the paper casualties of a hole punch, only more jagged. Cornelia bagged them up, wondering how much things like gloves and evidence bags cost. She'd never thought to ask before.

'We've got the same logistics problem here, too. To the north is the Observatory, and there's always someone there. To the south, you're in a densely populated part of town. West is just a row of townhouses, and east would take you out by the Larix.' She squinted up over Cornelia's head. 'There're trees shading this area from view of the houses behind us, but some of them have dormer windows. Maybe Diana could—'

'She'll hex me for asking, but I'm on it.'

Cornelia fired off a text to Diana asking her to check in with the residents. Over the last year they'd made themselves known as well as they could locally, pulling out every stop in an effort to make information-gathering as smooth as possible. Luckily, Wrackton was filled with folk who saw little distinction between 'providing information to aid in an investigation' and 'gossiping about their neighbours'.

'When we go back, we can give Theodore the witchlight hypothesis, and he can try his hand at leading interviews with whichever witnesses Diana drums up.'

'I hope I'm not interrupting anything,' a soft voice said, and Cornelia and Mallory whirled, Cornelia's heart in her mouth. The fear, sensing an opening, clambered back into her head, loud and insistent that she was not safe, that she had not *been* safe the whole time she'd been outside, and Mallory's presence was but a balm for her reality.

A balm that had allowed her to forget, for a moment, that the world had anyone but her and Mallory in it, and what she saw was not a worldly reminder she particularly wanted.

Delilah Gabbott leaned on her cane, her expression withdrawn. Like she wished she hadn't spoken.

That made two of them.

Jacob's grave was just a few rows from where they stood, and Cornelia realised with a start that she'd forgotten that, too.

Pushed him out of her mind when the ground had swallowed him up. His face swam into her mind's eye and she blinked, staring at the ground by Delilah's feet. Delilah, who was presumably visiting the son that had been mentally tormenting Cornelia, even in death.

'Hello,' Mallory said, recovering first. 'Can we help you?'

It was a bold response from someone who'd been directing another witch to leap around an open grave.

'Dr Night Mayor, or Night Mayor Dr—'

'I hear she's Honourable now,' Cornelia added, realising a split second too late that that was not helpful.

Delilah swallowed.

'Honourable Dr Night Mayor Ray told me you were the ones who my son…'

Cornelia's eyes widened involuntarily, pure terror seeping in.

This was not a confrontation she wanted to entertain. She wanted to appear gracious, or benevolent. She wanted to settle for somewhere in the region of compassionate. It was – likely – not Delilah's fault Jacob had turned out to be a power-hungry prick, and Cornelia wanted to be the sort of person who could eloquently express that sentiment.

But she wasn't, so she continued staring at Delilah, her mind whirring.

'There's no easy way to say this, so I'll just come out with it. You were the ones my son hurt, and I'm very sorry about that.'

Cornelia froze. She didn't dare turn to Mallory.

'Ms Gabbott,' Mallory started. 'You don't need to apologise.'

'I do. Trust me, I do.'

They looked at each other for a long time before Mallory

recovered enough to say something. It was just as well, because Cornelia did not think she'd ever be able to speak again.

'We're sorry too. That it ended up like this. And we're sorry for your loss.'

Delilah swallowed and ducked her head, shuffling away. They waited until she was at Jacob's grave before Cornelia gathered up their stuff and called a taxi back.

'Thanks for that. Can you cover this tip, too?'

'So that's a big pile of fucking nothing then, isn't it? No offence,' Diana said when they presented their evidence in the research room.

'I climbed into a *grave*, Diana. *Twice*.'

'And you barely complained about it at the time,' Mallory said, a smile in her voice.

'You do worse just to get a good look at some horrible slug,' Diana added.

Cornelia didn't have a response that even bordered on intelligent, so she whispered a hex under her breath and Diana's teacup splashed onto the table.

'*Hey—*' Diana started, but Mallory held up a hand.

'Stop that,' she said mildly. 'We have a case.'

'An important case,' Theodore said, vaulting up from his seat with his hands on his hips. 'A case most vile and cruel. The case of the Wrackton Digger. I'm naming this one, Diana.'

Diana considered this for a moment. 'Fine,' she said.

Cornelia stood and wrote it on their whiteboard, and Theodore nodded his gracious acceptance.

'Is it odd that it's one Apparent and one witch?' Diana asked. 'Not that I care...' she added sotto voce.

'*Au contraire*, my little friend. Little, because you are shorter than me,' Theodore clarified unnecessarily. 'I have thought about this. You see, the only options available to the Wrackton Digger are those buried in entirety here: witches, demons, trolls and Apparents. So while their Occult status, or lack thereof, may transpire to be of enormous significance, what if they are approaching the grave-robbing in a sort of' – at this he swung his arms violently – '*clockwise fashion*?'

'There's only been two, so time will tell,' Mallory said, smiling at him.

'That was a good pun,' he said approvingly. 'Time will tell. Clockwise fashion. We are so collectively talented.'

'It is a good point,' Cornelia conceded. 'If the focus is on Wrackton, that is. Have we checked if there have been any—'

'Obviously,' Diana said. 'No similar reports of grave-robbing in Oughteron or any of the surrounding towns, a regional search turned up zilch.'

'So this is purely a Wrackton problem,' Mallory said. 'That's something.'

'Theodore suggested that it could be another ritual,' Diana said, chewing her lip. 'I talked to the neighbours who overlook Blackburn's grave, they saw nothing. I maybe talked a little *too* much, as I think they're now concerned that there is someone stealing random bones from the graveyard for necromantic purposes, but I did my best.'

'Almost nice job,' Mallory said. 'Theodore, is that enough for you to— Oh, he's gone already.'

Theodore had moved to the lab immediately, noisily lifting beakers out of a cupboard.

'Mallory, if you help me analyse these soil samples, I think that would be excellent day one progress. Cornelia, what did you have there? Paper? Your intrepid analysis is required! Lab coats, please!' Theodore exclaimed, pulling his cardigan around himself in obvious delight.

'Maybe just examine the paper fragments?' Mallory said to Cornelia. 'They're so small I don't want to destroy them, but if Theodore decides they're relevant we'll need to put them into the Magic Magical Machine for analysis. They could literally be something that fell off a recycling truck, or an ingredient in compost, but they could also be important and I don't want to ruin this for him.'

'No stone unturned,' Cornelia said. 'So glad we have an agency motto that can be used against us.'

'*One* of our agency mottos. I quite like "helping you detect the undetectable". I'm hoping we can really lean on the *helping* part for the rest of this case.'

'Then we can get back to bigger and better things, like our ongoing conflict between Cornelia and the rest of the Broadwicks and how that affects me and Mallory,' Diana said. Cornelia snapped her fingers and Diana shrieked at the hex that hit her eyebrow.

'Diana, what's the ETA on our interviewees?' Theodore called. 'I must also note that I am not seeing lab coats yet!'

Mallory repeated the relevant part to Diana as she rubbed her eyebrow, scowling.

'He's lucky I found someone useful for him. She's on her way.'

SIX

Diana had, in fact, turned up *three* someone-usefuls, the first of whom arrived promptly to meet them in the research room. Mallory stayed in the lab working on the soil samples with Theodore, who was full of a variety of helpful to distinctly unhelpful suggestions, and did not take kindly to Cornelia's request they close the partition door so they could talk to their contact in peace, despite insisting that Cornelia and Diana should, quote, 'run point' on the interviews.

Hayley Eason tucked a lock of strawberry-blonde hair behind her ear, glancing at their ostensibly blank murder board – Cornelia had whispered a spell to turn it around before Hayley got an eyeful of their process.

'Thanks so much for meeting us,' Diana said brightly, offering a plate of biscuits. Hayley took one hesitantly, then settled back in her chair. 'Cornelia, you remember Hayley Eason, from the Mayoral Offices.'

Cornelia had done a great deal of memorising when it came to the inhabitants of Wrackton, their connections, and their connections' connections. She knew Hayley as the (young) former partner of the former Night Mayor of Wrackton and Dr Ray's current assistant, but the message from Diana was clear: pretend the Undetectables had never had any reason to look into her before.

'I've been here before,' Hayley said, squinting at Cornelia. 'Not the basement,' she clarified. 'I'm friends with your sisters. Whatever happened to those parties? I was a big fan of the Samhain balls, they were so much fun.'

Cornelia cast a glance at the door to the lab, where Theodore was repeating his *clockwise fashion* arm movements to a captive audience of Mallory.

'You said you wanted to talk about the grave-robbing?' Hayley asked.

'Dr Ray— Dr Night Mayor Ray—' Diana started.

'She's Honourable Dr now,' Hayley said helpfully.

'Honourable Dr Night Mayor Ray, who we will henceforth call Dr Ray for purpose of simplicity—'

'I call her Priya,' Hayley added.

'Whatever,' Cornelia said. 'And I mean that professionally. What Diana is trying to say is that Dr Ray informed us that you were the one who called in the disturbance of Freya Evans's grave, and we wanted to hear a first-hand account, in your own words. Recorder going on, if you don't have any objections.'

Someone would have to transcribe the interview later for Theodore's benefit, and Cornelia knew in her heart that 'someone' would be her.

Hayley shook her head, then leaned towards the recorder to say, 'No,' emphatically.

Cornelia clicked the recorder on, rattling off the date, time and Hayley's name, and looked to Diana to start the actual proceedings.

Diana raised an eyebrow – still missing hairs from the earlier hex – and Cornelia grimaced. She had to do everything around here herself.

'Why don't you run us through what you saw that night. Can we confirm this was Monday last week?'

'Yes. It was early, about seven a.m. or just after. I go for a run most mornings and cut through the cemetery either on my way out or my way back. It all depends, really, on— Sorry, that's not relevant.' She smiled awkwardly. 'I was at Freya Evans's funeral last year – her aunt is friends with my mother – and I'd been at the burial, not in my official capacity as an aide to Honourable Night Mayor—'

'I thought it was Honourable Dr?' Cornelia interrupted.

'Not when she's the Night Mayor, the role is referenced differently,' Hayley explained patiently. 'It's been a while since we had titled Occulture, but that's how it used to be.'

'Don't interrupt our witness,' Diana said sweetly, and Cornelia felt herself parting with a retaliatory couple of eyebrow hairs. Someday they were really going to murder each other.

'As I was saying, I went to the funeral, so it's a grave I sort of… look at as I pass, if that makes sense. And that morning, I glanced over and saw the mound of dirt and just thought "that's strange", so I went over and saw it had been fully dug up.'

'What did you see?' Cornelia pressed. She took notes, her scrawling script crowding into the margins the way it always did, her thoughts moving faster than her hand could keep up with.

'A mound of dirt, like I said. Piled, like it had been dug up by someone. I looked at the gravestone to make sure it was Freya's – a bit of a shock that it was, honestly – and then I noticed the coffin was fully uncovered.'

'Could you see into the coffin?'

'No, the lid was still on.'

'Did you touch it?'

She smiled. 'I've spent enough time with Pri— with Honourable Night— I mean the Honourable Dr over the past few weeks that she has really impressed upon me the importance of never touching a crime scene.'

'What made you think it was a crime scene?' Diana asked, and Cornelia realised she'd left a long pause that Diana had hastened to fill. Her mind was starting to wander, song lyrics looping around and around in her head. She tapped her boot against the leg of her chair, fighting the urge to get up and pace the way she usually would if she wasn't leading interviews as her handwriting got more and more illegible.

Mallory said the pacing added to her mystique as a PI; Diana said it was a clear sign someone should've sent Cornelia for an ADHD assessment years before their friend Kingston had.

'It struck me as odd, so I called Observer Johnson and asked him if he authorised the disturbance – I would've seen an exhumation order if it came in to Dr— Honourable Night Mayor Ray,' Hayley said. 'He hadn't, so I asked him who the gravediggers were for this cemetery. I wanted to make sure it wasn't just a mix-up. He said all the cemeteries, except Vampire Cemetery, use the same gravediggers.' She paused, seemingly weighing up sharing the next part. 'He said, "Wrackton might be made of money, but it's not made of folk sensitive enough for the job." Honourable Dr Ray confirmed that she works with a couple of Apparent lads from Oughteron who come in as and when to operate the machines. She says they're the only ones authorised to do so.'

Cornelia glanced at Diana; they would be the boys they'd seen earlier.

'And Observer Johnson hadn't heard of the exhumation?' Cornelia asked.

'No, he was quite certain this was unauthorised. I called Honourable—'

'For the purposes of the tape, could we just call her Dr Ray?' Cornelia interrupted again.

'If you promise to stop interrupting, I'm sure Hayley will agree to anything,' Diana said through gritted teeth.

'—Dr Ray,' Hayley continued uncomfortably. 'And she came with Detective Inspector O'Sullivan and her team and they secured the area. Lifted the lid and confirmed the coffin was empty, then put it back as it was, but left the grave open for further examination.'

'Has anyone informed the Evans family about this?'

Hayley nodded grimly. 'Part of my job as aide. They're devastated. Losing a loved one is one thing; someone stealing that loved one's body is unconscionable.'

'Did you see anyone, hear anything on your runs that might be useful to note?'

'No, I'm sorry. I run with headphones in so I wouldn't hear anything. There's an older lady who walks her equally old dog every morning around the time I go out, but there's not another soul awake in that part of Wrackton that early.'

Hayley had nothing else to add, so Diana gave her a card and asked her to call should she think of anything useful. She said something about texting the twins about coming to visit, and Cornelia had to refrain from pushing her to the door.

When she left, Cornelia magicked away Hayley's cup and replaced it with a fresh one, adding more biscuits to the dwindling plate. 'Well that was dreadful. Who's next? Would Theodore perhaps like to take over *working his own specially asked-for case*, now, or—?'

The doorbell rang and Diana jumped up. Theodore and Mallory were still absorbed in their lab work, and hadn't so much as looked up at Cornelia's desperate attempt to be rescued from boredom.

'*Next* is much more unpleasant, and I apologise in advance, but she's also our second eyewitness. We got a nice little corroboration from Hayley.' Diana threw open the door. 'Mrs Blackburn! Lovely to see you in the flesh. It's been ages, hasn't it? Please come in, the kettle's on.'

Cornelia had just enough wherewithal to find a clean spoon as Mrs Blackburn shuffled into the room. She had a very small, very ragged, probable dog in her arms – Cornelia might've identified it as particularly mournful rat had Hayley not suggested 'dog' – and a very tired, very *done* expression on her face.

'May we first say we are tremendously sorry for your loss,' Diana started, but Mrs Blackburn scoffed.

'That's all anyone says. *Sorry for your loss, sorry for your loss.* You didn't believe me that he was poisoned, and now someone's taken my Paul out of his grave and he's barely cold!'

There wasn't a lot Cornelia could say to this, so she got up and made tea.

'Would you like a biscuit, Mrs Blackburn?'

'I'm *grieving*,' she spat.

Cornelia stared at her.

'Of *course* I want a fucking biscuit.'

She steadily ate her way through four biscuits as they set up the recorder, and asked her what she'd seen at the cemetery.

'I already emailed your Melody to tell her the grave had been disturbed,' Mrs Blackburn said.

'*Mallory* did mention that, yes,' Cornelia said, annoyance boiling in her stomach for reasons she couldn't identify. 'She said you contacted her and told her the grave was disturbed. That was last night.'

'You little clodhoppers found it today, you tell me.'

'We aren't really police,' Diana said. 'We're PIs. Helping you detect the undetectable. While we do occasionally work with the police on certain cases, there's a distinction.'

'But you digress,' Cornelia said. She threw down her pen and assumed her pacing position, following her footsteps over the floor tiles as she moved over and back, over and back, across the research room.

Diana glared at her. 'I suppose I do. What made you think Paul— Mr Blackburn's grave was disturbed?'

'I had a little plant pot, and it was moved. Can't have been the wind. It was a pot of flowering ivy, brought from the place we first met. Little bits of confetti or something scattered around it. *Someone* was there. Paul didn't have many friends left alive, so it can't have been another visitor. We go see him every morning, you know. Me and Maisie.' She clutched the probable-dog-now-known-as-Maisie closer, where it tremored against her shoulder. 'We go for a little walk and we tell him about our plans for the day. This is the first morning I've missed a walk, and it was only because I knew that terrible, *awful* little bastard was being buried beside his long-suffering father, and I didn't want any part in it.'

It was hard to tell if she meant 'bastard' in the pejorative 'he's a murderer' sense, or if she felt really strongly about the circumstances of Jacob's birth. Cornelia wasn't sure she wanted to know.

'That's understandable. Did you touch the grave when you discovered the plant was moved?' Diana prompted. They knew the answer to this – there had been no plant pot to see.

'I took it back with me,' she said. 'I don't want anyone touching Paul's things, especially if he's not there to bite their fingers off.'

'Do you still have it?'

'Yes.'

'Could we have it?'

'Why?'

'We could run some forensics tests on it, maybe determine if magic was used around it,' Cornelia said.

Provided she hadn't mauled it to the point of any trace evidence being gone for good.

'Why?'

'Because it could be useful in identifying who took your husband's body,' Diana finished patiently.

'What's it worth to you?'

'Mrs Blackburn,' Cornelia said, her own patience completely worn out. 'We want to find the person who took your husband's remains. I don't know what you know about decomposition, but he—'

'Deserves to be placed back in the ground to rest,' Diana finished hurriedly.

'Yes. So any leads you have, any stone we can turn over, we want to do that.'

'I want to talk to the Night Mayor,' Mrs Blackburn snapped. 'I want to have a meeting. *With her.* I want *her* to speak to me, not that infant she sent last time. Halo, or whatever her name was.'

'Hayley. She's Dr Ray's new aide, so she's quite senior.'

'I don't care about that. Get me Dr Ray, and you can have your plant pot.'

'Fine,' Cornelia said, and made the call there and then, securing an appointment for two days' time, which mollified Mrs Blackburn enough into begrudgingly promising to surrender the plant pot once she'd met with her, and, more importantly, agreeing to leave.

'How did that go?' Mallory asked, nudging open the partition door. 'I heard her leave,' she added, smiling wryly.

'She has potential evidence but is refusing to give it over to us unless she gets an audience with the Night Mayor,' Cornelia said.

'What kind of evidence?' Theodore shouted from across the lab. 'I'm eavesdropping! Something damning, I hope. A photograph of the Wrackton Digger in action. An electronic device belonging to the killer. The discarded undergarments of a quick-change incognito!'

'A plant pot she insists was moved before he was dug up. She also said she saw—'

The doorbell rang, interrupting her.

'That's Freya's family now, hold that thought,' Diana said. 'Theodore, you sure you don't want to…? Thought as much.'

Freya Evans's family had been even more distraught than Mrs Blackburn, but had even less information.

'So that's a bust,' Cornelia said after they left, scribbling PLANT POT and PAPER on the whiteboard. 'But Theodore should at least be able to get that plant pot.'

'Splendid work, truly stellar,' Theodore said grandly. 'Looks like you need to talk to the two gravediggers Observer Johnson hires when the mood suits him, and probably Observer Johnson as well?'

'*I* don't need—' Cornelia started, but one glance from Mallory and Cornelia closed her eyes in defeat.

'I think if you hasten, the three of you can squeeze in a visit to him today. This case is coming together *very* nicely. I should try being lead more often, I'm getting so much done,' Theodore said.

It was testament to how much they generally liked him that the rest of the Undetectables didn't set upon him with a large iron-lined box and leave him at the edge of the Redwoods.

'Worth a try,' Mallory said, stretching. 'Come see what we've been working on before we go. Spoiler alert—'

'I think you mean *soiler* alert. 'Cause it's soil.'

'Hah,' Mallory said, but there was an obvious smile beneath

it. 'The soil samples just gave us composition of the soil. No blood, no obvious magic trace. We didn't get anything physical other than the paper. Little fragments that you'd expect, but nothing obviously or even possibly associated with the grave-robbing. Unless you count this bit of crisp packet from 1993.'

'Which I don't,' Theodore said. 'See you later.'

SEVEN

Back when Cornelia was twelve and her sisters were sixteen, the entire extended family – even the worst-behaved uncles and aunts and great-whatevers from Imogen's side – had descended on the Observatory for Ethel and Agatha's Naming Ceremony. It came later for twins for reasons Cornelia had been unable to establish, as she'd had hers at seven (it had been just as eventful, probably, but she didn't have as clear a memory of it, only that Grandad Cornelius was regretful at having made the trip). Had Agatha and Ethel been triplets, their ceremony wouldn't occur until they were twenty, which Cornelia also found lacking in explanation.

There had been an incident that Cornelia still refused to speak of because it wasn't her fault. Curtains should not be flammable by default, and twelve-year-olds with short attention spans shouldn't be asked to carry candles, even if they're trying their hardest to focus.

The curtain had been replaced, but Observer Johnson's opinion of her had not.

They stepped into the main hallway of the Observatory, and Cornelia trailed her fingers off the marble skirts of Hecate and Morrigan, mothers of the Ternion, where they stood in a niche, hands clasped.

'Do you think he's even still here? Not like him to not immediately sweep down and growl at me for existing,' she said, almost pleased with herself for thinking of something the old Cornelia would say. The one who didn't have to pretend her body wasn't screaming at her to lock herself in her bedroom, to never leave her house again, that it wasn't safe, wouldn't be safe, had never been *safe*. She wasn't much of an actor, but her recurring role in the play she liked to think of as *Appearing Normal and Unhindered by Inexplicable Horrors* had thus far successfully stopped Diana interrogating her on why she was suddenly incapable of doing things that had previously been as easy as breathing.

Even breathing came with challenges, these days.

'I'm up here,' a voice called, and the Undetectables looked up to see Observer Johnson crouched at the opening to an attic space. 'Can you all climb?'

Cornelia looked to Mallory, who nodded shortly. She had no idea what it was like for Mallory to live in constant pain, but remembering to check in with her was one of the few memory-related things that took her no effort at all.

They clambered up an ornate ladder – Diana was wearing platform boots so impractical there was almost a catastrophe – and emerged into the glass dome in the roof of the Observatory. Midnight-blue stained glass and hand-painted stars in glorious constellations faded into a view of the sky so crystal clear that

Cornelia thought she could simply walk off the edge. It was one of the few places in Wrackton she'd never been, though she'd always wanted to see it. It was used for special ceremonies, though what they were and why they happened wasn't something Cornelia had ever felt particularly motivated to find out.

'I bet at night the painted sky merges perfectly with the real one,' Mallory whispered.

Observer Johnson looked uncharacteristically neutral to see them, organising flowers on a shrine in the centre of the room, even if Cornelia noticed his gaze wavered slightly when he spotted her. She pulled her jumper sleeves down, anxious sweat pricking under her arms, and lifted her head, trying to appear unbothered. This was a nice glass dome, and she was here with her best friends. Her ride-or-dies. Her fellow investigators. Her Mallory.

Before she could interrogate that last thought too hard, Observer Johnson cleared his throat.

'You said this was about burials and interments,' he prompted.

'Yes,' Mallory said. 'We were wondering what you could tell us about the process of burials, particularly in the witch cemeteries.'

'They're not only *witch* cemeteries – we lay Apparents to rest there, too,' Observer Johnson said, rubbing a hand over his lined face. Cornelia wondered what he'd look like if he smiled. 'But primarily, yes, "witch cemeteries" is correct.'

Mallory waited, as he had not only not fully answered the question, he had given her information she already knew.

As much as Cornelia had wanted Theodore to do this himself,

the thought of him bungling such a simple information-gathering exercise by over-egging it wasn't worth needing to rescue their reputation later on, especially over something so inconsequential.

The boredom was starting to seep in again, heightening her fear. She needed to keep herself on task. Distractions equalled peace. She needed hundreds of small distractions a day. This could be one of them if she threw herself into it.

'I don't do any of it myself,' he continued. He hadn't paused for that long; Cornelia tended to think many thoughts in the time it took the average person to complete one. 'I did for years, but it reassures folk when someone is in charge of the burial and someone else is in charge of the ceremony. They feel they're in safer hands.'

'Who typically helps?' Cornelia asked, before Mallory could.

'After years of searching, I found two brothers from Oughteron. Ian and… Lee, I think. Maybe the second one is called Stewart, I don't really deal with the one who isn't Ian. They're hard workers, always here promptly, respect the customs, even when they're varied. Apparents, naturally. The only burials they don't help with are faerie and vampire, for obvious reasons. They've overseen witch, Apparent and demon burials, have been on hand for troll entombments, though we don't get many of those.'

'Would you say they're trustworthy?' Diana asked.

'Indubitably,' Observer Johnson said. 'I hand-picked them. They are the only ones, besides myself, authorised to dig on any burial land here.'

'Have you, or they, noticed any disturbances at any graves

recently?' Cornelia asked, sounding too enthusiastic to her own ears.

'First I heard of anything wrong was Freya Evans's grave, which I assume you are here to ask me about, but I heard that through Dr Ray and her aide, Hayley whatsit. I remember faces, not names,' he said sharply.

Trolls were uncannily good at remembering faces; Observer Johnson was not brilliant at remembering names to go with them.

'They asked me to keep an eye out. If you three are here, that must mean there's something Occult going on.'

'We're following a line of enquiry at the behest of our client,' Mallory said politely. 'You mentioned the brothers are the only ones authorised to dig on any burial land – what exactly does that mean? Do you mean in a magical context, or ceremonial?'

'As much as Occulture likes to stand on ceremony, I mean in a magical context.' He snorted. 'We used to have a free-for-all, but now it's wards and approved tools – even with the approved tools, one could not simply dig up a body. Hence Dr Ray and her aide's *interest* in myself and the boys.'

'Curious, then, how it's happened anyway,' Cornelia said.

'I have accepted that it makes me a suspect, but I have no need for bones. Should I *want* bones, I would have returned the graves to their previous states, and no one would be any the wiser. I told Dr Ray this, and I am telling you now: I had nothing to do with it. And in my opinion, the boys like their work too much to do something like this. Besides, this would be showing initiative they don't have,' he mumbled sotto voce.

'When's the last time your boys were in Wrackton for a burial?'

'Earlier today, but I haven't needed them since sometime last week. Time before that… there was a run on demon burials for a while there, so we were slammed. Deaths are like buses,' he said. 'They will always carry on to the final destination one way or another.'

'Could we have a number for Ian or… his brother?' Mallory asked.

Observer Johnson pulled out his phone, frowning. 'Is that all you need, or would you also like to take some of my hair?'

As Observer Johnson was bald, this was an offer that Cornelia was willing to refuse.

'Speak now or allow me to sit in silent contemplation.'

Mallory raised a slightly timid hand. 'Where's the toolshed for all the burial grounds? We're going to need to see it.'

Cornelia weighed up staying with Diana and potentially risking her asking if she was okay, or going with Mallory and trying to manufacture the power of distraction, which is how she found herself a few steps behind Mallory in the pretty Memorial Garden at the rear of the Observatory. She'd paused to look at the Ternion memorial tomb (the garden was aptly, if a little obviously, named) which she could only remember looking at once before, when she was small. The tomb itself was relatively underwhelming, given how much of a big deal the UML and the former Night Mayor had made about their *Visit Wrackton* campaign. For something meant to honour the three main goddesses of Occulture, it was just a marble slab upon which sat a fountain decorated with little pentagrams and a sculpture of three disembodied linking hands in the middle, denoting Hexana, Blair and Elisabella.

'Do you think they're actually under there?' Cornelia asked, and Mallory turned back to stand with her. 'The Ternion.'

Mallory shook her head. 'I read somewhere that the tomb is ornamental, though it's impossible to know with this place. Their remains are somewhere in Wrackton, but nobody knows where. I assume the Night Mayor does, and probably the Ghoul Council.'

'Weird, to think about it. Even goddesses die.'

It was a morbid thought impulsively expressed, but she could trust Mallory not to make it weird.

'They don't have one for Hecate or Morrigan,' Cornelia said suddenly, looking around. 'There's statues inside, but I don't—' She stopped, the end of the sentence deserting her.

Mallory chewed her lip thoughtfully 'I have always wondered why— Sorry, what was I saying?'

Cornelia couldn't remember Mallory having said anything at all, or what they'd even been talking about, and they crossed to the tool shed in amicable silence.

Mallory unlocked the heavy door – it was less *shed* and more *beautiful, tiny cottage* – her kitbag at the ready. Across the garden, Diana emerged from the Observatory with her phone in her hand. She'd voted to stay outside, ostensibly to contact the gravedigger brothers, but largely to avoid seeing any 'fucking spiders or weird little flying pricks'. Cornelia always thought that was a perk of going anywhere people didn't normally venture.

'What are we looking for?' Cornelia pulled on her gloves as Mallory surveyed the space.

'Signs,' Mallory said. 'Of what, I don't know, but we may as well just finish this case up so Theodore can feel he's done a good job. That sounds horrible. I know it sounds horrible. I think Theodore is so good at so many things, but he's not a *leader*, he's a… goddess, saying "follower" sounds so…' She shook her head, and Cornelia let it slide.

She wasn't wrong. There was just no nice way of saying it.

'If it makes you feel better, my gut is telling me this case is a complete waste of our time and whoever is doing it is trying to be a nuisance,' Cornelia said. 'I do enjoy how your version of half-arsing an investigation is virtually identical to most people's whole-arsing it.'

'Can you take photos of those shovels?' Mallory continued, a blush creeping over her cheeks. 'He'll want soil samples, see if we can get something circumstantial. Otherwise it's trying to find a shovel in a world of shovels. It's likely pointless because they are used to dig grave sites all the time, but our second motto is "no stone unturned".'

Cornelia lifted the camera she'd had dangling around her neck and obliged as Mallory kept looking. She'd pulled her hair back into a ponytail, a sure sign that her brain was working overtime.

Mallory examined the shovels for prints and pulled tapings off the handles that she affixed to backing cards. 'Some prints here, but that's to be expected, given that they're used regularly. I'm not actually expecting the Wrackton Digger left anything behind here, especially as what Observer Johnson said is pretty definitive – our only real suspects are the gravediggers, which makes it both easy and incredibly difficult to pin it on them.'

'Do you think?'

'If Dr Ray or Sully had found anything already, there wouldn't have been a second grave-robbing,' Mallory said grimly.

'Fair point.'

'Although I say they're Theodore's— *our* only suspects, but… there is one other viable option at this time.'

Cornelia got it at once. 'You're wondering if they could've been somehow persuaded into doing it by someone else?'

'That's my current hypothesis. Two random people— Sorry, brain jumped ahead,' Mallory raised a hand. 'Bodies, even in varying states of decay, are heavy. It's not a one-person job, even if there was witchlight travel involved. The Digger likely has an accomplice, which again points to the gravediggers as likely culprits. We're no strangers to two killers working together, so it's a viable supposition. However, two *random* people carrying partially skeletonised remains would be suspicious, while two people whose job it is to cart coffins around and dig holes would get away with this easily. If the Wrackton Digger was not one or both of them, it's possible they were used *by* the Digger.'

It was genius, and in another world Mallory would probably be a criminal mastermind. As it stood, she was too nice and—

The thought was interrupted by Mallory holding out a hand. For one illogical moment, Cornelia thought she meant for her to take it. Her hand twitched towards the soft curl of Mallory's palm around her latex gloves.

'Can I have a beetle?' Mallory prompted, after what must've been several years of Cornelia staring at her and thinking a million unconnected thoughts. 'A magic trace is the last potential piece of evidence we'll get from here.'

'Yes, of course.' Cornelia reached smoothly down the front of her jumper and dropped a box into Mallory's hand.

She felt safe in this shed, she realised. It was warm and a bit damp and cobwebby, and it smelled of earth and something else comforting. Soap, or detergent. And it was emanating from Mallory every time she turned her head, her ponytail flicking.

'All right, Lawrence VII,' Mallory said, addressing the beetle. 'Do your thing.'

'Then we can conclude today's performance of Forensic Investigation Theatre, and hopefully Theodore will be satisfied with our routine findings and move the investigation on himself.'

And Cornelia could get back to trying to swerve the screaming call of the Void.

As Lawrence walked on the shovel, Cornelia's phone buzzed again.

(FKA) MOTHER (DO NOT ANSWER)

She sent it to voicemail – a service she did not and would not ever check – and ignored Mallory's quizzical look. They'd have to try harder than that to get hold of her.

Lawrence VII flickered and Mallory and Cornelia both startled.

'He's… no,' Mallory said, sounding disappointed.

'There's some kind of trace there,' Cornelia said, excitement creeping into her voice. Real excitement, at seeing *Sonata lutumae* do what they did best. 'Lawrence just doesn't know what it is.'

'Did you see what colour he flickered? I thought it was white,' Mallory said uncertainly. 'But I can't be sure.'

'It was too fast to see, it was like a camera flash.' Cornelia frowned, reaching into the back pocket of her jeans for a battered lavender notebook, scribbling this observation down. Mallory had given her six of these and she was down to her last one, the others lost to time and misplacement. All too often objects just disappeared from Cornelia's hands by a process that felt magical but was not. Too much was going on in her brain at all times to remember every single thing happening in the present. If she could hang on to this notebook, someday she was going to do a PhD for the simple purpose of spiting everyone who'd looked at her sideways for her dissertation topic.

She'd probably need to be medicated first.

'Let's go again,' Cornelia said, handing over a second beetle from the top of her boot, and got her phone ready to take a video.

This time, she caught the burst of light.

'This is different to the time they detected plant magic,' Cornelia said. 'That time they flickered green then back to orange. This time it's a burst of light, or energy, then back to orange.'

'A bug in the bug?' Mallory suggested.

'Or they're onto something.' Cornelia put the beetles back in their boxes and safely into Mallory's kit, alongside her fingerprint tapings and soil samples. Mallory surveyed the shed one last time before they left, Cornelia already feeling bereft at the idea of stepping outside. Mallory had a habit of making her feel safe.

'—thanks,' Diana said loudly, and Cornelia pushed the shed door open.

Diana's nose wrinkled in frustration as she put the phone on loudspeaker.

'Hi, my brother said you're asking questions about the Wrackton graves?' a voice said.

'Yes, I'm just wondering if you remember Freya Evans, or Paul Blackburn?'

'I don't think so, no,' the voice said. Friendly, yet mildly bewildered.

'Are you sure? You must remember Freya Evans, she died last year. She has a big family, a husband, lots of in-laws.'

'Oh yeah!' the voice said, in a tone that suggested the owner was hoping Diana would drop it.

'And Paul Blackburn was a centenarian, his wife—'

'Mate, that's *Mrs Blackburn*,' a second voice whispered.

'Oh yeah, I remember her. Awful. That he died, and that she was so unhappy.'

'Right. Just wondering if you've been to those graves lately, seen anything?'

'No, I don't think so,' a voice said – they were similar enough that Cornelia was having trouble distinguishing them; the expression on Diana's face suggested she was, too.

'When's the last time you were in Wrackton? Either of you,' Diana asked.

'Besides today? Erm… Few weeks ago? Demon burials. A run on them.'

'Observer Johnson said something about buses,' the second voice said.

'And you haven't been here for any other reason?'

'Not sure,' a voice said uncertainly. 'We'd… we'd remember that, wouldn't we?'

Mallory frowned.

'I think it could be really helpful to us if you *could* remember,' Diana said sweetly.

'Has anyone ever asked you to do anything you didn't want to do?' Mallory asked.

'All the time,' a voice said. He didn't seem to notice Diana was no longer speaking.

'I mean against your will. In an Occult sense,' Mallory clarified.

There was a pause.

'I haven't the faintest idea,' the voice said. 'Ian, mate, do you?'

'Nah mate, I think we'd know. Right?'

Diana pressed a fist to her face.

'Well, thank you for your time. We'll be back in touch with more questions as and when they come up,' Diana said.

'Cheers, Diana. And hey, let us know if you change your mind on that thing.'

Diana hung up.

'So I take it that was Lee-Stewart-Ian?' Cornelia said bravely, half expecting Diana to rip her head off. Diana rarely couldn't steer an interview in the right direction.

'Ian *Stewartson* saw nothing useful. He thought I was calling to suggest his brother, Lee Stewartson, had dug up the wrong grave and was ready to rip his head off. I'm still furious,' Diana said, though there was a smile playing across her lips.

'Why? We've had bad interviews before,' Cornelia said.

'He's an opportune salesman,' Diana said, trying not to laugh. 'Apparently the Brothers Dim want to set up their own funeral home, and he wanted to know if I was interested in being a first customer.'

'Should we consider that a death threat?'

'Who knows. Who cares. What did you get? Any leads, any hints that they did it?'

'A potential hypothesis, all going well.'

Diana's phone buzzed again – Cornelia jumped, afraid it was hers – and her eyes practically shone as she answered.

'Hey,' Diana said breathlessly.

Mallory and Cornelia both turned and mouthed an over-exaggerated 'hey' to each other, and Diana hit Cornelia with a tiny hex. Mallory pressed her hand to her mouth, smothering giggles she normally refused to even entertain during work hours.

Diana in love was a very different sort of Diana, even if she refused to acknowledge it.

'Yes, Taylor, you can come help me and my childish idiot friends, we're heading home for a scintillating afternoon of lab work now.'

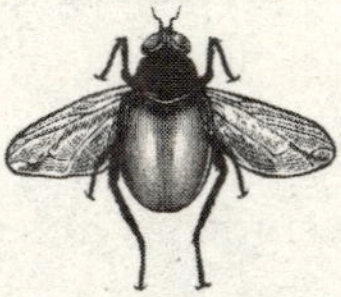

PERIMORTEM II

They liked it when the papers started reporting on them. Call it vanity, or a desire to be recognised. Little pieces, little snippets, a prelude to the sonata that was still to come.

They missed the point, though. People always tried to force a conclusion before the end.

They knew the act of burial was closure for the living. That the buried weren't always dead to start with.

To bury was a means to an end. To reap the rewards of a carefully executed plan, a project that is theirs alone. Their victims – they liked *victims*, an accurate word that didn't soften the circumstances – had no idea they were dying, had no idea they were already dead, had no idea they were buried six feet under, in a tomb of their own making.

They liked the panic. Each victim heralds a week-long affair – mark your calendars, this is the main event. The panic builds to a crescendo that lifts the hairs on the backs of their arms. Goosebumps, tears. A solo standing ovation.

It would be a matter of time before the papers figured it out.

Before someone put the pieces together. They were digging their own grave.

That made it all the better.

EIGHT

'Run it again,' Theodore suggested.

Mallory, perched on a stool next to the Magic Magical Machine, gritted her teeth and tried again. She was conscious of her friends, mere feet away in the research room, laughing and joking as they finished the murder board – despite this not being a murder in the strictest sense.

'I don't think we have a sensitive enough test to isolate whatever the beetles picked up,' Mallory said, sighing at the results from her various tests. 'It could be that they picked up a trace of the wards, and there is no separate magic trace to be found. I think we can ask Sully to check the fingerprint database for the partials we pulled off the shovels – though we know they belong to Ian and Lee, it could help you build your case. The only other thing I can suggest is that you go back with more beetles – perhaps these ones are contaminated? Though if they're contaminated already, we might be out of luck with magical lab work, and we should— *you* could focus on the information we've gathered so far. Cornelia reckons this is all the Digger being a deliberate nuisance. I think we'd be wise not to... get our hopes up about this being a particularly big or interesting case.'

'Wisdom is in the eye of the beholder,' Theodore said. 'You're quite right, Mallory. Probably high time I visit the scene myself. I can have Diana contact Detective Inspector O'Sullivan about the fingerprints. She can send any findings to you at the Mayoral Offices, so you can get back to work.'

The Machine beeped again and she brought the chart around the partition to Theodore.

'See? It's also possible it's just an area of high concentration of old magic. It could be picking up old spells from the graves around the area. I've always assumed magic hung around.'

'An ingenious suggestion,' Theodore said, staring at the chart. He wrapped his cardigan around him, bending so his nose was inches from the paper. 'I think we need a clean soil sample. It may be that we can devise a way to isolate different elements, but without knowing exactly what's in the soil already, this is likely a pointless exercise. And I harbour no secret desire to waste your time! All I care for is the unveiling of the truth – no matter the villain, we can be greater than their devious plan! I can get the soil sample, if you'd rather go discuss the minutiae with the others. Also, you look like you could use a sit down.'

Mallory pulled off her lab coat and smiled tiredly at Theodore. Over the last year, Theodore had settled into a more subdued version of himself, more akin to the Theodore she'd grown up alongside. Though she still watched him, still scrawled notes in her Theodore Cold Case Notebook, the events of last year – his attempt to possess her, his constantly disappearing into the Mayoral Offices, the fact he was secretly communicating with Katherine the ghost – had all but been forgotten.

He'd apologised, once, for possessing her, and then skilfully avoided any and all references to it. He'd got his job back, the bowels of the Mayoral Offices were no longer accessible, and they had all studiously avoided mentioning that the Broadwicks had (in all likelihood) murdered Theodore. It was like they had mutually lifted the rug and shoved everything underneath it.

Seeing him now, happily humming at such a pitch that his cat ears were vibrating as he set up beakers and test tubes, filled Mallory with such a sense of fondness, she couldn't help but tell him about it.

'Theo?'

'Hm?'

'I just want you to know that my favourite times, some of my fondest memories, are about us working together on cases. I hope that never changes.'

Theodore pulled her into a hug so quickly she almost fell over, the tops of his cat ears brushing against her chin.

'I will never stop being grateful that of all the basements in all the world, this was the one I died in.'

She squeezed him, feeling a buildup of static, and left him to it while she went to the research room.

Diana and Taylor were curled around each other on one of the sofas, Taylor's green hair spread out over the seat cushions, and Cornelia was illogically standing on her desk, gesticulating so wildly the sleeves of her jumper billowed as she moved.

'What's going on?' Mallory asked.

'Cornelia's recent brush with poverty has spurred her into action,' Diana said.

'She's on a mad one,' Taylor said.

'No, listen,' Cornelia said, jumping down. 'It's a genius plan. And not just a plan, but the gold standard in PI activity: a stakeout.'

'I'm listening,' Mallory said. Cornelia's eyes were practically shining. It was a notably total one-eighty from her earlier, obvious boredom with the case. Something had changed, though Mallory couldn't say what it was. She contained too many multitudes for Mallory to be able to pin her mercurial moods down.

'I know our previous attempts at stakeouts haven't gone all that well,' she said.

'You can say that again,' Diana snorted.

'I *know* our previous attempts at stakeouts haven't gone all that well,' Cornelia repeated.

'Because?'

'Because I got bored, and I was morally opposed to following someone who wasn't a murderer,' Cornelia said. 'Now shut up and let me finish.'

'I think you should shut up and let her finish,' Mallory said.

Diana was trying not to laugh. Taylor had chosen to stare at their sparse murder board, a muscle twitching in her jaw.

'We don't know what the Wrackton Digger is up to – their aims, their goals, their intentions. Apart from considering earlier that this is all a deliberate waste of time on the Digger's part, all we know is that someone is doing *something* with the bodies of the recently deceased in the dead of night. Perhaps those someones are the gravediggers' – Mallory noticed she'd written LEE AND IAN STEWARTSON on the murder board – 'or perhaps they are being directed by someone Occult to dig. A demon, or… well, a witch or troll or vampire or faerie with a big mallet. We can't discount that perhaps the wards are old, or Observer Johnson is wrong about their effectiveness and someone has been able to circumvent the wards, extract the bodies, and climb into a car with single-handed strength even the trolls would fear. Or witchlighting away. Or there's two of them, like Mallory suggested,' Cornelia added, catching Mallory's eye.

'Just tell her what you're proposing,' Diana said. 'And don't think I haven't noticed you're suddenly very into this case you've done nothing but moan about since we took it on.'

'I'm older and wiser now,' Cornelia said.

'It's been one single workday!'

'I *propose* we catch them in the act. Now that the papers have picked up the Wrackton Digger' – Cornelia held up a fresh copy of the evening edition of the *Wrackton Gazette*, where on the third page there was a small report on the disturbed grave and a quote from the Evans family (Mrs Blackburn apparently declined to comment) – 'it's possible it'll expedite their activities. We have no idea how or why they're choosing their victims, but if we take the fact that both victims died a year and two months-ish ago, we could hypothesise that *that* is the unifying feature between them.'

'And we figured out that there are several folk who are coming up on a year-and-three-months anniversary tomorrow. The next few anniversaries aren't for some weeks yet,' Diana said.

'All of which suggests that *tonight* is the best time to try catch them out, and if not, we keep looking for a pattern. I'd like us to try to build up a picture of what the Digger is doing before this gets away from us. Get something concrete quickly.'

Mallory had to admit it was actually a good plan.

'I don't understand why you're so into—' Diana started.

'We could split off in pairs and take as many cemeteries as we can,' Cornelia continued, as if she hadn't spoken.

'Oh fine, don't listen to me,' Diana muttered.

'There's only four of us,' Mallory pointed out.

She was loath to interrupt a good flow, but she was getting better at redirecting Cornelia when she started down a path that didn't fully make sense, or wasn't the best use of resources. Diana called it 'good leadership', but Mallory still felt like she was being a killjoy a lot of the time.

'Pairs would limit us to two cemeteries. If we send Theodore to—'

'But what if we recruited extra helpers? Taylor and Diana go to one, Felix and Kingston to another, me and you—'

She broke off, but not before Mallory felt a swoop in her stomach at the pairings.

'And what about me? What pairing do I get?' Theodore threw open the sliding door, having been summoned by Mallory's mention of his name. 'Fear not, Cornelia. It is my executive decision that I shall remain here. Hold down the fort. Do a little spot of haunting. That'll be my next book, Diana. *The Haunting of Broadwick Mansion*. Utterly original.'

'I don't want to overstep your executive decision-making, but I think you should go with Diana and Taylor,' Mallory said, eyeing them whispering on the couch. Taylor was curled in Diana's lap and neither gave any indication that they heard any of this.

'Oh, much worse!' Theodore complained. 'You want me to third-wheel. Fine, I will be your Reliant Robin, but I will not like it. That's a sort of car, Mallory. Older than I. Classic, I believe. My uncle owned one, used to roll it down the hill with the handbrake off for fun.'

'It's just to try keep them on track,' Mallory said, trying not to laugh at any of this. It was hard enough to get Theodore to accept she wasn't laughing *at* him, but at the fact that even in his greatest displays of enraged chagrin, he was, unfortunately, hilarious.

'And you think Felix and Kingston are going to do a better job?' Diana asked, surfacing for a second – Theodore was clearly far enough away that he hadn't interfered with her hearing aid.

'Felix commits to any bit they participate in, they'll keep Kingston in line. That's an *actual* directorial decision, by the way.' Mallory grinned at the scandalised look Diana threw her.

'Any special requests for the kit?' Cornelia asked.

'Cameras, warm outer layers, a blanket to sit on, some snacks, something warm to drink, and a tactical nap,' Mallory said, already heading for the basement door.

Annoyingly, there were four possible grave targets spread across three cemeteries. With coaching from Mallory, Theodore assigned Taylor, Diana and himself to the bigger witch cemetery, where Paul Blackburn had been dug up. Cornelia had hypothesised that, as the cemetery had just been hit, it was least likely to be targeted again. The other anniversary burials were in the demon mausoleums, and an Apparent in a tiny cemetery a few roads over from the Larix. Kingston and Felix took up the mantle in the latter, and Mallory and Cornelia took the mausoleums.

Mallory privately wondered if they were on the right track with burial anniversaries-plus-some-time, or if there was no way of knowing a pattern until one emerged. She caught herself and laughed quietly – Cornelia had been right, she was incapable of half-arsing anything to do with her work.

The evening was cool, the sun only beginning to set as they went – the perks of it being late spring. Mallory was ready for properly warm days that made it easier to move, not having to rely so heavily on her heating pads and hot water bottles. The heat created other problems, of course – there was always something going wrong in her body – but it was better than the cold.

'Is here a good place?' Cornelia asked.

They stood at the highest point of the demon cemetery, shielded from view by an ancient tree and the stone walls of a particularly ostentatious mausoleum.

Throughout her twenty-two years, Mallory hadn't had much reason to visit, and she was looking at it for the first time with forensic appraisal. It was oddly pretty, set out like a scaled village of the dead: smooth black granite monuments with gothic roofs in neat rows on labelled paths, meticulously maintained to appear as a quiet, lifeless oasis. Dead leaves crunched underfoot and moss-covered tree limbs criss-crossed between the shining crypts. A perpetual autumn.

'This is perfect,' Mallory said, checking behind her. 'I have good visibility all the way down, and we're pretty hidden here. If someone comes along, we'll know.'

'Hopefully the Digger pops in before midnight and we can head home. Maybe watch a film, if Diana and Taylor can bear to have air pass between their faces for a run-time of ninety minutes. And if you're feeling up to it – it's been a long day, thanks to Theodore.' Cornelia spread the blanket on the ground and motioned for Mallory to sit. 'I forgot! I managed to finish my UBI application, but I'm confused – is that per *day*?'

'It's per week,' Mallory said, smiling at her. 'And plenty of people live on it solely and are comfortable.'

A constant refrain within the agency had been how much trouble they'd be in if Cornelia ever lost access to the Broadwick fortune, but Mallory hadn't considered how lost Cornelia would be if this day ever came. She counted herself lucky every day that the Unified Magical Liaison and the Ghoul Council insisted on taking care of everyone without fuss or the sort of bureaucratic nonsense Mallory sometimes saw on chronic illness support forums.

'I can't believe other people live like this. All those times you and Diana made fun of me I thought… I don't know. I think I just thought everyone had some level of not caring? Especially in Wrackton. I knew we – as in, *the Broadwicks* – had money, obviously. I'm not a total idiot, and I didn't think we should hoard it when others might need it more. How could I have been this unaware?'

Mallory had some ideas, but didn't think it helpful to express them.

'You'll figure it out,' she said instead. 'You always do.'

Cornelia paced around, something else she was going to say on her lips, but whatever it was got swallowed and replaced with an all-too-familiar haunted look.

'Are you okay?' Mallory peered at her. 'You've gone all sweaty.'

'Yeah, yeah, I'm fine. The cold, the air or something. Don't worry,' she said tightly.

It was not cold in the slightest, and the air had not changed.

'No, I *am* worried. What's wrong? Are you sick?'

'Just leave it,' Cornelia said.

As much as Mallory didn't want to, she left it, as she had the countless other times she'd noticed something was wrong and Cornelia had brushed her off.

'Can we talk about your family, then? It's peripheral to all of this.'

'What about them? They're a bunch of murdering murderers.'

'We *think*,' Mallory reminded her. 'We only *think*, because a ghost deigned to show us a memory that may or may not be real.'

'If that's not really how she knows Theodore, then I don't know what to believe. What's that got to do with anything, anyway?'

'I noticed you rejecting calls from Imogen. I also noticed this was a habitual rejection of calls when you gave me your phone earlier. She's tried every few months to get in contact. You don't *have* to talk to her, I just wondered how you felt about it all.'

Cornelia threw herself down on the blanket, staring up at the sky.

'Sky's real pretty tonight,' she said, ignoring what Mallory had just said and patting the blanket beside her instead.

'We're on a stakeout,' Mallory said, her heart already beating faster.

'We can do two things, come look at it.'

Mallory carefully lowered herself back on the blanket, leaving deliberate inches between her and Cornelia. It was barely ten p.m. and darkness had swallowed up everything in the sky but pinpricks of starlight and the milky glow of a gibbous moon.

'Stars,' Cornelia said, lifting a hand to trail it across the sky between the tree limbs. 'Possibly the most beautiful thing in existence. With notable exceptions, but they're up there.' She paused. 'You know – and you can't tell Diana this, she'll never let me live down being a romantic at heart – I've always thought the perfect date would be a picnic in the roof of the Observatory. Having seen it today, I doubly think it.'

'That would be nice,' Mallory said, trying carefully not to imagine what that would look like.

'Not that I've been on any dates recently. Not since Beckett, actually, which is… goddess, eighteen months ago. He always wanted to go *do* things on dates. Go see things, go look at things, go fancy places for dinner. And at the time I was torn between Being an Adult in my first proper relationship, and just… being comfortable with him. Going to do things wasn't about having fun, it was about him being able to say "look, I am performing a relationship", if that makes sense?'

'It does,' Mallory murmured.

'I always imagined myself with a friend, first and foremost, and a partner as a bonus. Beck and I were friends, obviously, but he wasn't a *partner* in the larger sense of the word. I was always trying to temper his reactions to things, or explaining why certain things were offensive or whatever. He didn't really believe in me, when it came down to it.'

Mallory made careful, small sounds of agreement.

'Diana thinks,' Cornelia started, 'that I—'

But she never finished that sentence, whatever it was going to be.

Her phone buzzed and she held it up to her face with a huff of exasperation.

'I'm going to block her, I swear— What the fuck?'

LIKELY: ETHEL BROADWICK

She'd answered it before Mallory could say anything. She shifted closer to listen in, her head pressed gently against Cornelia's, their shoulders touching. Cornelia absently grasped Mallory's fingers as she spoke and Mallory froze.

'What the hell do you think you're doing, calling me at this hour, and also at all? I'm working for a *living* right now. If Imogen, who I *refuse* to refer to as Mother, told you to call me, you can tell her to fuck right off.'

A strangled reply came through the phone on a loud, crackly exhale. 'Cornelia?'

'Mother?' Cornelia said. Mallory could feel the tension in her voice.

'Cornelia, you need to come home,' Imogen Broadwick said, her voice taut. It sounded as though she was or had been crying.

'Are you in Wrackton all of a sudden? Did you come all the way back here just to bully me into talking to you? This is pathetic. Tell Ethel she's dead to me. Tell Agatha if she tries anything I'll kill her myself—'

'They're gone,' Imogen said. 'Agatha and Ethel. They've been taken by the Wickermere Reaper. I need you to come home. Come to Wickermere.'

NINE

24:29:57

Cornelia wasn't sure how they got back to Broadwick Mansion, but she dimly suspected Mallory had taken charge. That Mallory had pulled the phone from her hand, had spoken to Imogen in a calm, reassuring tone and squeezed whatever details she could out of her, then got a taxi and the rest of the Undetectables – core members and freelancers alike – to abandon the stakeout and assemble in the basement.

Agatha and Ethel abducted. Agatha and Ethel. Agatha and Ethel.

'Is this real? Have they actually been taken by the Wickermere Reaper?' Diana demanded, her face flushed. She, Taylor and Theodore had literally run home.

Cornelia found herself on a chair where Theodore had taken to patting her on the head and making vague, rumbling shushing noises. She illogically thought that he was slowly transforming into a cat, day by day.

'What is a Wickermere Reaper?' Taylor asked.

'Ostensibly a serial killer – Apparents were found dead up in the Lake District last year and it made headlines, but Occulture didn't really care until they started going after Occult folk. Imogen said the Ghoul Council has taken over the investigation, but we knew that already because Cornelia asked Dr Ray about it weeks ago and she said to talk to the Broadwicks, given they basically *are* the Ghoul Council, as they're part of the special cabinet—'

'But the Ghoul Council usually passes these sorts of things over to the UML, who pass it on to us,' Diana said, moving to sit by the wall so she could hear.

'Is now a good time to ask what a Ghoul Council is?' Taylor interrupted. 'I thought, the way you go on about the Broadwicks, that it was like the Apparent House of Lords, or whatever the feck it's called. A government branch that made decisions about decisions?'

'It's like a special research branch of the UML that specifically deals with ghosts,' Mallory said. 'There are seven members in the cabinet who have some say in UML business, but anything with ghosts, or that they decide are ghost-related, are in their jurisdiction.'

'It's as though nobody even listens to me,' Theodore said, still patting Cornelia on the head. 'Every word I choose is of express importance! I tell you every day what the Ghoul Council does to me personally, and you just don't listen, though now I say that, I realise it is not the time for airing such foibles. It is a special branch of government that governs itself, up in Wickermere. A place I would never like to set foot, even if I could travel so far. The Broadwick family has been entrenched in its existence for… well, forever.'

Felix and Kingston burst in the door – Felix was wearing what could only be described as a burglar outfit, and Kingston was wearing a pair of Felix's dungarees. Cornelia felt the urge to laugh hysterically at how seriously they'd taken the stakeout that had suddenly fallen way down the list of priorities.

Agatha Ethel Agatha Ethel Agatha Ethel REAPER REAPER REAPER

Mallory repeated what she'd just told the others, which wasn't much. Nobody seemed to know where to look, which suited Cornelia. She couldn't say if she'd ever had a panic attack before, or if she was having one now. All she could think was that she was shutting down, her voice not responding to her efforts to say something, her limbs not answering her requests to jump into action.

'The Wickermere Reaper victims have all been in the Lake District, but they've been recovering bodies in the vicinity of Wickermere – that's the town where the Ghoul Council is situated, and where the Broadwicks have been living for the past few years, allowing us to have the run of this house,' Mallory said patiently, ushering Theodore to his iron chair. 'I get the impression the house belongs to the Broadwicks, but requires a Broadwick to be involved in the Ghoul Council proceedings for the Broadwicks to be able to continue living there.'

Theodore grasped Cornelia's arm in a spray of static and brought her with him, forcing her to sit as Mallory kicked on her laptop and threw a marker to Taylor so they could get writing on a fresh murder board.

'Last reported Occult abduction was earlier this year, and that was the one that really kicked Occulture into being afraid.

The Ghoul Council and the UML responded by doubling down on trying to minimise the problem – the usual methods of gaslighting and outright lying, it seems,' Mallory said.

Cornelia heard the snippet of news podcast that had blasted across the cemetery play in her mind: *Do not fear do not fear do not fear.*

Taylor dutifully wrote on the board while Diana pulled out her phone.

'Reports say five victims,' Diana said, standing to write on the other side of the murder board. 'Does Imogen know for certain the twins have been taken by the Wickermere Reaper?'

'She wasn't at her most articulate, but the Broadwicks and the Ghoul Council at large seem to think so. So far, the only people who know are us, the Ghoul Council and the UML, but they don't want anyone else knowing until they know Cornelia is safe. They're sending a driver to collect her, so we'd better get her packed.'

She nodded to Diana, who immediately started tapping on her phone. Cornelia had to assume she was making a list, and she wanted to help, but couldn't.

'Is it likely someone would come for her?' Kingston asked. 'Isn't she safer here, away from Wickermere?'

'I don't know,' Mallory said, casting a worried look at Cornelia. 'They want her where they can keep an eye on her. They seem to think the Wickermere Reaper is targeting the Broadwicks specifically, but until we get further information…'

'You should get your things together,' Taylor said, squeezing Diana's hand. 'We can hold down the fort here. Can't we, pals?' She shot a meaningful look at Felix and Kingston and

Theodore, who all nodded solemnly.

It took far too long for Cornelia to understand what Taylor was saying.

'No, I'll go alone.' Cornelia struggled to her feet. She didn't feel like her body was hers.

'Absolutely not,' Diana and Mallory said in unison.

'We should really come too,' Felix said. 'As fun as it would be to play PI full-time, I don't want to leave any of you.'

'No,' Cornelia managed. She needed them to understand that this was her mess. Her stupid family, her stupid sisters.

'This is an Undetectables case,' Mallory said firmly. 'Even if we're not officially hired. We're coming, and we're helping you find them. We're going to get them back.'

Cornelia nodded. It was all she could do. The thought of getting in a car and driving all the way to Cumbria at this time of night was horrifying. Stuck in a cramped space, wasting hours and hours, when she could be doing *something.*

Agatha Ethel reaper dead dead dead dead dead

She went to her room to pack but found herself standing motionless, staring at her bed. She didn't even know where to start. None of this felt real. Mallory and Diana waited a generous five minutes before tiptoeing in behind her, closing the door softly.

'Taylor, Felix and Kingston are putting our kits together and finding wellies and raincoats,' Diana said. 'Theodore is supervising.'

Mallory didn't say anything. Bending carefully, she pulled Cornelia's suitcase from under her bed and set it on top of the duvet, before moving to the wardrobe and selecting clothes methodically. Occasionally she'd hold something up to show Cornelia, who didn't respond, so she'd revert to Diana, who was rummaging around in Cornelia's underwear drawer and cursing the lack of matching socks.

Within minutes, the suitcase was full and Diana was zipping it closed. Mallory took Cornelia's hand and led her to her own bedroom, sitting on the bed while she got her own stuff sorted. Diana came back with a cup of tea, which she pressed into Cornelia's hands with the instruction to drink, and the pair of them were packed in moments, their suitcases by the door next to the kit bags Felix and Kingston looked far too pleased to have assembled.

'I don't know why they're so smug. They're a pair of fuckin' eejits who didn't know the difference between a Kastle-Meyer test and a beetle box,' Taylor said to Diana, who kissed her with such force she almost knocked her over.

'I love it when you talk science to me,' Diana said.

Cornelia barely registered any of this.

'Mallory,' Theodore said, beckoning her down the hall.

Even in Mallory's clear attempt to be out of earshot, Cornelia could hear enough. Every sound was amplified like she'd cast a hundred listening spells, and her skin itched under her jumper.

'—don't know if *all* of you should go, when we've got a case here,' Theodore was saying quietly.

'She needs us there. This is more pressing. I can do both, I need you to—'

'Naturally! Obviously! She's one of ours, we must do what we can. No matter my feelings on the twins, I cast those aside in the face of—'

'—we will be back and forth, Theo. We'll likely need the lab—'

'Fine. Okay, I understand. The Digger case can wait until your triumphant return.'

Theodore gave Mallory a hug, then she was beside Cornelia. 'Your mother said a driver was coming, but I think we should witchlight there.'

'Genius idea,' Diana said. 'I was just about to suggest it.'

'We know you're the resident motherfucking genius,' Felix said, raising a beautiful eyebrow. 'But there really is a time and a place for it.'

Cornelia nodded. Witchlight sounded preferable to getting in a car. She couldn't get in the car.

They're gone. They're gone. They're gone

'Can you— I'll do it,' Mallory said, and took Cornelia's phone again. The time flashed up: it was just after half past ten, which was impossible to accept. An age had passed from when she was in the cemetery with Mallory.

'Imogen, it's Mallory. No, Cornelia's all ready to go, but could you do us a favour? Is there a witchlight somewhere you can leave in a prominent position? Cornelia isn't going to take the car you're sending. Well, this will get her there faster. Yes, I understand. Thank you.' She hung up. 'Witchlight on the table in the dining room, she said. You're going to have to do the honours. *Can* you do that?'

Cornelia had no idea what she could do, but she nodded anyway, visualising the dining room. The horrible drapery, the coffee and greige decor that made her want to scream or be sick whenever she saw it.

The suffocating feeling of a place she couldn't escape from.

Wickermere, and Rowan House, had been a pleasant escape for years – so many bugs, so many places to be by herself, so much room to just exist in dungarees and wellington boots and not care about dressing up unless she was dragged to some sort of dinner. It was where she was most permitted to be herself – until she became a teenager and those expectations changed.

Going back felt like climbing into an old skin suit that didn't fit anymore.

'Okay we need to hold hands, but also get our suitcases in, somehow,' Diana said.

A sudden surge of memory, of hearing Agatha and Ethel whispering in the hallway outside her bedroom.

'How do we know this isn't some kind of play?' Cornelia asked quietly, her hand frozen in mid-air.

'Usually there are actors involved, and a plot,' Theodore said.

'A hoax. An attempt to get me back in contact with them,' Cornelia continued.

Mallory's blue eyes stared into hers, the irises shifting as she scanned Cornelia's face.

'I haven't ever heard Imogen Broadwick cry before,' Mallory said finally. 'And I hope I never do again.'

It didn't quite answer Cornelia's question, but if Mallory was sure…

Agatha Agatha Ethel Ethel lost forever

'Driver's still coming,' Mallory said, checking Cornelia's phone again. 'I'll tell him he's just bringing the bags. Felix, or Taylor, can you…?'

They both nodded.

'We can take our kits if we wear them, I guess. I need my—'

Diana had thrown her meds to her before she had to say anything, zipping her suitcase back up.

'Everything essential in the backpacks and kitbags, and the rest will find us.'

Diana eased Cornelia's bag onto her back for her with a tenderness that made Cornelia want to scream. Felix, Kingston, Taylor and Theodore stood in the hallway like a rag-tag guard of honour.

'Keep an eye on the place,' Diana said to Taylor, who kissed her one last time.

'Ready?' she asked Cornelia and Mallory.

Cornelia wasn't, but she nodded again anyway. She gripped Mallory's and Diana's hands tightly, squeezing her eyes shut. The last – and only – time she'd done this, it had hurt, but there was nothing but emptiness where any kind of feeling should be. She held the picture of the witchlight sitting on the huge mahogany dining table and together they stepped through, landing in the middle of the dining room Cornelia had not wanted to re-enter.

Only it wasn't a dining room anymore. It wasn't even the right room. The table was there, two witchlights bathing it in warm orange light, but so were seven pairs of bewildered eyes staring at the Undetectables as they collected themselves. Cornelia noticed stacks of coffee cups and a truly excessive murder board as she tried to regain her composure.

An alarm started whistling somewhere above their heads.

'Cornelia?' Imogen asked, rising from her seat. 'What the *fuck* are you doing?'

TEN

23:55:57

Being home didn't suit Cornelia, insofar as Rowan House *could* be considered 'home' – while she'd reclaimed Broadwick Mansion, Rowan House was a different kettle of fish.

Perhaps it was the effects of the witchlight, or the fact Ezra had motioned for a short blonde faerie to jump up and run for the door, pressing a crystal against the frame so the screaming would stop (the faerie had grimaced apologetically at Cornelia as she let herself out of the room).

Perhaps it was the fact she had pictured this very table in the dining room she'd had many an uncomfortable and/or unhappy family dinner in, but instead it was in a room she'd never seen inside before. Gold shiny plaques covered a wood-panelled wall, and a matching placard on the door read *WAR ROOM*, which was a Ghoul Council tradition Cornelia was aware of – 'Mother's in a War Room, darling, you must leave her be' was a constant refrain she overheard being said to Agatha and Ethel over the years – but had never experienced.

Whatever it was, Cornelia stared around at the familiar, expectant faces of the Ghoul Council sitting cabinet and felt eight years old all over again, unsure of the expectations being put on her, and knowing she was failing no matter what she did.

But perhaps that was the shock talking.

Mallory hadn't let go of her hand when they landed, and she squeezed it now, pulling Cornelia back into the present. Back into herself.

'Bit late for a meeting, isn't it?' Cornelia said. 'I didn't think you usually worked past eight p.m.'

'Emergency protocols. You could consider answering your mother,' Ezra Broadwick said, peering over his glasses with an expression that made it clear it wasn't a suggestion.

'Okay. Imogen, I followed your instructions exactly, I was not aware I was picturing the wrong room. But what I am doing is the least of your concerns right now! I'm here because you demanded I come home. So, *tada*.'

She lifted her free arm, kitbag bumping against her hip, for an impromptu jazz hand.

'Yes, well,' Imogen said, fluttering a hand. She looked remarkably different since Cornelia saw her last, which had been two Yules ago.

Or perhaps Cornelia was finally seeing her for the murderer she'd always been.

Ezra Broadwick leaned over and took Imogen's hand, pushing his glasses up with his other. Cornelia's father looked at her in the inscrutable way he always had, detached somewhat from the reality of the child he'd produced, as though he'd failed on his third attempt.

'What happened to Agatha and Ethel? Tell us from the beginning,' Cornelia demanded.

'Diana, Mallory, nice to see you both. I hope you've been keeping well,' Imogen said stiffly, as though Cornelia hadn't spoken.

Cornelia's eyelids fluttered as a stab of annoyance shot through her. She'd been away too long and had forgotten this particular family quirk; even in the face of her daughters being missing, *abducted* by a known serial killer, Imogen Broadwick valued propriety over anything else.

'Where are my sisters?' she ground out.

'Oh, they're *your sisters* now, are they?' Imogen scoffed. 'You've spent years pushing them away, and now...' She wrenched her hands free of Ezra's and stood. 'I need to be alone.'

She stormed out of the room on spindly heels, the *clomps* audible as she moved swiftly to another part of the house.

'It's good to see you, Cornelia. In spite of the circumstances,' Harry Foster said, clearing his throat.

The eyes of the Ghoul Council had not left Cornelia, and she allowed her gaze to flick up to the speaker's face.

Harry Foster, the Ghoul Council's demon barrister. His sallow, lined face betrayed nothing, though it never did. Cornelia had always thought him to be fond of her. Agatha and Ethel – *Agatha Ethel Agatha Ethel* – had called him Uncle Harry for most of their lives, but had forbidden Cornelia from doing so also. She had no idea why she'd gone along with it. She had vague memories of the twins constantly leaving her out of things, conspiring against her, until she'd met Diana and Mallory and it stopped mattering. Her family was elsewhere now.

'There's no need to needle at her, Harry,' Dot admonished, pushing her glasses onto her head with a pale, wrinkled hand.

Dorothy Early was a witch Cornelia had known her entire life and *did* consider to be an aunt. She'd been friends with Cornelia's grandfather. Cornelia had long suspected Dorothy had been in love with him, as she could think of no other explanation for putting up with his cantankerous nonsense for as long as she had. Cornelia had barely known him, but his reputation had been made clear through snippets of stories.

'Harry. Auntie Dot,' Cornelia said, nodding to them. There was a wild sense of panic in her chest, and she was sure she wasn't behaving normally. 'Sorry to crash the meeting. I suppose if I was going to ever successfully interrupt a War Room meeting for any reason, this is a good one.'

Harry huffed lightly with mild amusement as Dot stood stiffly.

'Ezra, I'll ask Lucy to check on Imogen,' she said, moving to the door. 'We'll pause the meeting.'

Cornelia looked back to Ezra. 'Ez— Father. Dad. Please. I came here as fast as I could, I want to know what's happened. Who discovered they were missing?'

'Lucy did,' Dorothy said, coming back to sit down. 'She found the empty car outside the Rowan House gates.'

Ezra rubbed a hand over his face. 'We're in a meeting, Cornelia.'

'A meeting, I hear, is paused,' a familiar voice chimed in.

Cornelia was reasonably certain their name was Nova Khan, though they'd never met. She just recognised their voice as *the* Nova Khan who'd issued the soundbites that news podcasts had been eating up over the last few months. Nova was a small, slight troll, their dark features and warm brown-grey skin flawless, their entire demeanour glamorous in a way that would make any faerie (read: Felix) jealous.

'Nova, don't start. She's a Broadwick too,' the unfamiliar witch sitting beside Nova said. She threw an elbow into their ribs for good measure.

Cornelia took her in. She was pale and dark-haired, and before Cornelia could form any further impression of her, the witch flashed her a smile that transformed her whole face, briefly revealing a tiny tooth gap Cornelia wanted to see again, leaving her feeling oddly dazzled.

'Paused or not, your mother and I agreed that it was best for you to come back to Rowan House so we could guarantee your safety. This meeting is not for you.'

'But my agency is here,' Cornelia said. 'To help.'

She was starting to remember more of why it had been easy for her to stay away for as long as she had – every single interaction Cornelia had with her parents was an unrelenting battle of wills, where she was certain they were adhering to a set of unspoken principles that didn't have any bearing on the real world, but did have a bearing on how much Cornelia could tolerate being around them.

'Cornelia…' Ezra said, rubbing his forehead. 'We haven't forgotten your silence, though we're willing to overlook it in these circumstances. However, you can't just barge in here, making demands…'

Annoyance and fear co-mingled, making it hard to think of an argument. Just as she was considering witchlighting back out of Rowan House, Mallory squeezed her hand twice, shorthand for 'let me try'.

'Mr Broadwick,' Mallory said evenly. 'We are a highly respected private investigation agency. The UML has endorsed our involvement in cases' – a truth only belied by the fact they still made it immensely difficult for the Undetectables to make wholly legal manoeuvres – 'and crucially we've solved many cases, including murders. Particularly serial killers. Imogen told us you believe your daughters were taken by the Wickermere Reaper. We just want to help you find Agatha and Ethel.'

Ezra inhaled, presumably preparing to politely tell Mallory to fuck off, but Harry spoke first.

'Let them listen in.'

Cornelia's mouth twitched into something resembling a smile.

'Harry. You can't be serious?' Ezra said.

'I defer to you and your judgement in all things but matters of family,' Harry said. 'And unfortunately, this is family.'

'We'll have to start the meeting again,' Dorothy said. 'Restart the minutes. Won't take long. Sit down, dears. I'm sure you're exhausted from all the travelling.' She sat back in her chair and winked.

'Fine.' Ezra said. 'Begin again, Dot.'

Mallory pulled her hand free and they got themselves situated. Mallory had her notebook out in an instant, while Diana folded her arms, observing.

Cornelia's whole body was filled with energy she couldn't expend, her knee bouncing so hard she hit the underside of the table. The pain brought her back into her body for a moment.

None of this felt real.

'War Room meeting of the Ghoul Council. Present members: Harry Foster, esquire, Dorothy Early, minute keeper,' Dorothy said, tapping on a stenotype as she spoke. She seemed practised in doing both at once.

'Nova Khan,' she said, nodding at the troll next to her, who bowed their head.

'Olivia Reid,' she said, nodding to the witch with the dazzling smile.

Olivia was in her late thirties or perhaps early forties, by Cornelia's estimation. She flashed the smile again and Cornelia forced her gaze away.

'Ezra Broadwick, presiding. And guests Cornelia Broadwick, and… I can guess, Diana Cheung-Merriweather, and Mallory…'

'Hawthorne,' Mallory said quietly.

'Of course.' Dot nodded. 'Previous attendees were Imogen Broadwick, and Lucy Caldwell, who are both now in a private assembly. We may now begin.'

Cornelia had no idea how the Ghoul Council could stand all this performative bullshit. Her sisters had been abducted – could already be dead – and they were pissing about with order and notes and minutes. She could feel a vein of fury pulsing through her, the only feeling she could fully name.

'Very well.' Ezra placed his hands on the table. 'This is an emergency War Room consultation regarding the disappearance of Agatha and Ethel Broadwick, both aged twenty-six. Their car was discovered empty at the gates of Rowan House approximately forty-eight hours ago' – he checked his watch to confirm and Cornelia choked back an exclamation at how long it had taken them to get in contact with her – 'and it has been brought to our attention that they may have been taken by the serial killer known as the Wickermere Reaper. The action matches the modus operandi of the individual, who is believed responsible for the disappearances and deaths of Apparents Hodgson, Bell and Kaur, and Occult folk Howard, Warren and Carson.'

He gestured at the murder board, which had all of this information pinned neatly on it. Cornelia's eyes watered behind her glasses, that last name ringing a dim bell.

'This killer is well-established. We believe they have a motive of targeting the Ghoul Council, and our goal now is to find a way to have the twins returned to us without harm.'

'How do you know?' Cornelia asked.

Ezra shot her a look she knew well, but she persevered.

'How do you know they've been taken by the Wickermere Reaper?' The name felt leaden in her mouth.

'It was brought to our attention.'

'How?'

'That doesn't matter. What matters is—'

'How the *fuck* can't it matter? Surely that's the most important part of this? HOW did you find out they were taken by the Wickermere Reaper? No news outlet has released this, but it had to have happened. *How?*'

'Cornelia,' Mallory whispered. 'Let them finish, we can ask later.'

She was right, but Cornelia didn't like it.

'I can fill them in,' Olivia offered.

Ezra sighed, and Olivia tapped her long fingers on the table in front of her. 'The Wickermere Reaper has a well-established pattern: they choose a mark, abduct them, bury the mark somewhere underground, and those close to the mark have three days, or seventy-two hours, to find them.'

Cornelia, knowing all this already – though still not clear on the mechanics of it – flashed back to the calls she'd ignored and felt a swoop of rage-tinged guilt. The Broadwicks hadn't tried very hard to get in contact with her. They'd waited over a day to even start. There were only twenty-four hours left before the twins—

'Cornelia's right – how do we know any of this?' Diana asked, shifting slightly in her seat. 'How is the Wickermere Reaper notifying anyone of their intentions, and how are the families recovering the victims… afterwards?'

'That is… varied,' Olivia said, when it was clear nobody else was going to speak up. 'Information has been withheld from the public to prevent panic, and to prevent a copycat. In this case, the pattern of behaviour is identical to previous Wickermere Reaper abductions. Three days is how long we have to recover the twins alive. Less now, obviously. It took a while for the involved authorities to recognise that the cases were localised in Wickermere. We ourselves were instrumental in linking the Occult kidnappings to the prior Apparent ones. "We" of course meaning the Ghoul Council and the UML.'

'Wickermere's not really a thing anymore, though, is it?' Cornelia said, the words coming out before she'd realised she was going to say them. 'I've been wondering this, wondering why they called them the Wickermere Reaper when it's not a proper town. You don't even see it on Lake District maps anymore. How does the Reaper know about this place?'

'Unauthorised Apparents who come close to the area know to give the town a wide berth,' Harry said obtusely.

'Thanks to Cornelius,' Dot said, nodding reassuringly when Cornelia forced herself to make eye contact.

A rush of fondness for her favourite almost-family member flooded her, though it was immediately replaced with numb dread.

'The wards Cornelius Broadwick created send anyone curious enough to see an abandoned village back the way they came. There are additional wards to protect Rowan House from intruders – hence the alarm going off upon your arrival here,' Olivia added. 'Cornelius left Rowan House to this generation of the Ghoul Council cabinet, and the protections will remain in place until such a time as Imogen and Ezra step down from their positions, and the next Council will decide how best to maintain the secrecy of the Ghoul Council. It's essential, UML-approved, and concerning to us that the Wickermere Reaper has chosen Wickermere as the location for their crimes.'

It never felt good to remember that there was nothing normal about *Being a Broadwick*, but it felt worse when Mallory and Diana were listening too, even if they – or at least Mallory – wouldn't judge her for it.

'So how do the… the victims get recovered?' Cornelia asked. It was a question that had plagued her as she'd read articles and listened to podcasts reporting on crumbs of information, and it had never got any clearer. 'If Apparents can't come in.'

'It's complicated,' Ezra said. 'Involves search-and-rescue and intentional access. Cornelius had fail-safes for the Wickermere wards, but these have added to the delay in recovering victims. We are viewing our position here as an advantage.'

'Local police are Apparent and were unwilling to get involved past the initial protocol, and assisting in ancillary investigation tasks,' Dot said, still typing. 'Not equipped to handle Occult matters, the poor dears. So, the UML has directed the matter to the Ghoul Council locally, for monitoring and management. Now, Harry Foster. Our chief strategist for the emergency operation. Your discussion.'

Harry shuffled papers in front of him. 'The goal for the Ghoul Council, I must state, as I have many times over the past two days, is to get the girls back. I thought we might examine the pre-prepared strategic frameworks, as they may assist us in the matter over these crucial twenty-four hours.'

Cornelia fought to take in what was being said; a quick glance at Mallory, who was scribbling as fast as her wrist would allow, told her that she didn't need to listen, and a quick glance at Diana told her that whatever Harry was saying was utterly useless bollocks.

He fell silent, having used a lot of words to say nothing at all.

'I think we can open to questions,' Dot said. 'Nova?'

'I wonder, were the pre-prepared frameworks stress-tested for a matter of urgency?' Nova asked smoothly. 'Clearly there is an escalation of events here. It's worth considering the Apparent victims were practice, and the Broadwick twins were the true targets. After all, Agatha and Ethel represent the family, which in turn represents the Ghoul Council. They would be far more easily accessed than Ezra and Imogen, but could be utilised as leverage.'

'What kind of leverage?' Cornelia asked. 'Has the Wickermere Reaper asked for anything?'

'I am not so sure that we should be negotiating with terrorists,' Nova retorted.

It was not quite an answer.

'A fair point,' Ezra said tiredly.

'*Is* it?' Cornelia exploded. She stood up, chair dragging over the hard wood with a squeal, and neither Mallory nor Diana moved to stop her. 'Are you seriously suggesting the official Ghoul Council stance is to not negotiate or try to appeal to the killer in any way, *just in case* this is targeting the Ghoul Council?'

'If you knew half the work that went on within the Council walls, you would agree,' Nova said.

'They're right,' Dot said. 'It can't be discounted.'

'I think Cornelia has a point,' Olivia added, tucking a lock of hair behind her ear. 'I don't believe we've seen any indication that this is different than the others. We have the old case files from the other victims, I think we should be examining those as a matter of urgent action.'

Mallory perked up at the mention of concrete information.

'This isn't a forensic examination,' Nova said. 'The police have done that. Poorly, I might add.'

'We have procedures in place for a reason,' Ezra said. 'The rules are for everyone, us included, not just for those we govern or advise.'

'I propose we put it to vote that we reconvene for a full Council sitting tomorrow morning, see if we can usher through an emergency action clause,' Harry said.

'I can get Lucy to action that immediately,' Ezra said. 'All in favour?'

Dot, Harry, Ezra and Nova raised their hands. Olivia took a beat, her eyes on the Undetectables, then she sheepishly raised her hand too.

'You can't be serious,' Cornelia said. 'If you waste any more time, they'll be *dead*. You'll have let your daughters die, and for what?'

'Cornelia—' Ezra started.

'No,' she said. 'What have you done, besides sit here? Have you done a location spell, even?'

'Cornelia, I *know* you would like to believe I was born yesterday, but we did attempt a *more* than cursory search for your sisters. It was the first thing we tried,' Ezra said sharply.

'Mr Broadwick,' Mallory said gently, placing her hand on Cornelia's. It was a warning as much as a comfort. 'You allowed us to participate in this meeting, which we appreciate. We would like to formally be brought into the case. We would like access to the police files, and to be permitted to investigate the Wickermere Reaper.'

'I can get Lucy to hand over copies,' Olivia said quickly.

'Great. Like Mallory said, let us take care of it,' Cornelia said.

'Now who's not being serious?' Ezra said. There wasn't a trace of surprise or resistance in his voice. He spoke to her like she was eight and had demanded to be allowed to sleep with worms in a jar next to her bed.

'Didn't you hear us? This is our *job*.'

'Cornelia's right, Mr Broadwick,' Mallory said. 'This is our job. The Ghoul Council have agreed over the past eighteen months that this is the case. The Night Mayor of Wrackton agrees. The UML agrees. The current circumstances should not alter that fact: we are a legitimate agency. Does it say anywhere in the existing procedure rules that you can't hire an external party?'

'Well—' Harry started.

'No, it doesn't,' Ezra said.

'But we'd need to pass a motion,' Nova said.

'In the event of an emergency, a selected higher council can pass temporary motions as long as they're not contra-indicated by existing policy,' Olivia said.

She was clearly on their side, or as much as a Ghoul Council member could be.

'Yes, that's the protocol. All in favour?'

'Of what?'

'Of letting the Undetectables' – Ezra said it like there was something unpleasant in his mouth – 'assist the Ghoul Council by conducting their own investigation into the Wickermere Reaper.'

'Pending what kind of clearance?' Dot asked.

'First-level. They can access the documents we received from local authorities, and speak to us, and enter and search rooms within Rowan House proper, but we reserve the right to not involve them in any internal processes, meetings or general Council motions, and to remove them from the case at any juncture,' Harry said. 'And they cannot question or speak to the families of the deceased. We cannot alert outsiders to unfolding matters.'

Dot, Harry, Ezra and Olivia raised their hands, Ezra somewhat reluctantly.

All eyes went to Nova, who raised an eyebrow. 'What?'

'It's majority rules, as we have two members absent. Subsection eleven hundred and twelve, line thirty-seven,' Dot said.

Nova stood. 'Fine. Have it your way.'

'We will,' Cornelia said fiercely. 'We'll find them.'

ELEVEN

22:30:01

'I have the case files,' Lucy Caldwell said, meeting them outside the War Room before Cornelia had even thought about where they'd go next. Ninety minutes had passed since they'd arrived and Cornelia hadn't felt the time go. 'Olivia let me know you were looking for them.'

She was a short, pretty faerie who Cornelia had met approximately once before, and she seemed to be a very junior member of the Ghoul Council.

'Your accent is the same as my girlfriend's!' Diana said.

'We're going to start getting you to put money in a jar every time you bring Taylor up unsolicited,' Cornelia said dryly, accepting the neat stack of manila files from Lucy.

'I have more,' she said, hurrying off to a desk sitting in the main entrance hall – Cornelia had never seen one there before, as the Broadwicks used to try to separate work from home life. A lot had clearly changed in Cornelia's absence. Lucy returned with a box marked *EVIDENCE* that did not look as though it should've been outside of a police station, but Diana took it from her, smiling gratefully in a way that seemed to disarm Lucy completely.

'I was just setting up rooms for you,' she continued. 'Cornelia's room has already been turned down, but if you give us a few minutes, we can accommodate all of you. That's the great thing about working in a castle – there's room for us all!'

'We'll take the guest house,' Cornelia said firmly.

Lucy blinked at her. 'I don't think anyone has stayed out in the Laurels in years. Let me just check it's—'

'We'll sort it out ourselves. I know where everything is.'

'All right so. I can have a late dinner sent over, I'm sure you're famished,' Lucy said.

'No,' Cornelia said quickly. 'We don't want anything from the house. We can just—'

Diana kicked her. 'We'll take the guest house, and I'd love dinner, just for tonight. Is there a supermarket nearby?'

If Cornelia was honest with herself, she'd never intended to bring Mallory and Diana to Rowan House. For as long as she'd known them – which was at least two thirds of her life – Cornelia had avoided the subject of Wickermere. She'd said goodbye to them every summer (and sometimes weeks before summer officially started) and would return right before school started back up. She'd retreated to Rowan House briefly when her degree ended and she'd had the Internship That Shall Not Be Discussed to contend with, but it had been a semi-nostalgic visit.

Now it felt tainted.

Her parents were murderers and her family made her sick,

yet here she was, leading her best friends in the entire world down the back steps to the boat-turned-guest-house. She was twenty-two years old and already feeling like she'd been alive for centuries, hungry, tired and frightened.

Agatha Ethel Agatha Ethel

She tried to see things from Diana and Mallory's perspective as they crossed the back lawn. Warm yellow light illuminated the windows of Rowan House, a veritable castle nestled in the Cumbrian fells. It had manicured gardens that gave way to forest, and had they arrived here by car, it would've simply emerged from the fog like a mirage as they turned the corner.

Ridiculous Broadwick nonsense, she saw now, passing a stone statue of Grandad Cornelius. She was grateful Diana and Mallory were taking in too much to comment on it. It was so dark she couldn't quite see the red glow of the markers denoting the shoreline of the lake, but she could hear the static crackle of the water growing in volume the closer they got.

'What is that?' Diana asked, pressing a hand to her ear. 'Is that coming from Lake Wickermere?'

'It's actually better known as Bonemarrow Lake,' Cornelia said, shoving her hands in her pockets as she walked. 'It does that.'

'This is where Theodore insists he'll be thrown into if he ever— if he's ever caught doing something against Ghoul Council rules,' Mallory said. Cornelia couldn't make out her face in the gloom, but there was a tightness to her tone, which softened when she added, 'He'd also point out that putting "lake" before a word ending in "-mere" is a linguistic redundancy almost as large a crime as saying "ATM machine".'

'Or "PIN number",' Diana added. 'Still, weird Theodore's heard of Bonemarrow Lake. I thought the whole thing was made up, honestly.'

'I imagine Theodore's read enough of the Ghoul Council pamphlets and done enough paperwork over the years that he knows more about this place than we do.'

'I'd be willing to bet he knows more than *I* do.' Cornelia fumbled in her pockets for the key she hoped she hadn't immediately lost. 'We'll be able to see the lake properly in the morning,' she continued. 'And you'll be able to see more of Wickermere; there isn't much of it left really, only Bonemarrow Lane. The entire village was shut down and burnt out before I was even born.'

It had never struck Cornelia as odd before – not consciously, anyway – but she could feel a *tone* from Diana, despite her not actually saying anything.

So, there was an entire village named after her family. So, one of the oldest and most important Occult councils in the known Occult world operated solely from an annexed branch of her parents' second mansion. That was normal.

'This is us.'

The Laurels was a shrunken version of the main house, gables and all. It had two bedrooms, a small black-and-white-tiled kitchen, a wood-burner stove built into the surprisingly large living room, and a bathroom that was fancier than Cornelia's bedroom in Wrackton.

It would do for the next two nights, or until they found the twins.

Alive.

'There's a double room upstairs, and the big bedroom is on this floor,' Cornelia said, awkwardly trying to light the stove. The house smelled like it had been aired recently, but had a stillness about it, punctuated by a grandfather clock ticking ominously in the corner, as grandfather clocks are wont to do.

'Dibs the double room,' Diana said after a beat, running for the stairs to lay claim to it before Cornelia could argue. 'You two can share. Mallory should have the bigger bed anyway, and not have to climb stairs.'

Cornelia stared after her, then chanced a look at Mallory, who was in the kitchen, studiously unpacking files onto the narrow kitchen table. She gave no indication she'd even heard what Diana had said.

'We should bring that table in here,' Cornelia said. 'Give me a second.'

She muttered spells to herself and the room rearranged itself the way she wanted it, leaving space for a murder board she summoned from her old bedroom in the main house. She moved the kitchen table to under the sitting room window. In the morning they'd have a clear view of the lake, and of Wickermere beyond it. Cornelia switched on a lamp.

'I can just witchlight back to Wrackton tonight,' Mallory said, resuming her file unpacking.

'What?'

'There's only two bedrooms, and if there's a chance you can get any sleep tonight at all, I think you should take it. Plus, Theodore is a little… put out… that we're abandoning him mid-case, even with Felix, Kingston and Taylor around to help. It's likely we'll find things to analyse here, so I'll need to go over and back anyway,' Mallory said, avoiding looking at her. There weren't many people Cornelia could make unwavering eye contact with, but Mallory was usually one of them.

'Don't be silly, it's a king bed. I actually think it's bigger than a king bed, so there'd be loads of room. I could just sleep on the couch,' Cornelia suggested, though she'd never actually done that and wasn't sure how comfortable it would be.

'Seriously, I'm fine going home,' Mallory said, opening the closest file and skimming it. 'You need to be here far more than I do.'

'We've shared hundreds of times before, this isn't any different.'

Though it *was* different, in a way Cornelia couldn't quite explain.

Mallory laughed awkwardly, and got to work setting up the murder board, writing two columns: *APPARENT* and *OCCULT.*

'The police file has photographs,' Mallory said, sticking them up.

'I'm here, I'm here,' Diana said, running back down. She'd changed into a comfier outfit, her phone clutched in her hand. 'I found a place that'll deliver to us tomorrow, so at least we won't starve while Cornelia is playing orphan.'

Cornelia hit her with a well-timed hex that made Diana smack herself in her own eye.

'For the love of *Blair*, Cornelia, it was a *joke*. We're *lightening the mood.*'

'My sisters might die, but GO AHEAD,' Cornelia shouted, her temper flaring.

'This isn't helping us find them,' Mallory said firmly. 'Both of you sit down. Opposite sides of the couch. And consider being quiet, while you're at it. Here's our case.'

She shuffled the papers in front of her, having made impressively short work of understanding the case at hand. 'As Ezra said, the Wickermere Reaper kidnaps victims and buries them underground, giving seventy-two hours to recover them. Cause of death is believed to be a lack of oxygen. They suffocate,' Mallory said matter-of-factly, though Cornelia could tell it was part of Mallory trying desperately not to panic her.

She wasn't like Diana. She was panicking, freely.

'How is the Wickermere Reaper taking their victims? I can't see Agatha and Ethel willingly following someone into the back of a van, but I've never been able to understand them' – or they her, for that matter – 'so I don't actually know what they'd do. The Council said their car was found empty at the entrance. We'll need to see that, when it's bright enough out.'

'How they're abducted isn't known – toxicology suggests there was no drugging involved, there are no ligature marks, no injuries other than... occasional perimortem wounds the authorities believe to be self-inflicted.'

'What kind of wounds?' Cornelia asked, though she didn't really want to know the answer.

'Broken nails and finger lacerations, like they were trying to claw their way out.'

A horrifying idea that Cornelia couldn't bear to picture, much less think about.

'So, if they're not being coerced physically...' Cornelia trailed off.

'It could be something more obvious. Farmer with a shotgun?' Diana suggested. 'Unlikely, though, if the Ghoul Council are involved.'

Cornelia shook her head. 'There has to be a magical component to all of this, otherwise we wouldn't be here.'

'I have considered it's possible a demon could coerce a victim to leave with them, but it would need to be someone *incredibly* powerful to keep a victim from fighting for almost three full days,' Mallory said.

Before Cornelia could formulate her next question, Mallory pre-empted it.

'To put it bluntly, the victims are, through an unknown manner, being placed in wooden crates underground and left to die. The authorities, with the help of the Ghoul Council—'

'Bureaucratically, surely? I can't see Nova Khan or Imogen Broadwick slumming it in wellies and a raincoat looking for the victims,' Diana said.

'Bureaucratically, yes. The Ghoul Council helped with allowing temporary access to Wickermere, otherwise impossible with the wards Cornelius Broadwick put in place. The bodies of the prior victims, buried in wooden crates, were found using cadaver dogs. The burial locations are spread across Wickermere. The town has a two-mile radius, approximately.'

'I'll look into that, see if there's a pattern,' Diana said. 'Maybe there's a way to figure it out in time.'

Cornelia wanted to tell them about the town she spent her summers in. Wanted to tell them about the abandoned village and the ways it used to come alive in her mind. Tell them about the plants, the unlikely friends she'd made, the ways

Wickermere had allowed her to shape herself into something even as the Broadwicks were trying to mould her into something else. The words just wouldn't form on her tongue, even as her jaw twitched, daring her to make a sound.

Nobody said anything else for a long moment and Mallory ploughed on after glancing at Cornelia's face. Whatever she saw there apparently suggested she should speak faster.

'Onto the victims,' she said quickly. 'The Wickermere Reaper is first thought to have emerged two years ago, when the body of Apparent man Max Hodgson was recovered – closer to the border of Ambleside, actually, than Wickermere – but his body wasn't discovered until ten months after his disappearance.'

Mallory held up photos of a body well into the decay cycle.

'Hodgson had a job in a popular tourist activity centre, and there were no established leads at the time – they briefly thought he was targeted by a customer, but that was an utter guess based on a suggestion from a witness trying to be helpful. A second Apparent, Terry Bell, was discovered late last year, about three weeks after his initial disappearance, where a local coroner put TOD at approximately a week to ten days prior to the discovery – this time the body was recovered half a mile from Bonemarrow Lane, within the Wickermere town border. Bell's murder was later linked with Hodgson's, and formed the basis of establishing the Wickermere Reaper's MO.'

'How did the authorities determine the three days thing?' Diana asked. 'The Council was reluctant to tell us how they knew the twins had been taken, but there *has* to be a way they're being notified, or this is all just a guess.'

The news had been infuriatingly unclear on the *how* of the

Wickermere Reaper. Cornelia wondered if the point had not been to report, but to keep people sitting up worrying about the Reaper for clicks and streams.

'In the first two cases, an ad was taken out in a local newspaper with a ransom.' Mallory held up copies of the ads. 'This information wasn't made available to the public, presumably because the Wickermere Reaper stopped using it as a method of communicating ransom.'

SEVENTY-TWO HOURS
TO LOCATE MH
———
SEVENTY-TWO
THOUSAND TO
RECOVER HIM

SEVENTY-TWO HOURS
TO LOCATE TB
———
THREE HUNDRED
THOUSAND TO
RECOVER HIM

Cornelia took them and pinned them to the murder board.

'Local authorities were unable to trace who placed them, or establish if there was any significance to the figures demanded. Terry Bell's family were well off – they spent their summers here every year – but the authorities were unable to determine how the Wickermere Reaper knew that, specifically.'

'I'm sure if you sat in any restaurant around here and listened, people with three hundred thousand going spare would make themselves known,' Diana said derisively. 'Apparents are fucking *weird* about money.'

'Did this appear online, too, or just in print?' Cornelia asked, ignoring her as her mouth finally allowed her to speak again.

'Just in print. It's believed that held up the discovery,' Mallory said, reading one of the reports in front of her. 'One of the families didn't read the papers, the other didn't ever read the ads.'

'Odd,' Diana said. 'Did any of the others report a different method of ransom notification?'

Mallory rifled through the case files. 'No. That is curiously missing from all of the reports. As is how Hodgson and Bell's families found out at all. Write that up on the board.'

Cornelia obliged, glad for something to do with her hands that wasn't tearing at strands of her own hair.

'Spring of last year, an Apparent courier by the name of Grace Kaur went missing en route to Wickermere, and was recovered about five weeks later, under the bridge that links here to the next town over. There was no ad this time, but she was well-known locally and her disappearance got more media attention. I remember seeing this!' Mallory said suddenly. 'I saw it when we were in Larkin Studios, Sandi Clementine was reading a newspaper. I didn't get to read the story, but I remember the headline.'

'And that's how the Wickermere Reaper got their name,' Cornelia said, peering over Mallory's shoulder.

'Yep. And then they switched to Occult victims. A demon named Ali Howard, recovered about a week after the deadline. Then a witch named Annie Warren, who was… *Hexana*,' Mallory said softly. 'They just missed the deadline. Her body was recovered seventy-five hours after her disappearance.'

This sobered them all for a moment. Cornelia felt the pressure building in her head. She wanted to scream and almost considered asking Diana to go outside and fight her, just to feel something.

She turned her attention to the photos of decomposing bodies, trying to channel the terror into something else.

If she was honest with herself – something she tried not to do very often – she was getting pretty sick of the constant low-level terror she'd been carrying around for the last eighteen months.

'This one had just started the decomposition process.' She pointed to the photo of Annie Warren's body. 'First and second instar maggots.'

'Please don't make me look at maggots, I beg you,' Diana said.

'This is useful, though! In several of our previous murder cases, the bodies were prevented from decomposing, or we came upon them immediately before any decomposition had set in. Bugs give us information about the bodies.'

'Doesn't that suggest the death *isn't* magical?' Diana asked. 'Could this just be a straightforward serial killer, no magic involved?'

'Good point,' Cornelia said. 'Why are they so sure they're being buried alive?'

'The coroner's reports say there were physical signs of anoxia,' Mallory said quietly. 'Skin colour changes suggest the burial sites were flooded with carbon monoxide. Carbon *dioxide* could do similar things to a body, but each coroner's report was careful to make the distinction.'

'What is the distinction?'

Mallory opened her mouth to explain, then closed it again. 'It's complicated,' she said instead. 'Again, this could be non-magical, but there would need to be an oxygen source if they really were to live for three days.'

Assuming the Wickermere Reaper *wanted* the victims to be recovered.

'Victims were found with bottles of water and food wrappers – in the case of Annie Warren, the autopsy confirmed she'd eaten not long before she died. They were unable to find any trace evidence at all that suggests the victims were ever held anywhere other than their burial site, which feels pretty conclusive to me. They're abducted at point A, buried at point B, and there's seventy-two hours to recover them.'

'To go back to Mallory's demon persuasion suggestion – a possibility, of course,' Diana said. 'We should probably ask how the Wickermere Reaper is getting victims from point A *to* point B without—'

'Witchlight,' Mallory and Cornelia said together.

At least the Wrackton Digger case had given them *something*. Cornelia wanted to go back and slap the hours-dead version of herself who had been bored – bored! – working on the Digger case. She'd do anything to go back to mundanity. To living in fear she couldn't rationalise.

'And if the Ghoul Council believe it's magical, as much as they tend to make our cases difficult, then I believe there are enough anomalies here to suggest it is magical,' Mallory said. She avoided looking at Cornelia directly when she added, 'and it suggests that wherever the twins are, they do have an oxygen source.'

Cornelia stared at the photos of the bodies, flashing back to cadavers and uni and a time she thought she'd just get a job working in forensic entomology. Her first internship had proved that assumption wrong; they'd picked on her for her focus and her attire and her 'general attitude', whatever that meant, and the whole thing was less about bugs and more about conforming to social standards.

But she remembered something else, too.

'Before I committed to my research on magic responses of *Sonata lutumae*, I briefly considered studying the infrared and thermal sensor capabilities of *Celyphidae lyrescua*. Lyreflies,' she supplied, mostly for Diana's benefit. 'They're like fire beetles, or kissing bugs, which are also called vampire bugs—'

'You'd know all about kissing vampires,' Diana mumbled.

'Or flat bugs,' Cornelia went on, ignoring her. 'They have strong infrared sensors because they bury eggs in carrion for a ready food source, and like the carrion to be as fresh as possible, as the heat helps the eggs hatch – to the point that they are *remarkable* at finding living things, particularly injured or dying living things, underground. And I originally thought how useful it would be for entomological rescue, maybe for victims buried under landslides. Of course, then I would've had to go somewhere like New Zealand where there are frequent landslides, or somewhere with natural disaster areas, and my supervisor said I was a natural disaster in the making and talked me out of that, so I didn't do it.'

'Was there a point to this study, and also to telling us about it?'

'I don't know how effective they'd be here, but I'd be willing to test it out. Throw everything at finding them. If they're underground, Lyreflies would find them.'

'Who do I call to get Lyreflies?' Diana asked, her phone already in her hand.

'That was the second problem with my research,' Cornelia said. 'I have no idea where to find them. They're so rare – incredibly endangered – and they only live for a day once they hatch. They will only lay eggs on the *Cephalanthera noxa*, or Sleeping Helleborine, which, as far as I know, just doesn't exist in the whole of England. Perhaps in the whole of Europe, and trust me, I've tried *everywhere*.'

'We'll park that one for a second, then,' Diana said, and Cornelia smiled at her.

She felt a bit like she might cry.

'Let's move on to the rest of the Occult victims,' Mallory said quickly. 'The most recent one is… goddess, they buried the lede. She's still alive.'

'What?' Cornelia grabbed the file out of her hands.

'She's *still alive*.'

'Not only that,' Cornelia said, feeling a burn of something like hope. 'We've heard of her.'

TWELVE

21:00:23

Mallory had always imagined Wickermere as a pretty tourist town like the ones her Apparent schoolmates visited at half-term when she was growing up – a place too hilly for her to navigate comfortably now. She'd casually count down the days until Cornelia's return, even if it meant partially wishing away her summers spent with Diana and Felix (and their various, ever-changing bandmates). Cornelia would text infrequently and Mallory always imagined her bored, in a picturesque little village, where the Broadwicks would outdo their generous Wrackton party output by hosting lavish events on fancy yachts or in private rooms overlooking a lakeside expanse. The sort of thing that would make the most important members of Occulture amenable to binding handshakes or signing dotted lines with decorative pens.

She'd never imagined Cornelia in a place this desolate. She tried to imagine her clever, creative, impulsive, curious friend surrounded by trees and fog and the darkest secrets of the Occult world.

Cornelia was but a grainy outline in the near distance that Mallory had to strain to pick out in the darkness. Mallory and Diana linked arms, taking careful steps along the dim witch-light line around the edge of Bonemarrow Lake. Conversation stalled as the fizz of static grew too loud to think over, let alone speak. The sound was familiar, from constant proximity to Theodore; it was the sound of hundreds, if not thousands, of semi-corporeal forces meeting resistance of any kind.

Ghosts.

His warnings about ghosts being thrown to the bottom of Bonemarrow Lake were a constant refrain. It had never, in all her years of knowing him, occurred to her to ask about the logistics of such a punishment.

'This isn't an official Lake District lake, is it?' Diana half shouted, fumbling to put her hearing aid into its iron-meshed case.

Mallory's knee grazed something and she stumbled, her hand landing on what felt like plastic boxes, until she realised it was a sprawling stack of cathode ray televisions – she'd only ever seen them *on* television, so it was both strange and sort of meta to see so many of them gathered together.

'No, but it should be,' Mallory answered after Diana had helped right her. 'These are old TVs,' she said, trying to judge how far the stack extended. They were arranged in a pyramid, leaving her to surmise that their location was intentional, if a little odd.

'Weird,' Diana said. 'Cornelia, what the fuck are— Oh shit, she's gone.'

Cornelia had all but disappeared. Mallory and Diana hurried to catch up, as her furious steps brought them to the other side of the lake. A second noise was layering over the fizzing of the lake, a slow, mechanical *thunk, thunk, thunk* that got louder with every step. Mallory's legs were just starting to cramp after ten minutes of walking past the vague shape of a treeline and an expansive nothingness she had to assume was a hilly field, pain spreading up her spine, when Cornelia turned sharply, hopping over an iron gate and fumbling with the catch so Mallory and Diana could walk through.

'It would help if you told us where we were going, you know.' Diana pressed a hand to her good ear, wincing. 'Or where the fuck we are now, or what that goddess-forsaken noise is.'

Mallory tried to catch her breath. It was quieter here than it had been halfway around the lake, but the clanking was still distracting. They were in a witchlight-illuminated lane with low-walled herb gardens and all manner of gnarled, wild-growing woodland around them. The fog was thinner here – Mallory suspected magical influence – and the space felt like something out of a fairy tale. Beyond the lane was the barely visible outline of what Mallory assumed was Wickermere village – though *village* felt like a generous description of what appeared to be one small street.

'It's just over here,' Cornelia said, a little breathlessly. 'They had hackberry trees, a whole row of them, and I'd stand and watch caterpillars collect and hope to see them pupate. Dot and Harry used to take turns bringing me out here whenever my parents were particularly exasperated with me, and introduced me to them. They've always been good to me.'

'Where is "here"?' Diana asked again. 'And who is or are "they"?'

Cornelia pointed into the thinning fog, and all at once Mallory understood where they were. A tiny traditional cottage with a sage green door, perfectly quaint in all ways, except for the massive factory – the source of the *thunk*ing noise – rising from the back of it, steam curling in a steady pillar from the slate chimney.

It was an image that Mallory had seen every time she used soap or took medicines from Occult-run pharmacies. An illustrated cottage on matte cardboard boxes or smooth wraparound bands bearing the words *WITCHES OF BONE-MARROW LAKE.*

This was the most prominent apothecary cottage industry in the known Occult world, wildly popular with a specific subset of Apparents.

'Even I'm impressed,' Diana said, slipping her arm through Mallory's. 'You good?' she asked in an undertone.

Mallory nodded. 'Just hate seeing her so… you know.'

'I hate it too,' Diana said. 'But we can't let her see that.'

Mallory was glad they were on the same painful page. They hurried after Cornelia, who was semi-patiently alternating hammering on the painted door and ringing the bell. A flash of light lit up the windows every time she pressed the button. It reminded Mallory of something she'd seen on a TV show once, but couldn't remember what it was before an older demon wrenched the door open, glaring down at Cornelia.

'Cornelia Broadwick,' she barked. Both an identification and a condemnation, somehow.

'I'm back in Rowan House,' Cornelia said.

'Obviously,' the woman retorted. 'What time do you call

this? I'll tell you, it's gone half past one.'

'It's urgent. We were hoping to speak to Stella.'

'At this hour? Why?'

The rest of the pieces were falling together for Mallory. When Cornelia hesitated, Mallory extricated herself from Diana's arm.

'We're the Undetectables, private investigators, urgently looking into the matter of the Wickermere Reaper. We'd just like a few moments of Stella's time, if that wouldn't be too much trouble.'

The demon leaned back, her pale, lined face scrutinising each of them in turn.

'She won't like that at all.'

'Please, Ruby,' Cornelia said plainly. 'I wouldn't ask if it wasn't urgent.'

The woman – Ruby – paused with her hand on the door, halfway closed like she still had a mind to slam it, then reached over and pressed a button on a panel on the wall.

Another woman – a witch – entered the room. She had a pretty shock of dyed hair, pink blush and dark pink lipstick contrasting with her alabaster-pale skin, making her age utterly indeterminate, though somehow similar to the more severe-seeming Ruby. Mallory wondered if *this* was Stella Carson, but the witch replied, 'She said no to whatever you're summoning her for, Ruby.'

'Go get her, Jo. This is important.'

The woman scoffed, but stomped off, her feet encased in green velvet shoes and making no noise as she walked.

'If Stella gets upset, you'll be asked to leave,' Ruby warned.

'She doesn't like strangers in the cottage, and she doesn't like business at home, no matter how close home is to business.'

It occurred to Mallory that Ruby, Jo and Stella made up the Bonemarrow Lake witches, despite Ruby being a demon, which made the moniker more than slightly confusing.

Mallory could feel panic radiating off Cornelia in barely constrained waves.

'Sit, then,' Ruby barked. 'Tea?'

'I can make it,' Diana said hurriedly. 'We don't want to trouble you.'

'If you'd wanted that, you'd have never darkened my doorstep,' Ruby said, but there was no venom in it, and she directed Diana into the kitchen.

Mallory took a grateful seat next to Cornelia, who wasn't so much sitting on the seat as perching on the edge of it like she was going to fly off. She had wrapped her arms around her knees, and Mallory nudged her to get access to her bag, from which she pulled out a recorder, her notebook and the case file they had on Stella Carson's abduction.

A younger witch came into the room, her light brown skin complemented by a cream woollen jumper, her expression concerned as she took in all their faces.

Stella Carson.

'Hi—' Mallory started, but Cornelia moved her hands rapidly, and Stella signed back, the sleeves of her jumper falling back to reveal forearms full of black and grey tattoos.

'She said be quick about it. And she said my regional dialect is still dreadful,' Cornelia translated.

At this point it should not have come as a surprise to

Mallory that Cornelia knew British Sign Language; she had always contained multitudes. So, knowing Cornelia would explain how this had come to pass at a later stage, she smiled and started the recording.

'Could one of you please state your full names, for the record?' Mallory asked, as Cornelia signed.

'Josephine June, Ruby Carson and Stella Carson,' Jo said, creeping back into the room.

'Better known as the Witches of Bonemarrow Lake,' Diana said, following behind her with a tea tray.

Cornelia, it transpired, *really* knew BSL, and she and Jo took turns translating for the rest of the room – though it was only for Mallory's and Diana's benefit – and Mallory felt a flutter in her chest at the idea that there were always going to be things she'd discover about Cornelia until the day they died.

'Can you tell us what happened the night the Wickermere Reaper took you?' Mallory asked.

I was in the garden that evening. That's the last thing I remember. The world closed in around me, and I woke up in a room, Stella said through sign as Jo took over translating.

'A room?' Mallory pressed.

Stella shook her head. *A box. Grey walls, painted. Wood? I felt like someone was watching me. But I had no...* Stella paused for the longest time. *No desire to leave. There was a bed, and food. A book to read. A toilet. The space was empty of colour. Empty of feelings. I waited. I didn't fight.*

Stella's eyes filled with tears and Mallory longed to stand up and hug her, hating that they were forcing her to relive this.

'Did the Wickermere Reaper speak to you?'

Stella shook her head. It took Mallory seeing it a few times to realise that Stella had a sign for the Reaper – she brought her index finger to her mouth, then made a circular sweeping gesture to represent Wickermere, and followed it up with a two-handed gesture that Mallory recognised as the swing of a scythe.

No, Stella signed emphatically. *The Wickermere Reaper didn't speak to me. I remember seeing someone, but I don't know who. I remember being surprised, then I blinked and was in another place. It was so… peaceful.*

'Peaceful?'

Yes. Her tears were falling fast now. *I waited, and I read.*

'What was the book?' Mallory asked.

It was about H. H. Holmes, the Apparent serial killer.

Mallory frowned. She knew that book; she did not like the idea of someone buried alive with it.

'How long were you in the box?' Cornelia asked and signed.

Even Mallory understood the reply: *I don't know.*

'Almost four days,' Ruby said quietly. 'She's my niece. She's been living with us since she was eighteen. They were the worst days of our lives.'

At this, Stella draped an arm around Ruby's shoulder and pulled her in for a hug.

Mallory put a hand on Cornelia's arm.

'We were under the impression that it was three days?' Mallory said before Cornelia could blurt out anything.

'We were given more time,' Jo said. 'And thank Elisabella for that.'

'How?' Cornelia asked.

'The Reaper gave us more time,' Jo said, as if it was the most obvious thing in the world.

'No, but—' Cornelia started.

'How did you escape?' Diana interrupted. Mallory had the sense she'd been patient up until now.

'She didn't. We found her,' Jo said, frowning.

'What?' the Undetectables asked in unison.

'We found her by ourselves. It should be in the case file,' Ruby said. 'No mean feat, let me assure you – Jo hasn't done a physical spell in years due to her asthma, and my magical prowess is, as you know, mostly in the lotions and potions area.'

Mallory, mildly embarrassed at her apparent oversight, opened it again, but there was a conspicuous lack of information about *how* Stella had been recovered.

'It doesn't say.'

'How did you find her?' Cornelia asked.

Lyreflies, Stella signed, fingerspelling the word.

'We followed the Lyreflies,' Ruby affirmed.

'Fuck.' Cornelia stood, raking her hands through her short hair. 'Where do you get them? How did you get them?'

'What's lit a fire under your arses?' Jo asked. 'We answered your questions, it's your turn to answer some of ours.'

Cornelia hesitated, and Mallory knew exactly what was going through her head. They'd been told not to tell anyone.

But this could be their only chance to find Agatha and Ethel.

'My sisters. We believe they've been taken by the Wickermere Reaper.'

Jo had barely finished signing this to Stella before she crossed the room to squeeze Cornelia's hands briefly, then signed rapidly. Mallory didn't understand what they were saying, but she recognised Stella's whole demeanour as one of heartbreaking optimism: she was reassuring Cornelia.

'Agatha and Ethel are strange girls, but they always bring us things they've baked, or plants they think we should have in the garden,' Jo said, tapping a slipper on the floor. 'They grew up into monstrous cretins, I have to say. But I am still truly sorry for your family.'

'When Olivia drops by later, we should ask if there's anything we can do for the Broadwicks,' Ruby said. 'She's a good sort, she'll be honest with us.'

'Or I could try sending for Harry or Dot. I can only imagine how desperate they are,' Jo said.

'You can help them by helping *us*,' Cornelia said. 'Please. We need the Lyreflies.'

'No can do, I'm afraid,' Ruby said.

We have pupae, Stella signed. *They're not ready. There's only one mature Lyrefly left, but it'll die in a few hours.*

Mallory didn't know what 'only one' meant in the context of finding the twins, but the look on Cornelia's face suggested this development was slightly better than 'shit out of luck' – but only just.

'It might be useful,' Cornelia said.

'We got lucky,' Jo said softly. 'And in part, it's thanks to you. When you told us about the shortage of Sleeping Helleborine the last time you were here, we started looking into its medicinal properties, got our hands on an import, and Stella found the Lyreflies. They only live a day no matter how many of them we have, and they're temperamental little creatures when it comes to reaching maturity.'

'Can I see the pupae?' Cornelia asked. Stella nodded and took her down the hall.

Mallory and Diana exchanged glances.

'How long do they take to, er, pupate?' Diana asked.

'How long is a piece of string?' Jo shrugged. 'I'm sorry. If they're not ready, there's nothing we can do. There has to be some other way we can help you.'

Cornelia clattered back down the hall with Stella at her side, a small box in her hands, presumably with the precious single Lyrefly inside. Her face was the sort of flushed it got before she became really upset.

'There has to be some way to help them along, or some way to find others. Surely you know someone who can—'

If they emerge in time, they're yours, Stella signed.

Cornelia pressed a fist to her mouth, and for a moment Mallory was afraid she was going to break down right there in the middle of Bonemarrow Cottage. Mallory lifted a hand, reaching for her, but Cornelia swallowed hard and cleared her throat.

'Do you have any enemies?' she asked Stella.

Stella laughed. *Of course we have enemies, we're a successful business.*

'We considered this at the time – the Ghoul Council put a lot of emphasis on this being the Wickermere Reaper's motivation, but I can't see how that was the case for the rest of the victims. Taken at random, given three days. If someone wanted to harm us, they'd have come for our Stella again after we got her back here.'

This, at least, was plausible.

'What about anyone who comes to the town? Vendors, couriers? Do you get customers coming here?'

Stella shrugged. *Town is warded. Few people come here, customers never come to us.*

Mallory's gaze flicked to Jo and Ruby, who didn't disagree.

'Anyone we employ is helping with distribution or remotely managing our social whatsits,' Jo said. 'We rely on their discretion to keep up the mystique of the Witches, so we pay anyone who works for us well.'

'Ever had any trouble with employees?'

Jo shook her head. 'Easiest way to keep a worker happy is to make sure their hours are good and their pay is great. We work to retain our staff.'

'And among you?' Mallory pressed.

'What about us?'

'What's your relationship like? You live and work together.'

'We live and work together, yes,' Ruby said. 'Jo and I have lived together since we were girls. Apparently, the kids are calling this sort of thing "queerplatonic", but for us at the time, it just made sense. We started this business from the ground up, then Stella joined us. We're a family.'

'Which means we do want to hex each other into oblivion sometimes,' Jo said fondly.

Almost dying made them so much nicer to me, Stella signed.

The barest of smiles broke through Cornelia's panic.

'What do you know of the other victims?'

'Ezra and Imogen paid us a visit while we were searching for Stella,' Ruby said. 'We knew the odds, but we didn't want to give up hope.'

'Hope is the one thing I wish we could bottle, we'd be made for life,' Jo said almost wistfully.

Mallory had, in the back of her mind, considered that Stella's rescue was not as legitimate as it seemed. There was nothing in what the Witches were saying to her that suggested they were involved. If anything, they'd beaten the odds.

If they could do it, the Undetectables would too.

'I have a thought, if you'd like to hear it,' Ruby said. Her expression was inscrutable. Jo was focused on signing, and her expression betrayed nothing but the words she was translating.

'Yes,' Cornelia said.

'Where did you say your sisters were taken from?'

'Their car was found empty at the gate of Rowan House, keys still in, engine running.'

'Within the bounds of the House, or outside?'

'Why?' Mallory said. 'I mean, why does it matter?'

'Because this entire town is warded against anyone not expressly granted entry. Doesn't entirely work on Apparents, but every courier, every gardener, every chef, housekeeper, vendor or whoever else needs to be in Wickermere is permitted to be here because the Ghoul Council allow it. You wouldn't notice the wards if you had permission to be here.'

'I know the Broadwicks are important to Occulture,' Diana said, making the deliberate understatement of the year, 'but what could possibly warrant that level of protection?'

Ruby's eyes narrowed. 'The Ghoul Council is shrouded in secrets, and those protections are old. Rowan House was the original meeting point for the Council, and they've never found a better place.'

'How do you know all this?'

'I'm old too,' Ruby said. 'It would take someone dangerous to so boldly threaten the Broadwicks in their own garden.'

'I hate to state the obvious,' Mallory started, about to do exactly that, 'but are you suggesting that the Wickermere Reaper is someone known to the Ghoul Council?'

Ruby raised an eyebrow, but did not elaborate.

'What did the ransom note say?' Jo asked suddenly.

'What?' Mallory yelped.

'The ransom note,' Jo repeated, a little impatiently this time. 'What did it say?'

Mallory's eyes met Cornelia's.

'What did yours say?' Diana demanded, recovering first. 'Why isn't it in the case file?'

'We had it in our possession right up until Stella was found,' Jo said. 'And then it self-destructed.'

'It was vague. Demands for a ghostlight from the bottom of the lake—'

'Is that why the lake is so fuzzy?' Cornelia interrupted.

'Yes. Don't interrupt,' Ruby snapped. 'Then, when we failed to produce the ghostlight, there was a second note, offering us an additional twenty-four hours. It contained information nobody should've known.'

'Which was…?'

'If you think I am stupid, just say that.'

'Sorry,' Cornelia said, surprisingly meekly for her. 'Did you offer the Wickermere Reaper a ghostlight?'

'Once a ghostlight is thrown into the lake, it's next to impossible to retrieve one without terrible repercussions.'

It wasn't quite an answer.

'So did you consider doing it at all?'

'Of course we did. The first thought, once we read that note, was *how do we get in*. Ghoul Council be damned. We tried and tried to figure out a safe way of doing it. People have died trying. Good people, losing their lives time after time over years' worth of attempts. Every time someone dies in that lake, it grows a little less safe.'

'Did you ask the Ghoul Council for help?' Diana asked.

'Oh, we asked them. They're probably still deliberating on it as we speak,' Ruby said sourly. 'The extra time wouldn't have helped without the Lyreflies, I can tell you that much.'

A short silence elapsed between them. Mallory couldn't tell what Diana and Cornelia were thinking, but she had a sharp sense that the Witches were telling the truth.

'Stella, do you know where you were standing when you went missing?' Mallory asked, rising from her seat stiffly.

Stella gestured to Ruby, who glared at her, but opened the front door and pointed so Mallory could see. 'She was standing there in the vegetable patch, tending to the tomatoes. I saw her through the window as I was cooking dinner, then five minutes later I glanced back out and she was gone.'

'How far from where she was taken did you find her?' Mallory asked, following Ruby back inside.

'Not far. Lakeside. There are no maps of Wickermere anymore—'

'I have an old aerial photo of the lake,' Diana said, producing it from Hexana-knows-where. Mallory constantly admired Diana's readiness. 'The Apparent police drummed it up from some forgotten archive, it was in Stella's file. Terrible quality. If you could indicate even an approximation…'

Ruby took it from her, and she and Jo looked at it carefully.

'There.' Jo tapped a long nail on the photo. 'Right there.'

Diana marked it. The burial site was barely five minutes from the cottage, close to the lakeshore. They'd walked right over the area on their walk here.

'Stella, could you tell me how you've been since?' Diana asked brightly. Jo brought both of them a short distance away, translating, leaving Mallory and Cornelia with Ruby. They had no experience of working with almost-murder victims, and asking for especially traumatic details in front of Stella felt wrong.

'How did she look?' Mallory asked quietly.

'Haunted,' Ruby said. 'Her clothes were rumpled, she was covered in dirt.'

'And how did you find her? As in, what did you find when the Lyreflies located her?'

'She was in a box. A big, mouldy wooden box, like a crate, but… Goddess, it was one of our old shipping crates, repurposed. The Lyreflies were relaying back this horrendous *thunk, thunk, thunk* as well as crackling from the lake, and that's when we knew. The whole time, she'd been less than half a mile away.'

Cornelia nodded at this description of the Lyreflies at work as if it made perfect sense, so Mallory, unwilling to interrupt to ask about mechanics, just had to hope she'd understand better later.

'I hadn't realised how big our crates were until I was looking down into one – size of a box room, easily. Stella was lying in the centre with her eyes closed, her hands on that book. I don't think she'd even realised she was *gone* until we pulled the lid off the box and light hit her face and she started panicking. Those screams... I never want to hear those screams again. She kept signing that she had something to do, but... I don't know. I never want to see anyone else go through anything like that again. Just never again.'

'Is there anything else about it you can tell us? Is the site still there?'

'We planted Wolfsbane over it, you should be able to find it when it's light out again. Once she was out and the police cleared the site, we didn't want her to have to pass by and remember it.'

'Are Stella's clothes that she was wearing still around?'

'Apparent police bagged them, but didn't take them away. They're in the hall cupboard.'

'We'd like to take them. We'd also like to take magic samples from all three of you. It might help our investigation.'

Mallory had carefully learned the language of asking; she would never protest if a suspect or witness refused, or asked for a warrant, or a lawyer. It was not the admission of guilt Apparent TV would like everyone to believe it was.

Ruby nodded, and Diana dug out fresh swabs and tubes. Ruby directed her to the cupboard and Stella dug out the evidence bag, her face impassive.

'We'll get out of your hair,' Mallory said. 'Thank you for your help. If we have more questions, would it be okay if we...?'

'Obviously,' Ruby said.

'We're here anytime. I hope you find them,' Jo said.

I know you'll find them, Stella signed. *They'll survive this.*

THIRTEEN

20:00:12

Darkness in Wickermere was different to darkness in Wrackton, where everything was overlaid with a neon glow at all times. Here, once the sun disappeared beyond the trees – if it even broke through – the only visible lights were from Rowan House. The sky was resolutely velvet-black and coated in thick fog or grainy mist, the grounds utterly silent but for the persistent fizzing from Bonemarrow Lake.

Cornelia used to love the feeling of being closed off from the rest of the world. At twilight she'd hear the insistent patter of moths at the window, frantically attempting to reach the light of her lamp. Deeper into the night she'd slip out and wander the grounds for nocturnal insects, or pay Stella's garden a visit, and she'd stumble upon foxes quietly watching her, or witness the majestic swoops of owls overhead.

Now it felt oppressive. The world was closing around her, the darkness a noose tightening with every passing second of the remaining hours.

It felt like a dream. Like a nightmare she recalled with a shock, over and over.

Agatha Ethel Agatha Ethel

She took off, the box with one lone Lyrefly clutched in one hand, the fingers of her other wearing crescent moons into her palm.

She heard Diana swear and felt bad about running off faster than Mallory could keep up with, but kept going anyway, uncurling her balled fist long enough to turn on her phone torch, aware that at any second the lake could produce one particularly effervescent fizz that would render her phone a useless brick.

'THERE!' she shouted, the *thunk, thunk, thunk* of the factory particularly loud. Cornelia had long hypothesised that the Witches had used a sound-displacement spell of some kind so Ruby and Jo didn't have to deal with it. Ruby would never admit to it. 'WOLFSBANE! OR ACONITE, IF YOU'RE BEING SPECIFIC.'

She repeated it when Diana showed up, Mallory close behind.

'Thank *Blair* you know what it looks like, I thought we'd have to come back in the morning,' Diana said, panting.

'There's no way you'd know this was a burial site,' Mallory said, dismayed. She swung her torch – Mallory was forever properly equipped for all eventualities – and caught the purple aconite flowers shivering in the slight breeze.

The Witches had done a thorough job of covering it up; nobody would know it had almost been a permanent grave.

'If this works, we can try it where the twins were… taken

from' – Cornelia swallowed – 'but Lyreflies don't live long. This one's youngest progeny are close to pupating and— You know what, now is not the time,' Cornelia said, before anyone else could. She opened the box and took out the sole *Celyphidae lyrescua*, stroking a gentle thumb over its shiny blue thorax. Lyreflies straddled the genus classification of flies and beetles for numerous reasons, although their wing structure was that of a beetle, folded away beneath the lyre-like shape of its body. It was moving slowly, as she lifted it to her ear and heard a melodic buzzing, interspersed with a droning click.

'This sounds like a plan of action, but… what are we trying, exactly?' Mallory asked.

'Heard of lyrebirds?' Cornelia asked Mallory, who nodded. 'They're mimics,' she explained to Diana, who had pressed close to her side in order to hear properly. 'There's a multitude of reasons why these are known as Lyreflies, but here's the main one.'

Cornelia placed the Lyrefly down on an aconite flower and pressed a thirty-second timer on her phone. It was an agonising wait and she curled her toes inside her boots, pressing her nails into her palm until the timer went off and she scooped the Lyrefly up again.

'Listen,' she said, and the Undetectables crowded around, Diana in closest.

There were the sounds of a shovel hitting the ground, a wooden lid dropping into place. Cornelia waited, holding her breath as there was nothing but fizzing from the lake for a few seconds. Then shuffling. Shouts. A melodious, clicking drone repeating over and over.

And then the Lyrefly screamed.

They all reared back, even Cornelia, who had been expecting it.

'What was that?' Mallory asked. She looked close to tears.

'An echo. Lyreflies can mimic the sounds of what has come before, which would make them useful in a disaster situation, which my research would've— Never mind. What I'm saying is that they can pick up strong vibrations, an imprint of something that has happened before. The ghost of sounds. As opposed to ghost sounds, which as we know, is an entirely different thing and many such cases have been made in the basement of my childhood home.'

The others didn't laugh, though Cornelia hadn't really expected them to. This was too serious, and she was shaking as she spoke.

'This is the site Stella was buried in, no doubt about it. Which means we need to go to the gates. Now.'

They went around Rowan House instead of through it – after throwing down a sound beetle and wasting precious seconds watching it flash green. It was a probable reaction to the Wolfsbane, but one Mallory determined was worth verifying – up half-staircases that turned through hedge-lined pathways that seemed to lead nowhere, Cornelia's phone light leading the way. She stomped over ferns that sparkled damply as the light passed over them until they were on the driveway, crunching through gravel and heading towards the two gates that led into the estate.

'This is the inner gate,' Cornelia said, pressing her hand to it. It sprang open at her touch and the three of them tromped down more gravel. Cornelia tried to slow her movements to let Mallory catch up, but her blood was thrumming so hard in her head. If she slowed down, she'd stop. She'd crash out, and they'd never find the twins.

'Here,' Cornelia said, stopping as she opened the second gate. A stack of police markers had been kicked to one side, clearing a path for other cars to drive through – the only sign anyone had looked at the scene forensically before it was destroyed. There was another few feet of gravel that gave way to a dirt track. 'This is where the Council said they were taken from – at the gate to Rowan House.'

Mallory already had on a pair of gloves. 'Where's the car?'

'Apparent police have it. Apparently.' Cornelia set the beetle down on the gate and set a timer. 'Where, I don't know – we can follow that up in daylight.'

'How do the wards work?' Diana asked, examining the gate. Only now did Cornelia notice that she had the paper evidence bag with Stella Carson's clothes tucked under her arm. 'Like, what's to stop any prick walking through these gates?'

'They'll throw you backwards repeatedly,' Cornelia said. 'I was told this was preferable to the wards on the Ghoul Council inner sanctum, which would, allegedly, kill you. But I'm uncertain if that was an empty threat.'

Diana nodded, camera in hand as she took photo after photo of the scene, or what remained of it, the flash a bright burst that cut through the darkness.

Their magical forensic tools might have limitations, but at least they had a chance of them still working on an otherwise totally destroyed crime scene. She thought about all the tests they could do – combing the area for hairs and fibres, for footprints, for tyre marks from another vehicle. For some sort of calling card from the Wickermere Reaper. But their business was undetectable, and they wouldn't find Agatha and Ethel with pure forensics.

Unless, of course, the Lyreflies hatched in time.

Mallory had walked quite a bit away, her torch in her hand as she quietly examined the ground.

'Impossible to tell which tyre tracks are theirs, there are tonnes of them overlapping, and the gravel is so deep that the tracks disappear.' She sounded disappointed. 'There's no other entrance to Rowan House?'

'Lakeside, the way we walked, but some parts of that path are so narrow you'd have to drive into the lake. Which, to answer your question, means no.'

Mallory nodded.

The timer went off and Cornelia scooped up the Lyrefly again, her heart pounding.

She heard tyres crunching over gravel, footsteps shuffling through stones. She heard the gate buzzer go and the quiet sounds of someone accepting a delivery. Days of sounds condensed into single notes.

Then she heard it.

A familiar car engine puttering up to the gates.

Agatha's voice – she was so sure it was Agatha – saying, *'I wouldn't mind, but Poppy has— Oh, hello!'*

The car doors opened. Two of them, Cornelia was sure. *Clunk, clunk.*

'*We understand,*' Ethel said.

Then walking. Away, she was sure.

Then nothing. The Lyrefly's antennae twitched and it clicked twice, then stopped moving for good.

Cornelia sank to her knees even as Mallory moved away from the gate, searching the ground for footprints that might match the twins'. Cornelia pulled a sound beetle out of her pocket, barely daring to hope, but the beetle flashed once.

Maybe they were defective. This was the second case where they'd been of no help.

Mallory shook her head as she returned, peeling off her gloves, and Diana slung her arm around Cornelia's shoulders, forcing her to stand.

'We got what we came for. Let's go back,' Diana said firmly.

Diana didn't let go on the walk back to the guest house, forcing them to do a strange, two-step shuffle that would've ordinarily annoyed her, but now felt grounding. Cornelia felt like she was on the verge of spinning out. She'd secretly wanted to hear Agatha and Ethel one more time – many more times, she wanted to find them *alive* – but she hadn't expected to hear their final words.

Still, the Witches had given them something to start with. She had seen the careful way Stella tended to the Lyrefly pupae and had heard the reassurances from all of the Witches. Cornelia's phone was filled with strings of sent texts and emails to any and all contacts she could think of that might be able to find her mature Lyreflies as a matter of urgency – Diana was typing one-handed as she walked, doing the same – because she knew, in her heart of hearts, that it wouldn't matter if they solved the case and unmasked the Wickermere Reaper if Agatha and Ethel were dead.

She glanced back at Mallory, who had slowed to a shuffle of her own, and stopped until she caught up. Mallory looped her arm through Cornelia's free one, saying nothing but staying close.

Her two best friends, the only things holding her up now, physically and mentally.

'Are you okay?' Mallory asked softly. A silly question, all things considered.

One she couldn't answer truthfully, because her thoughts, scrambled and rapid and disconnected, were returning to one common theme: she couldn't bear the idea of failing.

She'd been expected to fail at everything in her life so far. The Ghoul Council, though Harry had acquiesced to the Undetectables' demands to be let in, appeared to be doing so to keep Cornelia quiet. Her parents had concealed a ransom note, if the Witches were to be believed. The Broadwicks weren't taking her seriously. They didn't think she could do it.

She had to prove everyone wrong, and she couldn't begin to articulate this to Mallory. Mallory, who would understand completely, who would listen and offer an objective perspective. Who would be kind and considerate no matter how she felt. Doing so would be admitting that not failing was all she really cared about, when it came down to it.

A twist of disgust in her stomach almost made her gag.

Agatha Ethel

They were cruel strangers she'd grown up alongside – not with, always on the outside – and clashed against and been compared to at every step for the entirety of her twenty-two years on Morrigan's green earth. And yet they were only twenty-six – an impossible paradox of an age nobody should die at, and an age Cornelia could not imagine being.

It was as though the Whistler had made her realise her own mortality, and the Wickermere Reaper had forced her to acknowledge everyone else's.

She sucked in a breath, suddenly aware her lungs were constricting at the next jumbled thought that emerged coherent, on the tip of her tongue, ready to tell Mallory: that they had made a mistake in taking the Whistler case and starting the Undetectables all those months ago, and that all of this felt impossibly, inconceivably connected.

Agatha Ethel Agatha Ethel

'Cornelia,' Diana said, not as gently as she could've, given the situation.

'What?'

'We've been standing at the door for the last five minutes. Are you going to let us in, or…?'

Cornelia shook her head and realised she had, in fact, been standing and staring at the front door of the Laurels.

'Fuck, sorry.'

The cottage was cold inside. After a bit of deliberation and consulting the internet, Diana lit the stove and an orange glow cast long shadows across the room.

Cornelia threw herself down on the sofa, her leg bouncing.

'We need to verify if what the Witches say is true about the wards and authorised personnel.'

'Easily done, I got Lucy's number earlier and she said to contact her with any queries,' Diana said.

Lucy replied with a photo of the clearance list, which they gathered around Diana's phone to see.

'She said this is the Rowan House access list first, followed by the general Wickermere clearance list.'

LUCY CALDWELL
HARRY FOSTER
DOROTHY EARLY
EZRA BROADWICK
IMOGEN BROADWICK
AGATHA BROADWICK
ETHEL BROADWICK
OLIVIA REID
NOVA KHAN
CORNELIA BROADWICK
MALLORY HAWTHORNE
DIANA CHEUNG-MERRIWEATHER

A second photo showed the names of the Witches of Bonemarrow Lake, followed by various delivery drivers, couriers and staff employed by the Witches.

'No cleaners?' Mallory noted.

Cornelia couldn't remember if there had ever been any staff that weren't Ghoul Council members in Rowan House, so said nothing.

Diana paused while she waited for Lucy to type. 'She said they used to, but in the last few years – before Lucy's time, anyway – they've kept things incredibly locked down. Folk bring stuff on designated days, and that's it.'

'Maybe—' Mallory started.

'One of the couriers is the culprit?' Diana said, pre-empting the suggestion. 'I had considered that someone with a big van could use that to abduct folk, and it's a good start, but the days don't match up – the victim, Grace Kaur, *was* authorised to be here, but her days are all spread out and allegedly couriers can't enter Wickermere on a non-designated day without contacting Lucy for clearance first, and she said there was no such special clearance offered in the last few years – we're the first. A bizarre system, to shut down a whole village like this.'

Mallory bit her lip thoughtfully. 'That was quick work, Diana, thank you.'

'So the Wickermere Reaper is likely someone on the Ghoul Council, or one of the Witches,' Diana said, writing *UNAUTHORISED – ELIMINATED* beside the couriers' names. 'Question for Cornelia, mostly – did we know that the Ghoul Council was actually a Broadwick and Co. operation and not a joke we made among ourselves about their far-reaching power?'

Cornelia swallowed, but ignored the question. Every time she examined her reality, she learned that it was outside the norm, and it never got any easier to confront her general obliviousness. The money thing still hung over her uncomfortably.

'What was it that Ruby said? "It would take someone dangerous to so boldly threaten the Broadwicks in their own garden." Do we take it that she thinks all of this is about the

Ghoul Council? If that's the case, perhaps our hypothesis that Agatha and Ethel were the intended targets all along has some weight,' Mallory mused, sitting beside Cornelia, so close that her leg brushed Cornelia's knee. A pleasant tingle raced up her spine but she didn't otherwise acknowledge the touch.

'Why the fuck did my parents not tell us about the ransom note?' Cornelia found herself saying.

'It's assuming there was one,' Mallory said reasonably. 'We know the Witches got two, for whatever reason, but it doesn't mean that was the case for all the victims.'

'They were evasive,' Diana pointed out.

'A ransom note would make sense, but it has to be a ransom of something more than money,' Mallory said.

'That, or they're simply refusing to give Broadwick money to the Wickermere Reaper,' Diana said. 'Which they wouldn't do,' she added, after Mallory shot her a look.

Given that they'd cut Cornelia off, she wasn't so sure.

'It likely *is* something other than money. Otherwise they'd either be upfront about not paying the ransom – whether that's morally, in principle, or put to a Council vote – or they'd have paid it by now. We know the first two victims had ads demanding money, but neither family saw it in time. Perhaps the Wickermere Reaper evolved their MO to include a targeted ransom note. The Witches weren't asked for money, they were asked for ghostlights. Maybe the Ghoul Council have been asked for something priceless?'

'Worth more than their daughters?' Cornelia demanded, to which the other Undetectables had no answer.

'There's one other possibility to consider,' Mallory said

slowly. 'And it's that Imogen and Ezra already have an idea who the Wickermere Reaper is. Perhaps they've made these same deductions, and have come to the conclusion that it's someone known to them. By denying the contents of the ransom note, they're trying to force them to deviate from form.'

'A year ago I'd have said that was impossible,' Cornelia said, ripples of fear making her shiver despite the heat from the stove. 'But now that we know they killed Theodore—'

'*Think* we know,' Mallory said.

Cornelia felt a flash of annoyance, not at Mallory specifically, but at the idea there was any doubt. Katherine Vane had no reason to lie, as much as she did not seem a reliable source.

'We've pretty good evidence that they did. What's to stop them killing others? Or stop them abducting Agatha and Ethel, to make it look like they're not the culprits?' Cornelia asked.

'Because that was different. *If* the memory Katherine showed us was true, we don't know *why* they killed Theodore, but they've gone to great pains to conceal his death, with little evidence *or* suggestion it happened again. By comparison, this is flashy, attracting headlines, repetitive. It's different. I don't want to rule them out at this stage – we can't – but they're far down the list for me,' Mallory said. 'Besides, if it was entrapment to draw out the real Wickermere Reaper and they were *wrong* about the culprit, they'd lose the trust of the rest of the Ghoul Council, and of the UML if it ever got out that they were wasting police time and Ghoul Council resources like this. I don't think any of what we've seen of the Council suggests they have the first clue who the Reaper is.'

'It's elaborate,' Diana agreed.

'And as much as you don't see eye-to-eye, and the fact they've cut you off plays a part in this… worrying you like this?' Mallory said. 'Lying to you, not immediately telling you the truth? Calling you here at all, when they could've easily lied and said that you were somewhere safe away from the Wickermere Reaper's hunting grounds? They've done so many things to hurt you over the years, but this would be a step too far, even for them.'

Cornelia dropped her head into her hands. Part of her wanted to argue that this was *exactly* the sort of mind-game the Broadwicks might play with her, but she'd be arguing for the sake of it.

Mallory was right. This wasn't a hoax. Agatha and Ethel were out there, trapped, waiting.

'We should ask to meet with Imogen and Ezra now,' Mallory said, rubbing her eyes tiredly. 'Talk to them about the ransom note. Cornelia should do it,' she added as Diana raised her phone.

Cornelia dutifully sent a text, albeit making it as impersonal as she could.

Cornelia

The Undetectables request a brief meeting as a matter of urgency to discuss a pressing point in the case. Can you meet now?

Ezra

Your mother needs to rest. We can offer a private assembly at first light before the GC reconvenes

'Fucksake,' Diana said when Cornelia read out the text in her father's stiff, formal voice. 'Can't he just call it a meeting?'

Mallory tipped her head back against the sofa cushions, her eyes fluttering closed. 'Maybe we should rest, too. It's been a long day.'

Diana did not need to be told twice. She made tea and found fresh bread and cheese, acquired from Hexana knows where – but probably Lucy's doing – and a jar of onion jam that she hastily assembled into sandwiches, dishing them out on little plates.

Diana's phone buzzed as Cornelia accepted a plate, and Diana held it up to show Taylor's name on the screen, attempting to video call.

'I'm off to bed,' Diana said, not even bothering to hide the grin on her face.

'Try to keep it down,' Cornelia said, and Diana flipped her off as she climbed the stairs, her phone gripped between her teeth and her bedtime snack in her hands.

'Eat,' Mallory said after a minute. 'I can still go back to Wrackton—'

'No. To both. I'm not hungry, and we can share the bed.'

'You need to eat regardless. Just try a little. I know we're both treating you like you're made of glass right now, but it's because we're at a collective loss of how else to proceed.'

'At least you're honest,' Cornelia said, and made surprisingly short work of the sandwich.

She picked up the mugs and followed Mallory into the bedroom, running back to get more bread just as Mallory finished pulling on an old t-shirt that skimmed the tops of her thighs. She hurriedly pulled on a pair of patterned pyjama bottoms and climbed into bed.

Cornelia had already taken her pyjamas into the bathroom before she could question it. She was cagey for no reason, and was sure Mallory would notice, so she made a big show of loudly looking for something to clean her glasses with, as though that was the universal sign for 'everything's fine and I'm not suddenly aware of your every move and I don't know what that means either, but let's pretend it's not happening'.

'Your glasses cloths are here,' Mallory said as Cornelia ran back in, self-conscious in her giant bed shirt as she climbed in beside her, leaving careful space between them.

'I keep thinking about what they said about the twins' car being at the gates of Rowan House,' Mallory said, pulling the blankets up over her shoulders. She turned to face Cornelia with a hand curled under her face. 'And of the silence before the Lyrefly… expired. The footsteps stopped dead, like the twins vanished. Diana was probably onto something with the witchlights idea – I'm starting to hate how everything we do comes back to witchlights. But if there isn't another way into Wickermere, perhaps the Wickermere Reaper isn't forensically aware enough to realise they're narrowing the pool of suspects by taking the twins from inside the Rowan House wards?'

'You're right,' Cornelia said, staring at the pale pink polish on Mallory's nails. Flashes of the Whistler's face appeared behind her eyelids when she blinked. 'I keep thinking about Agatha's voice. She said "Oh hello!" like she was surprised, but I couldn't tell if it was "Oh hello, person I know" or "Oh hello, what are you doing here". And Ethel… Ethel saying "we understand", like they were… coerced, or instructed. But not in a way the Lyrefly could hear. Something internal, or silent. They'd protest if it was someone with a weapon. They wouldn't have got out of the car so quickly. But they did.'

Mallory nodded. 'I've observed enough of the twins over the years to know the Broadwick stubbornness is a family-wide trademark.'

Cornelia cracked a half-smile. 'Wait, what if witchlights can be used to circumvent the wards? We got into Rowan House when you and Diana weren't properly cleared, maybe—' She stopped as Mallory shook her head.

'Lucy said we were approved about five minutes before we showed up, and they've been wise to witchlight travel since we told the UML about it at the tribunal,' Mallory said.

'Are we sure? Have they tested it?'

Mallory chewed on her bottom lip thoughtfully, then sent a message to Diana, who called her back instantly.

'I'm busy, Mallory,' Diana said, her face flushed and her eyes bright.

'Sorry to interrupt,' Mallory said dryly. 'But we need you to ask Lucy something else for us.'

She relayed Cornelia's question about witchlights and hung up, finishing her tea.

Diana called back.

'They rigorously tested witchlight travel within Wickermere before the tribunal, as they'd got wind of the possibility and wanted a security check. You can't travel in here without clearance full stop, though you *can* travel within Wickermere if you are cleared to be here. If you could *deign* to not interrupt me for the next twenty minutes, I'd be so grateful okay love you, bye,' she said, before either of them could respond, and hung up.

'That answers that,' Mallory said, dropping her phone onto the bedside table. 'Whether they know it or not, the Wickermere Reaper is on that list Lucy showed us.'

Cornelia pulled the duvet over her head, teacup clutched precariously in her hand.

'It's going to be okay. It might not be good, or favourable. At times it probably won't even be tolerable. But I think it's going to be okay.' Mallory squeezed her hand briefly – so briefly that by the time Cornelia had extricated herself from the duvet, Mallory had already rolled over to the edge of the bed, leaving as much space between them as she could, or so it felt to Cornelia.

She wanted to ask her for a hug, or to hold her hand. She wanted to reach out and wrap her fingers in Mallory's t-shirt. Nothing they hadn't done before, or that Cornelia had ever thought twice about, and yet the idea of them casually touching felt ludicrous. She thought of Diana seeing it.

Why won't you admit how you feel about Mallory?

I don't know what you're talking about, Diana.

It hadn't been a lie, but it had changed everything. For the last year Cornelia had got more and more in her head, unable to shake the idea that Diana was seeing something that she couldn't see herself, leaving every single movement she made around Mallory more charged than Theodore in a thunderstorm.

She switched off the light, closing her glasses with a metallic *clack* of finality, and set an alarm for five a.m. The duvet rustling over her as she wriggled to find a comfortable position. Tears pricked the backs of her eyelids as a fresh wave of panic cascaded over her, as though her body had waited for her to be horizontal to distribute it evenly. She blinked them away, not sure they'd fall even if she wanted them to.

She listened for the sound of Mallory's breathing regulating, but it didn't come before she passed out herself, an ocean stretching between them.

One that Cornelia felt she could bridge permanently, if only she were brave enough to reach out a hand.

'Goodnight,' Mallory said quietly, right as Cornelia sank down into the darkness that claimed her from every angle.

PERIMORTEM III

They like to read. True crime, astronomy, psychology, sometimes turning to fiction if the mood struck, but facts were paramount to order, almost as essential as time.

A fact: history is told by the victors. People will accept someone's story told by another, shifting the lens until it becomes theirs. All too keen to discuss the horrors they've witnessed, as though that is the only facet of the story that matters.

Another fact: people will settle into horror very quickly. A hopeless agony with defined stages.

Day one it's denial.

Day two it's anger in its many masks – they liked it best when it manifested as panic. Audible, helpless, on-the-ground panic.

Day three it's bargaining.

They'd made it a waiting game. The bodies were in situ, two books in hand – one on the science of time, one on the stages of grief, a private joke with no punchline – and they'd wait for the day three domino to fall, for the lens to turn away from the bodies.

That's when they shone.

FOURTEEN

17:30:43

A few hours' sleep was somehow worse than none at all. Cornelia's eyes flicked open at the sound of her alarm – and at Diana's annoyed stomps across the floor above her – and she slid out of bed, anxiety thrumming through her like a drumbeat. Mallory took her meds and promptly witchlighted back to Wrackton with Stella's clothes, the beetles and the Witches' magic samples, leaving Cornelia and Diana to go back to Rowan House to tackle talking to the Broadwicks.

A prospect Cornelia was not much looking forward to.

'How do you want me to play this?' Diana asked. 'Do you want to appear competent and I your clueless, guileless side-kick in an effort to employ our usual methods of tricking people into giving us the information we want in a semi-legal fashion?'

'I think we can try that,' Cornelia said. 'Across the board, with all of the Council. Most of these people still think of me as a little gir— a child,' she said, tripping on the word.

Another thing in a long list of things she needed to figure

out about herself. She just wished the things bothering her hadn't become suddenly urgent and necessary in the face of a deadline, such as having just over seventeen hours to find her twin sisters before they suffocated to death, probably not far from where they were standing.

'Luckily this is one of my favourite roles to play,' Diana said, as a bedraggled-looking Lucy opened the front door of Rowan House.

'Diana, I hope the list was helpful!' She stepped aside so they could enter. 'Cornelia, your parents are strategising with some of the Council in the War Room. Might take a while longer yet.'

So much for the Council reconvening at first light, as it was just gone five a.m. – though Cornelia supposed it was the sort of lie she could fully accept, in the circumstances.

'I can check if they're ready to receive you, or else you can wait out here and speak to them privately?'

Cornelia and Diana exchanged glances. Privately would mean less posturing.

'We'll wait. I actually wanted to show Diana my old bedroom,' Cornelia said.

'I can get you some tea? Maybe some breakfast? Not much by way of appetite around here at the moment, but you should try to keep your strength up. I'll bring it up to you,' Lucy said, and then bustled off before Cornelia could object.

'We need to ask her more questions about the structure of the Ghoul Council,' Diana hissed. 'She's clearly game for helping us.'

'We should also ask outright if she's had any involvement, so we can eliminate her. The faerie thing is really handy sometimes,' Cornelia said. She led the way up the main staircase to her old bedroom, her left hand tracing a familiar path over the wallpaper as she walked. Diana took it all in silently as Cornelia opened the door.

Rays of light hit Cornelia's old desk in the window, bouncing off her old microscope. Dust motes rose up to meet them, the room exactly as she'd last left it – burgundy walls with cream trim and high ceilings, books and papers everywhere, her bed the only thing disturbed as it had been turned down. Cornelia sneezed twice for good measure, lost in vague flashes of memory. It was a relic of her past self, a memorial to a version she'd long grown out of, and was maybe never going to grow into in the first place.

Diana moved, as expected, to the wardrobe. Inside were things Cornelia had been all too happy to leave behind: dresses and skirts, and the one pair of heels someone had tried to force her into for a wedding when she was thirteen. They were items that had been given to her with the intent of helping her hold a shape she had to contort to fit into, but didn't *belong* to her. Like the first time someone called her a woman, and the word felt like a gift meant for someone else. It fit Diana and Mallory. It fit her effortlessly glamorous mother, and her sisters (*Agatha Ethel Agatha Ethel*) who relished the rituals they'd grown up in. Cornelia only revisited these discarded parts of herself, hidden behind the wardrobe door, whenever she was in Rowan House in some sort of painfully ironic, on-the-nose metaphor.

Diana frowned at it and closed the wardrobe again without comment.

'What did you want to show me?' she asked, breaking Cornelia's reverie.

'I wanted to give us a chance to talk to Lucy alone,' Cornelia said. 'And also try to find my old uni research on Lyreflies, see if I had any leads.'

She dug through the most recent addition to the room – a haphazard stack of folders and papers she'd discarded on her last trip to Rowan House. She selected a list of sources and tossed the folder to Diana, who flicked through it with her phone already in hand.

'Excellent work, detective.'

Cornelia squinted sarcastically, but was glad to have thought of something. No stone unturned. She didn't want to regret not trying.

Lucy tapped on the door, her arms laden with a tray of toast, croissants and a steaming pot of tea. Cornelia's stomach clenched at the idea of eating, but Diana handed her a croissant and made it clear by way of encouraging head movements that she wouldn't get away without trying.

Sometimes having friends that cared so much was the worst.

'How long have you worked for the Broadwicks?' Diana asked.

'About ten years now, I'd say,' Lucy said. 'I would've been in my early twenties, yeah. Why?'

'Oh it's silly. We've grown up knowing Imogen and Ezra were important in the Ghoul Council, but I guess I've never really understood what the Ghoul Council *does*.'

Diana was laying it on a bit thick, but Lucy didn't seem to notice.

'Ah, I can't really be telling you trade secrets, now.' She laughed nervously.

'Oh nooo, nothing like that. Just broad strokes, really. Like I'm five,' Diana batted her eyelashes. 'What *is* the Ghoul Council?'

Lucy cast a glance over her shoulder, and took another step into the room.

'Officially, we've one main goal – or one main *ghoul*, if you get me. Anyways,' she said hastily, 'we are dedicated to the research and management of spectral activity in Occult matters across the UK. We've also got special branches in Ireland, Italy, France, North America, India, Hong Kong, and one in the Fair Kingdom as well.' She counted on her fingers for a second. 'There's probably more that I'm not privy to, but those are the main ones. And I say "main ones", but some of them are just one fella in a tiny office that could double as a toilet cubicle. All very important, of course, but there wasn't room for two of us in the Irish cubicle, so I was delighted to be invited over here, to the main branch. I'm lucky the Broadwicks saw something in me.'

Diana made noises of being impressed and Cornelia kept her mouth shut, working on quietly taking Lucy in. She had a face you'd automatically trust. Cornelia understood for the first time, with a lash of well-buttered shame, that the Ghoul Council *was* the Broadwicks, and they the Ghoul Council. They'd hired Lucy as the pleasant face at the forefront. They had Harry and Dot as stalwarts, and had filled out the Council with Olivia-who-she-wasn't-thinking-about-because-that-was-both-stupid-and-pointless-but-also-a-distraction-she-didn't-need-or-want-because-this-wasn't-harmless-flirting-

and-rejection-time, and Nova. Nova, who she had a hunch served as the sole contrarian. Proof to the UML that the Broadwicks weren't *completely* surrounded by yes-folk.

'It must feel pretty special, to be chosen,' Diana said brightly.

'Imog— my parents don't easily pick favourites,' Cornelia said, confident that Lucy wouldn't easily clam up. 'But when someone earns that trust from them, they're privy to all sorts.'

'Ah, not at all,' Lucy said, waving a bashful hand. Cornelia had seen Taylor do this particular hand gesture enough to know it was some sort of intricate Apparent ritual used to ward off the concept of 'notions', which Taylor had explained as 'having ideas above your station' and Cornelia had taken to mean something akin to 'self-esteem of any regard'.

'Oh, I don't believe that, after they invited you here!' Diana said. 'I bet Imogen and Ezra have you doing all sorts. Especially now, with the Reaper case.'

'Sure look, everyone's on edge and I'm happy to help where I can,' Lucy said. 'I've been compiling addendums to the dossiers for Imogen, making sure everyone's airtight and we know where everyone was. Can't be too careful, if the Reaper is trying to get at the Council, it's completely understandable that we'd want to be sure nobody was at risk of being dragged into the mess simply by being in the wrong place at the wrong time, or even targeted!'

'What dossiers?' Cornelia asked.

Lucy's eyes widened fractionally. 'I… can't say. I'm sorry, I shouldn't have even mentioned it, it's just we're all on edge. We're rule followers. That's probably what Imogen and Ezra saw in me when they brought me here – a commitment to the rules of the Ghoul Council, our management goals and our aims. They take trust here so seriously, and it's not easily earned. Nobody is more worried about the Reaper than the Broadwicks, I can tell you that much.'

'What kind of management does the council do? See,' Diana said, changing tack as Lucy hesitated, 'we have a ghost in our house. I live in Broadwick Mansion with Cornelia and Mallory, and our office is in the basement.'

Cornelia made sure her face was relaxed, methodically eating her croissant. She was awake enough now to remember she had vowed not to participate in anything that could be construed as taking anything from her parents, but it seemed a shame to waste a perfectly good plate of pastries.

'Theodore, right?'

'Yeah! Do you know him?'

'I write a lot of the paperwork for him,' Lucy said.

'We've noticed there's a surprising amount of paperwork involved in his management, but I wonder if that's all there is to it, with Samhain ghosts? The set-up around here feels to me like there's got to be more to it. There aren't that many Samhain ghosts wandering around…'

Cornelia hated to admit it, mostly to avoid the inevitable gloating, but if there was one thing Diana was particularly good at, it was buttering people up.

'Yes,' Lucy said, smiling a little as she shifted further into the room. 'There is more to it, but I don't know if I should—'

'Have a croissant,' Diana said. 'They'll only go to waste otherwise.'

'Oh, alright.' She sat next to Diana on Cornelia's bed.

'So does that mean there are other kinds of spectral disturbances the Ghoul Council deals with, then?'

'It's mad actually,' Lucy said around a bite of croissant. 'Before I started working here, I'd no idea how extensive the work would be. I sort of thought it'd be a lot of fluting about. A cultural role with no meaningful function. I'm a Junior Clerical, so I don't know all the ins and outs, and I certainly don't know what goes on above me, but I'm responsible for maintaining Cornelius's wards and keeping folk away from the lake, authorising clearance and so on. I also log artefacts given to the Council, and arrange UML and Ghoul Council appointments for the Relic Room – lots of fascinating old Occulture stuff in there. I haven't seen it all, but many an object of Occultural significance, even a crypt, I've heard, is to be found within its walls. Occasionally, I get to do some big girl jobs – your friend Theodore, for instance, falls under my remit. Though I usually send that on to the Mayoral Offices. I met him once, actually.'

'When was that?' Cornelia asked sharply.

'It was when he was still alive, we had a brief conversation,' Lucy said, almost apologetically. 'His name crops up quite often. Unusual things, Samhain ghosts.'

'Are there many ghosts under your remit?'

Lucy licked some croissant flakes off her fingers, waving her free hand. 'No, no, he's the only one! I imagine I'm only allowed to write up the amended rules and so forth for him, so he knows where we stand on Besiegement-like activities – that usually comes down from the UML, we have meetings, and then decide the new directives – because he's on Broadwick property. I bet if he was anywhere else, I wouldn't have a thing to do with him. I'm sure there's a secret vault somewhere that has all the names of all the Samhain ghosts we know of, but Theodore's the only one in Wrackton, and the only one I've ever had any kind of contact with.'

Knowing, as they did, about Wrackton's second Samhain ghost, Katherine Vane, it stood to reason that Lucy just didn't know about her. As a faerie she couldn't lie, but it felt bizarre to Cornelia that she'd be so blatantly unaware of what was in the Mayoral Offices. The Ghoul Council and the UML and former Night Mayor Vincent Van Doren were so interlinked before Van Doren had died – died at the hands of his son, whose face would *not leave Cornelia alone*—

'Do you know anything about Agatha and Ethel's disappearance?' Cornelia asked, ignoring Diana's irritated glare.

'Well, I know they're missing? How are you holding up, love?' Lucy asked.

'I'm fine. Or,' Cornelia amended, 'as fine as can be expected.'

How *fine* that was, was up to individual interpretation.

'Oh, did you mean was *I* involved? Goddess, no. No, never!' Lucy said.

'We had to ask,' Diana said cheerfully. 'We'd be bad investigators if we didn't. Listen, I wanted to ask you, why's the lake like that?'

'Bonemarrow Lake? What about it?'

'It's just that Theodore thinks if he misbehaves badly enough, he'll go in there in a ghostlight. I keep telling him that's beyond preposterous,' Diana said, with a lilting little laugh.

Lucy's smile faltered.

'It *is* preposterous, isn't it? It's not like that's a lake full of ghostlights out there?'

'There have… historically… been measures necessary to control the population of Samhain ghosts. You have to understand, the risk of the Besiegement Curse is so high when it comes to ghosts who are not amenable to management. The options become deeply limited.'

'The what?' Diana asked.

Cornelia stayed silent, watching.

'There are rules around interacting with ghosts,' Lucy said uncomfortably. 'And while a lot of it is bureaucratic in nature, plenty of it is legitimately geared towards safety. The Ghoul Council are incredibly strict in how certain interactions can be carried out. Séances must be properly facilitated by a trained professional, all interactions with any potential Samhain ghost not suitably motivated to follow the handbook must be monitored carefully. Otherwise, the proximity of a ghost can lead to a Besiegement. It hasn't happened in a long time, barring some near misses – we're talking well over a century, when the Ghoul Council started lobbying the UML to really push the public safety messaging. Apparents took it too far, living in fear of ouija boards' – Lucy snorted – 'but strangely, all the horror films helped reinforce the safety aspect. Their ideas weren't *wrong* – in terms of impact, they're not far off the reality of the dangers of a Besiegement.'

'What *is* a Besiegement, though?'

'Ah. Prevention of the Besiegement Curse is our foundational concern, really, in the Ghoul Council. That, and preventing a resurgence of the Vampire Wars, but that's by the by. The

Besiegement Curse is, as the name suggests, a curse – an old one. If a ghost is given unfettered access to a person's body – such as through a séance – they can, effectively, claim it as their own, though it's not as simple as—'

The door to the War Room slammed open and Lucy leapt to her feet, gone before Cornelia could stop her. She and Diana followed Lucy out, and Cornelia shut the door behind her, glad to be out of her old bedroom.

'Imogen,' Cornelia said, brushing croissant crumbs onto the stairs as she hurried into the entrance hall where Imogen and Ezra stood, talking quietly. Neither looked as though they'd slept. 'Mother. We need to talk, now.'

'Absolutely not,' Imogen said, staring after Lucy, who had run to her desk with such impressive speed, she might as well have witchlighted. 'We told you everything we are cleared to share.'

'But you *didn't* tell us everything.' Cornelia felt a burn in her stomach, the fiery sense of injustice she'd carried since she was ten and was getting 'could try harder' results in her school report cards that had heralded the start of Ezra looking at her with constant mild disappointment, and Imogen pursing her lips instead of pretending to indulgently listen to anything Cornelia had to say.

That, and the fact they'd lied to her about talking in the morning. It had been a classic Ezra 'we'll see', meaning 'never', and she hadn't recognised it in the moment.

'We've told you everything we can.'

'We met with the Witches of Bonemarrow Lake,' Diana said. 'In an effort to gather as much information as possible relating to the former victims, to try paint a picture of who might want to take your daughters. And we learned something interesting.'

'They talked to you?' Ezra said, just as Harry exited the War Room.

'Ezra,' Harry said, his brow drawn in concern. 'This isn't the place.'

'I'm sure it's—'

'Esquire means something around here,' Harry said. 'It is my job to prevent us implicating ourselves in any way, particularly when that is unnecessary.'

'"Implicating yourselves"?' Cornelia spat. It was on the tip of her tongue – the last time the Broadwicks *implicated themselves.* Katherine's memory of them was as good as her own now, she could see them telling Van Doren that they'd killed Theodore. '*Hexana forbid* we have to go to the Night Mayor to smooth things out for you. Oh, but of course, you can't just go to Honourable Dr Night Mayor Ray now, can you? Because she actually plays by the rules you seem to care about so much.'

'I heard she was in line for a knighthood,' Nova said silkily, appearing at Diana's side. 'She *does* strike me as someone who would relish being called "sir".'

Dot, clearly responding to the commotion, wandered out of the War Room with an eyebrow raised. She glanced at Imogen and pulled a subtle face at Cornelia that forced her to bite back a smile.

'Cornelia, I am willing to overlook your outburst because we are all in a state of shock,' Ezra said carefully. 'But if you're going to continue being here, with your friends, we have got to talk about your temper, and how adults behave in adult spaces.'

'Oh leave her be,' Dot said, rubbing Ezra's arm in a way that was partially aggressive, partially calming.

'The Witches told us something interesting that's not in the case file,' Diana said, subtly stepping in front of Cornelia. It was just as well, because Cornelia was about to hex the lot of them back into the War Room.

'I'm sure whatever they told you, we already know and don't need to discuss it outside the War Room,' Imogen said. Despite the effortless grace, she was always a hair-trigger away from blowing up. It never ceased to surprise Cornelia that anyone would wonder why she was Like This, when the evidence was right here.

'Worth checking, though? See, they mentioned the Wickermere Reaper sent them a ransom note when Stella Carson was abducted,' Diana said. 'And we were wondering if, perhaps, that might be relevant to establishing MO. Perhaps would even help us get your daughters back?'

'Diana, you are a guest in my *home*—'

'Stop talking, Imogen,' Harry said in warning. 'We have systems in place for a reason.'

'We don't have time for any of this,' Nova said, flicking a dismissive hand. 'Olivia?'

It was a summons rather than a request.

Olivia, who had been lurking in the doorway of the War Room with a book tucked under her arm, made eye contact with Cornelia as she passed, treating her to another flash of a smile. It reminded Cornelia of something that felt, impossibly, like home, if only she could put her finger on what it was.

She snapped back to the situation at hand.

'Imogen, let's get you some tea. Keep your strength up. Tensions are high, but our ability to cope is higher. That's what you'd always say to me,' Dot said, taking Imogen's arm and leading her away.

This left Diana and Cornelia looking at Ezra, who was carefully unmoved.

'We just want to know the facts, so we can help,' Diana said, her tone unusually cool. 'You've invited us into your home and onto the case. We're a trusted agency, but we can only do our best work if *you* trust us. We're all on a deadline – I know you're more aware of it than we ever could be, but I guarantee that everything could be sped up if you would just show us the ransom note. We had a look at the one the Witches were sent, and—'

'But that self-destructed,' Ezra corrected.

Diana paused, a small smile on her lips.

Cornelia always felt an urge to clap when Diana did this, though she'd never tell her. The slam-dunk of it all.

'So you agree,' Diana said, somehow managing to keep smugness out of her tone. 'There *was* a ransom note? For them. And for you.'

Cornelia had never actually heard her father swear, but she could practically see his neurons lighting up with every single curse word he knew and then some.

'Your mother would rather…'

'I don't care,' Cornelia said softly. 'I don't care what she'd rather. I know she'd rather a lot of things, but the fact is that if you don't tell us what the Wickermere Reaper demanded, Agatha and Ethel could die. They could die, and I'll be all you have left.'

Ezra blinked. Once, twice. Stalling.

'There'll come a day when you're better able to understand everything that's happening here,' he said finally, shoving his hands into his pockets. 'That note and its contents don't matter. It's misdirection. It won't get the girls back. Keep doing what you're doing, by all means, but if you keep flaunting our guidelines, I will have no choice but to ask you to stand down. Now if you'll excuse me, I have to keep my family together.'

He walked away, wingtips clipping the tiles.

Cornelia was dimly aware she was shaking.

'Are you okay?' Diana asked.

Cornelia turned on her in an instant.

'What do you fucking think? What the fuck kind of question is that?'

She didn't wait for a response, stomping back up the stairs as if she was going into her bedroom.

FIFTEEN

16:04:37

'Never again will I make fun of you for how big Broadwick Mansion is when *this* is your other house. Broadwick Mansion is your tiny little townhouse compromise. Also – Wickermere? Surely that's not *Broad*wickermere. Please tell me it isn't. Actually, don't confirm or deny that, it's more fun for me to believe it's true,' Diana said, leaning in the doorway of Agatha's room.

Her hair was in a ponytail, and she'd pulled on the white overalls Mallory had taken to insisting they wore to crime scenes where evidence might still be present.

She had clearly judged that Cornelia had cooled off just enough to be poked at again. This was the way their friendship manifested: in barbs and pushing and hexes and showing up for each other. Diana was closer to the sort of sibling Cornelia always wished she had, though it made her feel sick to think of it now. It took all of Cornelia's strength, on her days when she was too afraid to set foot outside or full of panic at the idea of doing anything normal, to return those barbs with her usual level of ferocity.

'Shut up,' Cornelia said, which Diana maddeningly took to mean yes. 'They used to live here full-time, before Agatha and Ethel were born, and then they divided their time between official Ghoul Council bullshit and other UML-centric bullshit until they, evidently, became the bullshit themselves after Grandad Cornelius died.'

Cornelia wiped her hair back from her forehead impatiently, looking back into Ethel's room where she'd been working for the last hour.

She'd identified the biggest difference between Agatha and Ethel as people, and it was the sliding scale of chaos. Agatha was orderly, everything in its place, whereas Ethel – though she outwardly presented that same neatness – clearly used her bedroom as an outlet for the gremlins that lived within her. Diana had suggested they draw straws – as if Cornelia didn't know she'd cheat – but chaos was something Cornelia could work with.

It made her a bit sad to see how similar she and Ethel were in a lot of ways. There were papers strewn across her desk and piled on top of books on the bookshelves. Half-finished bags of sweets hung out in the open top drawer of her dresser next to socks that had been balled up in mismatched pairs. Plants clinging to life hung from ceiling baskets. A taped-up schedule that Ethel had scribbled on again and again until Agatha's neat, round writing had established a new – clearly more efficient – schedule.

There were theatre tickets pinned to a little board next to her vanity alongside photos of friends Cornelia barely recognised, the twins posing on beaches and family skiing trips Cornelia had declined on the basis of it being the worst-sounding thing she could possibly do with her time, and she solved murders for a living.

All of it was a bit sad. She'd hated them as a kid, hated being compared to them, hated how badly her parents wanted her to be, in essence, the third twin.

But here she was, rummaging through their belongings like it might tell her something, *anything*, about who had taken them.

'I haven't found anything interesting in Agatha's bedroom, except for her mystery bedside drawer of fun, should you like to see the one – that is one, single – toy she keeps in there that I don't think has ever been used,' Diana said. 'And as soon as those words were out of my mouth, I realised that that might not cheer you up the way it cheered me up. It's hard to not be open season on the Broadwick twins.'

Cornelia cracked a smile at Diana's uncharacteristic fluster.

'Honestly, it's entertaining enough to see you fear me biting your head off. I'm still trying to make headway here, I have to basically imagine what it would be like to walk around inside my own brain when I drop things.'

'And what a time that would be,' Mallory said, climbing the stairs. She nodded approvingly at Diana's overalls and struggled into her own.

They somehow looked nice on her.

Beside her was a large carrier bag overflowing with bottles and beakers.

'Taylor and Kingston packed up some things they thought we'd find useful, like a mobile lab. I assume Kingston used his power of knowing things to divine that, but they've put all sorts in here, including the Sprinter, of all things.'

'I miss the Sprinter. Poor thing barely gets a look-in since we got the Magic Magical Machine,' Cornelia said.

The Sprinter was the first of Mallory and Theodore's magical forensics advancements – essentially a spell identification database, much like the Apparent concept of a fingerprint database. It had given Cornelia the idea to look up a way for Mallory to carry around a modified binding spell she could use on her legs on her really bad pain days, when compression was what helped most. She'd replaced the spell once, after the Whistler case, and Mallory still wore the crystal around her neck.

Cornelia supposed it was comforting, to have the spell there, and that it didn't mean anything else.

Not like the gloves Mallory had given her that time, that she kept in her pocket and went to monumental effort not to lose or misplace. Or the limited edition, impossible-to-find record Mallory had tracked down and given her last Yule that she thought she'd run into a burning building to save. Or the fact she'd gone out of her way to find the Lawrence sound beetle colony and Cornelia thought of her every time she opened their vivarium.

Not like that at all.

Mallory finished zipping up as Diana filled Mallory in on what Lucy had told them.

'I'm going to go down to her desk and try to talk to Lucy about the dossiers, see if I can get my hands on them. I can't imagine anyone else on the Council is going to be *quite* as forthcoming, but if we're right that it's someone with access to Wickermere, I think those alibis are going to be necessary,' Diana finished.

'Did she give any indication that she thought anyone was lying about their whereabouts when the twins were taken?' Mallory asked.

Cornelia shook her head. 'No, she said they were to "make sure" everyone was "airtight", which, thinking about it, suggests they're conside ring there's a leak in the Council, as opposed to a Reaper *on* the Council.'

'I'll try asking Lucy outright if she has any suspicions. She is, as Taylor would say, an absolute dote, and if anyone hurts her I shall riot,' Diana said.

'How's Theodore?' Cornelia asked. 'And do we have any evidence to go on?'

'He wasn't there, but left a detailed note,' Mallory said, passing over a torn-out notebook page upon which the words *MALLORY SHOULD YOU ARRIVE WHEN I AM NOT PRESENT THE MATTERS HAVE BEEN TAKEN IN HAND!!!!* were scrawled in Theodore's hand.

'Usual self, then,' Cornelia said.

Mallory smiled. 'As for the evidence, the beetles from both Stella's and Agatha and Ethel's crime scenes appear to be wholly contaminated, as expected – I got what I can only describe as a miasma of a result. I need Theodore to help me interpret that chart. I came back here because we need to get samples from the Ghoul Council as a matter of urgency, so if we *do* find anything physical to go on, we don't have to waste any more time.'

'That's going to be tough, given how much of a stickler for rules they are – or that Harry is, specifically,' Cornelia said.

'I know, but needs must. There was one other thing,' she added. 'I need Theodore to look at it too, but I found some kind of red physical trace on Carson's shirt. I thought maybe it was brick dust, but I'll need him to look at the chart, I've left the Magic Magical Machine running on it. I'm hoping it's something that could link back to the Wickermere Reaper.'

'The next best thing to magical forensics *is* regular forensics,' Diana said, struggling to pull her overalls off without taking her shoes off, though she was undoubtedly quoting either Mallory, Theodore, or both of them.

'Exactly. Maybe someday we'll get a case that has normal traces that can be investigated with normal methods. Blood spatter, or… something that doesn't involve anyone's family.' Mallory pulled on latex gloves. 'Where do you want me?'

Right here, Cornelia thought, and then shook her head. Her thoughts had been less clear than usual lately, but that was weird. It was as though Diana had lanced through the logical part of her brain and made her doubt every thought she'd had since.

'I'll be back,' Diana said, finally free of her overalls. 'Hopefully with something actionable.'

'Thank you,' Cornelia said, turning back to Mallory. 'I'm trying to do a "what would I do" scenario, but apply it to my sister, who I am discovering is more like me than I am comfortable confronting.'

Diana looked between them and then shut the door to Ethel's room, leaving them alone in the mess.

'If it's just a "what would Cornelia do" situation…' Mallory said thoughtfully.

She walked backwards to the door, closed her eyes, and moved forwards slowly, hands aloft.

'I would walk in and immediately drop my stuff here,' she pointed to a pile of shoes and jackets behind the door, her eyes still closed. 'If I had anything important – documents, things I wanted to look at – I'd leave them unopened here,' she pointed to the desk. 'And then if I had gone through the documents but wasn't ready to address the contents, I would put them in a safe place.'

'Bottom drawer,' Cornelia and Mallory said at the same time.

'Every time. Remember when you lost your university accommodation acceptance letter and tore your room apart?'

Mallory had been so sick then, her face pale and drawn, but had turned up at Cornelia's panicked summons, walked into her bedroom and immediately found the letter in a drawer with her jumpers. Cornelia remembered looking at her like she'd performed a miracle.

She knelt next to the bedside table and Mallory pulled out the bottom vanity drawer, laying out a plastic sheet and emptying the contents one by one, arranging neat stacks of documents.

Cornelia crouched beside her and took photos, then flicked through the pages for anything interesting. Mostly old bank statements, various club memberships, a fancy witchlight, a residency application for a botanist position in Spain, and then something that made Mallory hiss so vehemently, Cornelia was sure she'd hurt herself.

'Don't panic,' Mallory said. 'But this is weird, and probably relevant.'

A stack of at least seven letters, carefully handwritten on thick cream paper, addressed to both Agatha and Ethel, from Lyle Whitlock, prisoner at Foxland Hall.

'Why the FUCK are the twins writing to the Dollhouse Murderers?' Cornelia said, reaching to snatch the letters from Mallory, who deftly moved them out of her grasp.

Her hand brushed Mallory's sleeve, and even through the gloves and overalls she felt something swoop into her stomach that made her pause.

'This one says he's newly single, so probably just the one Dollhouse Murderer,' Mallory said, appearing not to notice Cornelia's inner turmoil. She handed over half the sheaf and Cornelia scanned them.

'Started about five weeks after he went to prison, last one was from…'

'A week ago, if this is the last one.'

Cornelia was already on her feet, checking the desk for more letters, then ran downstairs to the hall, past a confused Diana who was leaning so far over Lucy's desk to look over her shoulder at her computer screen that her feet were practically off the floor, to the sideboard where post was often left. Nothing for either twin.

'This is disgusting,' she said, bursting back into the room.

'What the fuck is going on in here?' Diana asked, following her back up a few moments later.

'Fuck is right,' Cornelia said. 'They've… I don't even know where to start.'

'The twins have been sending letters to the Dollhouse Murderer,' Mallory said. 'Weird, mundane, how-do-you-do letters with no substance in them – he's written replies on the back of them. There's at least one a month, no indication that they've been discussing anything strange, no threats, nothing that worries me. Could you—'

Cornelia was already on it, whispering revealing spells and decoding spells and anything else she could think of, but nothing changed in the letters that indicated there was magical concealment afoot.

'What if there's something secret in the text? What if they contained a spell or instruction hand-coded in, no magic involved? Maybe the Wickermere Reaper and the Dollhouse Murderer are in cahoots,' Diana added.

'Say that again,' Cornelia said.

'Cahoots?'

'No, the first bit. What if someone here was forced to act on behalf of the Dollhouse Murderer? Or *wanted* to? What if the twins aren't really missing at all? What if all of this is yet another fucking mind game?' Cornelia asked. She could feel her temper rising, mingling with wild panic.

Diana had her phone out and was through to Sully in moments, relaying what they'd learned before she'd even said hello.

'That's… weird,' Sully said when Diana finished.

'You can say that again,' Cornelia said.

'I won't, though. What do you need from me?'

'We need to visit him,' Diana said. 'We need to talk to him face-to-face, and ask what he's doing.'

Sully sighed. 'I can't facilitate that, I'm sorry. We could request it, but his visitors will be limited, and I heard he's amassed quite a following in the wake of the murders.'

Mallory frowned so deeply that she wrinkled her nose, and Cornelia bit back a smile. It was one of Mallory's greatest vexations – the celebrity that came with doing the worst things a person could do, and how many people would rush to treat Whitlock like a hero. At least with Jacob dead, he couldn't have anyone running around after him.

Even if it didn't feel like he was. They'd watched his body be put into the ground, and Cornelia still had a creeping sense that he was watching her every move.

'It's also not something I'm particularly *willing* to facilitate,' Sully went on. 'Can't you ask the Broadwicks?'

'No,' Cornelia said shortly. 'We can't.'

'Right. Apologies, but I'd better be off.'

Diana hung up, tapping her phone off her forehead.

'We've one other option,' she said. 'Someone who probably *owes* us a favour at this stage.'

'And who I'd be willing to bet the remaining money in our agency account has dealings in the town where Whitlock's detained,' Mallory added, catching on.

It took Cornelia another second, and then she grimaced, accepting defeat.

'Fine. Call Grey Quinn.'

SIXTEEN

13:58:05

Cornelia longed for the days when they got away with being an utterly amateur agency that could steal magical DNA samples and be done with it. Legitimacy as an agency had pushed them into having to hide their illegal manoeuvres better.

They waited for the Ghoul Council to break for breakfast, busying themselves in the first-floor hallway in a manner that made Cornelia feel very small, awash with glimmers of childhood memories of doing almost this exact thing. The main difference was the frisson of anxiety blooming in her chest whenever she checked the time, which was often.

Once the issue of the letters had sunk in, Diana relayed what she'd found at Lucy's desk.

'Proof, mostly, that the dossiers do exist – on her desktop she's got a file called "DOSSIERS_ALIBIS_IB",' Diana said, a distinct note of pity in her voice. As much as she seemed to enjoy manipulating powerful people, she got no joy out of manipulating the kind or generous. It was something Cornelia liked very much about her, even if she'd never tell her. 'From what I gather, she doesn't have any specific suspicions about any of them. The sun shines out of Imogen's and Ezra's arses, Harry is so wise and proper, Dot is so kind and beloved, Olivia is so smart and pretty' – not that Cornelia had noticed – 'and Nova… Of all of them, Lucy seems the most apprehensive about Nova.'

'What do *we* know about Nova?' Mallory asked. 'Apart from them being a troll.'

'And the official spokesperson on the Reaper case for both the Ghoul Council and the UML.' Cornelia explained what she'd surmised earlier about them – that Nova had been hired as a way to show that the Broadwicks were open to opposition.

Mallory nodded thoughtfully. 'Did you get the actual alibis out of her?'

'As best I could. It appears the Ghoul Council are operating on the assumption there was a breach, rather than considering the possibility that the Reaper is one of their own.'

'Good to know that one of the most powerful governing bodies in all of Occulture are so susceptible to fallacies,' Cornelia said bitterly.

'If they weren't, there would never have been a need for the Undetectables,' Mallory said. It was so small a comfort it was practically not one at all. 'Anyway, the alibis!'

'Imogen and Ezra were off the grounds – Ezra said that he was driving to the next town over for something. Olivia was just coming back in on foot from a walk, Nova had left not five minutes prior to them getting the ransom note—'

'How did they get it? The note. How was it delivered?'

'Lucy said she was in the kitchen and suddenly remembered something, ran out to her desk to get it, and found an envelope there addressed to the Broadwicks.'

'Not to the Ghoul Council?'

'She said the Broadwicks specifically,' Diana said. 'I'm thinking that sounds like demon persuasion magic. Or a coincidence.'

'Which, as we know from Theodore, is unlikely,' Mallory said. 'Who else?'

'Harry was in his office in the Ghoul Council Headquarters. All of this would ordinarily be verifiable, but there was a glitch in the way the wards recorded the comings and goings right at the time they think the twins were abducted. Which does admittedly bolster their theory that it was an external breach, but only if it's true.'

'It also makes their alibis a pile of shit. None of that is verifiable,' Cornelia said, running her hands through her hair. 'And all we have are crumbs. Thanks for following that bread trail, though, Diana. If we can properly figure out how the wards work, we could maybe see if there's another fallacy they overlooked.'

'I can do that. Bear with me!' Diana dipped out, leaving Mallory and Cornelia to continue waiting.

If there was one thing Cornelia hated, above anything else, it was waiting. She tried to write up what Diana had told her, but kept throwing down her pen to tap her head against the wall behind her, the agony of waiting a viscerally uncomfortable one.

'Do you think there's anything to the security breach?'

'It's either legitimate, and Cornelius Broadwick missed a trick when he was setting up the Wickermere and Rowan House wards, or the more concerning prospect of someone on the Ghoul Council attempting to cover their tracks.'

Cornelia didn't know what to say to that, and didn't speak again until Diana bounced back almost an hour later, brandishing photos on her phone of a modular diorama of Rowan House and Wickermere. It wasn't as extensive as her Wrackton one had been – made with love and care and time, when time wasn't so precious – but the bare bones showed a hulking estate with fenced grounds for Rowan House (and the Laurels, where they were staying), a dip that would become the mile-wide and two-miles-long Lake Wickermere, trees and trees and trees that choked the landscape. Across the dip-that-would-be-lake was a smaller building Cornelia recognised as Bonemarrow Cottage, and across the back Diana had built a vague approximation of Wickermere village.

'Seeing as Wickermere doesn't exist on any coherent map anymore, I pieced this together as best I could. There are no proper photos of Wickermere village, apart from some archival images I was able to find from the 1950s,' Diana said. 'I'm trying to understand the Wickermere Reaper's possible movements within the borders of Wickermere, look for any weak points, see if we can eliminate other possibilities, assuming the Reaper is using witchlights. And, most importantly, see if the distance from the abduction sites to burial sites has any bearing on where Agatha and Ethel might be. I think it's telling that Stella was buried so close to the Witches – I just don't know what it is telling *us*. Any sign of movement?' She pointed downstairs. 'I tried to listen at the door, but got nothing.'

'They've a cloaking spell in place,' Cornelia said grimly.

Mallory put down her phone, rubbing her eyes. 'I've been trying to see if anything in the area was built using red brick, or if there are quarries that might produce it, but it's not even hypothesising at this stage, it's guessing. It could be vomit, it could be mould. It could be literally anything. It might not even be relevant, but I want to feel like I'm doing *something* with the time we have.'

They fell silent for a moment. Cornelia felt tense, not knowing when the Council would vacate the War Room, unsure they ever would, unable to really focus on anything except getting in there and doing what they had to do.

'I'm thinking about what Lucy said.' Mallory tapped her fingers on her legs, her back against Ethel's door, her legs reaching across the hall to Agatha's. 'That the Ghoul Council has physical archives. Given how cagey Ezra was, we have to assume whatever the Wickermere Reaper wants is something bigger than money, that the Ghoul Council doesn't want getting out – or doesn't want falling into the wrong person's hands.'

'He also said it was a distraction, that he doesn't believe it's going to get Agatha and Ethel back,' Diana pointed out.

She flicked through the profiles on the Ghoul Council members Cornelia had tried to complete while Diana was working on the diorama. She'd done better than she thought, managing to fill out the profiles with information she'd gleaned from online reports and her own memory.

Dorothy Early had been a member of the Ghoul Council with Cornelia's grandfather, Cornelius Broadwick III, and had retired at least three times to Cornelia's memory, but kept coming back as a consultant. Harry Foster had been a late addition to the cabinet, mere months prior to Cornelius's death. Nova Khan had been hand-picked by Ezra and Imogen when they stepped into Cornelius's role. An online article from an Occult political journal suggested exactly as she'd thought – Nova was there to be controversial. She couldn't find anything on Olivia Reid, except for a couple of journal articles on mass spectroscopy in spectral activity that she bookmarked to read at a time when her family weren't in danger.

While Cornelia had known on some level that the Council was made up of experts in various fields and that Harry wasn't the only one, learning that Dot was a physicist, Olivia a biologist, Nova a former ecologist, and Lucy a former political scientist had been surprising. Her parents had political backgrounds that were largely inherited, though she had been surprised to learn her mother had started out in thanatology before she'd met Ezra Broadwick. It was an uncomfortably similar a path to the life she had chosen for herself.

'Could it be someone in the UML?' Diana asked, before lightly tapping herself on the forehead with her pen – a pink, fluffy thing that tickled Cornelia's nose just to look at it. 'We know it's someone with Wickermere security clearance, never mind.'

It was as likely as anything that the Wickermere Reaper was downstairs, anxiously anticipating a cup of tea and a cucumber sandwich lovingly assembled by Lucy.

It made Cornelia want to throw up, but not enough to tell anyone how she felt about it.

Especially as she didn't *know* how she felt. Everything since the Undetectables had taken the Whistler case had shown her everything was corrupt. It would be some time before she could really reach into herself and examine it all, but that examination wouldn't – couldn't – take place until this was all over.

The War Room door finally opened again, signalling the break for breakfast, and as soon as the final murmurs spread down the hallway to the dining room, Nova dipping outside for a smoke, the Undetectables descended the stairs as one.

Glasses and cups were spread across the table among witch-lights, papers, diagrams that made no sense and a whiteboard that seemed to still be debating policy and procedure. Her eyes landed on the wall of placards. It was not, as she'd first suspected, a Best Council Member of the Month wall, but a memorial for former members, starting with someone called E. Dorren and ending with C. Broadwick. In between she saw A. Waldorf – a name she recognised with a start, as Aurelius Waldorf had been accidentally instrumental in them identifying his great-grandson in the Dollhouse Murderer case – more Broadwicks than one could shake a stick at, an errant Van Doren, and then a line of special memorials for Wickermere Divers, who had, it seemed, one by one perished year after year in Wickermere Lake, until it came to an abrupt end some years back.

Cornelia shook herself back into the room, taking in the whiteboard and groaning as she realised how much time the Council had been wasting with it while they'd been waiting upstairs.

'Better to not look at it,' Diana suggested. 'Lest you explode from rage.'

'Okay, how do we do this? What order were they sitting in?' Mallory asked, evidence bags at the ready. Cornelia lined up *Sonata lutumae* boxes, a marker in her hands to label them.

'This is where Harry was sitting last night.' Cornelia pointed. 'My parents were at the head of the table. That's my mother's signature lipstick shade.' She indicated a crystal glass, the rim stained rosy pink. There was a book on her seat, tucked under her jacket so that Cornelia couldn't read the title.

'And that's Dot's lipstick, so that's definitely her seat,' Diana said.

'Who's on her left?' Mallory asked.

'That'd be me,' Olivia said sheepishly.

Cornelia gripped the edge of the table to stop herself jumping with fright.

'Hi.' Cornelia smiled at her. Mallory looked between them and continued pulling samples.

It was a pity, because if Olivia somehow happened to not be a murderer, Cornelia was sure Mallory would really like her. She made a mental note to tell her about the journal papers.

'Meeting going well?' Diana asked casually, setting a beetle down on Imogen's glass.

Olivia bent to get a closer look.

'Are these the…?'

'The beetles from my undergrad dissertation? The very same,' Cornelia said. 'Olivia is a biologist, Mallory. Maybe she could give you some pointers, or help you with assignments if you need it!'

She could not explain why those words were coming out of her mouth, but they were.

'Oh, thanks. That would be cool,' Mallory said, in a way that suggested she did not think it would be cool at all.

'If you're trying to figure out which one is my glass, I actually took mine with me,' Olivia said apologetically. 'But if it's a magic sample you're after, hand over a swab.'

She quickly swabbed her own mouth and Cornelia dropped it into the sample tube gratefully.

'I'd get out of here ASAP, everyone's planning a short breakfast.'

'We're almost done, we just need—'

'Imagine seeing you three in here,' Nova said, sweeping into the room. They looked down at Cornelia over their glasses with an amused expression on their face, that made Cornelia feel at once as though she was in danger.

'Just doing our jobs,' Diana said, while Mallory calmly continued to collect samples.

'Harry would love this. He'd love the violation of privacy, the chance to flex some UML rules he doesn't get to work very often.' Their smile was dangerous, as they twisted a witchlight between their fingers.

'We have clearance to investigate Rowan House,' Mallory said. 'That includes everything in it. I hate to suggest there's any kind of violation of your civil rights here, but we've got a lead, and the lead is meaningless without your cooperation.'

'I can ask my mother to facilitate this,' Cornelia said, hating it. Hating the bare idea of acting like police, like it was okay to trample over people's rights just because it made their lives easier.

'You won't have to,' Mallory said. 'They know we're on a time crunch. Either their sense of propriety outweighs their need to find Agatha and Ethel, or they've something to hide. Or a secret third thing. But the Broadwicks won't resist this if they're forced to make a decision. It's better not to have a debate over it.'

'Nova,' Olivia said. Their gazes met, and Olivia flashed them a grin that made Cornelia's stomach flip.

'She's got me there,' Nova said wryly. 'Normally I'd be all over this, absolutely burying you in tribunals and whatever else I felt like. But you are on a time crunch, I can appreciate that. Besides, it's not like the Broadwicks will be around much longer in the same capacity.'

They held a hand out for a swab.

'What do you mean?' Diana asked, and it was unclear how much she was feigning interest.

'They've made no secret of their regrets in bringing me into the fold. Harry and Dot were all for it – apparently a cabinet of yes-folk raised too many questions with the UML. There's really only so much sycophancy one can take before it becomes utterly tiresome – my patience for it ran out some years ago.' Nova dropped their sample into the proffered tube.

Before Cornelia could relish her hunch being right, Dot's head poked around the door.

'Heads up,' Dot stage-whispered, her ruby pendant pinging gently against the doorframe. 'Thought I heard your voices. Time to break up the secret meeting. They're cominggg,' she sing-songed, winking at Cornelia.

'I found it,' Nova said, handing over the witchlight. 'Lucy's desk, like I said. Along with my lighter. It's becoming a respawning location for lost things, that's the third time this month.'

'It would help if everyone stopping having a relaxed approach to the concept of "personal belongings",' Olivia said.

'Silly. I keep losing my things all over the place,' Dot said, sighing. 'I'd forget my head if it wasn't screwed on. Take whatever you need, dears, but be quick about it.'

Mallory finished up and Olivia followed them both out as Cornelia and Mallory sat on the chairs in the hall, trying to appear casual. Olivia made a show of looking at something on her phone as Ezra and Imogen passed. Imogen's gaze slid over Cornelia, signalling a freezing-out that had been a long time coming.

The panic, the pressure, all of it threatened to force her to her knees and she swallowed. She still had time to fix it. Still had time to prove herself.

Every bone in her body wanted her to go back to Broadwick Mansion and stay there, rotting away in a room with curtains drawn to shut out the rest of the world. Every fibre of her being wanted her to give in to the darkness that had been threatening to overwhelm her for the last eighteen months.

Somehow, finding Agatha and Ethel had become a light at the end of a dark, dark tunnel. It was a thought that made her feel she was losing her mind.

'If you need anything else, just let me know,' Olivia said, when the Broadwicks were out of earshot. Her face crumpled with concern. 'You must be so worried, Cornelia.'

Cornelia bit her lip. 'I am.'

She just couldn't say *what*, specifically, she was worried about.

'We need to get going on testing,' Mallory said pointedly. 'Diana, do you have everything sorted? We're travelling back now.' She nodded politely at Olivia, who stared after her as she passed.

'It's so funny,' Olivia said, as Cornelia spent far too long adjusting her jumper. 'She reminds me so much of me.'

SEVENTEEN

12:03:59

'Well, well, well. Look who deigned to return,' Theodore said acidly, as Mallory passed through the witchlight and into the research room in a frightening spill of colours and emotions, worse than the last time she'd witchlighted. She wrapped her arms around herself, a lance of emotional pain as bad as her worst physical pain jabbing through her heart.

'Mallory?' Theodore stood up from his iron chair, his face creased with concern. 'That was a joke! I am over-the-moon delighted to see you! You're my favourite, don't tell the others!'

Cornelia and Diana stepped through right after her.

'Hey,' Diana said, her hand pressed to her heart. 'I thought I was your favourite!'

'Sorry, still not used to witchlight travel,' Mallory gasped, straightening with difficulty.

Theodore's face was filled with concern as he patted her gently on the shoulder, static flying. Truthfully, she didn't think she would ever grow used to witchlight travel; the expediency was not worth the emotional turmoil. She both longed to give

Cornelia a hug and never see or touch her again.

Ever since Diana had accused Cornelia of having feelings for Mallory, Cornelia had gone out of her way to create distance between them. There were moments they both seemed to forget, their closeness as common as Diana's was with literally everyone, and then Mallory would do or say something and it would start all over again, the casualness of it disappearing. She shouldn't have made sharing a bed weird.

And yet, there was the demon mausoleums. The *we should do that sometime.* It was both unbearable and baffling and she regularly wondered what she would do the next time Cornelia came home with a partner. Mallory had been warring with her desire to tell her the truth and have her reject her outright, or to maybe take some time away on her own and try to get over her without her heart falling out of her chest every time Cornelia looked particularly nice.

Especially when she always looked particularly nice.

'We need to get going with our samples we collected, and quickly – we've got a meeting,' Mallory continued, finally able to get a full sentence out.

'A *meeting.* How mysterious and beautiful. The fleeting nature of existence—' He looked to Cornelia and closed his mouth with a snap. 'Oh! Mrs Blackburn allowed me to collect the plant. I had a minor issue trying to alert her to my presence as she had a doorbell but no door knocker, so I just paced around outside her house and then eventually started howling like a wolf knowing it would set off the little dog – I think it's a dog, Mallory, but it might be a rat in a jumper, I could not possibly say without closer inspection – and it *did* set off the little dog and she told me never to darken her doorstep again, but I got the plant. That is the conclusion.'

'Then let's look at that while we're here. I need your help interpreting multiple sets of data,' Mallory said, smiling at him. She felt equal parts relieved he was managing the investigation so well on his own, and guilty for ever doubting him.

'These hands are yours, as are these eyes,' Theodore said. 'Also, sorry Diana and Cornelia. You are all my favourites in unique and special ways. Any luck finding the twins?'

Cornelia shook her head stiffly, and Theodore wrapped an arm around her in what was clearly an attempt to soothe her, though Cornelia appeared anything but.

'Also, Mallory, I am intrigued by that sample chart the Magic Magical Machine spat out in your absence. Don't look so alarmed, I didn't *touch* the Machine, but I determined you were testing the red stain? I thought some sort of natural stone or brick dust upon visual inspection, but it has a sort of… mould-like quality to it that made me ponder if it's environmental. I took a teeeeny tiny sample from it, ran an acid test, so I don't believe it *is* brick,' Theodore said, patting Cornelia on the head, oblivious to her discomfort. 'I have written some hypotheses on the murder board.'

'The Witches said they found Stella in a mouldy box,' Mallory mused. 'Diana?'

'I'll take a look. We have some calls to make, which means you need to stick with Mallory, Theodore,' Diana said, eyeing Cornelia. She subtly tilted her head at Mallory, the meaning clear: give her space.

'I can get the new samples ready for the Machine if you want to fill me in on the Wrackton Digger?' Mallory wanted him to know she trusted him to keep the case going in their absence, even though the Wrackton Digger 'case' felt like running around with crayons compared to the Wickermere Reaper.

'I have been writing case notes.' He held up his notebook as he followed her into the lab. 'And as case lead, I would like to host the meeting. Even though there are only two of us present!'

'Be my guest.'

With exaggerated movements, he found his place, licked a finger, and tapped the page as Mallory rounded the iron partition and woke up the Magic Magical Machine where it had been idling in her absence.

'Regarding the case of the Wrackton Digger, we now have a third incident of an attempted grave-robbing.'

Mallory paused with gloved hands on the Ghoul Council swabs. 'What?'

'A third. This morning.'

'Shit,' Cornelia said, coming out to join them. She had the twins' letters from Whitlock in her gloved hands.

'I attempted a solo stakeout,' Theodore said, clearly delighted to have doubled his audience. 'I sent Felix, Kingston and Taylor home not long after you all left, then regretted it. Alas, I am one, solitary, single ghost, and cannot be in multiple places at once. I chose the smallest witch cemetery; there was an attempt at a demon mausoleum.'

'Shit,' Cornelia said again, shrugging on her lab coat.

'Right?' Theodore asked. 'Horrible luck! Rotten timing! Flawed assumptions! And now I will continue this horrible-luck streak by delivering a smash-cut of the *second* piece of bad news, which is that the mausoleum was so old, it was unmarked. I did go find young Kingston and asked him to help me out with maps and such, and I rummaged around the remaining records in the Mayoral Offices, but it seems anything about that part of mausoleums is lost.'

'Where was it?'

'On the north hill, at the very edge. I always thought it was quite lonely out there.'

Right where Mallory and Cornelia had been sitting when they got the call.

'I wonder, did the Wrackton Digger see us?' Mallory asked Cornelia, who had gone even paler.

'You mustn't blame yourselves,' Theodore said. 'I have it in hand. I have a potential eyewitness to question – Taylor said she'd pop in today to help tidy up, I can get her to help me with questioning, you needn't look so *alarmed*, Mallory.'

'I'm not alarmed, I'm glad you're accepting help,' Mallory said tiredly.

'Can I continue?'

'By all means.'

'I think I've helped advance the case a little. See, I was softening the effects of the one-two hit of bad news with a little sprinkle of good news.'

'What did you get?'

'It's quite mysterious, really. The beetles weren't particularly receptive to me at the demon mausoleums – their reaction was muted, and I wondered did I contaminate them somehow? But I followed procedure. I think this strongly suggests the Wrackton Digger was there. I also got soil samples, I was about to test them when you showed up. *And*, I hasten to remind you, I *did* get the plant pot.'

'Excellent,' Mallory said. 'That's wonderful, Theodore. Thank you. Actually, one more thing – do you happen to know anything about a Besiegement Curse?' Diana had filled her in on Lucy's half-formed explanation, and it was needling at her.

Theodore recoiled in alarm. 'Where did you get such a wretched notion from?'

'Is that a yes?'

'*Is that a yes.*' Theodore turned with a flourish to rummage through a stack of Ghoul Council handbooks until he threw up his hands in defeat. 'I had a pamphlet… It's a possession curse of hideous ramifications. And quite theatrical, too – it's not just *possessing* someone, it's what I like to call Possession Theatre. You can't say the victim's name or they take everyone in the vicinity down with them! Awful stuff. Ghoulish, one might call it, Mallory. And the Council has been trying to connect the dots with, if I might say, a frankly *dull* pencil, because they think my Samhain ghost status and their Besiegement Curse that allegedly finishes on Samhain are somewhat *related*. Preposterous nonsense if you ask me, which they never do. They're dreadfully afraid of the concept of possession and keep reinforcing the risks and dangers of me participating and how that would result in, as you well know—'

'Being Isolated in a ghostlight and tossed in the bottom of Bonemarrow Lake forever, yes,' Mallory finished, having heard this many times before, though feeling a fresh chill as she thought of the lake itself in all its fizzing, hissing glory. Wondering if there were ghosts like Theodore down there.

Ghosts who had broken the rules.

'I cannot overstate how *obsessed* they are with reminding me of the consequences of possessing anyone or even being seen to *contemplate* possessing anyone, like thought police. As if I would *ever*—' He cut himself off with a jolt, and Mallory knew he was thinking about the time he sort-of-tried to possess her.

Mallory had rationalised it as something he'd felt was necessary in the face of the mind-fuckery of that particular case, where poisons and magically mind-altering air had made untangling it next to impossible. Cornelia had reacted so… She didn't know how to describe it, and didn't want to revisit it. Both because revisiting it risked his safety in Wrackton, and because she feared talking about it would cause the trust they'd shakily rebuilt since to crumble into nothing.

Theodore made a show of clearing his throat, as though a ghost could need to, the subject clearly off-limits to further questions. 'You know what all our samples mean, don't you?'

'That we've got work to do?'

Theodore drew himself up to his full height, cat ears a-quiver.

'Well, yes. But also. It's time for the best thing we can do as private investigators with a penchant for science. Mallory Hawthorne, it's time for a forensics montage.'

For the next hour they solidly worked on their respective clues in companionable silence. Cornelia sat motionless beside Mallory, beetles walking up the arms of her lab coat, her expression vacant. She had got nothing from examining the letters.

'He's on the way,' Diana said, buttoning her lab coat.

'Who is *he*?' Theodore asked suspiciously, as Mallory rearranged the charts she'd printed out of all the sample results.

'He'll be here soon,' Diana went on, either ignoring him or not hearing him. 'What do we have?'

Theodore held up Mallory's printed graphs and shook his head. 'No matches from the beetles.'

'Did you test us?' Diana asked.

'We have those as controls,' Mallory said, pointing at a separate stack. Ghoul Council sample vials lined the edge of the table – ruby-red curls of smoke for Olivia, Dot, Ezra and Imogen, a blue-grey one for Nova, a sapphire-blue curl for Harry, and a green sample for Lucy, though that had been for the sake of thoroughness.

'It's funny,' Theodore said. 'The beetle samples were so contaminated, almost like there were hundreds of magic samples in it all at once.'

'Funny ha-ha, or funny demonstrating the limitations of the scientific analysis methods we have at our disposal?' Cornelia asked, snapping into the room.

'Both. Decidedly both. But a little less on the funny ha-ha, I expect.'

'Does that suggest we need to try devise a more sensitive test for magic traces?' Mallory pressed a hand to her cheek, thinking.

They'd tried working out *what* the Magic Magical Machine was actually picking up when they tested magic. It could identify a magic source – witch, demon, troll and so forth – and Mallory and Theodore could occasionally match the signature to a specific person, but magic seemed to have a chemical signature, subject to change and manipulation. It would never tell them *who* a culprit was, merely point them in the right direction.

She hoped someday to write the definitive guide with all these questions answered. When she had more time, and had done enough to be deemed a legitimate scientist.

'I think this is about the *amount* of magic used – the strength of the trace, so to speak. If, as you say, the Wickermere Reaper is someone on the Ghoul Council – a horrid thought, really. Dreadful pinnacle of corruption. But, say that's the case. The folk in Wickermere may use similar types of magic, and the beetles are picking up everything, rather than a particularly strong trace of something specific.'

'So it doesn't actually help us, is what we're saying,' Diana translated.

'There's also the wards – they could be the problem. Same thing we had in the Wrackton Digger case – the beetles didn't quite react properly.'

'I thought it was the beetles themselves,' Cornelia said. 'but maybe that's it. Shit.'

'Ah, the wards. Frightening, how the plot thickens in the Wrackton Digger case every time you turn your backs, isn't it?'

'How so?'

Theodore pulled his cardigan around himself and sucked in a breath, like he was listening to something. Then his expression cleared. 'I forget what I was saying.'

'How's that plant pot doing?' Mallory asked, conscious of the time and in no particular mood for what she considered to be an obvious attempt by Theodore to get her worried about the Wrackton Digger case.

'Ah!' Theodore pirouetted on the spot. 'I have been *contemplating* it carefully from all angles, so that we might—'

There was a crash. A terracotta pot and Theodore's soil samples shattered across the lab floor, along with most of Mallory's samples from the Wickermere Reaper case.

Theodore froze. 'Mallory, I'm so sorry. I'm so, so sorry, my hands just—'

'It's fine,' she said shortly, forcing a smile onto her face, pushing down the burning desire to snap at Theodore. It wouldn't help to point out that this was bordering on incompetence. 'We have the charts, we haven't got time to do deeper tests on the physical samples anyway. The plant pot wasn't likely to show you anything, so it doesn't matter. Just clean it up, please?'

'Of course. Oh Mallory,' he said mournfully. 'I am so, so sorry.'

They heard the clatter of footsteps outside and Diana swore, snapping her fingers to clean up the former clue before Theodore had even reached the ground. Mallory got to the door first, not looking back to see Theodore recognise their visitor.

'I'm going to start billing for the time I spend in this establishment.' Grey Quinn ran a hand down his jacket lapel. He had a soft t-shirt on underneath, which was undoubtedly as casual as Quinn got.

The last time Mallory had seen them interact, Theodore had thrown his cat ears at Quinn; they were natural enemies, owing to Quinn's part in Theodore's eternal cat costume, though this was one-sided. To her surprise, Theodore sat quietly in his iron chair, his arms crossed thoughtfully, rather than defensively.

'Before I begin, what are you indebting yourselves to me *for*?' Quinn tapped a tasselled loafer against the tiles.

'All we can say is that the debt won't be with us, and this is time sensitive,' Diana said, hands on her hips like she was modelling her lab coat.

'No?' His tone was interested. 'Who would that be?'

'The Broadwicks,' Cornelia said shortly.

'Interesting.' Grey Quinn sank back in his chair, appraising Diana. 'What could possibly be so pressing they couldn't come to me themselves? That they'd send an intermediary who has, and I mean no disrespect, significantly less influence?'

'It's definitely not potential murder or abduction,' Theodore said. 'That would be ludicrous if it was the case. But it's not.'

'Family emergency,' Mallory said smoothly, still prickling with annoyance at Theodore. 'It is at their discretion to tell you about it.'

'And what do you need from me?'

'I need you to get us in to speak to someone, in Foxland Hall.'

'Interesting,' he said again. 'Why would you think I had any access to a category A prison, much less any sway over prisoners, prison guards, or visitation procedures?'

'Let's not play ignorant, it doesn't suit you,' Diana said. 'We know you were in the pocket of the Apparent prison services and were heavily involved in Van Doren's for-profit plans for Wrackton when he was alive. It's not a stretch to imagine that one of the first-known Occult serial killers in an Apparent prison has renewed the potential for new investors, and thus given you an opportunity to strengthen your connections. We don't have time for coyness, Grey.'

His mouth twitched and he shot Theodore a glance.

'Fine. Who?'

'We want to speak to an inmate named Lyle Whitlock. Today,' Mallory said.

'As in *Dollhouse Murderer* Whitlock? That was your appellation, wasn't it?'

'Can you do it or not?' Diana asked.

His gaze flicked over Cornelia, whose jaw was twitching, her leg bouncing so hard she was shaking the sofa they were all perched on. Something akin to pity flickered over his features, so quickly Mallory wasn't sure she'd seen it, and then he stood. 'Give me a moment.'

He strode into the lab and settled against one of the benches, pressing his phone to his ear with a flourish.

The Undetectables waited in tense silence, Theodore peering around the corner at him.

'He shouldn't do that,' he said mournfully. 'There are chemicals in there, they might eat his suit.'

'Would serve him right,' Cornelia said.

'Would it?' Mallory asked.

Cornelia smiled. 'I've no idea.'

Quinn came back shaking his head. 'Not today, not this week, but perhaps next week at the earliest?'

'That's no use to us, sorry,' Diana said. 'Time is of the essence.'

'We can get you your own lab coat,' Theodore said.

'Why on earth would you do that?'

'Protect your clothes. Dangerous in the lab, and you're here a lot.'

'I know I keep saying sorry, which is ironic because I'm not in the slightest,' Diana said, 'but since when did you two not want to kill each other?'

'I've never wanted to kill him,' Quinn said archly. 'I was merely instrumental in the cat costume – though I maintain he was not having fun that night. I'll keep an ear to the ground for you, Diana,' he said. 'Adieu,' he added, directing it at Theodore, before striding out.

'The ear to the ground is undoubtedly because he can't pass up the idea of a Broadwick debt,' Diana spat. 'Waste of my fucking time.'

'That was nice,' Theodore said, prompting the remaining Undetectables to swivel their heads as one to look at him in shock.

Mallory recovered first. 'What?'

'Nothing, nothing. I wanted to talk to you a bit more about the mausoleum soil, though…'

'Can it wait? If you need help, keep going to Felix and Kingston, or I can ask Taylor to drop in after work later. Worst case, pop in to see Dr Ray, she'll be… not *happy* to help, but obliging.'

'She may even put her second-best intern on the Case of the Misbehaving Printer,' Theodore said. 'I'll hold down the fort. I'm sorry again, Mallory. Hands like butter, but a heart of gold.'

She wished she could trust him fully.

'We have to go now,' Diana said abruptly, scooping up Mallory's charts.

'It stops hurting after a while,' Theodore said mildly.

'What does?'

'Whatever ails you as you pass through the light.'

Mallory didn't know if that was reassuring, or a worrying insight into Theodore's general state of mind.

EIGHTEEN

9:01:45

'FUCK,' Diana shouted, looking up from her diorama, making Cornelia yelp and Mallory jump and pull a muscle in her neck at the same time. She gripped it, wincing. They'd only been back from Wrackton a few minutes and Mallory and Cornelia had started going through their hypotheses again.

'Look. They lied to us. They fucking *lied to us.*'

Cornelia and Mallory shuffled closer to where Diana had taken up a section of the floor with her model. She'd placed blue witchlights to mark the physical boundary lines in front of tiny Rowan House, as well as little red witchlight markers showing where the other Wickermere Reaper victims had been recovered. She'd expanded it using satellite maps of the adjoining Apparent towns so they could see where the victims had been taken from, yellow lights marking the abduction sites. It was still impressive.

'Lied how?' Cornelia demanded.

'Okay, I'll hazard that "lied" is a bit strong. Maybe they didn't even know what they were implying, if we're right that they're unaware the Wickermere Reaper is someone on the Council. But they said, repeatedly, the twins were taken from where?'

'The gate to Rowan House. The police report they gave us—' Cornelia started.

'—said *at* the gate,' Mallory said.

'And when we went out to the gates, we saw markers on the ground and…'

'Assumed,' Cornelia said through gritted teeth. They couldn't afford to make mistakes like this, not with how little time they had left. 'We fucking *assumed* they meant the outer gate.'

'And there was no way to tell, because the gravel ate up any tyre marks,' Mallory said. 'Diana, this was a great realisation to make, but I'm not sure this helps us?'

'No!' Cornelia said, launching to her feet. 'She's right! The semantics don't matter, except they *do* – the Ghoul Council think the *outer wards* glitched and someone external was able to get access to Wickermere. But that's not it. There are two sets of wards. *Only* the outer wards failed temporarily. The internal ones were fine. The Wickermere Reaper didn't cover their tracks properly. They fucked up.'

Mallory's eyes widened as she took in the realisation. 'We're right, then. It's someone we've met. And if they've made one mistake, they'll make another.'

Cornelia felt like she was suffocating.

'I don't understand how they're overlooking this as a possibility,' Diana said. 'I know, I know, we've wormed our way around UML directives before – the time I got Grey Quinn to bodily drag us onto his property so we weren't "entering" springs to mind. But for the love of Blair, if they'd just *think*— Unless they can't. Unless Harry is convincing them not to.'

'It'd be more likely Belissima again, or something similar, than one demon convincing an entire Council – although maybe the twins contacting Lyle Whitlock has something to do with it,' Mallory mused, then shook her head. 'No. I'm not one for hunches, but that doesn't feel right to me. I think this goes beyond simple demon persuasion, or filling the air with hallucinogens. The call is coming from inside Rowan House, and the Council can't see it.'

Imogen, Ezra, Harry, Dot, Nova, Olivia.

Cornelia had clung onto the idea that her parents were maybe behind this whole thing. That it was a hoax, a grab for power. They'd murdered once before, she could imagine them doing it again. She thought of Harry and Dot and how they'd acted as extended family when she didn't have any. How easily that could be delineated between the past and the present. How helpful Olivia and Nova had been, and how that could simply be manipulation. She wondered if they were doomed to keep trusting people who shouldn't be trusted, or if they were going to become cynical and awful as time wore on, afraid of betrayal.

'It's like Jacob all over again, isn't it,' she whispered. 'It's always going to be someone we know. We're never going to be safe again.'

She'd never managed to get the words out before. Never managed to put a description on the feeling she'd carried around since the day Jacob—

'No,' Mallory said, with a surety that took Cornelia by surprise. 'We know now not to trust anyone – not that we have been. Any rapport we already have can be used to our advantage. We will be wary of help from anyone but Lucy. We don't let anyone get close, and we don't answer any questions, but we find answers to as many of ours as we can. We still have time, and I'm more confident about this than I was when we woke up this morning. We have moves we can make, it's not over yet. We're going to find them, Cornelia. Alive.'

Cornelia didn't miss the sharp look Diana gave Mallory; she knew that Diana was admonishing Mallory for promising Cornelia they could solve this case, but she couldn't find it in herself to doubt her.

'Where is it?' Diana asked instead.

'Where's what?'

'The car,' Diana said. 'The twins' car?'

'The police still have it – the report says it got sent to Vehicle Crimes, about an hour from here,' Mallory said. 'We could request it gets released, but I don't know how long that'll take.'

'We don't have time for any of this. We need to get into the Ghoul Council,' Cornelia said bluntly. 'We need to find out what the Wickermere Reaper wants, and see if we can give it to them.'

'So glad we caught you,' Diana said breezily as she followed a rumpled Lucy to her desk.

'Can I help you with anything?' Lucy juggled her keys in one hand and a reusable coffee mug in the other.

'Let me get that for you.' Diana took the cup from her. 'You must be exhausted.'

Cornelia stood back as instructed; she'd been too tired to

argue. Mallory hadn't spoken much since they'd decided to come here, every movement stiff and clearly painful, but she said nothing and Cornelia didn't want to push it.

'We're just waiting on Ghoul Council clearance,' Diana said cheerfully. 'Say, there isn't any chance you could take a look? I know the security system is rigorous, and we'd rather not lose limbs going in there.'

'Oh Diana, I don't know about that,' Lucy said, waking her computer monitor and peering at a clearance list. 'I can't see if it's—'

'I imagine it's just taking a while to get sorted. Low priority,' Diana said, waving a hand. 'But we'd really appreciate if you could speed it up somehow?'

'Well…' Lucy looked at the three of them: Mallory, leaning against the front door – for support, mostly, but it had the added benefit of seeming nonchalant – Diana, who was her usual put-together self even in an oversized shirt, cycling shorts and with her hair piled on her head, and Cornelia, who was doing her best not to give the game away by being too impatient.

'I suppose in the circumstances, seeing as they're locked in a meeting now, waiting would be a bit silly when I can just…' She typed for a moment, rapidly pulling up screens and muttering to herself.

Cornelia had no idea how Lucy was even going to permit a ward bypass, until she reached into a locked drawer and handed each of them a black crystal.

'Mind you don't give those to anyone else – without Rowan House clearance at an absolute minimum, they'll take your arm off. Literally.'

'What is this?' Cornelia asked, looking at it. She'd known there was a reason she couldn't enter the Ghoul Council Headquarters – Dot had made absolutely sure she knew it was a threat to her life and not just a suggestion – but had never actually seen the method the Ghoul Council used to enter their inner sanctum. It was smooth obsidian, and Cornelia recognised it as one of the crystals that had stopped the alarm when they'd landed in the War Room the night before.

'It's a key of sorts. Disables some of the Headquarters defence mechanisms. But like I said, you can't pick that up again until you're sure you've got clearance – you're in the House so it won't see you as a monumental threat, but the Ghoul Council Headquarters will try to protect itself above all else. There's only two here for authorised visitors – I'm giving you my one as the third, so I can't come in with you.'

It did not fully answer Cornelia's question of what the crystal *was*, but given that she'd been able to accept witchlights into her heart and mind for her whole life, she could probably stand to not press for further details.

For now, anyway.

Lucy pressed a key into Diana's hands and gave them rapid instructions to place the crystals on a small shelf beside the Ghoul Council entrance and take two steps back. The Undetectables found themselves at the vaulted door at the rear of Rowan House, scarcely able to believe their luck.

'That gets less adorably lucky and more incompetent-seeming the further into our careers we get,' Diana whispered. 'There was no way that should've worked.'

The warning of not accepting help rang in Cornelia's ears,

but she pushed it down. Lucy was a faerie and couldn't lie. She wasn't involved.

'She trusts us,' Cornelia said. 'She trusts *you.* We just… used it.'

'Can we hurry up?' Mallory checked the time, chewing her lip. The now-familiar swoop of terror at the impending deadline filled Cornelia's stomach and she thought she might vomit.

They lined up the crystals and Diana turned the key before jumping back. They waited to see if the Council Headquarters would recognise them as intruders, but nothing happened. They gathered up the crystals and stepped directly onto a narrow spiral staircase that Mallory valiantly took without complaint, even as it seemed to extend down and down into the darkness, one tiny witchlight illuminating the way every few steps, until they emerged into a narrow, coffee-coloured corridor with black wood doors extending as far as the eye could see, lit by thousands of tiny witchlights, like a star field.

'This explains the "remodelling" excuse for moving the War Room into the main house,' Cornelia said, leaning against the wall. Mallory looked as though she might pass out. 'There has to be a better way than stairs.'

'Where to?' Diana asked, hands on her hips. She'd barely broken a sweat.

'You're the motherfucking genius,' Cornelia said, sharper than was warranted.

'We need to start with their offices,' Mallory said. 'Imogen's and Ezra's. That ransom note has to be somewhere— Shh!'

Cornelia froze at the sound of slow footsteps, a door creaking, and a familiar voice saying, 'You know my loyalty is to the Broadwicks.'

So much for locked in a meeting.

'And Nova's isn't. I'm saying be *careful*, Harry. I might be out to pasture, but you've life left in you yet. No matter what they try to say,' Dot said, emerging into the corridor.

She paused at the sight of them.

'Fuck,' Diana whispered.

'Did you get clearance for this, Cornelia? Although seeing as your limbs are intact, I'll have to assume that's the case. What are you up to?'

'Unearthing secrets, finding a killer. You?' Diana asked, stepping forward.

'Right, yes. I'm sure the Broadwicks are happy for you to be running around in here. Forgive me, I'm not used to seeing you all grown up,' Dot said, laughing a little.

'Listen, Dot, we've been hoping to talk to you,' Diana said. 'Cornelia says you're an old friend of the family, so maybe you can answer this – who'd have it in for the Broadwicks?'

'Goddess, what a question! In this line of work, you have to be so careful,' Dot said, glancing over her shoulder. 'You learn who you can trust and you look out for each other where you can.'

'We keep hearing things to the contrary,' Diana said, tapping her thumb and middle finger together – a pre-agreed signal for Cornelia to go on without her – and she and Mallory stayed in the hallway while Cornelia walked purposefully down the corridor, reading wall plaques until she found the right room, and casually entered her father's office. Sage green with wood panelling, same as his office in Broadwick Mansion.

There was no telling how long it would take before Harry heard them talking.

'I appreciate you can't share Ghoul Council secrets, but we get the sense there's something personal to taking Agatha and Ethel, and who's better placed than you to tell us if that's the case?' Diana asked cheerfully.

Cornelia closed the door behind her and forced herself to focus, Dot and Diana's muffled voices a constant reminder that there was no time.

'—blame Cornelia for wanting to know what's happened to her family,' Diana was saying.

There was no time.

She felt her breath catch and she forced herself to calm, taking in the office properly.

Everything was laid out neatly in obsessive little rows. It was easy to see that his only progeny who actually had his genes was Agatha. The rest of the family were as chaotic as Cornelia, even Imogen. She opened drawers at random, and stopped. The only thing out of place was a file on top, carelessly stuffed in with a label that made her skin crawl.

THE UNDETECTABLES

And it was an inch thick.

She pulled it out and shuffled through the pages. Every single case they'd worked over the last eighteen months. Every piece that had appeared about them in the news. Every invoice they'd been sent. Copies of emails Cornelia had laboured over. All of it there, on heavy ice-white paper. She took photos and put the file back, and opened another drawer beneath it.

There was nothing but a folded piece of paper at the bottom, which she took out and held up to the light.

> BRING ME ELISABELLA
> YOU HAVE SEVEN HOURS TWENTY MINUTES
> AND FIFTY-THREE SECONDS

It counted down before her eyes, the numbers flicking by.

This was the ransom note.

'Harry! What a surprise to see you here!' Diana exclaimed.

Her time was up. Head spinning, Cornelia had just enough mind to open the office door, striding down the hall with the note clutched tight in shaking fingers.

Dot and Harry looked at her with surprise, though regrettably not with confusion.

'"Bring me Elisabella". What do they mean? Her body's buried in Wrackton, why haven't you gone and dug it up already?'

'Now Cornelia—' Dot started, but Harry held up a hand.

'Leave this with me. Go head them off,' Harry said.

Dot hesitated, but eventually nodded, her lips pursed. 'Go easy on them, Harry. This is her family too.'

Dot flashed Cornelia an apologetic look and ambled up the corridor.

'Well?' Cornelia demanded.

'Cornelia,' Harry said patiently. 'Let's be reasonable about this. I can either call Ezra and you can have a distinctly more unpleasant conversation with him, or you can hand over whatever it is you have and we chalk it up to mild hysteria over your sisters going missing. We won't mention it again, but you hand it over now.'

Cornelia was utterly speechless. The only things coursing through her were a heat that she thought would blind her temporarily and the concept of the colour red, but Harry wasn't finished.

He sighed, looking more like the honorary family member she had adored her whole life. 'You can't do this anymore, Cornelia. I know you used to get out of everything by being clever, but there are consequences now. I am duty-bound to report this to the UML in the next thirty days. The Undetectables will be fined – it's nominal, but it's not the kind of thing you want on your record. I *hate* that I have to do this to Ezra and Imogen, especially with their last child, but—'

He caught himself, but it was too late.

'You think they're already dead,' Cornelia said, the words hot in her mouth.

Diana and Mallory were utterly silent during this exchange, though Diana looked perilously close to exploding.

'I didn't say that.'

'You did, actually. "Especially with their last child," as if I'll be all they have left when this is over.'

'I am a realist, Cornelia. Even if were possible, we can't give them Elisabella.'

'Which means you fucking *have her somewhere.*'

'We have to think of the risks,' Harry said. 'The Ghoul Council have one main goal – an annex to the UML's goal of upholding the Do No Harm Charter – and it is to prevent a resurgence of the Vampire Wars. If it were possible to hand over Elisabella, we would have to choose not to. The Ternion cannot be of this earth, in any capacity.'

'Okay, I have questions,' Mallory cut across. 'Sorry. But firstly, it sounds like you physically have Elisabella's remains somewhere, which I would've thought was impossible, for a number of reasons.'

'*I* don't physically have her somewhere. No one "has" her.'

'That doesn't really answer the question,' Mallory pressed.

'It doesn't, does it?' Harry pressed his lips together.

'There's a vault somewhere, isn't there? Occult objects. A crypt, or a relic room,' Cornelia accused.

'Who told you that?'

'I've lived here my whole life,' Cornelia said, suddenly aware that Lucy could be held responsible for how much they'd manipulated her. 'Every summer, I've sat and listened at walls, picking up bits and pieces, here and there. Do Agatha and Ethel know? Is that why they're gone?'

'Nobody knows *anything*. If we knew, we'd have them back.'

'You have her remains here somewhere,' Cornelia said again, certain of it. 'The Ternion's remains are meant to be buried in Wrackton, in the memorial garden. But they're not, are they?'

'Verification of the exact location of the Ternion's remains would involve disinterring our existing monuments, which is an unconscionable act of sacrilege. And even if it wasn't, even if there were other possibilities, I couldn't just *tell* you where they are. I don't think you understand you are now a *liability* to this process—'

'I know that. They dragged me here for that reason alone,' Cornelia said.

'Notwithstanding. It is not as simple as handing over Elisabella's remains. The Broadwicks – your parents – don't want…'

'Don't want to save their daughters? Have been advised not to, because you think they're already dead?'

Harry pinched the bridge of his nose before staring Cornelia right in the eyes. '*Can't*. What the Wickermere Reaper is asking for is impossible, and they are too proud to admit it.'

Cornelia was dimly aware that the ransom note was shaking in her hand, her fingers white from effort.

Harry eyed her with something akin to pity. 'Walk with me,' he said. She could feel his fondness for her was still there. She crumpled the note in her hand and walked alongside him, her friends bringing up the rear.

'I have no problem with you looking into things here, but we can't be underhanded about it. Whoever the Wickermere Reaper is… you can't come by the knowledge accidentally,' he said carefully.

There was no trace of him using demon magic on her, it felt like he was trying to convince her the old-fashioned way.

'We – the entire Ghoul Council – are doing everything we can. If you believe nothing else, believe that.'

They'd reached the bottom of the staircase and Cornelia had just managed to slip the corner of the note into her pocket as she took a step forward. Harry opened his mouth when a sensor sounded and he threw out a hand, blocking further passage, as spikes extended from the walls across the stairs, a soft *beep beep beep* the only warning they'd have had.

'Give me the note,' he said calmly.

'What note?' Cornelia tried, but he stared at her until she

meekly handed it over, hating herself for not thinking faster on her feet.

'I will say this to you once,' he said, his hand closed tightly around her fist. 'Do not fuck with me. The rules are in place for safety. They're not a joke. This is not a game.'

'It's just SO UNFAIR,' Diana wailed, throwing herself to her knees, her bag clutched tightly to her chest. 'AGATHA! ETHEL!! WE'LL AVENGE YOU!!' She raised her fists and howled.

It took Cornelia a bewildered second to realise what was really going on, and then she and Mallory grabbed her under an elbow each and Diana made a show of not wanting to move, hyperventilating dramatically.

'She's very fond of them,' Cornelia said. 'This has been hard on all of us.'

Harry looked at the note in his hand and stuffed it in his pocket. Wordlessly, he pressed his own crystal to the wall and the beeping stopped, the spikes retracting. He stayed close behind, his eyes never leaving Diana, until they were safely back in Rowan House.

'Tensions are high, let's not make them higher. I got Ezra and Imogen to let you stay, I can just as easily undo that.'

He slammed the door in their faces and Diana adjusted her shirt, opening her bag so Cornelia and Mallory could see inside.

'Thank fuck for that – I thought I'd never get these files out.'

NINETEEN

7:00:11

'That was quite a performance,' Mallory remarked to Diana once they were safely back in the Laurels. Cornelia pulled the curtains shut and cast a cloaking spell.

'Thank you, I think it was one of my best. I am definitely hitting peak pretend-hysteria years at the ripe old age of twenty-two, but we can try to squeeze a few more out before it stops working.' She pulled a stack of files out of her bag.

'I didn't even see you sneak away,' Cornelia said, trying and failing to keep a tone of awe out of her voice.

'And neither did Harry,' Diana said smugly. 'I spotted Imogen's office when we first arrived, but figured Ezra was the one with the ransom note and was going to run in on our way back out anyway – a gamble that has very much paid off, because I present to you: Imogen's staff dossiers!'

'How?' Cornelia demanded.

'Lucy has a printer behind the desk. Everyone else here appears to be allergic to technology – I suppose the proximity to ghosts would do that to a Council, but even still. I had a hunch she prepared physical documents, and that they'd contain more than just Lucy's alibis. These files are *thick*.'

'First, though, what exactly did the ransom note say?' Mallory asked, holding up a hand to stall Diana. 'I know it requested Elisabella, but what else?'

'It just said "bring me Elisabella" and a countdown timer,' Cornelia said, surprised at how choked up the idea of an actual ransom note made her feel. Even if Imogen or Ezra were the Reaper, the intention was, clearly, to let the twins die if an exchange wasn't made. 'Nothing else. If we assume that the Wickermere Reaper is someone on the Ghoul Council, they have access to the Ternion's remains – they could ask the UML to allow them to be removed from Wrackton, easily, even ignoring what Harry said about it being sacrilege or whatever,' Cornelia said.

'But if that was the case, the Reaper wouldn't *need* to demand them if they know where they are, would they? They'd just go get them, or make someone on the Council do it for them,' Diana said.

'Unless it's meant to be an impossible request?' Mallory suggested. 'We've heard before that the Ternion aren't in that grave by the Observatory, but I did think that was Wrackton's entire tourism appeal as an Occult town. So the Reaper needs to know how to circumvent the gravedigging wards in Wrackton, *or*, if Elisabella's remains *aren't* there, they'd need to know precisely where they are. Maybe they're in the crypt Lucy spoke of. Or maybe the Wickermere Reaper genuinely doesn't know.'

'Good point,' Diana said.

'It feels sadistic,' Cornelia said, an uncomfortable hunch building in her stomach. 'The first ransoms were placed as adverts – maybe that was a mistake, and the Reaper thought they'd find them in time. Or, maybe it was meant to be impossible. Maybe it's not about the v... the victims at all – it's about those on the ground waiting. We saw in the police reports that there was evidence the victims ate and drank, right? And Stella told us it felt peaceful – that doesn't fit with our understanding of serial killers. I don't think this is about the victims at all, I think it's about us. Not *us*' – she gestured to Diana and Mallory – 'but all the families. They've all been asked to do something impossible. Stella was rescued via a lucky loophole. We don't know if the others got a magical ransom note, but if we assume they *did*, they were all likely asked for something impossible.'

'I can follow that up. Harry's "rule" be damned,' Diana said, her phone in hand.

'No, I think I'm right. It's about the impossibility of the request. The Bonemarrow Witches were meant to give the Reaper a ghostlight, the Broadwicks – and the Broadwicks specifically, not the Ghoul Council – Elisabella... it's meant to be agonising. We are in agony because the Reaper wants us to be, because the Reaper thinks this can't be done.'

The surety burned through her, white-hot and louder than the maelstrom of feelings she hadn't yet identified.

'Okay,' Mallory said, after barely a moment of consideration. 'Let's work on that assumption. I'm going to ask Kingston if the Ternion are actually buried in Wrackton, he'll know faster than anyone else.' She drafted a text, biting her lip. 'I'm also going to ask him and Felix to check in on Theodore.'

Cornelia smiled a little at that, some of her anger deflating. Mallory had not taken to Kingston in the slightest when he'd first showed up, but after his almost-death and having to adjust to life with an ostomy bag, as well as countless hospital appointments and surgeries, he and Mallory had become something akin to friends. It still made her happy to see Mallory appreciate Kingston's scary-good ability to know things, and trust him to help.

'I think you're right, Cornelia,' Diana said, pressing her fists into her eyes. She seemed exhausted, her usually flawless hair showing signs of stress. 'With the Whistler and the Dollhouse Murderers, it was about power, status… this *could* be about power again, but it feels less… focused. There's some context we're missing, and I think this is it. It makes sense for the Wickermere Reaper to be some sort of… reverse sadist.'

'It's as good a hypothesis as any,' Mallory said, looking at her phone. 'Felix says they're on it, and that Kingston is getting ready to go look for the Ternion.'

'Then let's look at these dossiers I so lovingly stole for us,' Diana said.

'They had one on us,' Cornelia said, suddenly remembering as she fumbled for her phone.

'What do you mean?'

'I mean I found a file in my father's office about every single case we've worked – except Katherine Vane, thank Hexana, though alarming, seeing as they *should* know she's in there. Everything else, though. It stops just before the Wrackton Digger.' Cornelia shivered as she spoke. It was too much to bear to think about them watching her that closely. That she'd thought she'd spent the last eighteen months out from under their thumb, the last few months living separate to them.

'Should we be concerned, or should we be annoyed at ourselves for not anticipating that the Broadwicks might've cottoned on to where such large volumes of their own money were going?' Diana asked.

It was a fair point, but Cornelia felt it was more sinister than that. 'This wasn't *the Broadwicks*, though, this was them using their position of power on the Ghoul Council to spy on us, essentially.'

'Everyone has been telling us since we started how much of Occulture is in the Broadwicks' pockets. It's probably time we start believing them.' Mallory divided the staff files so they had some each to look at. 'Harry has been denied a promotion every year for the past six years. Possible motive, wants to get the Broadwicks where it hurts?'

'And he thinks they're dead already, based on what he said earlier. Though that could've been a slip, rather than a belief,' Diana said, not looking up from her file. 'So, possible motive: harm the Broadwicks or force their hand? If they're out, he gets the promotion.'

'We heard what Dot said – his loyalty has always been with the Broadwicks. I didn't understand it at the time – still don't, really – but I remember hearing how he and Dot were behind my parents stepping into Grandad Cornelius's job. I'd find it hard – though not impossible – to believe he'd want to hurt them, after all this time,' Cornelia said. 'Does that line up with our sadist hypothesis?'

'It's a question of if the Broadwicks were always the end target, or if it became clear that it was *possible* to target the Broadwicks after the Wickermere Reaper got away with it multiple times prior. Like an escalating challenge, so to speak,' Mallory said.

Cornelia had only been half-listening to the reply, the words washing over her as she leafed through Nova's case file. 'Whoa,' she said, sitting up. 'Nova's been on probation – extended probation – for the last few months.'

'Why?'

'It just says "acting under the assumption of impunity".' She scanned the rest of the file. 'Mother dearest didn't include transcripts from hearings, but they eventually reinstated them and left them on probation. Which feels… unlike the Broadwicks, without an extensively considered reason.'

Growing up, Cornelia hadn't been able to make a decision on anything without it turning into a multi-day negotiation. Mostly, she'd shout or show them a PowerPoint she'd made, and mostly they'd say 'we'll see' and discuss it without her present. They hadn't wanted her to leave formal education, and had *ideas* about which Apparent universities she should've applied for, which institutions she should go seek work at as an entomologist. They hadn't liked the idea of the Undetectables one bit.

'Is it not better and less dangerous to keep someone like that around instead of sending them out into the world? Particularly if there was any wiggle room to "acting under the assumption of impunity" in the first place,' Mallory said.

Cornelia had to agree: that angle felt more the Broadwicks' style. Years later and she was still convinced they'd never actually *liked* former Night Mayor Vincent Van Doren, but rather liked what he could *do* for them.

'The extended explanation seems to suggest they did it for

the good of a project they were working on, which I suppose means there was a grey area when it came to what was punishable. But would it piss Nova off enough to resort to murder – or to turn their murderous intent towards the Broadwicks?'

Diana rose to write on the murder board, starting a motive column.

'Lucy has repeatedly applied to be a special project manager, they originally head-hunted her from the Irish branch to be a Junior Clerical Officer,' Mallory said. 'Makes me feel bad we manipulated her this morning, she's not been having the best time of things. They keep turning her down – the last letter states that they need her in her position, and they've offered her a nominal raise as consolation. She did essentially say this already, but there's nothing new here that would give me pause.'

'Poor Lucy,' Cornelia said. She had no idea what a Junior Clerical Officer got paid in one of the most secretive and influential organisations in Occulture, but she thought about what her parents had and how easily they could pay Lucy well.

'Dorothy and Olivia… oh, there are *redacted* parts of their files here. And – *Hexana*, there are files on Imogen and Ezra. They keep dossiers on *themselves*?' Diana said, aghast.

'It almost adds an air of transparency to the whole thing,' Mallory said.

'Except it more seems that they're ready to toss each other into the fire if needs be.'

'It sort of explains everything about how Occulture works, doesn't it? They've got all these rules and regulations and ideas about how the world should function, but they're ultimately drowning under those ideas instead of living any sort of meaningful life,' Mallory said. 'Keeping files on themselves, possibly on each other, in an effort to make things transparent, when it's anything but.'

'It explains so much about you,' Diana said to Cornelia. It was the first real barb she'd got in since they'd searched the twins' rooms, and Cornelia illogically wanted to sob from how temporarily normal it made her feel.

'What do Dorothy's and Olivia's files say?' Cornelia choked out, her voice rough.

'Dorothy and Olivia are special projects managers – Olivia got the job Lucy applied for. Dorothy retired a few years ago but they brought her back – she initially wanted to take over Cornelius's role about fourteen years ago, but by that stage she was a couple of years from retirement. Like Cornelia said, she keeps coming out of retirement to be a special consultant.'

'She's been around as long as I can remember, longer than Harry, even,' Cornelia said. 'Imogen and Ezra think highly of her, she was a good friend of my grandfather's. They must think highly of Olivia, too, if she was able to rise through the ranks so quickly. Anything on project specifics?'

'There's an ongoing historical project – it was resurrected about fourteen years ago. It's called… hang on.' Diana muttered a spell and held the page close to her face. 'Do we have any matches?'

Mallory looked like she was going to struggle to her feet, so Cornelia got up first. Mallory pointed tiredly to the mantle, where Cornelia found a lighter.

'Project HAUNT,' Diana said, holding the page up to the flame. 'Historically Accurate Undertakings of Non-Corporeal Telemetrics. Rolls off the tongue.'

'What the fuck does that mean?' Cornelia demanded, as Diana continued reading silently.

'Seems to be about the range of reach of a ghost? I'm guessing like how Theodore can't leave the bounds of Wrackton – didn't he say that if he goes too far into the Redwoods, he gets pinged back into the basement? So, that. And their ability to communicate through the lake. It's all redacted, but I can just about make the words out. Cathode ray… OH! Is that what the stack of TVs is about, down by the lake's edge?'

'I bruised my shin on them,' Mallory said. 'And made a mental note to ask you what on earth they were for. I thought maybe they were an art installation, but this makes more sense.'

'I would get told off for climbing on them,' Cornelia said, scrunching up her face. 'But it never occurred to me to ask what they were for. They were just normal to me. Wait, fourteen years ago – that's when Grandad Cornelius died.'

Cornelia had a flash of memory of a hot summer wriggling around the garden with an ant hill, Agatha and Ethel talking about burying her alive so they didn't have to share car snacks with her, as though she couldn't hear them. She couldn't remember exactly what she said, just the unimpressed look on Agatha's face when Ezra had told them to get ready for Wickermere, and felt a sick swoop in her stomach, like there was something significant about that day.

'I don't remember exactly, but Ezra said… something.' She rubbed her forehead, wiling herself to remember, but also afraid of what she'd unearth if she did.

'Anything else?' Mallory asked Diana, rescuing Cornelia whether she meant to or not.

'Olivia joined Dot on Project HAUNT after Imogen stopped working on it a couple of years back, but had previously been assigned to something called Project TRIAD.'

'Could that be a euphemism for the Ternion?' Mallory asked. 'Does it have any details?'

Diana shook her head. 'No. It was either put on hold or ended two years ago, when Olivia fully took over Project HAUNT solo – that lines up with when Theodore started getting much more contact from the Council, doesn't it?'

Mallory nodded. 'He's always found it stifling, but it ramped up around then for sure.'

'Everyone's worked on Project TRIAD, it seems, barring Lucy. That appears to be Ezra's remit. Project HAUNT, on the other hand, has had everyone barring Lucy, Nova and, interestingly, Harry. It seems to be Imogen's pet project.'

Cornelia took the redacted page from her, scanning it herself, the lighter shaking. She wondered when she'd last eaten.

'Right,' Diana said, finishing scrawling on the board. 'I think we start from the top down. We talk to Olivia' – Cornelia felt an annoying thrill at that – 'on the assumption that Dot will probably tell your parents what we're pursuing.'

'And how do we do that? Surely Harry'll have told them what we just did.'

'And admit that someone let us into the inner sanctum of the Ghoul Council? That it was possible to manipulate our way in, while they're actively wondering who let the Wickermere Reaper in? No. Harry won't tell anyone what happened. Not yet, anyway,' Diana said, with more confidence than was warranted. 'And don't worry – I've got a plan.'

TWENTY

5:58:02

'So you're saying it's in my own best interests to tell you what you want to know?' Olivia repeated.

As far as Diana's plans went, this one was particularly hare-brained.

She called the front desk just after half four to get Lucy to invite Olivia over to the cottage, but when there was no answer, Diana pulled Olivia's number out of the staff dossier – 'We don't have time to get this in a more legitimate manner,' she reminded a slightly scandalised Mallory – and asked Olivia to come urgently to the Laurels.

That had been Cornelia's suggestion – bring the questioning to them, away from prying eyes. Diana had made it sound like they wanted to interview her about the twins, but Olivia became utterly aware within the first thirty seconds that this wasn't going to be a friendly chat, and Cornelia wanted to rip her own skin off.

Instead, Cornelia stood up and made tea, keeping an ear out for what Diana was saying.

'And what we want to know is what's going on,' Diana said. Her tone was casual, practically friendly. 'The Broadwicks are reaching a point of particular desperation – I'm sure you've noticed it?'

Olivia nodded stiffly, glancing up as Cornelia brought in the tea tray. She regarded the cups with particular suspicion and opted to hold hers in her hands, elbows resting on her knees, gaze steady.

'I think it's palpable. Nobody *wants* to say that they'll eventually start taking frustrations out on those around them, particularly those closest to them, but… it's not a stretch to imagine that might be the case. Jobs lost, folk held accountable for things that are beyond their control…' Diana said.

Olivia frowned, and Cornelia knew in that instant that Olivia was much too clever for this kind of tactic. She'd respond to honesty, even if she herself wasn't honest, much the way Mallory would if she was in this position.

Before Cornelia could say anything, Mallory swooped in.

'We've no proof of any of that, though. In terms of actual proof, we saw the note,' she said.

'The note,' Olivia repeated.

'Yes. We saw the ransom note, and we know what the Wickermere Reaper is asking for in exchange for Agatha and Ethel's lives.'

Olivia paused, clearly weighing up some options. 'How did you surmise there was a note?'

'We're really good at our jobs,' Mallory said quietly.

'Right.'

'But you know what it says?' Mallory continued.

'I do.'

'Why would the Wickermere Reaper think the Broadwicks would have access to something like that?'

It took Cornelia a second to understand Mallory's tactic: if Olivia somehow *didn't* know what it said, Mallory wouldn't be the one to tell her.

'I don't know.'

'You do,' Mallory pressed. 'We *all* know you do. Obfuscating the truth stops us getting the twins back. We need to know why the Broadwicks doing *this* could possibly be worse than the safe return of Agatha and Ethel. Why it's worth letting them die, instead of just giving the killer what they want.'

Olivia paused. Cornelia searched her face for a scrap of anything that suggested dishonesty, and only found hesitation.

'There are things we do here that are not public knowledge. That are not for *anyone's* knowledge outside of the Council. I really can't make that any clearer. It's about safety, Mallory. I get why you brought me in here, but...' Olivia stared down into her cup. 'I can't help you. Or give you the answers you want.'

'Tell us about Project TRIAD,' Diana said.

Olivia blinked, but had the wherewithal not to ask how they knew, or pretend she didn't know what they were talking about.

'I don't think going there is going to help anyone. That project hasn't been active for some time, and when it was, it was nowhere near ready.'

'What do you mean?' Cornelia had been trying to stay quiet, but the words burst out of her.

Olivia inhaled sharply and set her cup down. 'I assume you know what it is, if you're asking me?'

'We are speaking of the Ternion here, aren't we?' Mallory said.

Cornelia longed for a day when they worked a case that had absolutely nothing to do with the Ternion or their mothers.

'It's what we call a legacy project. Project TRIAD – Ternion Recovery, Identification, Authentication and Demarcation. We like initialisms around here.' Olivia smiled briefly. 'It's believed the Ternion's remains were covertly moved out of Wrackton some years ago – at the top of the last century. They were exhumed, though the Observatory memorial remains in place. However, some folk were convinced that the Ternion's bodies were still in Wrackton, just in unmarked graves, and they were determined to find them, to honour them again. Caused an upheaval, the Council made it so that only authorised personnel were able to dig in any of the graveyards. I've seen old photographs, it was like a large family of frenzied badgers took over Wrackton, just digging and digging. Today, we don't fully know where those remains are located – Wickermere was thought to be the most likely location, as at the time a fledgling Council had just installed itself here permanently, after years of formation and dissolution. Prior Councils didn't have a focus,' she added, anticipating Mallory's next question. 'It was years before they settled on ghosts in general. The original name was the Council for Ghosts, Hauntings, Occulture and Unusual Liaisons, which eventually led to the division of the council into what we now know as the UML, and the Ghoul Council.'

Her speech was pressured, like she really wanted them to understand what she was saying and why.

'We haven't finished Project TRIAD. They could be

anywhere in Wickermere. To a degree, the Wickermere Reaper may know we don't have the technology *or* magic to properly search deep enough into the land for any and all hidden burial sites. I personally don't think they're buried here – I believe their bodies are somewhere in Wrackton, and they never left. I also believe that if the Broadwicks had the means to recover your sisters, Cornelia, they would've by now. There's a reason they had so much support on the existing Council when it came time to take their positions as heads – they follow the rules to a fault. They embody everything the Ghoul Council is meant to be.'

If only that were true.

'How long did you work on Project TRIAD?' Diana pressed.

'About two years, before I was directed to other areas of Council work.'

Meaning, Cornelia surmised, Project HAUNT.

'What did you do there?' Cornelia asked, careful to put it in past tense.

'I worked with Imogen and Dot, occasionally Ezra over the years, but I was fairly junior. I did a lot of solo archival work, sifting through photographs and that.' She smiled wryly. 'Not much science in it, but it's important work. Too much of Occult history has been lost to time.'

She didn't offer to speak on her current work.

'How long have you been working with the Ghoul Council?' Mallory asked.

'About six or seven years now. I used to work with the UML – a minor department concerned with magical illnesses in historical contexts. I had an interest in para-anthropology, even wrote papers when I could, but if the Ghoul Council asks you to join, you don't say no.'

'And since then, have you had any trouble within the Council? Say, any issues with promotion, or being asked to do roles that didn't suit you?'

'Are you asking if I had any reason to harm Agatha and Ethel? No. And I have no reason to want to bring any harm on the Broadwicks, either.'

'Have you seen anything, heard anything suspicious? Anything that's worried you, in the last few days, or years?'

Olivia shook her head. 'Everything we do here is worrying in its own right. All I can say is, whoever is doing this… it's someone who knows a lot, but not enough.'

'So you think it's someone known to you?'

'I didn't say that.'

'What are you saying?'

'I'm saying rumours escape, and there are folk within the UML who would do anything for a seat at that table. We say loose lips sink ships, but they do it in the night – when people are tired, or in the pub, or not thinking. You become so accustomed to keeping secrets in a place like this, you forget what's common knowledge, even among colleagues. There's been a history of hiring faerie staff on account of the honesty, but it backfires more often than not.'

Cornelia thought of how easily they'd manipulated Lucy and felt a pang of guilt she tried to push down.

'You're thinking it's, what, corporate espionage?' Mallory asked – the only one of them capable of keeping incredulity out of her voice.

'I can't say much more,' Olivia waved a hand. 'Whatever the Wickermere Reaper knows, or thinks they know, it could be from any of us. Even I've been guilty of slipping up in the past – ultimately, you can't know what would tip off someone looking for something specific. Work is tough, we all make mistakes, have arguments. You wouldn't believe how hard I fought for location spells as a first resort, and they didn't even—' Olivia stopped. 'But of course, we're doing our best.'

'What did you say?' Cornelia whispered. She could feel the red mist descending again.

'We're doing our best,' Olivia repeated. 'We want the girls found safe and sound—'

'No, you said *how hard you fought for location spells*. Please tell me Ezra didn't lie to me and they did, in fact, take that simple measure?'

Olivia had gone pale. 'The Broadwicks had their reasons for not following—'

'They could be *dead*, Olivia. DEAD. And you're saying the *foremost Occult council* didn't try *looking* for my sisters using the most *basic* of magic? What kind of world do we live in? What kind of existence can *anyone* have if Imogen and Ezra *fucking* Broadwick can just decide not to bother with common sense? If they never take any fucking RESPONSIBILITY?'

Cornelia didn't realise until she'd finished that she was shouting, her whole body quivering with rage. She either wanted to throw something across the room or burst into tears, and she wasn't sure which would come first.

'Cornelia,' Mallory said sharply. 'Stop.'

She turned back to Olivia, whose brow had furrowed, but

had remained remarkably unshaken by any of this. 'Do you have a better location spell than we do?'

In its heyday, Bonemarrow Lane and the accompanying Wickermere village side streets had been impressively picturesque rows of grey slate houses and shops, whitewashed cottages with thatch roofs, a thriving little village side street surrounded by greenery framed against the hills that rose up beyond it, a line of trees the only thing dividing it from the edge of Bonemarrow Lake, shielding it from full view. A hidden Occult town in the centre of beauty.

Now, it was a husk. The stone structures stood, but the roofs were gone, whitewash blackened with soot, businesses shuttered, homes abandoned, rotting wooden windows and doors shuddering in the slightest breeze.

Cornelia stormed ahead of the other two as she followed the distant glow of the location spell that drew them ever-closer, a combination of terror and hope seizing her middle, cold sweat dripping down the inside of her jumper – not that it mattered, as it was misting lightly.

'What happened here?' Diana asked, trotting to keep up, Mallory trailing behind but waving away any attempts to stay in step with her.

'It used to be a popular Occult tourist spot about fifty years ago, and for whatever reason – probably paranoia – Grandad Cornelius decided it had to go, completely.' For Mallory's sake, Cornelia paused, even though she wanted to run towards the location spell, her heart barely able to contain the hope that they were about to find the twins. She pointed to what she thought was an old bookshop – based solely on the fact the remains of a wooden sign swinging from an iron bracket still said *OOK*. 'I used to sneak down here as a kid – I'd follow Agatha and Ethel, and when they were off doing goddess knows what, I'd play in the ruins until it was time for dinner.'

'And leaving the beautiful charred remains was meant to keep tourists away?' Diana asked, looking around. 'The film potential. The photography potential. The *book* potential of this place is off the charts.'

Cornelia set off again, walking backwards briefly to look at her. 'The wards and the lack of habitable space have done wonders – there's nothing else in Wickermere but trees and fields full of trees. The only thing left behind was Rowan House and Bonemarrow Cottage.'

'I can't see the glow anymore.' Mallory slowed to a stop as she peered around.

Cornelia squinted, and mumbled another location spell. A bright glimmer at the end of the row made her speed up.

'Could you at least wait for Mallory!' Diana exclaimed, her hands on her hips as she moved. 'And me, for that matter!'

But Cornelia was gone, running down the line of houses and stopping at a low-roofed cottage, soot rising up the walls, but the building still intact, red and black mould covering the sides.

A gentle glow lit the driveway where a car sat, burnt to a crisp.

Cornelia ran to it, her heart in her mouth, but it was empty.

'This is Agatha and Ethel's car,' she said breathlessly. 'It's here, it's possibly been here the whole time, which means

Vehicle Crimes never saw it, which means *someone* was trying to cover their tracks.'

'Are you sure?' Mallory asked, the familiar snap of her pulling on latex gloves audible in the still quiet of the dead village.

'I'm sure.' Cornelia crouched to point at the dashboard. 'Notwithstanding the location spell, see that melted plastic on the dashboard? Their friends gave them little dolls of themselves for their birthday years ago, because… I actually can't remember why and it's not important, but Ethel stuck it there so they could "remember their values", whatever the fuck that means. It's been moved into every car they've had since – they've always shared. Plus, the reg plate is still kinda readable. It's theirs.'

Mallory opened the passenger door, where it creaked and groaned and looked like it was going to disintegrate in her hands.

'There's no way we're getting evidence out of this. How did it even get here, when it was meant to be with Car Crimes or whatever they're called?' Diana asked. 'Covering tracks is one thing, but surely even the most incompetent of police would've noticed it wasn't sent over?'

'Accounting for the delay in someone getting a tow truck to come, the nature of the crime and the fact the Ghoul Council are probably intimidating to Apparents, it's likely it was overlooked. It's in the report that it was sent, so if Lucy told us it was, it's because she *believed* it was. It was true to her.'

'But why destroy it so obviously?'

'We can assume they didn't want us to find it,' Mallory said grimly. 'Which means there may have been *something* to find.'

Cornelia pulled a beetle box out of her boot and placed it carefully on the hood of the car, but nothing happened.

'I think this is a manual fire,' Diana said, sniffing. 'I can smell petrol underneath all the rest of the disgusting smell of burnt car.'

Cornelia heard a cough and looked up, but Diana hadn't moved.

'Did you hear that?' she asked, but Diana pointed at her ear and shook her head, fumbling in her pocket to put her hearing aid back in. She'd taken it out for the walk around the lake.

Mallory looked around, confused.

Cornelia heard it again, followed by a wail of despair, and scrambled to the door of the cottage.

'Hello?' she shouted, wrestling with the door handle.

'Cornelia?' Lucy's distant voice sounded from inside the house. 'Is that you?'

She was sitting in the least affected room at the back of the house, on a bed that looked too clean and new next to the mould that ran up the walls and the window frame. There were bottles of water, a box of various packaged foods, and a stack of books.

'Diana!' she said as soon as she saw her, then burst into tears.

'What happened?' Diana knelt beside her, slipping an arm around her shoulders and passing her a tissue.

Never let it be said that Diana was not astonishingly well prepared.

'I've been sequestered,' she sniffled. 'Until the twins are found.'

It partially explained why Diana hadn't been able to contact her.

'You're not locked in,' Cornelia said, confused. Her boot caught on something that looked like a long, bent nail, and she kicked it away from her. 'We got the door open with no issues. Come with us.'

Lucy shook her head, tears rolling off her face before she blew her nose noisily.

'Harry,' she said, fresh sobs choking any more words she might've said.

'Did he put you here?' Mallory asked.

Lucy nodded.

'And is he using demon magic to forcibly sequester you here, in this' – Mallory paused, looking around – 'establishment, instead of in any of the dozens of rooms in the castle where you work… ed?'

Lucy nodded, trying to compose herself. 'I know how it looks – I know it looks terrible, it looks—'

'Like you're being held captive by an Occult government entity?' Diana suggested.

'Yes, but… oh, Harry thinks I… that I…'

'Gave information to the Wickermere Reaper?' Cornelia said, the guilt hitting her full-force. She'd underestimated Harry – of course he'd go and report Lucy as soon as he'd found the Undetectables in the Ghoul Council Headquarters.

'Yes.' She looked vaguely surprised. 'How did you know that?'

'It's kind of our whole job,' Mallory said gently.

Much more gently than she had with Olivia, Cornelia noted.

'He told me someone attempted to breach the Council earlier and that they think someone's been passing information to the Wickermere Reaper – he said he wasn't formally accusing me, like, but he said I was presenting a danger,' Lucy said. 'I don't know who could've breached the Council, he knows the wards are too strong, but — he brought me here. I can't leave this room even if I want to. Even if someone else tells me to. It has to be him. And I'm not allowed to talk to anyone else on the Council, in case I glean any more information or am used against the Broadwicks. It's just until it's over. And he said it'll keep me safe from the Wickermere Reaper.'

To Cornelia's surprise, she felt hot tears prickling her eyes and blinked them away. This was *entirely* their fault. Instead of the Council looking inwards, they'd put two and two together and made a false imprisonment.

'Why did he pick here?' Cornelia asked, kicking the doorframe.

'I don't know, he said it was better I was out of Rowan House, but still… close. I think it might be my fault that the twins…'

'Lucy, did you see the car on fire outside?' Diana said quickly.

'What car?' She sniffed.

'Agatha and Ethel's.'

'That was meant to be off with the forensics lads, I thought? How'd they manage that?' She stood and tried to look through the window, but found herself turning around in circles before saying 'Oh, fucking forget it' and plonking herself down on the bed, arms folded.

'We don't know,' Cornelia said, trying to be soothing, but she was distracted by Mallory, fresh gloves on, who was examining something on the wall. 'We were wondering if you knew, but that's all right. Did Harry say anything else?'

Lucy shook her head mournfully. 'He's right. I shouldn't have told them anything.'

'Told who?' Diana asked.

'The Wickermere Reaper. Whoever they are, they must've… I must've…'

'This isn't your fault, you know.' Diana patted her shoulder.

Cornelia felt the tears coming again and made to go into the hallway.

'If you'll excuse me,' Cornelia said, smiling what she hoped was a normal smile, but somehow felt like she was showing far too many teeth.

She took a deep breath, regretting how mildewed the gulp of air smelled, and let it out. A creeping sense of terror had spread up her limbs, and a little voice in her head told her she was too far from the safety of the Laurels. Too far from the safety of her bedroom back home. She walked away from the room, wiping the one tear that had fallen with her sleeve, and came to a door at the end of the cottage that was almost completely hidden by large crates. She pulled her sleeves over her hands, trying not to brush off the disgusting walls.

She opened the door and found two large crates, roughly connected, holes bored in the sides and a makeshift lid leaning against the wall, studded with what Cornelia realised were coffin nails.

'Mallory?' Cornelia called, spotting a familiar logo on the side of the crate, beneath which read the words:

WITCHES OF BONEMARROW LAKE

A chill ran through her. Just like the Witches said: a large crate, repurposed. This was what the Wickermere Reaper was putting their victims in.

Mallory found her and took in the crate, then pointed up to the corner of the ceiling where it met the walls.

'And the floor in the corner, where the carpet has peeled up. What do you see?'

'Red… I see red stains,' Cornelia said, looking at the rivulets of angry-red mould. 'Mould? The Witches said the crate was covered in mould, you and Theodore said—'

'That it was something biological, yes. That's not mould, though. It's algae. Red algae. An *abundance* of it. But what does the algae and the crate tell us, above anything else?'

'The Wickermere Reaper's been here.'

TWENTY-ONE

4:43:20

Attempts to get Lucy out of the burnt house were futile – between sobs she spun and staggered and couldn't set foot outside the room she was in, so they did the next best thing: Cornelia went outside and called her mother, who was already on the way.

Cornelia shouldn't have been surprised, but it was a small kick in the stomach. Perhaps part of her wanted this to be simple; for Harry to have trapped Lucy here alone because he was big-bad-evil and she could get on with dealing with more trust broken in the face of another serial killer unmasked.

They were met at the top of Bonemarrow Lane, next to the shop bearing the *OOK* sign, by Imogen, Ezra and Harry, who were bearing down on them like they thought they were about to meet the Reaper in the flesh.

'This would want to be worth it,' Harry said mildly, upon seeing them. 'You triggered a ward. The by-laws state that no unauthorised member of the public, regardless of relation or circumstance, shall enter a location of exile as determined by the Ghoul Council Member's Charter, subsection C, part—'

'This was a trap,' Mallory said, just as Cornelia was

wondering if Harry rehearsed his recitation of various Ghoul Council laws, or if he made them up on the spot.

'What?' Imogen pressed a hand to her chest. She was prone to exaggeration, regardless of her guilt, but this gesture seemed lacklustre at best. Ezra didn't say anything, his hand on Imogen's elbow.

'That's all you have? "What?"' Cornelia said. 'You put Lucy here as *bait*. You think she's something to do with it, don't you? And instead of, I don't know, *finding the twins before they fucking die*, you're pissing around with faerie bait. What does the Fair Kingdom think of that, Harry? Surely there are by-laws stating it's—'

'Cornelia, go back to Rowan House. Stay *inside* the house this time,' Imogen said. 'And stop interrupting us.' She seemed spaced out, the same way Mallory did whenever she took her heavy-duty meds.

'You were already on the way here, if anyone's interrupting it's YOU!' Cornelia shouted.

She was dimly aware she'd settled back into the terrible parental dynamic of her youth, and was bordering on acting childish, but couldn't find it in herself to care. The mist had descended again, red and hot and angry.

'And what we do with our time is none of your business!' Imogen snapped.

'You've *imprisoned* a faerie in a burnt-out house in Bone-marrow Lane in an effort to trap the Wickermere Reaper, and think that's not worth an interruption?'

'Cornelia, shut up,' Ezra said sharply. 'You don't know what you're talking about.'

'Oh, sorry, should I have whispered that? Are we afraid the

Wickermere Reaper is hiding in the bushes, listening in?'

'I am not talking to you about this Cornelia,' Imogen said, lifting her chin. 'Hexana knows we don't have the time.'

'And whose fault is that? Do the rest of the Council know you're keeping Lucy here?'

Harry blinked rapidly – a sign he was about to whip out more by-laws, no doubt – and Cornelia took that as a yes.

'Is there anyone else here?' Ezra asked, cutting across whatever Imogen was about to say. 'Did you see anyone? Hear anything?'

'Just Lucy,' Mallory said. 'Nobody else.'

Imogen sighed. 'Go back to the Laurels, pack your things, and I'd better find you in your bedroom later, Cornelia. Blair help me.' She took a step closer, forcing Cornelia to take an involuntary step back. Her boot scuffled the blackened surface of the path. She stared into her mother's icy blue eyes, her jaw clenched with the effort.

'And just let us do our jobs. If it behoves you, you'll permit me to do so. Keep working on whatever it is you're working on, but know that whatever I do here, this is my domain. These are my decisions. Mine and your father's,' Imogen amended, like she forgot he was there. She pressed her thumb and forefinger to the bridge of her nose. 'This is giving me a headache. Goddess, Cornelia, you're only back and you're already driving me to a darkened room.'

It hit her like a slap. The reminder that their rules and secrets mattered so much more than family, that everything they stood for was flimsy and worn and a lie. Whatever happened within the family would always be secondary to the parts of their lives that were on view.

'Are you going to free Lucy, or is she to remain sequestered until she's the next victim?' Cornelia pointed back up the lane at the house.

'Why would you say a thing like that?' Harry asked. 'She's been sequestered because she broke the by-laws she's bound to as an employee of the Ghoul Council.'

Cornelia exchanged a glance with Mallory, her scalp prickling the way it did when a demon was trying to use persuasion magic on her. Mallory shook her head almost imperceptibly.

'There is no reason you couldn't sequester Lucy in a different location, or make her impossible to approach,' Mallory said.

'She *was* impossible to approach,' Harry said. 'That's why we're here, to check in on her.'

'And it took you this long to come for her? She could be dead,' Cornelia said.

'Not now, Cornelia,' Ezra said tiredly, adjusting his glasses. 'She agreed to these rules when she joined. The rules are paramount to everyone's safety. The UML agrees – we deal with transgressions in our own way. It was not done lightly, but it was done with the full agreement of the Council.'

'I know you want there to be some kind of conspiracy over and above the one we're dealing with, but there isn't,' Harry said. 'There is a killer at large, targeting Wickermere, and we are taking the steps necessary to defend ourselves.'

'How did you decide on sequestering so quickly? I don't understand how this got rushed through all the meetings,' Mallory said.

'It didn't,' Ezra said. 'There's a reason she wasn't in several of them.'

It was such a simple, nothing sentence that it made Cornelia's blood run cold. It cemented for her something she'd feared, deep down, about the world she lived in. It wasn't just shamefully opulent and beneficial to her family. It wasn't maintaining the status quo through rules and appearances. It was by-design dangerous, and calculated, and callous.

It was not a pleasant thing.

To face her father, telling her with a muted shrug that they had sent their least-respected Council member out in disgrace to sit somewhere the Broadwicks would turn their noses up at having to walk past, as a punishment or an effort to trap the Wickermere Reaper – she wasn't sure which was worse.

'So this is… authorised cruelty? You're allowed to lock up members of your cabinet in burnt-out hovels whenever you feel like it?' Cornelia could feel the injustice burning through her like a hot knife. 'A punishment, before you even know for sure if she's done anything wrong?'

'She has,' Harry said.

'Rules are rules, Cornelia,' Ezra said.

A disgustingly familiar refrain.

'We have to protect the Ghoul Council to keep everyone safe. All of Occulture. That's why we brought you and… and the girls here, every summer. Why the building is warded, why we've needed to know where you were at all times.'

That almost explained the dossier he'd been keeping on the Undetectables. She wondered if he knew she'd seen it.

Ezra stopped, out of steam, as though he'd just remembered Agatha and Ethel were still missing.

'Cornelia, listen,' Harry said, his tone kind. 'It is our

understanding that Lucy may have passed important information to an individual affiliated with the Wickermere Reaper, if not the Wickermere Reaper themselves. Everything happening here is above board.'

'Except you think the Wickermere Reaper was going to come here, and that's why you've trotted down from the War Room like the world's slowest cavalcade, minus the horses, despite Agatha having that really intense horse girl phase when she was thirteen—'

'That's not possible,' Harry said, and Cornelia's scalp prickled. Definitely demon persuasion magic.

'Well, maybe it was Ethel who had the horse phase,' Cornelia said, like her mouth had decided to take the rest of her sentence in its own direction. Something that happened frequently *without* the presence of demon persuasion magic, but she knew that wasn't what she meant to say.

'Maybe,' Harry said, smiling tightly.

Mallory put a hand on Cornelia's arm and she tensed.

'Harry, we have one tiny question,' Diana said sweetly, speaking for the first time. She'd been watching everyone, Cornelia realised. Watching their faces.

Ezra inhaled, the exhaustion of the last two days obvious and heavy. He raised an exasperated hand.

Harry was looking at Cornelia as he had often over the years, amusement at his favourite honorary nibling, about to regale him with stories of insects.

'We're just wondering how the car got here without alerting your wards,' Diana said.

'What car?' Harry, Imogen and Ezra said in unison.

'Funny how that's become the Council theme song,' Cornelia said, motioning for them to walk with her, back up Bonemarrow Lane to see the remains of Agatha and Ethel's car.

She was not expecting Imogen to burst into tears, but she did, and it was as disturbing as it had been when she'd first called.

'It's their car,' she sobbed, pulling at Ezra's arm.

He looped his free one around her shoulders and nodded to Harry to take a closer look. 'It is theirs, isn't it? We let the Apparent police take it, it should surely… I'll be having words with their supervisor next week,' Ezra said firmly.

'I think we've bigger questions,' Harry said.

'Yes,' Cornelia said. 'Like who brought Lucy down here, and how come they didn't see the car?'

'Harry brought her down here,' Imogen said, recovering. 'It was a mutually agreed-upon location. We know the Bonemarrow Lake witches don't come into the village, Nova and Olivia come for walks or runs or what have you in this direction so they could check in on her without her being permitted to speak to anyone. The car… is a surprise, but the wards were only to alert to people. Harry, can you ask Lucy if she saw or heard…?'

Cornelia scrutinised their faces – all three looked genuinely worried. Ezra had the sort of pinched, tense look he'd had about his face in the weeks after Grandad Cornelius died. Imogen… Cornelia had never seen her mother look so broken, and there was a tension about Harry's face that she didn't recognise. Probably because she was seeing him in a whole new light.

To be on the Ghoul Council meant there was an absence of goodness, no matter how nice folk seemed on the surface. Like politicians, people in power – *niceness* didn't paper over the hideous, immoral, illogical decisions they were making day in, day out, hiding behind the passivity a cabinet or board provided them. Mistakes were made, decisions were reached, Lucy was sequestered. Someone is the Wickermere Reaper.

Her scalp prickled again, trying to persuade her to think about something else, and she fought against it. It didn't make sense that her parents would trust Harry to question Lucy right now – unless he was making them think they should.

'Well, if Harry brought her down here, and only Harry can talk to Lucy, and Harry is adamant that he didn't see the car…' Mallory said slowly.

'I don't like what you're implying,' Harry said, after a pause.

'How surprising,' Cornelia said. 'It's still a question that I'd like answered. Unless the Ghoul Council wants to debate on it for several weeks first, of course.'

'I'm sure you would,' he said smoothly. 'But there are legal implications to me divulging anything that might be interpreted as evidence.'

'Nothing will be entered into official evidence without agreement of the local authorities, who'd need to verify our information anyway,' Mallory said. 'And at present, we are not working with anyone other than you. So you've nothing to lose. That is, unless…'

'That kind of tactic doesn't work on me, I'm afraid,' he said.

'Afraid of what?' Diana asked, tilting her head.

He eyed her with suspicion.

'Mallory, you're a guest here,' Ezra said evenly. 'I am asking you not to overstep. We are pleased you want to be here for Cornelia, but if you and Diana both continue sticking your noses in, we will have to ask you to leave.'

Imogen's sobs had quieted and she had her hands over her face.

'I have one last question,' Diana said. 'Sorry, totally hear you on the overstepping thing, won't happen again. This is mere curiosity.'

'Ask,' Imogen said. 'Then get back to the Laurels.'

At least she'd given up on the moving back into Rowan House portion of her demands.

'How do the wards work? I know Cornelius Broadwick – may he rest in peace, of course – set up the original wards, but people keep talking about them and I'm just… I'm just so confused,' Diana said.

Cornelia thought she was overdoing it, but Ezra seemed to buy it.

'It's a highly sophisticated magic system, that has been digitised for the modern age. Every time someone authorised crosses into Wickermere, there's an alert. If they're not authorised, they're pushed away from the perimeter. It goes from the top of Bonemarrow Lane there' – Ezra pointed to just beyond where Lucy was sequestered – 'all the way around Wickermere, which is about two miles, approximately. It ends about a mile into the forest at the back of Rowan House. The gates to Rowan House will only permit someone authorised to pass through, or they'll be thrown back. With the multi-layered approach, someone who could have access to Wickermere would not have automatic access to Rowan House – that would need to be granted separately. This is regarded as one of the finest security systems the UML has ever seen – patented, of course, by my late father. Very high tech, requires a great deal of knowledge to navigate.'

'Is that why Lucy had a sticky note with the ward passwords stuck to the front of the monitor?' Diana asked. 'Or someone who wasn't Lucy,' she added hastily.

Ezra's eyes flashed, but his expression didn't change.

'Only authorised personnel can enter the property, so it's not that much of an issue. It occasionally… glitches… but with the multi-layered approach, the Ghoul Council remains safe.'

He seemed unaware that the system could be tampered with by someone who actually knew how it worked, and wasn't bullshitting his way through a sales pitch. He also seemed unaware that the Ghoul Council was the problem.

It was almost sad.

'And if that's all?' He took Imogen's hand. She seemed spaced-out again, and Cornelia wondered if she'd taken something.

She wondered if she had any going spare.

'My rates are fair, for any further questions,' Harry said, and it took Cornelia far too long to realise he was making a joke, of all things, at a time like this.

He ran a hand over his face. He looked as exhausted as Cornelia felt.

'I will tell you something for free,' he said quietly as Imogen and Ezra walked away. He gestured his intentions to go in to talk to Lucy, and Ezra shot him a thumbs up. 'They don't know what they're messing with.'

Cornelia wondering if that was an admission of guilt, or if Harry was truly being more intelligent about all of this than the Broadwicks were.

TWENTY-TWO

3:26:33

They were running out of time. Mallory watched Cornelia pace across the cottage sitting room, which was not big enough for pacing. She repeatedly came dangerously close to crushing Diana's diorama until Diana hexed her so hard, she fell onto the couch beside Mallory.

'Sorry,' she gasped. 'Did I hurt you?'

Mallory shook her head tiredly. She was at a point where the pain was so intense it was floating above her. There was a chance she had a few more hours in her before she started vomiting.

Illogically, she thought of her unfinished course assignment. All the reading she hadn't done for cell and molecular biology, appearing as a cursor on a blank page in her mind, and felt a twist of guilt for even going there at a time like this.

'The Broadwicks seemed genuinely shocked by the car being in Bonemarrow Lane,' Mallory said, trying to refocus.

'And Harry was definitely trying to persuade us – magically, as well as regularly – not to keep pressing on the Wickermere Reaper Trap 2000,' Diana said.

'I don't think sequestering Lucy out there can be anything other than a deliberate trap, *but* – we do need to consider the logistics of it. If the Wickermere Reaper is, for argument's sake, Harry, why would he deliberately put Lucy in the very place he'd been working? Unless the twins were the final victims, and he has no intention of continuing,' Mallory mused. Her brain wasn't working at full capacity; she could feel her thoughts sludging along. 'And if it *isn't* Harry, it means someone else within the Council – Imogen, Ezra, Dot, Olivia, Nova – was instrumental in convincing Harry to select that location.'

'It feels like a taunt,' Diana said. 'To place her there, with the crate down the hall. The evidence of the Wickermere Reaper's workshop steps away from where Lucy was being held.'

'Right – which would tie into our hypothesis that the Reaper is a sadist. I would also like to note that Ezra did not seem to understand how the wards work.'

'He was using every buzzword known to man and then some, which suggests this is how it was explained to him, perhaps by someone who *also* doesn't know how they work.'

'But we've seen them in action in Wrackton,' Mallory went on, thinking of the cemeteries, as well as the Mayoral Offices. 'That's how they were keeping folk out of the Offices post-explosion. Except they didn't work on Theodore, which suggests there *are* ways around them, if you're familiar with the system.'

'As much as that would make me wonder if the Reaper is someone *not* on the Council, I did try to connect to the internet inside Rowan House and couldn't, because there wasn't any. There's a closed intranet that Lucy uses for the printer and, seemingly, watching soap re-reruns, but that's it,' Diana said.

Mallory did not ask her how she'd managed to find all that out in the short time she'd spent at Lucy's desk, and instead privately delighted in how *good* Diana was at her job.

'None of this is getting us any closer to finding the twins. They're out there, in Wickermere somewhere. We might've walked on their graves,' Cornelia said quietly. She had gone unnaturally still again, and Mallory wanted to kneel beside her and pull her into a hug, but the pain was too great for both of them, and Mallory couldn't make any of it stop.

'They're not dead yet,' Diana said firmly. 'We are not panicking. We don't panic. We have clues, we just need to slot them together. Any of the Ghoul Council look particularly mouldy to you?'

'It's algae,' Mallory said absently. 'And it could be any of them.'

'It couldn't be Olivia,' Cornelia said.

Mallory tried not to react to this. She couldn't say she hadn't noticed the way Cornelia looked at Olivia. It didn't *matter*, because it didn't mean anything, but it hurt all the same. She'd been preparing for the moment Cornelia visibly moved on for over a year, and it did nothing to stop the pain of it flooding her, mingling with the physical pain until she couldn't tell where she started and it ended.

'Cornelia,' Diana said. 'I am being nice to you, because I am desperately sorry about your sisters, and the fact your family are really terrible and evil and possible murderers. But in the words of my girlfriend: would you ever fucking cop on to yourself?'

She said it so fiercely that it made Cornelia laugh, a loud, long laugh that bordered on hysterical, until tears fell and then she was sobbing and Diana wrapped her in a tight hug and Mallory, at a loss for what she could do, consumed as she was by physical agony, reached into her bag and took her emergency pain meds, despite only taking her regular ones a few minutes prior.

Her phone rang, and it startled Cornelia enough into pausing sobbing and looking up at Mallory as she fumbled to answer it.

'That's good.' Diana patted Cornelia on the shoulder. 'You were going to get tears in tiny Lake Wickermere, and it's not actually designed for water.'

'Kingston?' Mallory said, the phone crackling. 'How'd you get on with the Ternion and Besiegement stuff?'

'Mallory?' Kingston's voice was strained. She could hear Felix in the background. 'I'm still working on that, but I have— I need to relay a message from Theodore, and Felix tells me I should insist you don't panic.'

'Good start.' A sense of dread curled in her stomach.

'Theodore would like you to know that in pursuit of the Wrackton Digger, he has discovered another disturbed grave – his own.'

'What?' Mallory said.

'What?' Diana repeated.

'What?' Cornelia moved closer to listen. Mallory pulled the phone away from her ear to put it on speaker, tilting it towards Diana.

'The Wrackton Digger has moved to Oughteron?' Mallory asked.

'No?' Kingston cleared his throat. 'No, he's buried here in Wrackton. Absolutely beside himself about it. Oh, can you say that about a ghost? Is it offensive? I've never been able to figure that one out.'

'Who's buried?' Diana prompted.

'Theodore,' Kingston said. 'But he's not now, his body's gone. Well, his remains. Can't imagine there was much of him left.'

'Full decomposition takes approximately five to ten years,' Mallory said automatically. 'He's been dead eight, so it would be mostly skeletonised remains, maybe some tissue left, but not much.'

The fact helped dull the sense of betrayal she felt at Theodore lying to her that he didn't have a grave close by. She'd never seen it and had been nineteen before it had even occurred to her that she *could've* gone to Oughteron visit his place of rest, but he'd quickly disabused her of that suggestion.

'No, Mallory,' Theodore had said when she'd floated the idea. 'Do *not* stand at my grave and weep, I am quite literally not there. Plus, I feel it is bad enough for young minds to have to hold the cognitive dissonance of "dead" and "semi-corporeal ghost" in one's head without adding a place of grieving into the mix. You cannot grieve me in a way that matters, because I'm…'

At that he'd trailed off, and she'd never questioned it again.

'Gross,' Kingston said appreciatively, pulling her back to the conversation. 'Felix was trying to calm Theodore – Taylor asked us to check in on him, but Theodore's gone back to the cemetery. He was really upset, said I needed to tell you at once.'

Mallory closed her eyes and Diana took the phone from her.

'Can the pair of you not take care of it? Or at least stall, until Taylor's finished work? I can ask her to come help.'

'Knowing that time is of the essence there, I'd like to say yes, but I've never seen Theodore this upset.'

The Undetectables had. Mallory had, the day he'd attempted to possess her.

The idea of the Besiegement hit her again and she shivered.

'We need you here. Just Mallory,' Felix said quickly, the muffled sounds of them taking the phone from Kingston crackling through the speaker.

Mallory looked to Cornelia, who held her gaze, her eyes red-rimmed but still bright, her lashes long and dark. Only her opinion mattered.

After what felt like an age, Cornelia nodded once, and placed her hands over Mallory's legs so that the familiar pressure of Cornelia's binding spell spread up her aching muscles.

'Go.'

The research room looked like a hurricane had hit it. Mallory crouched amid a scattered mass of printouts and charts, things written in Theodore's hand, books and couch cushions, the murder board in tatters. She cast a longing glance into the lab, wishing she'd had more time with all their forensic evidence, knowing every 'quick' trip into the lab sucked up three, four, five hours and they didn't have that to spare.

They barely had any time at all.

'Yes, yes, everything looks terrible, gather your things and let's *go*,' Felix said, gathering up the books and notes Mallory had been looking at and bundling them carefully into her arms, waggling their car keys. 'I shudder to think what Kingston's doing out there, unsupervised.'

Mallory settled back against the heated car seat, feeling a tiny degree of relief as the meds and binding spell and warmth combined in delicious alchemy, even as a song that sounded remarkably like a lot of crows screaming blared over the car stereo.

'Mallory does *not* want to listen to *Crowcaine Real Estate Dreams* and give you lyrical feedback,' Felix said firmly, turning it down.

Kingston leaned forward so he could talk to them both, unruffled.

'How goes it with figuring out which Council member is the Wickermere Reaper?' Kingston said, breaking Mallory out of her sense of relief to turn her head just enough to look at him sharply.

'You know the drill at this stage. I drink blood and I know things.'

It was a concession she had to make; after the last year and a bit of having Kingston around, Mallory was still struggling with how he seemed to know just about everything.

'And yet you don't know how to pack for tour,' Felix cut in.

'Oh, shit,' Mallory said. 'I forgot that was this weekend, I didn't want to take you away from your own work! I can call a cab back?'

'Don't worry, I have Langdon packing for us all, I just couldn't resist,' Felix said, smiling fondly.

'Yes, why was that again?' Kingston said, pretending to think. 'Oh, because I am "a menace" and "so filled with packing ineptitude" that Felix would rather "suffer Langdon going through my wardrobe and stealing half my fucking clothes than deal with you packing two left socks and one pair of underpants for an entire three-week tour".'

Mallory did not ask how a sock could be specifically left.

'Did you get anywhere with the Ternion?' she asked, trying to stuff the things Felix had foisted on her into a bag.

'Boy did he,' Felix said, then swore as someone in a particularly massive SUV cut across them. 'WHERE IS THE SPORT OR THE UTILITY IN DRIVING LIKE A DICKHEAD?' they shouted out their open window. 'Sorry, sorry, continue.'

'I will say that I think Observer Johnson is growing sick of the sight of me, but he *hasn't* told me to go away. I did get him to find this for me.' In the rear-view mirror, Mallory saw him reach into the pocket of his leather jacket for a folder he'd bent in half to fit, passing it to her. 'This is an old map of Wrackton. One of the last remaining maps, after the Mayoral Offices originally exploded. Which is to say, the time you blew it up wasn't the only time.'

It was truly wild to Mallory just how much the actions of their past followed them around in the wake of the events of eighteen months ago, to the point that she almost didn't hear what he said.

'What do you mean, *originally*?'

'I said what I said.'

Felix reached back to poke him in the shoulder.

'I don't know,' Kingston amended. 'I know they exploded

before, and your time was the second time. But just look at the map.'

The paper was fragile – so fragile it shouldn't have been jammed in his pocket like that – and directed her to a large spot in an otherwise sparse town. While Wrackton wasn't big today, it was hard to imagine it so empty.

'The Observatory used to stand where the Mayoral Offices are now,' Mallory said.

'Right, and Elisabella's, Hexana's and Blair's graves were supposedly right there, on the Observatory grounds, in a special burial site marked for the revered. I suppose the Apparents would call them saints or something.'

'Why would they change that? There's no Ternion memorial around the Mayoral Offices.'

'Folk preferred to remember the Ternion as goddesses, and not as ordinary mortal witches. There was a decree passed, and they were removed. Thus, the memorial by the Observatory was built. Pre- or post-explosion, I don't know.'

This lined up with what Olivia had told them about the Ternion's remains, and with what Observer Johnson had half-explained when they'd met with him, what felt like an age ago but had barely been a day.

'And everyone just… agreed to this? Not the townspeople, they—'

'Weren't happy about it,' Kingston said.

'The people of Wrackton? Unhappy about something? Unprecedented,' Felix said. 'Almost there, wrap it up so Mallory can calm down a ghost.'

'No, everyone did not agree to it. It was regarded as "highly controversial", which is history-speak for "a fucking disaster". I suspect if vampires still had magic at the time, they wouldn't have tried to make the Ternion appear mortal.'

'Why?'

'I think, and I'm using myself as anecdotal evidence here' – he gestured at himself, the poster boy for coming back to life – 'that that's part of our general power, as vampires, and not just a me-specific thing. As much as I'd like to think of myself as the most special boy, I'm pretty sure we're all meant to be immortal. If vampires were mortal, the war would've stopped much sooner. And if the *Ternion* were mortal, we'd probably want to be better or unified or some shit, I don't know.'

'You're so eloquent it astounds me every day,' Felix said, blowing him a kiss.

'It's a reductive way of looking at it all,' Kingston said, inching forward to press his face to Felix's shoulder. Their easy affection made Mallory smile; it was about time someone treated Felix properly.

'So, do we have any clue where the Ternion went? Is there an unmarked grave? Are they anywhere?'

'I don't know yet, but I can keep trying.'

'Langdon has called me seventeen times in the time it's taken to get this far,' Felix said, swinging the car towards the cemetery.

'Quickly,' Mallory said, too tired to find her own notebook among the pile of notes and papers she seemed to have amassed, even as she saw a flash of lavender somewhere down the bottom of the bag. 'Do you know anything about something called a Besiegement Curse?'

Third time lucky in getting answers, she hoped.

'A possession curse, yes,' Kingston said, folding his tattooed hands so the words *KING SHIT* were visible across his fingers. He was such an unlikely-seeming scholar, in so many ways. 'It's an antiquated concept, but back when séances were all the rage for Apparents, they had to have an Occult person present, usually someone well versed in the rules, to prevent it happening.'

'But what is it? A ghost possesses you, and then what?'

She had a flash again of Theodore trying frantically to communicate with her last year by knocking on the door of her mind, the way she felt she was losing herself to him, not sure what was hers and what was his.

'They can walk around in your body, talk, think and act like you. Access places ghosts usually can't. Potentially travel outside the boundaries of the place they're contained in, though that's the more extreme Samhain ghost variant. In a séance scenario, if you break the circle while communicating with a non-corporeal ghost, any manner of ghost can communicate with you, or through you, and sometimes that's permanent.'

'Sorry, *any manner*? Are you saying there's more to ghosts than the Samhain variety?'

'Are you saying Apparents are so afraid of the concept of death that they resort to *metaphorical* allusions to grief by using metaphysical paranormal phenomena that shapes a dark underworld of existence that only becomes known to you if you manage to purchase haunted property?'

'Yes,' Mallory said. 'I always assumed ghosts in general were a metaphor. I'd only ever heard of Samhain ghosts growing up, anything else seemed unreasonable. Even those times folk wanted to go to the séances they'd hold in the Larix basement or whatever, I always thought that was an Observational activity, rather than actual magic. And now I feel silly for thinking there were only Theodores in the world. Sometimes the way he talks, you'd think he was the only one.'

Even though she knew that wasn't true.

'Of course there's more than just Theodore. They're all over the cemeteries, in every single orifice of the Observatory.'

'There's one in this car right now,' Felix said. '*Booo*th of you out, and make it as quick as you can.'

'There could actually be a ghost in here,' Kingston said. 'We'd have no idea.'

He ran around and opened Mallory's door in the time it took her to get her seat belt off, and held out a hand to help her up. 'Part of me thinks the Undetectables keep getting tangled up in things that are, ultimately, connected,' he said quietly.

Mallory remembered the twins' letters to Lyle Whitlock, and shuddered. 'Any particular connection you can see?'

'When you asked me about the Besiegement, I got this sense...' He gestured at his stomach, where the outline of his ostomy bag showed through his t-shirt. 'Whoever the Reaper is, they are *very* concerned by the idea of a Besiegement Curse.'

It wasn't what she'd been expecting him to say.

'Part of me hopes you're completely off base.'

She spotted Theodore standing over a grave, his hands on his head in pose that, if this was a painting, could only be described as 'utter despair'.

'Mallory!' He rushed to meet her as she hobbled over. 'You came.'

'Kingston called. Theodore, what—'

'The Wrackton Digger has *me*.'

'I thought you were buried in Oughteron. You *told* us you were buried in Oughteron!'

'I didn't want to make you feel you should come to my funeral.'

'WE KNEW YOU AFTER YOU DIED,' Mallory shouted. 'Sorry for shouting.'

'I know. It's just you were so young, and I was so anxious about protecting your little minds from horror.'

'We FOUND YOUR BODY,' Mallory shouted, not bothering to apologise this time.

'I know, I know. I'm sorry. Erroneous decision. Can we walk any quicker? No? Slower! Slower is better. That's okay. Slowly, with haste.'

And then they were looking at the grave. *His* grave, a temporary oval marker with a small placard attached to it.

THEODORE
JAMES WYATT
199[illegible] – 2017

It had no message on it, no remembrance of who he was as a person. Someone had scratched out the year he'd been born.

It had been such a short life.

Mallory looked at Theodore, the tear tracks stark against his cat whiskers, surprised to find her own tears spilling steadily.

'That's why I didn't tell you,' Theodore said quietly. 'I didn't want you to come here and look at this place as somewhere I was. Emphasis on *was,* now that my body is NOT HERE,' he said, pointing at the empty grave below them. 'I don't know what they want from me. I don't know why they'd take my remains. I bet they're totally skeletal at this point. What does anyone want with a bag of bones?'

The answer on Mallory's tongue was 'necromancy', but it didn't feel either appropriate in the situation, or necessarily correct.

She wiped her eyes aggressively, not even sure why she'd been crying in the first place. Theodore was here and queer in the semi-corporeal sense. That had to count for something, even as his murder hung over her head, officially unsolved. She opened her mouth to tell him about the Broadwicks, to let the truth come spilling out, not caring if it was more for her own comfort than Theodore's benefit. All of it, everything they knew, everything they'd seen.

And then she stopped, her mouth snapping shut.

They weren't far from Van Doren's plot, had stood several feet away from Theodore's grave and not known it as they watched Jacob be lowered into the ground.

But Jacob wasn't there anymore.

His grave was open.

His body was gone.

TWENTY-THREE

1:31:56

'Do you have *any* fucking idea how big two miles is when it's in any direction?' Cornelia exclaimed, throwing her phone down onto the sofa.

They had an hour and a half left. Minutes. Somewhere out there, Agatha and Ethel were choking. Or they were waiting for Imogen and Ezra to swoop in and save them.

A muscle in her jaw had started aching, pulsing in time with her rapid heartbeat. She wanted Diana to have all the answers. She needed it to all be over. She was certain the agony was in the waiting.

When Diana didn't respond, still absorbed in the Ghoul Council dossiers as though they'd shake out a clue, Cornelia felt rage rising in her. 'Or how *reticent* the local – also, not fucking local! – police are about their search dog availability? Keep asking if I mean cadaver dogs, which I FUCKING DON'T, because I would SAY THAT.'

'Let's not panic,' Diana said for the millionth time, barely looking up. 'Someone has to be sensible, I've appointed myself that role today.'

'Shut the FUCK up,' Cornelia snarled.

To her surprise, Diana did, even though Cornelia was being horribly vicious.

The rage reached her lungs. A tunnel closed in around her vision, like there was only the countdown and her anger and the hopelessness of it all, memories of being taken and locked in a cage and almost dying playing out in horrible technicolour in her mind.

Her breathing was ragged. Blood rushed in her ears, her heart rabbiting so fast it hurt. She sank to her knees, or else was lowered by Diana, who was trying to talk her down but her voice was getting lost in the rushing sound, the fact that air would not come into her lungs, that she couldn't move.

And then Mallory was right there, her face inches from hers.

'Breathe in,' Mallory said firmly. 'Breathe with me. In. Hold it. That's it, let it go. In. Hold it. Let it go. In. Hold it. Let it go.'

She'd taken Cornelia's hands with the same assurance as if she'd dragged her onto a life raft. At Mallory's prompt, Cornelia mechanically responded to five things she could hear and four she could feel, her chest loosening and her lungs willing to accept air. Diana kept rubbing her back, and the tunnel vision expanded just enough for Cornelia to sit back on the floor with a thump and pull her knees to her chest.

'I'm okay,' Cornelia said. It wasn't a lie, exactly, but she was *alive*, at least. 'Tell me what's happening in Wrackton. Distract me for a minute.'

'If the Ternion were moved, and the Observatory was moved and the Mayoral Offices built on top of the site… could that explain literally everything wrong with that place?' Diana asked, looking at Kingston's map after Mallory had filled them in.

Or mostly filled them in. Cornelia had the sense Mallory hadn't told them everything.

Mallory had never been a good liar, and there was something in her voice, her eyes, that told Cornelia she was processing something, which meant she'd share it later, when she was ready.

Mallory was one of the few constants in Cornelia's life she'd never have to doubt.

'Good point,' Mallory said after a pause. 'I hadn't thought of that, but you're right. Kingston said something about how every case we work on seems to be linked in some way. And while I try not to give him *too* much credence…'

'Theodore's Coincidence Theory,' Diana said.

The actual theory – which was more of a working hypothesis and had absolutely not been peer reviewed – amounted to an event occurring twice was a coincidence, but a third time was serial, while a lone occurrence was an outlier. It strangely made more sense when Theodore said it.

Cornelia wiped her glasses lenses for the fifth time. She felt adrift, her heart in her mouth as the seconds counted down. She was aware of every single one as it passed, her senses heightened. She felt on the verge of another panic attack, if that's what that had been.

'It lines up with what Olivia said, about Wrackton folk being sure the Ternion were buried in unmarked graves somewhere. There was really nothing else?'

Mallory shook her head. 'Which begs the tentative question: are Imogen and Ezra somehow right, and the Wickermere Reaper asking for Elisabella's remains is just a distraction? Like asking the Witches for a ghostlight – a time-wasting manoeuvre.'

'Well thank Elisabella we didn't spend any time on it,' Diana said absently, still poring over the dossiers. Cornelia imagined pushing her into the lake for ten long, glorious seconds, which were interrupted by a soft knock at the door.

She stood, tension descending over her. She expected to see her parents on the other side of the door, or Harry, his face grave and bearing bad news. That they'd run out of time, ahead of time, and that was that. That whoever was there would herald an irreversible change in the facts of her life as she knew them.

She almost didn't want to open it. Leave the truth on the other side.

Instead, Olivia stood on the other side, holding an envelope between two fingers. Cornelia involuntarily smiled when she saw her. Mostly from surprise.

'Sorry to bother you, this arrived at the main house. Addressed to you, Cornelia.'

'Who even knows we're here?' Cornelia reached for the envelope, but Mallory intercepted with a pair of tweezers.

'Sorry, need to be overcautious at all times,' Mallory said to Olivia's quizzical look. Something in her tone told Cornelia she wasn't sorry at all. 'Where did you say this was delivered to?'

'Came with the post. I was giving Dot and Nova a hand with some admin stuff while Lucy is… Anyway, we found it. Like you said, not many know you're here, so I figured it was something urgent.'

Mallory stared at her with what Cornelia could only describe as 'open hostility', which was so un-Mallory-like that all Cornelia could muster was a mumbled thanks.

'I'll leave you to it.' Olivia hesitated, then turned back. 'Cornelia, I just want you to know that I am here if you need me. I'm bound by all the same rules, but if I can help… I'll help you. All of you.'

Her gaze flicked between Cornelia and Mallory, her face open and honest, and it made a thread of dread curl in Cornelia's stomach.

'Thanks,' Mallory said, all but shutting the door in her face. 'We'll let you know.'

She held the tweezers carefully and set the envelope down on the table.

'What's that?' Diana asked, coming closer.

It was, by all accounts, an envelope. White heavy paper, Cornelia's name typed neatly on the front.

'Maybe it's someone trying to sell me a car. Or extend a warranty for a car. Or maybe it's tickets to something,' Cornelia said, with hope she didn't have. Her gut was telling her otherwise – this was something bad.

'Beetle me,' Mallory said. Cornelia complied.

Instantly, the beetle flared green.

'SHIT,' Mallory said.

There wasn't time to go back to the lab.

'It's magic,' Cornelia said. 'So there's that.'

She ripped open the envelope when Mallory gave her the go-ahead nod, and she and Diana crowded around.

I'LL GIVE YOU A HINT
BUT I'LL NEED ELISABELLA'S SOUL FIRST
12:11:02

Cornelia's blood ran cold.

The timer had refreshed, giving them an extra twelve hours. She should've felt elated, relieved, *happy* even, but the words written above it made her shiver.

'That's a taunt,' Diana said. 'And that's rude.'

'It has my name on it,' Cornelia whispered. 'Why does it have my name on it?'

'And why did we get an extension on the deadline?' Diana asked, taking Mallory's tweezers to hold it closer to her face.

Not that there was any point. It would self-destruct like the others, and any prints or additional magic they could pull off it would take too long. The beetle had the sample, that would have to be enough to help them later, when it was all over.

'It's possible everyone got an extension,' Mallory said slowly. 'And that this is just part of the Wickermere Reaper's sadistic MO. Taunting folk when they're at wits' end, desperate for a lifeline.'

'We know the Witches got more time, even if Jo and Ruby weren't forthcoming about how – if everyone got more time, why wouldn't they be upfront about it? Surely it's more evidence that could've helped find their— find them?' Cornelia demanded, still reeling.

She didn't think she could take much more of this. Any of it. She was so close to witchlighting back to her bedroom in Wrackton and never coming out again, the old panic needling at her, telling her she wasn't safe.

'Would you? Say you're Apparent. Or anyone – aside from the Witches and us – dragged into the Wickermere Reaper case. You've been waiting for the authorities and the Ghoul Council to help. Waiting, and waiting. And you're thrown a lifeline in the form of this' – she waved the note stiffly – 'only for it to transpire that you can't fulfil the terms. And then you have to accept you're party to the failure to recover your loved one. So if you don't mention it, you don't have to have anyone say it was your fault, and you can keep blaming the Wickermere Reaper, and the people who were supposed to help in the first place.'

'That's genius. Disgusting, but genius,' Diana said.

'But why me? The last letter went to the Broadwicks.' Cornelia was being indignant, she knew, but it felt better to argue semantics for a moment than face the fact that the Wickermere Reaper was communicating with her directly.

'If we're right, and if this is a game the Reaper is playing with the families of the victims, the Broadwicks are possibly being too boring for their liking,' Mallory said, stretching her shoulders carefully. 'We've been actively running around trying to find out things, while the Wickermere Reaper is in the War Room listening to meetings. The most exciting thing we know of was Lucy being sequestered – the Reaper might be trying to shake things up. They're trying to rattle you. Don't let them, as far you can manage.'

Diana brought her a glass of water and Mallory threw back more painkillers.

Cornelia closed her eyes for a second. 'Logically, what does it mean, "bring me her soul"?'

Mallory's eyes widened, that sparkle of her brain working

overtime behind them. 'That's just it, isn't it? We took *remains* to mean *physical*, and assumed it was a *different* request to the Witches being asked for a ghostlight. I don't think Ghoul Council has her bones – I think her remains and her soul are one and the same. And that's why whoever the Wickermere Reaper is hasn't just gone and got Elisabella for themself – they can't.'

'Because you can't get into the lake without dying,' Cornelia said. 'As per the placards on the wall.'

And everything she'd ever been told about the lake over the years.

'But maybe if – like multiple members of the Ghoul Council – you'd worked on a secret project around the lake, you'd know of some stone left unturned. Some way that it *might* be possible, but that the Reaper wouldn't want to try themselves,' Diana said, catching on.

'A legitimate ransom,' Cornelia said, the words leaden on her tongue. 'The Wickermere Reaper gets to feel clever, gets to enjoy the families panicking, but has been asking for something attainable. So if you can't do it – if you can't drum up the money, or the object, or the remains of a goddess of Occulture – you have to live with the consequences of your own failure.'

'That's it,' Mallory said. 'All of it. We're right. The Reaper's been asking for Elisabella's soul all along, and it's at the bottom of Bonemarrow Lake. I think she's a Samhain ghost.'

PERIMORTEM IV

People say it's the hope that kills you, but they thought it was the aftermath. The realisation that it was never hope, but a bargaining chip. That the next phase was depression, and then full surrender.

They never could see it coming, even when it was in front of their faces, plain as day.

Folk saw what they wanted to see.

Two bodies began to press at the walls of their final resting place. Nails scrabbling at the edges, looking for a way out, as though it wasn't a one-way system.

Perhaps hope was the catalyst of death.

TWENTY-FOUR

12:02:35

Cornelia shoved open the door of the War Room without waiting for anyone to answer her knocks – that were more like a rain of hammerings – and strode in, the new note held aloft.

The Council ignored her, staring at the table, at the first ransom note that was disintegrating before their eyes. Tears rolled down Imogen's face as Ezra hid his in his hands.

Dot looked as though she might be sick, the others solemnly stoic.

It felt like the closing scene of a play – one with an unexpected encore.

'I need to ask a question about Project HAUNT and I need you to answer it honestly, or we aren't getting Agatha and Ethel back,' Cornelia burst out, slamming her hands on the table so hard the witchlights bounced.

'Cornelia,' Dot said gently, reaching across the table to her. 'Time's up, now.'

'I got a stay of execution.'

It took a moment for that to sink in. For Ezra and Imogen to lift their heads, for Harry to half-rise from his seat, for Nova to lean back with an eyebrow raised. For Olivia to look shocked, for Dot to press a hand to her mouth.

'If this is a joke—' Ezra started.

'It's not,' Mallory said quietly.

'And we need to know if Project HAUNT figured out a way into Bonemarrow Lake.'

'Why?' Imogen asked.

'We just need you to tell us,' Cornelia said steadily, her gaze lingering on each of them. The esteemed Ghoul Council, which had wasted three days and done nothing to save Agatha and Ethel.

Olivia, who'd brought them the note. Harry, who'd behaved oddly in imprisoning Lucy. Nova, who was the resident contrarian. Dot, who looked ready to collapse from the stress of it all. Imogen and Ezra, who had, in all likelihood, no matter what Mallory said, killed Theodore. A council of some of the (allegedly) most brilliant minds in all of Occulture, presenting a united front, unaware that one of their ranks was betraying them every single second of every day that had passed since the Wickermere Reaper took that first victim.

The Reaper was using undetectable methods of imprisoning and killing their victims, had unknowable motivations ('sadism' was plausible and likely, but Cornelia had always considered sadism to be a sad way to live one's life. To boil over with rage at the world, to be so deeply unhappy inside that a person would enjoy torturing others. She'd never understood why sadists didn't just resort to turning the metaphorical knife inwards, like everyone else did) and was hiding in plain sight. By all rights, the Undetectables were walking right into whatever trap the Wickermere Reaper had set with the deadline extension, but Cornelia knew – in her absolute heart of hearts, she was unshakeable in this belief – that the Reaper wasn't aware that the Undetectables knew this was a game. It was enough to crystallise a tiny flicker of hope within her.

'It's unethical for us to speak on Council projects without a motion to—'

'Harry,' Nova said silkily, cutting him off. 'If you don't shut up about motions, I am going to take my size eight shoe and shove it up your—'

'We tried,' Imogen said, interrupting. 'For years. Long before us. The banks of old TVs were an attempt to use the electrostatic charge the lake gave off like a signal. To fine-tune a channel of communication. We had special operations where we sent in divers' – that explained the Wickermere Divers memorial wall, then – 'and we tried sending in boats with trained divers inside. We tried special suits, we tried spells, we tried… we tried everything. Every individual we sent in – voluntarily, we were utterly transparent about the nature of the mission after the first – died, no matter how prepared they believed themselves to be. Every single one. Apparents, who stumbled upon Wickermere before your grandfather *graciously* ensured Apparent safety by shutting down and erasing the town, died horribly. We *tried* to find out what's down there. We failed. Now *why. Do. You. Want. To. Know?*'

Despite it being phrased like one, it didn't feel like a question.

'The Reaper sent us a note,' Cornelia said. She didn't have Diana's acting prowess. Any time she'd been forced to in their cases she'd been horrible at it, but this felt easy. Pretend the Reaper isn't in the room. Pretend not to know. 'They asked for Elisabella's soul, in exchange for twelve more hours. They've offered a clue. We joined the dots.'

'I doubt you've joined anything. I told you before, this was a waste of time,' Ezra said. 'A distraction!'

'I think they're serious,' Cornelia said, pushing back slowly and firmly.

Mallory's hand brushed the back of her arm and she felt buoyed by her presence, by Diana's presence, by the power they had, both collectively and over the Reaper. They were getting closer. Half a day was enough time. It had to be.

'They must've known all along you had some way of finding Elisabella. They're being generous enough in offering us another chance, a *last* chance to get Agatha and Ethel back.'

She worried briefly that she was laying it on too thick, then shrugged it off.

'No,' Harry said. 'It's unprecedented.'

'There is a way,' Olivia started slowly, but Dot shushed her.

'Don't give them false hope. Cornelia's stubborn, she'll do anything to get them back,' Dot whispered.

'We've lost two daughters, we cannot lose our last one,' Imogen said. 'And we *would* lose you. There isn't a way.'

Perhaps it was deploying 'daughter' against her like a needle-nosed weapon, or the fact of the Council, some of the most important people in the known Occult world sitting there, staring at the charred remains of a ransom note after three days of utter inaction, but Cornelia felt a whip of rage build up inside her.

'Give me the room with my parents,' she said.

Nobody moved.

'NOW,' she shouted.

The rest of the Council stood up. Dot hovered, but Ezra waved her on with one dismissive finger. Mallory checked to make sure Cornelia wanted them to leave too, but Cornelia nodded.

'I know what you did,' Cornelia said, shutting the door firmly behind them.

'What?' Ezra said, at the same time Imogen said, 'When?'

It was consistent of them.

'I know *everything*. All those times you made me feel like I wasn't good enough to be a Broadwick? You were doing me a favour, actually. I don't want to be like you. When this is all over, I'm changing my name.'

'Cornelia, this is not the time for this.' Ezra set his glasses on the table in front of him, pinching the bridge of his nose.

'It's the perfect time. All my life you've underestimated me. Treated me like a problem to be solved, managed, *hidden*. But I was always listening. I never understood why you couldn't tell I was *always* listening.'

They weren't words she had planned on saying, but once she'd started, she found she couldn't stop. Every wretched thing that being back in Rowan House had made rise up within her was spewing out of her, thick and bilious.

If she was looking into the face of the Wickermere Reaper as she said them, so be it.

'I know Bonemarrow Lake is full of ghosts. I know the

Council is more powerful, more influential over the UML and the rest of Occulture, than any of you would like to admit. I know Lucy's been sequestered in a fucking *hovel* in Wickermere because you don't see staff as people. You don't even see *people* as people, or anyone less than a Broadwick as being worth your time. But you also don't see your own children as anything other than bargaining chips. You let me in here, my friends in here, because it was better to have me in the way than somewhere the Wickermere Reaper could get me – not because you actually cared, but because you feared someone could use me against you.'

The realisation hurt, but it was refreshing. If neither of them was the Reaper, they'd underestimated her in a way the real Reaper hadn't. If one – or both – of them *was* the Reaper, it was exactly how she was supposed to think they thought of her. Both assumptions were wrong. They didn't know her at all.

'Cornelia—' Ezra tried.

'DON'T FUCKING INTERRUPT ME. *LISTEN* TO ME. I know you've continued throwing ghosts into Bonemarrow Lake – don't ask me how, but I *know*. I know you've been looking for the Ternion's remains, and I *know* someone in this building knows *exactly* where Elisabella is. I know, because *you* know someone here accidentally passed information to the Wickermere Reaper, who is somewhere out there laughing at you, all while in the middle of murdering your daughters – who are probably wondering why the fuck you haven't come to save them.'

They didn't reply – she expected, at the very least, a correction on the wrong Reaper assumption, given that neither

Broadwick was capable of not correcting her at the best of times – and Cornelia figured it was time to let everything else out. No better time to confront your murderous family members than in the midst of another murder.

'You don't seem to have wondered why I've pulled away from you over the last few months. You didn't bother asking – you kept trying to contact me, sure, but it was to pull me back into the family fold. Maintain the status quo so nobody asked any embarrassing questions, like "why isn't Cornelia home for Yule?" or "what's Cornelia up to these days?" – although saying that, you probably have good answers for the latter thanks to the *extensive* surveillance you've had me and my friends under. Extensive, but sadly incomplete. And instead of asking *any* questions, you cut me off because you thought I'd come crawling back to you, begging for money. I might have zero financial skills but I will *never* ask you for anything again. AND,' she said, hammering in the final nail before either of them could speak, 'I know you killed Theodore. He probably got too close to figuring out one of your projects, right? Stumbled upon something damaging, and you offed him out of self-interest.'

The words hung in the air between them. Strangely, she felt no sense of satisfaction for having said them. She knew, deep down, that no matter what she said – how angry she got, how eviscerated the pair of them were by the time she was done – they'd never give her what she needed.

Her parents blinked at her, Imogen dabbing a handkerchief under her eyes. If Cornelia didn't know any better, she'd have said they were confused.

'Much to unpack there,' Ezra said eventually. 'But if we start with Theodore – you're wrong about that. Whoever told you we were responsible is lying to you.'

Cornelia didn't think she believed him. She also didn't think it mattered.

'What benefit would there be to lying about that?'

'I… don't know,' Imogen said. 'But we didn't… we *didn't*. We don't really know what happened to Theodore. It was quite a confusing night, do you remember, darling?' she asked Ezra. 'The power went, and… Of course we didn't kill anyone, that's a silly accusation.'

Cornelia thought she might believe her, but didn't think that mattered either.

In any case, she'd overplayed her hand.

'The rest of it, that's true?'

'The parts relating to the Council – these are closely guarded secrets, Cornelia. Things nobody should know anything about,' Ezra said.

'I know about Project HAUNT. I know the objectives. And I know about Project TRIAD. That you've all worked on both of them. That you still work on TRIAD now.'

Imogen lifted her chin, but thought better of whatever she was about to say.

'Your information is faulty, Cornelia. If such projects existed, it would be nonsense for every member of the Council to work on them. The security risks alone would be catastrophic,' Ezra said.

Sometimes his desire to correct her was useful: he'd confirmed the contents of the dossier, and accidentally confirmed he was still working on TRIAD.

'Okay, so assuming you both still work on TRIAD...' Imogen squinted, and Cornelia nodded her assent. 'All right, assuming *Ezra* works on TRIAD. Is Elisabella in the lake?'

Ezra looked to his wife for support. Or perhaps it was permission. Imogen gave him a tight-lipped nod, and looked past Cornelia as she spoke. Her eyes were colder than ever.

'The Council believes her soul could be in the lake, yes.'

'*Could* be?'

'We don't know enough about the inner workings of Samhain ghosts to be able to say for certain if Elisabella is in there, if she's whole, if she's recoverable. We will admit to finding it quite useful to study Theodore Wyatt in a natural environment following his untimely demise, as it gives us real-world data to apply to the ghosts here. Incomplete data, but better than nothing.'

'Say she is down there. How do you get her back up?'

'You don't. I have already told you this. The lake is designed to destroy anyone, Occult or Apparent, who goes into it alone.'

'Is that true?'

Ezra pointed to the wall of placards. 'The Ghoul Council takes the Do No Harm Charter very seriously. A huge portion of our work goes to preventing the resurgence of the Vampire Wars, as you know, and there were efforts in the past to ascertain the risk factor of housing Samhain ghosts in one localised area – meaning, in this case, Lake Wickermere. Too many died as a result.'

'Died how? Be specific.'

Ezra swallowed, but it was Imogen who spoke. 'It's worse than death. A single Samhain ghost in our domain is strong enough to raze an entire town, perhaps an entire city. All that energy contained in one location, the fury of being locked away in a ghostlight for however long… the Besiegement Curse has claimed the lives of too many. We got close to it happening again some years ago, and we have abandoned that aspect of the project.'

'But what did they do? What were their methods?' Cornelia asked, a hunch building. She needed Mallory and Diana to examine it with her.

'You're welcome to the dossier,' Imogen said. 'Satisfy your curiosity.'

She might as well have said 'and fuck right off'; the tone was indistinguishable.

'We are in an impossible position, Cornelia,' Ezra said. 'The Wickermere Reaper is asking us to choose between all of our lives and Agatha and Ethel's. We'd lay our lives down for you. Whatever it takes. But this… ghosts are a force of nature. Something that can't be overcome. Something money can't solve.'

He looked defeated, then. Cornelia could see the man before her was not the stoic he'd presented himself as, but someone who fought hard to veneer his life in rules and rituals and laws in order to preserve his standing in the world. A man who was now realising no number of rules, no amount of wealth, would ever be enough to stop someone hurting you if they wanted to.

The door cracked open.

'Sorry to listen in, but we'd like the dossier, please,' Mallory said.

Cornelia glanced back at her, saw the look in her eyes that

said there was an idea churning behind them, and nodded. 'We'll take it.'

'Hopefully then you will understand where we're coming from. Where we're always coming from, despite your evidently misplaced anger and hurtful, untrue diatribe. We want our beautiful daughters to live long, happy lives. Be mothers, and wives, and grow into strong women,' Imogen said.

Cornelia heard Mallory softly repeat this, and then Diana, her head poking into the room from beneath Mallory's armpit, snorted.

'What?' Imogen asked. 'It's true.'

'I think it's quite obvious that you don't really know your children. Don't know any of us,' Cornelia said. 'I've been wondering where Agatha and Ethel are, you know. If they're holding onto the belief that Mummy and Daddy will come to the rescue. If the life they're meant to lead is still stretching out before them. Or if they've given in to the panic. That so much time has passed. If they're wondering what amount of money was too much to hand over to get them back.'

Cornelia was being vicious, but she didn't care. They deserved vicious. They deserved rage.

A black ring binder straining to hold hundreds of pages appeared at a wave of Imogen's hand. She passed it to Cornelia.

'Cornelia, it is not my fault that you've never wanted to share anything with me. I don't know you because you've deprived me of the opportunity to,' she said, her voice cracking. 'You push me away, you don't tell me anything about your life. You turned up with that boy that time, and I thought you were finally settling down, figuring out your life.'

'That boy died,' Cornelia said. 'And he didn't know me either.'

Beckett hadn't been what one might call a *good* boyfriend, but he wasn't a bad one. She'd learned a surprising amount from him, the whole breaking-of-sacred-covenants aside.

'Maybe someday you'll grow up and accept your place here. We don't have time for any of this. Once again, Cornelia can't handle the attention being taken away from her for half a second,' Imogen snapped, the tears dissolving into rage.

'We're done here,' Mallory said quietly, putting her hand on Cornelia's arm. 'We've work to do.'

Cornelia sat hunched on the floor in front of the sofa, a cup of tea in her hands, while Mallory, perched above her, kept exclaiming 'They're idiots!' as she turned page after page in the dossier.

'Any second now you'll tell us what you're talking about,' Diana said.

'What do I keep saying about magic?'

'That it takes too much energy to do?'

'The other thing.'

'That it's literal,' Cornelia said, sitting up. Her hunch was growing, Mallory's scientific analysis confirming what Cornelia knew to be true.

Which the Wickermere Reaper must've known, too.

Mallory smiled at her. 'Yes. I had this sense when we were eavesdropping—'

'Shamelessly, even though I couldn't hear that well. Awkward silences are the most likely to make my ear ring, so it was more like Mallory eavesdropping with trepidation, and me shamelessly making her repeat what was being said,' Diana added.

'—that they hadn't considered the literal description of what they were saying was relevant—'

'That you can't go in *alone*,' Cornelia finished. 'The Wickermere Divers went in *alone*. The Apparents who died, died *alone* – I'm not going to think about that too hard, it's too sad.'

'Yes! This dossier pertains to what is probably an amended Project HAUNT report that was shared with the whole Ghoul Council, and likely the UML too, if Imogen was happy for us to read it.'

'Common-ish knowledge,' Cornelia said. 'What was it, a directive?'

'Yes. There were operations involving sending in *solo* Occult folk to try to recover… anything, really, from the lake. They've been trying to figure out how to access the lake without dying. If I had to guess – and you both know I don't like guessing, but it's more a hypothesis than a standard guess – I'd say Project TRIAD was resurrected right around the time the Broadwicks took over from Cornelius. It sounds like Ezra handles it solo now, despite what Olivia said about it ending. Someone *had* to have suspicions about the ghostlights and Elisabella.'

'Not just the Reaper, but other Council members too – maybe that's why TRIAD shut down,' Cornelia said.

Amid the panic and the genuine terror, she felt a bubble of normality at bouncing ideas off Mallory like this. She was a constant bright star in the centre of the universe. Cornelia fell into orbit around her so easily, it was like she was meant to be there.

'This is a file here relating to someone called Edwin Dorren. Index eighteen,' Mallory said, scanning the dossier and flipping to the back, using her hand to hold her place. She pulled out a slim paper packet, a slow smile creeping over her face as she examined the contents.

'That name rings a bell.' Cornelia had seen that name in some context, but could only dimly picture it, lost in the general soup of her thoughts.

'He started the initial legacy project that splintered off into TRIAD and HAUNT respectively. No, wait, his great-great… maybe add a few greats, but it's a long line of Dorrens who've been involved in Ternion-related Ghoul Council happenings. This Dorren – the last Dorren, from about sixty years ago; strangely, there doesn't seem to have been any since – died in an unrelated incident.'

'Hotly anticipating the part where we get to the point, if this is from sixty years ago,' Diana said.

'I'm getting to it – they've kept a note he had in his personal effects, from a few weeks prior to his death.'

<u>The clue has always been in the name.</u>
Power of three! Cornelius main opposition without evidence.
Convince necessity regarding the drafting of the TRIO bill with respect to future HAUNT and TRIAD Ghoul Council ventures near the lake. Convene <u>tomorrow</u>?
Assess findings with/after risk assessment (QED: initial test w/ two successful)

'After his death, there was a pause in all lake-related ventures, until we get to a redacted death that I think we can surmise was a HAUNT-related incident, and that was in Cornelius's cabinet, so about fifteen years ago – the Broadwicks were there for that.'

'What does that mean?' Diana looked between them like they were playing ping-pong.

'I'm getting to it. The Council sent in one person at a time on each mission – seems to be a special operation of Project HAUNT. Over the years it looks like there were a couple of cases where individuals fell or dived in themselves.'

'What happened to them? Like, afterwards – if the fear is, like Imogen said, the Besiegement Curse, what happened to them?'

'That is redacted, but it doesn't seem anyone survived for long.'

'Why not. Why not do a little more murder. Why not work for the Ghoul Council, where you too can become a ghoul,' Cornelia snarled.

'This is the interesting bit. They all took a tincture before getting into a – this bit's redacted, but I assume some sort of special boat – with – redacted, I'm guessing modified – diving gear, administered by… "WBM forward slash RC or JJ".'

'Ruby and Jo,' Cornelia said, already climbing to her feet.

'Does someone want to tell me what the fuck you're talking about, or should I go back to Wrackton and leave you to it?' Diana snapped.

'Sorry – you know how magic is literal?' Mallory said, turning to her. 'How I got Langdon to cross the Mayoral Office wards last year by holding his hand' – Cornelia blinked, taken aback. She had no knowledge of Mallory and Langdon going into the Offices together, and realised Mallory had just never told her, which made her feel weird in a way she couldn't shake – 'and you neatly sidestepped the UML directive preventing us from setting foot in Oakpass Manor—'

'By getting our good pal Grey Quinn to bodily drag us onto the grounds, yes,' Diana said. 'I get it, you think that two people could survive in the lake, because everyone keeps saying "alone"?'

'No! Edwin Dorren wanted to send *three* people into the lake years ago, because the clue was in the name. We've always known the Occult power of three. He, as suggested in his note, tested it with two people, and it *worked*. But the Council were afraid – *Cornelius* was afraid. He wouldn't have been in charge then, but we can assume his word carried weight. The Council avoid risks. But Dorren succeeded with two people, it just doesn't sound like he got to present his evidence!'

'He did die, though. I hear what you're saying, but he, crucially, did die,' Diana said fretfully.

Cornelia peered over Mallory's shoulder. 'Kicked in the head by his favourite horse.'

Diana's expression remained concerned.

'The Wickermere Reaper is a sadist, as we've said a hundred times at this stage. But they're asking for something *possible* to achieve. It's meant to be difficult, or *appear* impossible, but the point of it is to leave us feeling complicit in the deaths of Agatha and Ethel for failing to produce Elisabella. And I think that's another reason why the Reaper sent the revised ransom note to you, Cornelia – *you* could force the Council into giving you the answers in a way the Reaper couldn't, in endless meetings, without blowing their cover. The Reaper knows about Dorren's hypothesis – of course they do. But the Council still believe in the solo nature of the mission.'

'None of the Lake Divers had death dates in the same year,' Cornelia said, suddenly remembering where she'd seen Dorren's name: the wall in the War Room. 'I was looking when we went in to get the samples – fuck, that was only a few hours ago. Anyway, I noticed and thought it was strange, then thought it was just another example of Ghoul Council bureaucracy, and then forgot I'd thought it at all because it was, like, nine hundred thoughts before I'd moved to do sampling.'

'That was an evocative visit to the inside of your brain, thanks Cornelia,' Diana said. 'Okay, so we're proposing to actually go into the lake together?'

'I think I was proposing two of us do,' Mallory said. 'Someone needs to stay on land, keep an eye on the Council.'

'There's no way I'm letting you go into a ghost-riddled lake without me. I will literally go down with this ship.' She gestured between the two of them, and then her face fell. 'Fuck. Ghost-riddled means I won't be able to hear, and if there's no way of knowing what's in there, I can't risk…'

'Becoming ghoul dinner?' Cornelia said.

'Or something that would mean it was over for all of us bitches, and not just me.'

'All three of us going in would be a total suicide mission. Two of us going into the lake is just sending in the clowns.' Mallory smiled.

It was almost reassuring and so it took a second for Cornelia to understand what her friends were saying.

'I am partially outraged you'd still go ahead without me, but I think we'll find this isn't about me. I promise I'll kill you clowns myself if you get possessed by angry ghosts. I won't call you clowns again because I am legitimately fearful you're going to die, though I think Mallory – and Dorren – is right. It's so simple, so brilliant, so completely Occulture. *Two* people!'

'We do need to bear in mind …' Mallory hesitated, and Cornelia was sure she didn't want to hear what was coming next. 'The fact Imogen gave us the dossier so willingly, so *readily*, makes me wonder if…'

If Cornelia had to guess which of her parents was most likely to be the Wickermere Reaper – which of them had killed Theodore, which of them called the shots – it was Imogen.

'But what if Cornelia makes a mistake, and dies?' Diana asked.

'Cornelia's right here,' Cornelia interrupted. 'What's the tincture and when do I do it?'

'We,' Mallory corrected. She looked exhausted but determined.

As horrifying a concept as the whole thing was, if she had Mallory with her, Cornelia could do anything at all.

Even die.

TWENTY-FIVE

10:09:59

Cornelia pressed the Bonemarrow Cottage doorbell so rapidly, there was a lightning flash through the window. She followed up with the thunderous roll of her own voice shouting through the letterbox. Mallory hurried to catch up with her, clearly in pain, but she refused to go back to the Laurels despite Cornelia's suggestion.

'For the love of Elisabella, have you *completely* lost your manners?' Ruby demanded, ripping the door open. 'I don't like this habit of calling after midnight.'

She scanned Cornelia's face, and whatever she saw there made her step aside.

Stella strode up the hall, suspicion on her face. *What are you doing?*

Cornelia signed, *Saving Agatha and Ethel* – or, more accurately, *Me save twins*. She loved how straightforward signing was. The whole world would be better if everyone was able to be this direct all the time – before remembering Mallory needed her to translate aloud.

'I need the— What's it called, Mal?'

'Tincture,' Mallory supplied, and Cornelia finger-spelled it out.

She'd learned rudimentary BSL when she was younger and spent a lot of time foraging for insects in the Bonemarrow Cottage gardens – occasionally Stella would come out to see her. Between Stella and Ruby, Cornelia amassed an unusual vocabulary – sign words for various plants and insects, alongside the basics. She'd had a deaf lab partner in her final year of uni and got much better when she had someone to practise with. Stella could lipread, she knew, but Ruby had explained to eight-year-old Cornelia that Bonemarrow Cottage was Stella's house, and in Stella's house it was better to make the effort for Stella, instead of expecting Stella to do all the work.

It was a revelatory lesson on ableism – on audism especially – at such a formative age, and it was quite possibly thanks to Ruby that Cornelia had started to really question the way the Apparent and Occult worlds worked in general. She shuddered to think what kind of dickhead she could've turned out to be if the only adults she'd had around her were the Broadwicks. As it stood, she considered herself to only be a bit of a dickhead, but she had the whole rest of her life to fix that.

The twins would be there to see and be unimpressed by it. She'd make sure of it.

The one you gave the Ghoul Council, Cornelia continued. *To the people who went into Bonemarrow Lake.*

And they didn't come back! Stella signed. *I'm not helping you. This is stupid.*

Cornelia, Ruby said. *Don't make me get Jo down here.*

We need it. Please.

Ruby and Stella shook their heads as one.

You can't, Stella signed.

'They died,' Ruby said to Mallory as she signed, like she was imploring her to make Cornelia see sense. 'Every person we sent in there, Hexana help us, they all died. The Ghoul Council absolved us of any responsibility – there were hearings, extensive hearings, that concluded we followed protocol – but I cannot tell you what it's like to look into the eyes of someone who is willing to die for "the greater good" or what have you, and give them the poison that permits it. Besides, Stella's the one who made it.'

'Mallory figured it out, they didn't take it literally enough—'

'What do you mean?'

'I mean we think they made a mistake, sending only one Ghoul Council member in alone. They think you can't go in alone to the lake. We have evidence to support our idea that we go in together,' Mallory added quickly.

Ruby froze and Cornelia started stumbling through translating what Mallory said, restarting twice. It wasn't just the speed of signing – it was her desperation to get it right, to make Stella understand what she needed from her, that made her fumble.

Stella impatiently tapped Ruby on the shoulder to sign firmly, *WHAT DID SHE SAY?*

Ruby signed rapidly and Stella shook her head frantically, saying *no* over and over. Cornelia was pretty sure Mallory didn't need a translation for that one.

Please, Cornelia signed.

If Stella agreed, the others would be convinced. The Witches of Bonemarrow Lake worked surprisingly similarly to the Undetectables – if one could be convinced, the others would typically agree.

Please. We need to get them back. This is the only way. We're on borrowed time.

I'm sorry we couldn't help, Stella signed. *Sorry the Lyreflies didn't hatch in time.* She scrunched her eyes closed for a moment. *You're right. This is the only way.*

Cornelia launched herself at Stella, enveloping her in a hug. *Thank you*, she signed, pulling away.

'Fucksake,' Ruby said, but she was already unlocking the door at the end of the hall that led to the factory. 'This will take some time.'

'We were hoping you wouldn't say that.'

Ruby eyed Mallory, who Cornelia could see was doing her best impression of someone not on the verge of collapse.

'Use the time to rest. I'll have Stella text you as soon as we're ready. I need three hours, minimum. Scratch that, we'll meet at first light.'

They didn't need to be told twice.

Mallory fell into bed, though Cornelia had to be convinced by Diana, who was not taking any shit. Mallory privately wondered if Cornelia was grateful for the coercion; a reason to sleep that wouldn't feel like a selfish decision.

'Not to tell you what to do, but you're not going on a suicide mission on no sleep. That's stupid. We do many things as an agency, but we try to limit actual gobshite-level activity. Let's go.'

Diana shooed her into the bathroom and turned to Mallory. 'Keep an eye on her. Don't forget your meds.'

'Yes, Mother,' Mallory snorted, unable to hide how secretly happy she was that Diana was looking out for her. No matter how much time she spent around her friends, little reminders they loved and cared for her lifted her heart every single time.

Diana grinned at her, delighted. 'I'm going to tell Taylor you said that. But also, and on a serious note – for the love of Blair, don't die tomorrow. I love you both and I would be… upset.'

Cornelia came back and took off her glasses wordlessly. Mallory showed her that she'd set alarms – four of them, all for pre-five a.m. – and Cornelia turned off the light.

Mallory drifted off into an uneasy sleep, one filled with trepidation, the knowledge that her meds weren't going to have worn off by the time they got up and she'd still be drowsy, the knowledge the twins were out there somewhere in a hole in the ground and there was a chance they'd fail. That they'd die a horrible death in the lake. That she was wrong.

That she'd have to die knowing she'd failed Cornelia.

She woke to a scream.

Mallory rolled over, fumbling for the light.

Cornelia was bolt upright, the blankets clutched to her chest, tears streaming down her face as a strangled 'No! No! No! No! No!' escaped her over and over again, looking at nothing, her eyes filled with terror.

'Cornelia!' Mallory shook her, but Cornelia batted her off, fumbling with the blankets in an attempt to flee, her legs tangled in the sheets. She looked truly petrified.

Mallory pulled Cornelia against her, stroking her hair. 'Shh, hey, Cornelia! Hey, it's okay. You're having a nightmare, it's okay.'

Cornelia gasped, pulling away from Mallory for a second. Tears still flowed freely down her face. Mallory whispered again, gently, 'It's okay,' and Cornelia pressed her face into her shoulder.

Mallory let her sob and sob until she was ready to sleep again, stroking her hair and saying nothing more than 'It's okay, you're okay' over and over, the lie huge between them, but also not a lie at all: for the moment, Cornelia was safe. Whatever darkness she was chasing, whatever was about to happen with her family, whatever had already come to pass.

'Sorry,' Cornelia choked out, her voice hoarse. 'Sorry.'

'Don't be. Has that happened before?' Mallory asked, though she wasn't sure how she could've possibly missed hearing Cornelia screaming into the night in distress. Even if there was a chance Diana wouldn't have heard her from across the hall with her hearing aid out, Mallory woke at every little unfamiliar creak and scuffle.

'I don't know. I think so,' she whispered. 'Always someone… always someone in the room,' she said. 'Jacob.'

'Jacob?'

'Yeah.'

'What does he do?'

'Just watches. Sometimes sits on the bed. I can *feel* the bed dip when he does it, even if I can't really see his face. Like the Hat Man, but real.'

'The Hat Man…? No don't tell me, I don't want to know. Jacob's not real, Cornelia. I mean he is, but he's dead. We saw him buried. He's decayed remains. We got him that night, and he's gone now. The Dollhouse Murderers are safely behind bars, even if we have conflicted opinions about how any of that should work. The Wickermere Reaper is someone else, and we're going to get them too. He's not here now.'

Even if the Wrackton Digger now had his body.

It had pained her not to tell Cornelia the truth as soon as she'd returned to Wickermere, but she'd been having an honest-to-goddess panic attack. The night terror strengthened her resolve. She wouldn't tell her until this was over. Until they were home safe.

'He never left,' Cornelia said, her voice cracking. 'He made me frightened. All the things he did, all the murder and harming Theodore and taking our sense of safety from us in Wrackton. He *never left*.'

She meant inside her, Mallory realised. The Jacob in her head.

'Have you been feeling like this ever since…?'

'He took me from Vampire Cemetery? Yes, and no. Initially I was angry, and glad he was gone. But then I found every time I left the house, I wasn't able to breathe, like there was always someone right behind me, or like I was going to end up in a situation I couldn't escape from. I'd go places and feel this overwhelming sense that I was going to die and nobody would help me.'

'I'd help. Diana would too. And Theodore, if you gave him a chance and could wait for a thesis on the benefits of helping.'

Cornelia coughed out a laugh, then grabbed the glass from her bedside table and drained it.

'Do you think you should talk to someone about this?'

Mallory asked tentatively. 'Somebody qualified. Because there's no shame in it. We've been through a lot, all three— four of us. I think it's affected us in different ways. Diana with her hearing loss, me with my...'

You, she wanted to say, but didn't.

'I've tried. Online, mostly. I found someone a few months back, but it's hard. A lot of the treatment wants me to "sit with or work through my irrational fears" and it's... not irrational, or even unlikely to happen again, in our line of work. If not me, my sisters. And this time, if the Ghoul Council is the target, maybe it *could've* been me. It still could! If the Reaper could take both of them, who's to stop someone taking me again?'

Mallory didn't know what to say to that, so settled for taking Cornelia's hand.

'We would never let anyone hurt you. *Never*. We'll go to the ends of the earth to bring you back. I'd find a necromancer. We'd do séances. We'd do whatever it takes to keep you around. You will never, ever die, Cornelia Broadwick, because we'd make you impossible to forget.'

'Ternion-level impossible?'

'Even more so.'

'Good, because we know shit-all about the Ternion, apart from their names.'

Mallory laughed, then slipped out of bed. Her body ached, but she took Cornelia's glass and padded out to the kitchen to refill it. The glow from the fading fireplace embers lit the murder board, a reminder of how little time they had left.

She handed the glass back over, and turned the light off again, fighting to get comfortable.

'Hey,' Cornelia said. 'Sorry. But do you think…'

'What?'

'Doesn't matter. You're probably not feeling well enough, anyway.'

She shuffled down further into the blankets, and Mallory turned over so she was facing Cornelia's back. Hesitantly, her hand shaking, she reached over and pulled Cornelia closer to her. She hoped Cornelia couldn't feel her heart rabbiting in her chest.

'Oh thank Blair,' Cornelia mumbled. 'I just needed to be reminded that I'm still alive, and I couldn't if there was nothing touching me. I'm not a ghost, I'm real.'

'You're real. We're both here. In a couple of hours we're going to find Elisabella. We're going to take down the Wickermere Reaper, we're going to get Agatha and Ethel back alive, and it's going to be okay,' Mallory said.

Cornelia squeezed her hand in the dark.

TWENTY-SIX

5:36:11

Cornelia woke to find that she'd wrapped her arms around Mallory, and Mallory's hand had come to rest in her hair. Cornelia left it there, unwilling to move, watching Mallory's eyes flutter open and looking away as she anxiously extracted herself from Cornelia's wild mess of curls. She elected not to wonder why she felt slightly disappointed at her reaction.

Ruby was already at the lake with Jo and Stella, the former of whom was disgruntled at best to be out of bed with the sunrise – even though Cornelia had always thought older people loved getting up early and had anticipated there'd be a time when she, too, enjoyed getting up at the arsecrack of dawn – and the latter of whom kept signing to Cornelia, *Ask someone else to do this.*

The Bonemarrow Witches were waiting on the pier, a wooden structure studded with witchlights and a sign that said *CAUTION! TURN BACK!* that was rapidly becoming invisible as the rising morning fog ate up anything more than two feet from where Cornelia and Mallory stood struggling into wetsuits. They were, as Mallory's interpretation of the redacted dossier suggested, specially adapted, but that didn't make them any less disgusting to wriggle into. A red-painted boat bobbed and bumped against the pier, static rising and hissing with every ebb of the lake's surface. It was to be the only thing standing between them and the ghosts within. That, and the aforementioned wetsuits, which Cornelia was starting to resent by the second.

As the boat bumped gently against the pier, her eyes focused and she saw that it was not paint, but algae.

'Just to be clear,' Mallory said. 'Ghosts have to declare a Besiegement before it's enacted, right? There's a point where they'd have to *say* or indicate "I'm taking over your body"?'

'Theoretically,' Ruby said, her hand on Diana's back.

Diana, wrapped in a furry coat she'd found in a wardrobe in the Laurels, was staring at the equipment she'd liberated from the attic of the Laurels, where Project HAUNT materials had gone to die – as much as Cornelia didn't want to take anything from the Broadwicks, it was property of the Ghoul Council and not *technically* a handout – which amounted to a sonar device she was studiously wrangling with. Given Diana's absolute amazement of the Magic Magical Machine, Diana monitoring them was the scariest part of the entire operation.

'Won't the ghosts destroy the sonar?' Cornelia asked, still battling the wetsuit. She'd tried asking what protection it would offer against ghosts. Jo had called her an idiot, but Stella had said there was a sparse layer of iron filaments inside which could offer *some* protection, though their heads would be exposed and they'd never successfully stopped anyone dying.

It was the equivalent of using a sock as a stab vest, essentially. But if the sock was surprisingly heavy and had an evil texture.

'It uses sound waves, so not technically, but we can't be certain. It's not picking up the contents of the lake well – there's high concentration in the centre. The TV bank is giving off interference, and the notes I saw—'

'Stuff the notes, anything of value is in the centre,' Ruby said briskly, as Jo signed for Stella. 'You get through that fog and there'll be a blue glow and you won't be able to pull yourself away from it. That's where you're headed.'

'Hexana protect you,' Jo added, even though she sort of looked like she wanted to stab the assembled members of the Undetectables if it meant getting in from the cold faster.

Mallory rolled her shoulders as Cornelia tried not to panic at the feeling of the wetsuit touching her neck. It had been bone dry when she'd pulled it on, but it still somehow felt clammy, damp seeping in from the fog. She knelt down to stare into the water, static preventing her from seeing the bottom, though she had been assured her whole life that it had unfathomable depths.

Given how many ghosts were allegedly hanging out at the bottom of it, that seemed likely.

This will taste bad, Stella said, handing over the tincture.

It was an unnatural sort of blue that drinks sometimes were. All it was missing was a puff of smoke shaped like a skull and crossbones, and it would be cartoonish levels of don't-drink-that.

'What's actually in this, or do I not want to know?' Cornelia asked, eyeing it nervously.

'It's a painkiller, essentially,' Jo said. 'Because if you touch that water, it's going to be agony.'

Cornelia licked her lips, her mouth suddenly dry.

'And it will help you find the centre of the lake,' Ruby added. 'Or more specifically, Elisabella.'

'Down it like a shot?' she asked Mallory, who nodded grimly, linking her arm with Cornelia's.

'Better than sipping it,' Ruby said as the pair nodded and tipped the bottles back.

'What, does it have one of her toenails in it or something?' Cornelia said, swallowing and holding up the empty bottle. It tasted disturbingly like tomatoes with an undertone of old hay.

'Don't be ridiculous,' Ruby said. 'It's grave dirt from Wrackton.'

Cornelia tried not to gag, and Mallory pressed a hand to her mouth as she forced the tincture down, blanching.

The fog started lifting, but Cornelia wasn't sure if that was the tincture kicking in.

'Sonar's ready. I can't see much, but the boat is showing up, so that'll have to do,' Diana said cheerfully. 'Please don't die out there.'

'This is one of the less intelligent things we've done as an agency,' Cornelia said, letting Diana squeeze her shoulder. 'Any final requests? Not too late to back out.'

It was, in fact, too late to back out, but Cornelia wanted to pretend she had control over the situation. They had to do this. It was the only shot they'd have at getting the twins back alive.

Mallory took her hand and Cornelia felt a jolt through her heart.

'Let's do it.'

It was warm. Unreasonably warm for a May morning, suggesting the lake's ambient temperature was not dictated by something as insignificant as the external weather. Cornelia rowed – figuring out the oars had taken a minute – her back to the centre of the lake while Mallory called out instructions, her hands clamped around her knees. Every stroke further into the fog made the air hotter and hotter, static fuzzing loudly as it hissed and popped off the sides of the boat. Water sprayed into the air as she lifted the oars. She'd left her glasses with Diana, who had disappeared from view practically the second they'd set out, and everything was coated in a filmy blur, just the two of them on the lake.

And several hundred ghosts.

The boat tipped dramatically and Cornelia put her hands out to the sides.

'They said don't fight it if this happens,' Mallory reminded her. 'If we go in, we go in.' She rummaged around the bottom of the boat and found the safety lines. She tossed one to Cornelia, fixing the other to the loops at her waist. 'And if we start getting dragged around down there, unclip or cut the line.'

She did not say that it was to give the other a chance to get back into the boat and survive.

Cornelia touched the blade at her waist. Normally, she'd be glad of the encouragement carrying such a dignified weapon, but it offered no comfort. It's not like one could stab a ghost, even with an iron knife.

The boat tipped again as they neared the blue glow that rose from the centre of the lake, more visible now despite the fog closing in around them. Cornelia's pulse remained steady and calm, probably thanks to the tincture.

The boat tipped a final time and they went over the edge, Mallory calmly allowing herself to be dumped into the water. Cornelia, despite her slowed heartbeat, flailed and fought it, getting tangled in her line while the boat floated away. There was a roar of static in her ears, like many old televisions bursting into life at once.

'Cornelia?' Mallory called, her voice muffled, and Cornelia kicked upwards towards the sound. She grabbed Cornelia's hand.

'She said try not to close your eyes.' Mallory's voice, distorted.

Cornelia felt she was disappearing into a dream. Her limbs relaxed, pulling her down, down, down.

Her brain tried to separate images from reality as her skin crawled, as though tiny insects had burrowed into her wetsuit and were making themselves at home in her skin. Even entomologists had insect limits, and this was Cornelia's.

Two realities spun out before her: the one where Mallory had her hand gripped so tightly it must've hurt, and the one where she was in a cemetery, a hand on her shoulder and a face she knew, and how immediately disarmed she felt, and the world around her disappearing as she tumbled and tumbled and found herself on her knees in a cage, that same face looking at her but everything changed.

She looked up to see Jacob wading towards them, his coat flapping in the breeze that whipped around his torso, water dripping from the wet curls beneath the beanie he always wore, sodden now.

She shook her head, flailing backwards, and he disappeared

like he'd never been there at all. Static lifted around her and Mallory disappeared from sight. She felt the tug of the dive line.

Gripping it with her hands, she pulled herself towards the boat and clambered back in, gasping, but safe. Inches of wood between her and the lake.

It took too many long, drawn-out seconds for Cornelia to feel a stab of panic until she saw Mallory surface, her hands taut on the dive line.

Cornelia reached out a hand for her, bracing against the far side of the boat, and helped pull her in.

She didn't let go as Mallory tumbled over the side of the boat, pulling her down with her.

She didn't move as Mallory stared at her, taking shallow breaths.

'Where'd you go?' Cornelia asked.

Mallory used her free hand to push her hair away from her face. 'Needed to try to get our bearings, see what we can see.'

'And?'

'Lots. Lots to see.'

'I thought it kind of shimmered like a mirage,' Cornelia said, her eyes on Mallory's.

'Mirage is a good word for it, it moved away the closer I got,' Mallory said. 'Weird observation, but it looked very… organised? There's plenty of ghostlights down there, but they were neatly arranged. Like there's some sort of ghost hierarchy. Which is strange, because surely we should've encountered some kind of ghost by now. Though it's unsurprising that nobody really knows what it's like out here, they weren't able to get any information out of the Ghoul Council folk who died in here, or the Apparents who wandered into Wickermere. Really not sure what it is about this Lake that screams “touch me, I’m not going to murder you”.’

The boat continued to bob gently on the surface of the lake, spinning slowly.

Cornelia felt a strange, insistent need to close her eyes, so she did. She saw flashes of what she could only describe as nightmares. Jacob, the Dollhouse Murderers, the cruel shovel of the Wrackton Digger. Theodore appeared to her and waved at her. Mallory floated in front of her, dead, burns covering her arms. Her sisters’ lifeless bodies, rictus grins pressing close to her face and whispering she was worthless.

Cornelia opened her eyes and saw Mallory had done the same thing, though tears had filled Mallory’s eyes when she opened them again, curled in around herself like her heart was breaking.

‘You were crying. You and Diana. You’re both dead. You both died,’ Mallory said, each sound fighting to break free of her throat.

‘We didn’t. It’s the lake, it’s the ghosts. I think we’re seeing histories mixed up with dream fragments,’ Cornelia said, though she wasn’t sure why she was so sure about it. She’d think about it properly later, if they survived.

She risked raising her head and saw vampire corpse after vampire corpse after vampire corpse floating, all fixing her with the same accusatory glare. She didn’t know what it meant. A woman lit in a soft glow swam towards her, hand outreached. Cornelia felt she knew her, but couldn’t say why or how.

‘She’s here,’ Mallory said. ‘Elisabella is here.’

There was nobody in front of her, but she grabbed the side of the boat and stepped out before Cornelia could do anything but grasp pathetically at Mallory's wetsuit sleeve.

For a split second, Mallory floated forward, and then her body was dragged down, down, and out of sight.

'MALLORY,' she shouted, her hand stinging where she'd tried to grab her.

Cornelia screamed, frustration tearing through her as the bubbles denoting where Mallory was disappeared in a swirl of fog.

Their history flashed in front of her eyes, seeing herself through Mallory's. Cornelia bouncing into the room the night Mallory thought Diana died, her eyes bright. Cornelia kissing Beckett in the Larix. Cornelia sobbing in her room, the funeral, wearing the gloves Mallory had sent her – the gloves she loved more than anything she'd ever owned – Cornelia's birthday, Cornelia in the suit she'd worn to Grey Quinn's Equinox Ball. Cornelia sobbing in the dark.

That one made her pause. She didn't remember that. Didn't remember being hugged by Mallory, or telling her about Jacob. She'd thought that was a dream.

'MALLORY!' She reached a hand out of the boat in desperation, colliding with her in a tangle of limbs as Mallory resurfaced and dragged herself over the side, kicking Cornelia and knocking her down even as she tried to cushion both of their falls so that Mallory was practically on top of her.

She took Mallory's hand automatically, wrapping another hand around her waist.

'Don't let go again. Please don't let go again. I can't lose you. I can't.'

Mallory buried her face in her neck, shivering. 'I saw her. She told me it was safe.'

'Don't. I don't trust anyone here.'

There was another flash of something like memory. This time Cornelia could see her and Mallory on the picnic blanket in the demon cemetery from above, her own hesitation when she'd accidentally suggested they should go on a date. The looks exchanged between them. Taking her hand when she'd answered the phone to Imogen.

The way she was always finding a way to touch her, brush against her skin, check in on her. The way Mallory had been the one to take action after the phone call, to stop Cornelia falling apart. The way she'd noticed Cornelia had not been okay and had deteriorated over the last year and a bit, even as Cornelia rebuffed every attempt by Mallory to check in on her.

A look at Mallory told her she was seeing it too.

A floorboard creak and Diana's voice, insisting she had feelings for Mallory.

All of it rising in her now, her limbs on fire, her heart beating furiously, telling her what had been in front of her this whole time.

The first thought she'd had when Mallory had been dragged away from her was that she'd never had the chance to tell her how special she was.

A thing she couldn't say aloud, for fear of breaking some kind of spell, something unspoken.

'It's not fair,' Mallory said softly, and Cornelia knew she meant this.

Them. The things they were seeing. The truth that hung between them.

'I mean, it is,' Mallory amended. 'You haven't done anything wrong. I'm just so sick of waiting, of biding my time. I keep giving you space, I keep trying not to say anything. I heard you and Diana talk about me last year, and then we're sharing a bed and you're sleeping wrapped around me and I let myself think that there's something there, but it's all a dream, isn't it?' She laughed a little; the sound was her heart breaking. 'This isn't real. This will never be real, and I am in danger of utterly destroying our friendship if—'

Cornelia reached up a hand and rested it on the side of Mallory's head, her thumb on her cheek, forcing her to look at her.

Mallory had bared her soul, and Cornelia knew what she wanted.

Knew that Diana was right.

Knew she'd always felt this way and had blithely ignored it for years, letting it stay out of reach of her consciousness.

'I just—' Mallory started again, her face tilting closer, and Cornelia kissed her.

She felt herself melting into it, pushing everything else out of her head.

It was as though her whole life had been one big lead-up to this.

She pulled back, searching Mallory's eyes to make sure this was okay, but Mallory closed the distance between them again, her fingers tangling in Cornelia's hair, one hand on the back of her neck, drawing her closer, kissing her deeper.

Cornelia wrapped her other arm tightly around her waist, pressure light but firm so she didn't hurt her, her brain telling her the wetsuits were in the way and she had just enough awareness to remind herself that removing any layers in this place was a bad idea, no matter how badly she wanted to get as close to Mallory as she could.

In the end Mallory was the one who broke away, gasping, her thumb still stroking Cornelia's cheek.

'We don't have time for this,' she said, her eyes on Cornelia's lips. 'Not now. We have to find… we have to find…'

Cornelia's vision swam again, the warmth of the water calling to her, asking her to close her eyes, step out of the boat, and sink down into it.

'Is this real?'

'I stopped kissing the love of my life to continue a case. I would say that's pretty real,' Mallory said, exasperated.

'Tell me something only Mallory would know.'

Mallory smiled, running a finger down Cornelia's nose, making her smile too. 'You know everything there is to know about me.'

'No, I mean something we can check later. Something we can point to, that's concrete. In case this is a dream.'

'This is something a dream would say,' Mallory said, pressing a kiss to Cornelia's cheek, her forehead, her neck, and Cornelia's grip on her tightened, her skin burning from the contact, and she had to fight to stop herself wrapping her hands in her hair.

'One thing,' she said instead, bringing her lips to Mallory's ear. 'One thing so I can know this really happened.'

Mallory paused, then tilted her chin so she was speaking into the tiny exposed section of Cornelia's neck. 'I've never in my life wanted four sugars in my tea.'

Cornelia laughed, incredulous. '*What?*'

'Every cup of tea you've ever made me has been wrong.'

'Why didn't you say something?!'

'You were so proud of remembering, I didn't want to tell you. I guess I was just happy I was worth remembering at all.'

'But wait. Wait! When we were twelve, you had tea and you said, "I can't have this with less than four sugars," do you remember?'

'That was *an Irish coffee* you and Diana insisted on drinking that Yule, and I refused to drink it because it was disgusting.'

Cornelia pulled Mallory to her, laughing so hard her body shook Mallory's too. She pulled back and wiped the tears from her face.

'That's a good one.'

The promise of later was enough to allow them to disentangle, Cornelia's thumb rubbing circles on the back of Mallory's hand.

'I think we've made it to the middle,' Mallory said.

'How can you tell? I can't see the banks anymore.' Cornelia squinted, suddenly aware of just how big a mile was in comparison to a human.

'Well, a whirlpool has formed right in the centre of that glow, and we're at the edge of it,' Mallory said, and then the bow of the boat got sucked down towards the deepest point of the lake.

Cornelia held her breath for as long as she could as the

boat sank lower and lower, feet of water rising above her head, until it felt like she would burst. She let it go in a gasp, only to realise she could breathe, and sucked in lungfuls of air, her head clearing as the light diffused into a cyan haze around her. She looked to Mallory, who rested her hand on the side of the boat, rubbing it over the algae-mottled surface and mouthing something at her that Cornelia couldn't understand as water rushed over and past them, the boat tipping ever down, down, down towards the bed of the lake.

As they got closer, it was clear just how many ghostlights littered the bottom of the lake, like shells or pennies in a fountain, glittering in the blue light emanating from the one they wanted. It was as though it had been waiting for this. Waiting for someone – some*ones* – to come and find it.

Leaning over the edge of the boat, Cornelia used her hands to move them both closer to the ghostlight, squinting against the brightness and wishing she had her glasses, or a camera. Everything was bathed in blue.

Which meant she could see the skeletons littering the bottom of the lake. Some were animal, but there were skulls and femurs and ribs and so, *so* many metatarsals that Cornelia felt a bit sick to think of the sheer number of folk who'd come down here and this was the last thing they'd seen. An underwater cemetery.

She pulled the boat closer to the ghostlight, Mallory helping once she realised what Cornelia was trying to do. The boat bumped over another skull and dislodged a witchlight from its orbital socket. Cornelia hoped they hadn't cracked the skull; that would've added insult to injury.

At last, they were upon it. Glowing so brightly it was practically audible, the ghostlight – *actual fucking* Elisabella – rested atop tangle of bones, another ghostlight attached to it like a limpet, this one dark and empty.

Cornelia pointed, signing *bag*, which was universally understandable. Mallory reached down to grab the bag from the floor of the boat, and the tangle of bones – possibly a complete set – moved around it like they were trying to protect it. Cornelia plunged her hands in and Mallory attempted to push the bones back, shaking free a large, bone-handled knife.

She met Cornelia's gaze.

These were probably Elisabella's remains.

Cornelia got the ghostlight – and its freeloading, empty companion – into a bag that she secured at her hip. Darkness descended and Cornelia scrambled to push the boat off the lake floor. Her hand connected with the bone handle of the knife Mallory had found, and she hesitated, tempted to shove it into the bag too, but decided against it. Taking unknown artifacts from ghosts was, perhaps, both reckless and a dick move.

The witchlight she'd dislodged brushed off her arm, a vague glimmer from within like the reflection she sometimes saw in a bug's elytra, or a human eye.

She sat in the boat properly, and Mallory's hand closed on hers. There was a shudder, and the boat jerked, like the lake understood they wanted to leave, the oars hitting the sides as the lake returned them, granting them permission to leave for shore.

TWENTY-SEVEN

4:10:54

It wasn't particularly reassuring to learn that nobody had expected them to survive.

When the boat docked and Mallory had clambered out, Diana was there, helping, before Cornelia had thought to hold out a hand to Mallory.

Then Diana and Stella began a rigorous process of poking them both in the shoulders repeatedly, finally ending in Diana throwing a – thankfully sheathed – iron knife at Cornelia. Predictably, it bounced off her shoulder, but made her exceptionally angry in the process.

'We don't have time for this, we're not *dead*,' Cornelia said. 'Thank you, Edwin Dorren and Mallory. But mostly Mallory.'

It's a miracle you aren't, Stella signed, but she looked happy to see them, handing Cornelia a towel while Ruby and Jo fussed over Mallory.

She'd gone pale, her arms shaking as she attempted to dry her hair. Cornelia wanted to offer to do it for her, but couldn't bring herself to ask.

The lake felt like it had been a dream. Like she'd entered another dimension and left with something almost tangible, but she couldn't bring herself to verify it had happened. Mallory had not looked at her since they left the boat. She could still feel the ghost of Mallory's lips on hers, her hands remembering the feel of her hips, her waist, but in the way one might recall a particularly vivid dream.

'Diana, I promise if we died in the lake, you'd know,' Mallory said. 'You didn't see anything on your sonar?'

'Just the boat floating around for an age, then it disappeared completely. You were in there for over an hour, we were convinced you weren't coming back. I was fully prepared for it to be Diana and Associates at the Undetectables. Taylor would've been promoted to full-time junior member so it wasn't just me and Theodore and a bunch of machines.'

'Nice to know we'd have been missed,' Cornelia said, accepting the hoodie Diana tossed to her and letting the towel fall to the wooden slats of the pier. She wriggled back into her clothes after a slapdash attempt at drying herself off.

'You would! I'd be continuing your legacy,' Diana said.

There was tangible relief on her face, so Cornelia couldn't be too angry about it all.

'What now?' She tapped the bag with the ghostlight in it. That, at least, was real. 'Do we try to draw out the Reaper immediately, or…?'

'We—' Mallory started, staring at Cornelia's upper arm. She looked down, confused, and saw a smudge of red, stark against the bottle-green fabric, that she initially thought was blood until she peered closer.

'Like Stella's shirt,' Cornelia said, looking back at the boat, bobbing in the water. The fact they could breathe.

I don't know what that is. Stella looked disgusted. *Burn the shirt, I don't want it back.*

But Cornelia thought she knew – and so did Mallory.

'I can't believe I didn't think of this before the lake – we were looking *right* at it,' Mallory said breathlessly. She was still pale, but her eyes were bright. 'I think this will help narrow it down! I need… I don't think I have enough lab equipment with me, what am I going to—'

'Microscope!' Cornelia said, picturing the one in her bedroom. She knew exactly what Mallory was talking about and felt a rush of hope again.

'Are you two going to finish a sentence so I can also know what's going on, or did the lake give you the power of secret language?' Diana demanded, and Cornelia felt herself flushing.

'I'll get the microscope, get yourselves back to the Laurels. Diana, help her,' Cornelia said, signing thanks to Ruby, Jo and Stella over and over.

Good luck, Stella signed, as they left the Witches of Bonemarrow Lake on the pier.

'I took a scraping off the boat, it's visually the same algae as in the place Lucy was sequestered,' Mallory said, her eye pressed to the microscope eyepiece.

She slid it to Cornelia, who looked at the two slide samples Mallory had hastily – but still neatly – prepared, one from Stella's shirt, and the other from the boat. Both samples had near-identical elongated cell patterns, regular segmented patterns along each 'branch'.

'Thank Hexana you brought all that back with you.' Diana turned the ghostlight around and around in her fingers.

She'd managed to detach the empty ghostlight from Elisabella's, and was, at her own insistence, 'thinking of a good hiding place for it'. Given that she'd hidden Blair's ring in a dollhouse for five months before getting around to telling anyone about it, Cornelia couldn't imagine it would be a stretch to hide Elisabella herself. She returned her attention to the algae samples, using precious seconds to try to spot any major differences.

'I'm holding an actual goddess in my hands, and that's not a line I'm using on a girl. I should use it on *my* girl, though. She'd like that,' Diana said.

'They're the same, aren't they?' Mallory said, ignoring Diana.

Cornelia nodded.

'What is all this for?' Diana asked finally. She had, in fairness, been quite patient.

'Like, what are we doing here?'

'The algae is how the Wickermere Reaper's victims are breathing while they're buried underground,' Mallory said patiently.

'And it's the same algae pulled off Stella's shirt, and presumably a modified relative of the algae we saw on the walls in the cottage Lucy was being held in,' Cornelia added.

Diana stopped twirling the ghostlight. 'Okay, so now we know the *how*, but I don't see how that—'

'Only someone who worked on Project HAUNT would

know the specifics of how the algae works,' Mallory said. 'It's been modified – it's readily available, it'll grow anywhere damp, but the Ghoul Council redacted this information. They all put Lucy in Informant Jail without trial simply because those were Council rules, I can't see them easily sharing information between projects – those redacted files were for internal use only. Nova and Harry didn't work on HAUNT, which makes them both unlikely to be the Reaper.'

'But that's not evidence,' Diana said. 'I know, I know, you two do the science and I do all the people stuff. But there's nothing to say the Reaper couldn't find the information somehow – someone has to redact the files, which means *someone* had the information. If Harry is the Reaper and is using persuasion magic on other members, he could persuade them to share the information redacted from the files. Maybe Lucy *did* pass information to—'

'Okay, okay, *fine*. If this helps convince you to narrow down our suspect pool, *fine*,' Cornelia snapped.

'When all this is over, we need to see a doctor about getting you a personality transplant,' Diana grumbled, but her heart clearly wasn't in it. Instead of replying as she usually would, Cornelia put her hands in her hair, pacing back and forth.

'We need something concrete in the next five minutes or we need to drop the clue altogether, we can't keep wasting time on— Mallory! Did you do a preliminary magic sample test on Stella's t-shirt?' Cornelia rubbed her hands together vigorously in a manner that Diana usually referred to as 'praying mantis, but worse'.

'No,' Mallory said slowly, colour draining from her face.

'And we can't go back and try it with the Magic Magical Machine, plus the beetles—'

'Fuck the beetles!' Cornelia said. 'No, no, I don't mean that. But what's the only thing better than magical forensics?'

'Regular forensics?' Diana suggested.

'Cornelia, I've done this *once*, with Theodore, in proper laboratory conditions. I've been reliant on the Machine, I don't—' Mallory started, but Cornelia was on a roll.

'You can do this. If there's a magic trace on that t-shirt, we can extract it manually like you would a regular DNA sample! We have the Sprinter— We need a chelation agent. *You* need a chelation agent.'

'We'd need something like boron, maybe, or—'

Cornelia tore out of the Laurels before Mallory could finish speaking, slamming open the door of the little greenhouse where Ethel kept most of her plant stuff, knocking over bottles of liquids. She swore under her breath until she found a little spray bottle and ran back to the Laurels.

'I have EDTA! Ethel has all sorts of plant bollocks out there, can you do it?' Cornelia panted.

'She didn't need you at all for that conversation,' Diana said to Mallory, who shushed her, snapping on a pair of gloves.

Mallory pulled Stella's t-shirt out of the evidence bag – her insistence on following protocol at all times meant it wasn't contaminated – and gestured at the bag of lab equipment they'd torn into to assemble the sample slides.

'Diana, can you hand me a test tube, some scissors, and set up a beaker of water over a heat source?'

To her credit, Diana did what she was asked while Cornelia

practically vibrated with impatience. Mallory cut up a section of t-shirt into tiny pieces, dropped them into the test tube and added the solution Cornelia had brought her. She worked steadily, barely looking up except to give instructions of things she needed. Real forensic science was a lot like magical forensic science, in that it felt impossible to achieve.

'There's a sample here,' Mallory said, a short while later – seconds felt like hours, so Cornelia wasn't sure how much time – 'but one major sticking point has occurred to me, which is that *Stella* is a witch. I don't have the samples from testing the Ghoul Council because Theodore destroyed them, and I can't compare the readouts from the Sprinter to what we find here, if anything. *If* this yields a magic trace, we— Scratch that, I have a magic sample from Stella! I didn't bother testing them when we'd figured out the Reaper was likely on the Ghoul Council, the swabs are over there! If we introduce the sample to a solvent, the magic DNA should take on the same colourways as when we put samples into the Machine, but it will hopefully be distinct enough that we can visually compare them. A lot of hoping, basically. Diana, set up the Sprinter?'

'The Sprinter, our old friend!' Diana pulled it out and hugged it. 'We thought we were too good for you, but we were wrong! Star of our show! Love of my life! Except for Taylor.'

Cornelia got the sense Diana was trying to mask a small amount of panic with outsized enthusiasm. It was almost working.

'I'm going to need card, or heavy paper, and… where are we going to find ethanol?'

'Wait, I can help with that!' Diana ran up the stairs and

came back down with a bottle of hand sanitiser, and Mallory and Cornelia got to work constructing two makeshift chromatography testing stations.

'With a little ethanol squeeze, and a *fucktonne* of luck, you too can… do science,' Diana said, leaning on the edge of the table as Mallory got the samples ready.

It was, for want of a better word, *scrappy* – they used pens to hang the paper in the solvent. Waiting to see if their t-shirt DNA sample would yield anything was *agony*, but a rust-coloured pattern appeared across the paper.

Two rust-coloured patterns, in fact.

'We have two distinct magic samples,' Mallory said breathlessly. 'The magic sample we got from the t-shirt *isn't* Stella's. It's likely the Reaper's. And while the colour isn't as distinct as it would be if we'd put it through the Machine, I *think* this is another witch sample, but let's see if the Sprinter can really confirm that.'

'Moment of truth.' Cornelia placed the t-shirt sample on the Sprinter. Much like an Apparent fingerprinting machine, the database of the Sprinter could only match a spell they already knew and had loaded into it.

The Sprinter beeped within seconds.

MATCH FOUND: REMINDER SPELL

'The Witches told us Stella kept telling them she needed to do something! It was magic! I *knew* the Reaper was going to fuck up eventually,' Cornelia said, some of the confidence in the Undetectables she'd had a day ago pouring back into her. 'And here we are. The only thing they're going to be reaping is consequences of—'

'I am satisfied that that's witch magic.' Mallory pointed at the screen after Diana nudged Cornelia out of the way so they could both see. 'The Sprinter isn't good at nuance unless we *give* it nuance – if it was witch magic performed by a non-witch, the Sprinter wouldn't recognise it. So neither Harry nor Nova could perform the spell. We can eliminate both of them. That leaves us with Dot, Ezra, Imogen and Olivia as possible suspects.'

'I'm really sorry your family possibly doubly sucks,' Diana said.

'Thank you,' Cornelia said, meaning it. 'Diana, I have a sort of plan, but I'll need you to pull out all the stops. We can't just confront the witches on the Ghoul Council, we need to do this softly, gently, and act like we don't have the upper hand.'

'Whatever you need me to do, I'll do. Well, almost anything. I'm not kissing either of your parents, for example.'

'What's the plan?' Mallory asked.

'Do you trust me? Both of you?'

Mallory and Diana nodded.

'Then follow my lead.'

'Just a second, I'm hiding the upper hand in a safe place,' Diana said, holding up the ghostlight with Elisabella in it. 'I'll keep the empty one on me as a decoy.'

'It's going in your diorama, isn't it?'

'Shut up, Cornelia.'

'Imogen, darling,' Diana said, moving to embrace her. The Broadwicks were in the foyer of Rowan House, standing around Lucy's desk like they'd never seen a computer before. Olivia was sorting through a stack of papers while Dot poured tea for each of them. Harry was pacing back and forth. Nova was nowhere to be seen.

If Imogen was confused by Diana's approach, she didn't show it. Her eyes were puffy from crying. Or perhaps from not getting enough sleep, from being the Wickermere Reaper. Cornelia couldn't stop looking at her like she was a murderer, like she or Ezra or Dot or Olivia could be the Reaper, and she didn't know how to feel apart from angry.

'I've had a splendid idea, but I don't suppose you'll like it. I want us to do it safely, and properly.'

'What is it, Diana?' Imogen brushed a lock of hair from Diana's face. 'You always were my favourite among Cornelia's friends. And you've been such a good friend to the twins, too, in absentia.'

Diana, to her credit, didn't flinch. 'It's so simple, I can't believe we didn't think of this before. We have a way – *you* have a way, with the Council, to contact the past victims.'

'We can't contact the families, we already told you this,' Ezra said.

'Yes, subsection eighty-four—' Harry started.

'That's not what she said,' Dot said. 'Listen to her. Could be the first good idea any of us has had in days.'

'I'm listening,' Imogen said to Diana, like neither Cornelia nor Mallory were there.

'I don't mean the families. I mean the victims.' Diana all but batted her eyelashes. 'Oh, it's so silly of us not to have thought of this before, but we should do it now.'

'Do what?' Olivia asked.

Diana smiled, saying the words exactly as Cornelia had told her to.

'All in favour of hosting a séance, say aye!'

TWENTY-EIGHT

3:09:02

The Ghoul Council readied themselves with surprising expedience.

'I don't have a *single* thing that would do for wearing to a séance,' Diana hissed as they gathered up candles from a storage cupboard near the kitchen.

'That's not the most pressing concern,' Mallory said fretfully, digging around a shelf of bottles and selecting one filled with what could only be described as 'violently green' liquid.

Cornelia had resumed pacing, unable to make herself focus on a single part of the task at hand. She was just glad her friends had better control of their executive functions.

'What could *possibly* be more important?' Diana asked, grinning widely.

'We don't even know if it'll work,' Mallory said. 'When Apparents do it, they just decide it's a little girl ghost, or a grumpy Victorian aristocrat, or their beloved grandmother, and they've no idea if they're being lied to or not!'

'Oh, don't worry,' Diana said airily. 'It won't matter if this works, we just have to make the Reaper *think* it's working. Unless the Wickermere Reaper is a Broadwick, in which case we're all fucked anyway.'

'I have some concerns about the scientific merits of séances,' Mallory said carefully. 'I've seen signs advertising them in the Larix, and I've ignored them. Mostly because I thought they were yet another *Visit Wrackton* tourism thing for Apparents. And while I know absence of evidence isn't evidence of absence, I have always assumed that ghosts needed to be… visible. Although Kingston suggested—'

'Oh no, they're real. Observer Johnson facilitates. I know Felix went to talk to Ben,' Cornelia said, hating herself for cutting across whatever Mallory was about to say about Kingston, especially when a look of genuine sadness crossed Mallory's face. Cornelia hastened to add, 'Not because they missed them – they did – but because Ben was the last one with the spare keys to their tour van and they'd lost the others.'

'Should we call Observer Johnson?' Diana paused, holding an impressive number of candles in one hand. 'Really up the ante, or whatever the phrase is.'

'No time, Nova will have to do. Assuming they can be convinced to help,' Cornelia said, straining to get the old cathode TV they'd found in a storage cupboard – thankfully in the main house and not all the way down in the Ghoul Council Headquarters – onto casters so she could roll it to the War Room. So much of this plan hinged upon their collective ability to be convincing. 'Otherwise there's no point in trying. It would be like bringing Diana into an operating theatre and hoping she knew how to perform brain surgery.'

'First of all, fuck you. Secondly, it's not like all of Occulture instinctively know how to talk to ghosts,' Diana said. 'Just because they're the Ghoul Council doesn't mean they know *everything* about ghosts. Maybe we can blag this.'

'Blag what?' a voice said, and they turned as one to see Nova leaning against the wall. It was unclear how long they'd been watching.

'I trust the Broadwicks have brought you into the fold?' Diana asked coolly.

'I'd much rather your version,' Nova said, examining their nails. They were wearing a long blue cloak, runes drawn onto their skin, and Cornelia bit back a smile.

No matter what Nova said, they were at least attempting to appear like they were helping.

'We want to speak to past victims of the Wickermere Reaper, try to see if any of them spoke face-to-face and could give us any clues that might help us locate the twins.'

It sounded a lot better than the truth, which was 'we are attempting to trap the Wickermere Reaper into revealing themself because we have no other option than to try get a step ahead of them before we present the bargaining chip Diana hid where nobody could find it'.

'You want to ask the dead what they can tell you about living?'

'Yes.'

They considered her. 'Okay.'

'Just like that? Okay? No red tape?'

'We have provision for emergency séances, as it happens.'

'If that's the case, why haven't you called one before now?'

'Because it didn't seem like that kind of emergency,' they said.

Dot led them into the War Room. The drapes had been replaced with silky black fabric. The lights were off, the table laden with concentric circles of candles. Witchlights glowed in the centre, warm white and electric blue.

Cornelia remembered looking at Mallory underwater in the lake in blue light and shook her head to clear it. Now wasn't the time.

'You can put the TV over there,' Dot said, and Cornelia wheeled it into position.

Diana dumped her extra candles on the table and put one in front of each seat. Harry, Dot, Imogen, Ezra, Cornelia, Diana, Mallory, Olivia, Nova. These would remain unlit for the duration of the séance.

Mallory got to work pouring out shots of absinthe, sliding them in front of each Ghoul Council member.

'Not for me, thanks,' Harry said, handing out carved sticks. 'Teetotal.'

Wordlessly, Diana poured a shot of juice. 'It's symbolic, apparently,' she said to Cornelia's look of confusion.

She jerked her head in the direction of Nova, who was sitting with their knees pulled up on the chair, eyes closed, robe folded around one of Harry's sticks on their lap.

'I'll take juice as well,' Olivia said softly.

Diana poured it and placed it in front of her, and Olivia flashed her a grateful smile.

Less dazzling than it had been the first few times Cornelia saw it, but now she *saw* what it was she'd instantly liked and speed-run a crush over: the way Olivia carried herself, her intelligence, the smile… they were all things she'd loved about Mallory since she was old enough to figure out her own likes and dislikes.

Silly, really, that it took an outside force to make her see the truth that had been right in front of her the whole time.

(Or, if she was being generous to Diana's attempt to alert her to her own feelings the year previously: outside *forces*.)

And there was no way to know if it had happened – if Mallory had happened, if they had kissed in that boat, if she'd told her the truth about how she felt – without asking. And if it hadn't… All of it felt impossible to think about, so Cornelia shoved it to the back of her mind.

Out of her peripherals she saw Diana look between her and Olivia – presumably Cornelia had been staring at her with the sense of dawning comprehension she felt written all over her face – then between her and Mallory, her gaze tracking like she was trying to X-ray the truth out of them.

It wasn't as reassuring as she'd hoped it would be.

'Where do you want me?' a voice said uncertainly, and Cornelia looked up with a start to see Lucy standing with her hands twisted in her dress.

'Ah yes, we'll need another candle,' Nova said, their eyes still closed.

As though Lucy hadn't just been falsely imprisoned.

Harry had the decency to look uncomfortable as Lucy sat beside Dot, settling into her seat as though nothing had happened. Olivia sat on Dot's other side, and Imogen, Harry and Ezra found their seats. Diana shuffled so she was between

Cornelia and Mallory, and Nova's eyes snapped open.

'I trust you all have your mistletoe?' they asked, raising the stick. 'No obvious jokes please. The wand is necessary for focus, particularly if we're calling up… *lesser* spectres.'

'I bet Kingston would love that as a band name,' Cornelia whispered, pursing her lips as Nova's head whipped around to look at her.

This Nova was very serious; it was suddenly clear why the Ghoul Council were as revered as they were, beyond the prestige that came with tradition. As much as she was loath to admit it, underneath that veneer of pretentiousness was serious work.

'Ground rules, before we begin.' Nova adjusted three small ceramic jars on the table, lining them up so they sat in front of their candle. 'No salt. We don't wish to anger the spirits. If we follow these rules, salt will not have been necessary in the first place. We must put our hands on the table, and we must not lift them. Not to scratch our faces, not to apply lipgloss, not to get up and run away. When we start this, we begin with the full knowledge that this is a group effort.'

'Almost sounds like a list of things that have happened in prior séances,' Cornelia said.

Nova fixed her with a look. 'It will be unsurprising to note that I have never had an incident, because those attending my séances have had the grace to listen, and the intelligence to respect the rules. Failure to do so is nothing you want to think about.'

'I'd like to know,' Dot said after a beat. 'Never too old to learn from you, dear.'

Nova looked briefly mollified. 'I suppose we must enter these things through complete informed consent. Should you let go of the table for any reason, there's a chance whatever spirits we call will attempt to engage in Besiegement. Given the likely volume of spirits summoned, it is unlikely you would be able to prevent a ghost accessing your mind, which may result in complete possession, and we would have to turn you over to the Ghoul Council.'

'What if we're already in the Ghoul Council?' Olivia asked nervously.

Far more nervous than a witch who worked with ghosts should be, Cornelia thought with a start. They should all be calm. This should be routine, and yet only Imogen, Nova and Dot looked remotely relaxed.

'Figure of speech, Liv,' Nova said. 'Everyone here needs to understand this on a very simple level: we are asking the spirits for a favour in speaking to us, we cannot judge them for wanting to take a bigger payment for services rendered. Understood?'

It was mildly shocking to see even Harry nod. Ezra didn't propose a meeting, Imogen didn't offer a platitude, Dot and Olivia stared grimly at the table in front of them.

The witches of the Ghoul Council.

One of them, the Wickermere Reaper.

'Now, I believe you wanted to lead the questions,' Nova said, looking to Cornelia. They reached for Harry and Olivia's hands.

'Nova, Harry, Dot, Olivia, Lucy,' Cornelia said. 'Imogen and Ezra,' she added as an afterthought. 'Welcome to the séance.'

'Is all this necessary?' Imogen said quietly, adjusting the absinthe in front of her so it sat squarely in front of her candle.

'It is,' Harry said.

'Let them do it right,' Dot said.

'Do not let go of the table until this is over,' Nova commanded.

Diana squeezed Cornelia's hand tight, then slipped her hearing aid out and into its case. They placed their hands on the table.

There was a faint blue glow from Cornelia's pocket, which she hoped the others couldn't see.

A physical bargaining chip she'd impulsively grabbed, should this all go the expected tits-up way.

'We call forth the spirits of Annie Warren, Ali Howard, Grace Kaur, Terry Bell and Max Hodgson,' Diana said. They'd agreed she had the clearest speaking voice under pressure. 'We ask you to reach out to your Occult brethren, and tell us who took you out of this world.'

Apparent séances were dramatic, and overwrought and unbelievable. Cornelia had watched enough mediocre horror films to know that it was all loud bangs and gasps and gusts of wind, knuckles on tables and fake possessions. And yet, when the room filled with static, the TV lit up with a faint green glow despite not being plugged in, and a light breeze lifted pieces of her hair across her forehead, she felt a flutter of terror.

Imogen straightened, and Cornelia was briefly glad they weren't required to join hands. There was no comfort to be found in her mother's well-moisturised grasp.

A lit candle in front of Diana sputtered, and the flame hopped to Diana's candle, then to Cornelia's, then to Imogen's, where the flame stayed lit as a soft voice whispered through the TV screen.

'I am. I am. *I am.*'

The hairs on the back of Cornelia's neck stood up. She hadn't expected this to work. Her eyes were glued to the TV screen as a gentle light pulsated through it like an afterglow.

'Spirit, identify yourself. Subsection twenty-eight, clause nine b, demands you do so by any means necessary,' Nova said.

Whatever fear had gripped Cornelia started to loosen; it was impossible to feel lost in a séance if someone was actively making it as unsexy as possible by throwing out handbook rules.

'*Max Hodgson*,' the voice whispered.

'Who killed you, Max?' Diana asked.

'*I don't know*.'

'Great start,' Nova muttered.

'Can you tell us anything? What you saw? How you felt?' Diana continued, undeterred.

'*I can tell you… they were… so gentle…*' Max whispered.

Imogen's candle sputtered violently and she flinched, but the flame held steady even as the wick smoked, runnels of sooty wax running onto the table, moving steadily towards Imogen's wrists.

'Max?' Diana prompted, but there was nothing more.

Imogen's candle extinguished gently and she visibly relaxed.

Cornelia looked to Nova, pressing her hands into the table.

'Just wait,' Nova said to her. 'They like to take turns.'

A sharper gust blew into the room and the roar of static filled Cornelia's ears.

This time, a match-strike flash lit the candle in front of Diana, hopping to Olivia's candle, and landing in front of Ezra, burning high and furious.

'*You*,' the voice whispered.

'Who are you?' Nova asked.

'*Wa...rren*,' the voice said.

Annie Warren. The final successful victim.

'Do you know who the Wickermere Reaper is?' Diana asked.

'*Yes*,' Annie whispered, the TV crackling so loudly Cornelia almost couldn't hear it. She saw Diana wince.

'Who is it?' Diana asked, her voice louder but still calm, straining to hear.

'*She's... here...*' Annie hissed.

The table collectively inhaled.

Ghosts using pronouns, eliminating suspects in your area.

The Wickermere Reaper wasn't Ezra.

'Is the Wickermere Reaper in the room right now?' Diana asked, after a pause.

Cornelia subtly glanced around, watching Imogen's, Dot's and Olivia's faces, but their eyes were locked on the candle in front of Harry.

'*Yes...*'

'Can you indicate, by way of lighting a candle in front of the culprit?'

Ezra's candle sputtered, the flame hopping to Olivia, then Dot, then Imogen, then back to Olivia and Imogen in rapid succession until it went out, leaving a curl of white smoke behind.

The static faded to a low crackle as they waited for someone else to approach. Cornelia could feel every single second drag by her.

'That was a waste,' Harry said. 'No offence.'

'We're not done,' Cornelia said, steeling herself.

She ignored Diana and Mallory's panicked looks as she leaned forward. Here it was. Unplanned show time.

'I have in my pocket what the Wickermere Reaper wants. Right now, on my person. I can see it out of the corner of my eye. I call upon whatever ghost can get a message to the Reaper right now. Can you tell them if they don't give me some kind of assurance that the twins are alive, well and able to be recovered alive, I will destroy it?'

Mallory gasped and Diana kicked her under the table. Cornelia flinched but kept going, staring into Dot's and Olivia's and Imogen's and Ezra's eyes in turn.

'What are you talking about, Cornelia?' Ezra asked.

'I'm taking matters into my own hands,' Cornelia said. 'We have what the Wickermere Reaper wants, but the Reaper has yet to make themselves known to us. There's no way of contacting them—' Mallory gasped again, softer this time, like she'd just realised something. Cornelia shook that off too. '—so if the Wickermere Reaper wants to play fair, they need to make themselves known. Who's in, ghosties?' Cornelia addressed the TV.

'Cornelia, stop,' Nova said.

'This is against the rules,' Harry said.

'You're being an idiot,' Ezra said.

'This is dangerous, dear,' Dot said. 'We don't do this—'

'What if we go bigger? I could right now call upon Elisabella herself – the divine one, in this room of her admirers.'

'Cornelia,' Diana hissed through gritted teeth. 'What are you doing?'

'Cornelia, you're not thinking this through,' Olivia said.

Cornelia ignored all of them, looking around at the Ghoul Council witches. Dot. Imogen. Ezra. Olivia.

Doing what she did best: being impulsive.

The Reaper expected everyone to follow the rules. *She'd* brought Cornelia into the game. Cornelia didn't respect authority, and she was done pretending she respected whatever the Reaper thought should happen.

Her philosophy in action again: the Reaper was just some (gender neutral) guy, and she was in this room, and Cornelia was going to play the game her way from now on.

Imogen, whose lips had been pursed through all of this, had just opened her mouth to say something when her candle flared, the flame jumping high enough that Ezra exclaimed aloud.

'*Open it*,' a voice whispered in Cornelia's ear. Insistent, like it was a thought she'd had herself, an idea she wanted. She could see herself doing it. How easy it would be. She had no reason not to, the little voice telling her it was the right thing to do. Her only option.

She whispered under her breath a spell to unlock the catch keeping Elisabella inside the ghostlight. On the third try, despite being weathered by water and the diatomaceous earth it had rested in for so many years, the ghostlight sprang open.

Every candle in the circles blew out, and Nova lurched forward, but an inner circle of candles relit one heart-stopping second later as the Ghoul Council looked on in abject terror.

A figure formed in the centre of the table, though Cornelia was having trouble focusing on her. She'd half-expected

Elisabella would be like Theodore, a semi-corporeal *person*, albeit one of goddessly proportions.

The other half of her was dimly aware she had done something she couldn't take back.

As Cornelia stared, she tried to take in what she was seeing. Elisabella stood on the table, the rich dark fabric of her skirt dipping dangerously close to the flames of the candles barely containing her, pale feet in slippers balancing carefully over the witchlights.

Water dripped down her long dark hair and her clothes, and Cornelia had the sense Elisabella was staring down at them – sensing, rather than seeing, as the more Cornelia looked, the fewer details she could pick out, like she was wearing the wrong glasses.

She couldn't see her face, couldn't see her hands, her body – other than 'vaguely tall' and 'vaguely person shaped' – as static swirled around her form like it was trying to hide her from view, but it was *her*.

'Fuck me, that's actual Elisabella,' Lucy gasped.

The War Room alarm sounded, and Elisabella raised a flickering arm. It stopped suddenly.

Actual Elisabella didn't appear to hear her.

The faces of the Ghoul Council were frozen in terror, hands pressed to the table. Cornelia was still trying to decide if any of this was her fault, where the idea to release her had come from, and was studiously avoiding looking at either Diana or Mallory even as the toe of Diana's shoe dug into the flesh below her ankle.

'War Room,' Elisabella read, looking at the plaque on the wall. Her voice was…

It was a normal voice, actually, which was both startling and made utter sense all at once. Everyone was transfixed by her, mouths moving in silent reverence. It was not the strangest thing that had happened to Cornelia today, so she was not as moved by it.

There was a chance this was all a dream, and by Hexana was she going to cling to it. Her mind let her awareness float up and away from the table, allowing her a moment to disappear into her thoughts.

Living in constant terror that had decimated her ability to thrive over the past eighteen-ish months had its occasional advantages, she had to admit.

An alarming thought occurred to her as soon as she'd freed herself from the frozen terror occupying her corporeal form, still at the table with her hands pressing to it with white-knuckle effort. Unbidden and confusing, she realised: Elisabella had not immediately pinged back to Wrackton. She *appeared* to be a Samhain ghost (and while Cornelia had only met two of those in her life, she had the uniquely transferrable skill of being able to identify arthropod species differences with incredible accuracy and felt qualified to make this determination based on the characteristics she had been trying desperately to see mere moments before) and the working understanding of Samhain ghosts was that they had to stay close to the place where they'd died – or, at least, where their remains were, if Theodore's recently revelation was anything to go by. Cornelia was waiting for her to vanish. Even if she had a goddessly show of – probably rational, given how long she must've been trapped in the lake – displeasure to get through first. Elisabella had to disappear.

'Quaint, how you believe the Wars can be fought in a room, and not out in the lands,' Elisabella continued. Cornelia felt sweat prickle beneath her arms as Elisabella moved between them. The air crackled with electricity.

'Elisabella,' Olivia said, recovering first. 'It is an honour. We have so many questions.'

'Elisabella, there is evil in this town. They want your corporeal form in exchange for the lives of two children,' Imogen said, speaking over Olivia.

Cornelia bit back an inappropriately timed snort. At twenty-six the twins were not children, no matter how much they acted like it.

Elisabella sank to her knees, static crackling. Nova had opened the pot in front of them and was busy daubing runes on the table with a powdery substance – salt, Cornelia guessed, though she couldn't be sure from this angle. That, or Nova was preparing to do a line at the end of the world. Everyone else was spellbound.

Elisabella crouched, a hand reaching out and hovering just above the candle line in front of Imogen. Cornelia wished she could *see* her.

'Your children are precious,' she said to Imogen. 'But in war, we have a lot to lose.'

'The Vampire Wars have long ended,' Diana said, finding her voice. 'You can relax now, babe.'

'I am not a babe,' she said.

Diana's mouth twitched, but she didn't continue.

'It amuses me that you call the Wars what they are,' Elisabella said. 'I know not what I am doing here. Why did you break me from my shackles, if not to free me?'

Her pattern of speech reminded Cornelia of Katherine, and of Theodore in moments where he was losing lucidity. Then again, Cornelia would also probably not be particularly sensible if she'd been locked in a tiny rock and left at the bottom of a lake for years upon years.

'Maybe Cornelia can answer that,' Nova said icily.

'I can't,' Cornelia said, trying to not sound like she was quietly imploding. 'But while you're here, we need your help.'

'Someone's trying to hurt in your name,' Mallory said quietly. Her eyes were wide and a tear track on her cheek made Cornelia want to reach across Diana to wipe it.

Something told her that wasn't the wisest move, so she kept her fingers firmly pressed onto the table, staring at the short nails she tried not to bite often.

'Nobody will hurt in my name,' Elisabella said. 'Blair, Hexana, come to me, my sisters in arms. COME TO ME!' She screamed, and the candles blew out again.

Nova vaulted to their feet, but it was too late.

They all watched it happen in slow motion.

The candle in front of Cornelia fell and Harry tried – ineffectually – to lunge for it, hands still pressed to the table, but it toppled, and the wax shattered.

The circle broken.

The rest of the candles snuffed out completely, smoke rising and filling the room with a scent reminiscent of birthday parties.

A whisper started up in the furthest corner of the room, passing through the TV where a bright white dot formed in the centre, growing stronger by the moment. The whisper was barely audible until it began to circle, cutting closer and closer until a voice screamed in Cornelia's ear, begging her to take her hands off the table. Louder than the voice that told her to open the ghostlight, more insistent.

It spoke to her in Jacob's voice, telling her she'd never be found.

It spoke to her in a terrified scream, telling her Agatha and Ethel died knowing she couldn't save them. Died in agony, gasping for their last breaths as the oxygen ran out.

It was a peculiar kind of torture, all told, for it continued for what felt like forever. Cornelia could feel herself tiring. Dot was looking at her with panic in her eyes, her hands firmly pressed to the table, urging Cornelia to look down, to look away, to focus on the present.

'Don't listen to them, Cornelia,' Ezra said, his gaze on the table. 'Don't look at them.'

She lowered her gaze, but flickers at the edges of her glasses showed her countless shapes coming to her – more than it seemed possible could ever be outside the lake, much less inside her parents' house, and yet they kept coming. All Occult, all drawn to the ferocity of Elisabella's cry.

'Starting to see why she was left down there in the first place,' Cornelia said, forcing her gaze down.

'Elisabella, we are an organisation founded in a world you left behind,' Harry said quickly. 'We are duty-bound to stop you leaving this room. The Ternion cannot walk the earth again, or—'

'And that's why the Wickermere Reaper wanted her,' Nova said.

'I ask you in the name of the Ghoul Council to stop!' Ezra commanded. 'All of you are in contravention of the rules!'

'Cornelia, shut your eyes,' Olivia said. 'You need to shut your eyes. Nova, do something!'

'I am *trying*,' Nova said, but Cornelia couldn't look, couldn't see what their efforts were, her eyes focused on the unlit candle in front of her.

'Take the salt and put it on your tongue.' Diana slid one of Nova's pots closer. Her voice was louder than everyone else's; louder than the whispers and everyone's frantic attempts to keep Cornelia safe. Always the voice of reason.

'Do it, quickly. It's okay,' she said.

Cornelia lifted her hands and poured salt on her tongue, resisting the urge to gag. It was almost sweet.

'Now swallow, and say you'll do what she wants,' Diana continued. So steady, so calm, even in the face of panic.

'I'll do what you want,' Cornelia said thickly.

'In your name, you'll let her walk,' Diana concluded.

'In my name, I'll let you walk.'

Someone screamed.

'CORNELIA—' a voice cut off.

The howl became a crescendo and Cornelia felt hands all over her. On her hair, her face, touching her ears, her shoulders, pushing her back from the table. She had the sense she wasn't in contact with the floor anymore.

That her corporeal body was floating.

That there was strange, warm light enveloping her.

That this was something horrifying.

Then she crashed back to the ground, hitting the floor hard.

Her eyes opened and she pulled herself up onto her hands and knees, taking in the horrified faces staring back at her.

All of their mouths were sealed shut with black wax that dripped down their chins. Mallory's and Diana's eyes were wide. The whole Ghoul Council stared at her, her parents and Lucy crying.

Only the flickering, watery figure of Elisabella was still able to move. She crouched over Cornelia, lifting a hand as if she was going to touch her. Her fingers were inches from her face, and then her head twisted, wrenching upwards at an unnatural angle.

'WITNESSES TO THE BESIEGEMENT.

OLIVIAHARRYDOROTHYEZRANOVAIMOGENLUCYMALLORYDIANA.

SAY HER NAME AND YOU WILL JOIN HER. THE BESIEGEMENT MAY COMPLETE INSIDE FIVE DAYS.'

The whispering died off and Diana was the first to move, grabbing the ghostlight and lobbing it at Elisabella. She disappeared into it, and so did the presence around her.

The static died, and the light at the centre of the TV faded to nothing.

Nobody moved, mouths still sealed.

Cornelia pulled herself to her feet, adjusting her jumper sleeves.

'What the fuck was that about?' she asked.

TWENTY-NINE

2:00:27

Nobody answered her.

Nobody except Diana, who said, 'You tell us, you absolute fucking liability.'

As the Ghoul Council and its members were wont to do, the room erupted in mild concern, peeling wax from their faces – it had gone on hot, so the skin beneath was red and angry – and babbling rules and instructions for further actions. Ezra's voice rose above the consternation.

'Everyone out and into the decontamination room.'

The ghostlight was gone from the table.

He opened the door and ushered his wife out first, and the ashen faces of Olivia, Dot, Harry, Lucy and Nova followed. Lucy and Dot both gripped Cornelia's shoulder as they passed.

It reminded her of a funeral procession.

She was getting quite sick of funerals.

'Councilfolk, you know the drill, and you understand the stakes. Do not say her name. Not in front of her, not to anyone else. You do not refer to the youngest Broadwick child by name,' Ezra commanded. 'As witnesses to the Besiegement, your soul will be claimed alongside hers should anyone in the vicinity of this site say her name over the next five days. There is a possibility that someone beyond the site could trigger the Besiegement should they become aware of what happened here. No matter what kind of pressure you feel you are under, subsection three b, part eight, compels you to refrain from speaking aloud the name of the Besieged, on pain of death.'

'We know,' Nova said. 'We were there when it was written.'

'Shut up, Nova,' Harry snapped. 'Repeating the rules is for the benefit of all, you know that.'

It would've been helpful to Cornelia to hear the rules properly laid out, for starters, but she was too shocked to find the words to ask.

'Why'd you do it?' Olivia asked. Her fearful expression was gone, replaced with something akin to… anger?

Cornelia shook her head. 'I didn't… I mean, I *did*, but—'

'We can talk about this later,' Mallory said.

'And we'll talk about the value of *hiding places*, too,' Diana said.

It occurred to Cornelia for the first time that everyone, in part, blamed her for what had just happened.

And that didn't feel entirely fair.

'I didn't—' she started, but Ezra spoke over her.

'You three, you need to go to the decontamination room. Nobody is to leave the grounds of Rowan House for the remainder of the time the Wickermere Reaper has allowed us.'

'We need to understand why Elisabella didn't immediately return to Wrackton—' Olivia began, but Nova waved a hand.

'Proof she's tied to Wickermere, I imagine.'

The rest of the Ghoul Council said nothing, and Cornelia saw the way they avoided each other's gaze.

Nothing about the séance had gone the way it should've.

Someone had interfered.

They knew, finally, irrefutably, that the Wickermere Reaper was among them.

'Decontamination. Now,' Ezra said, pointing out towards the mudroom. 'And the Council is in lockdown. That's an executive order. Decontamination and return.'

The Council filed out, Lucy clutching her face. She'd have been better off sitting in the Bonemarrow Lane hovel. Bringing her back had been a mistake.

'You do need to tell us what's happening,' Diana said, neatly catching Ezra by the arm. He let Imogen walk ahead of him without meeting her eye, Imogen's own expression guarded.

A weight sunk into Cornelia's stomach as another Broadwick illusion deflated before her: they weren't a unit. If it came down to it, Ezra and Imogen would turn on each other in an instant.

They knew the Wickermere Reaper was among them, and the set of Ezra's jaw spoke a thousand words he'd never dare to say aloud: he did not trust his wife.

'All we've been told is that the Besiegement Curse is bad, will result in full corporeal possession, and is frowned upon by the Ghoul Council,' Diana said. It wasn't a question, and Ezra responded accordingly.

'There isn't much else to it. We, perhaps, have a situation on our…' He trailed off, glancing at Imogen's chair. 'Bottom line is, if you say her name, all of us – every single one of us in this room – will be doomed.'

'To be clear,' Mallory asked, 'what happens if the Besiegement Curse is activated? I get the doomed-to-possession part, but is it… instantaneous?'

The unspoken part – *will it hurt if it happens?* – hung in the air.

'If the Curse is completed by someone saying her name, we believe there is a period of time to tie up loose ends. I suspect the idea of stepping into an unsuitable life, no matter how ready-made, has… consequences, for a Besieging spirit. Our understanding is there is time – a day, a month, any amount of time the ghost deems "enough" – for the Besieged to, effectively, close up shop. Get things in order. Then that's it – your body, your life, is theirs.' Ezra swallowed thickly. 'Your mother knows more about this than I do – much more. But this is what I know. To have a ghost take you over permanently is worse than death. Occulture has dabbled in necromancy, has tried for immortality—'

Cornelia opened her mouth to tell him what she knew about Kingston, and vampire magic, and immortality, and then stopped.

She'd never help Ezra Broadwick with anything but this case again.

He hadn't paid attention to the literal serial killer in his own house until it had become impossible to ignore. He was on the verge of crying in front of her. He was *frightened*, and not for Cornelia – he was scared the rules he'd so carefully built his life around were about to be so catastrophically broken. That's all he'd ever cared about.

And if he wasn't the Reaper, she had a creeping suspicion

that he, perhaps, wasn't as involved in Theodore's death as she'd once believed with utter conviction.

'I think not saying her name for a few days should be easy,' Diana said. She seemed remarkably unbothered by the whole thing. It almost stung. 'There's no need to worry.'

Ezra fixed her with a measured look.

'It wouldn't be much of a curse if that's all there was to it. The Besiegement Curse will leave you feeling *compelled* to speak her name. You will feel nauseated, you will feel like you are dying inside, and you will believe the only way to relieve your own suffering is to speak her name aloud. This is a lie. You must not.'

'Oh, is that all?' Cornelia said. 'All the money in the world, all the power of the Ghoul Council, and you think "just don't" is the solution? Reminds me of my teenage years, actually, where you thought "just don't" was a suitable alternative to, I don't know, *actually being my fucking parents*.'

Ezra looked at her – and really looked at her, she felt. Scrutinising her.

'Don't do this to your mother,' Ezra said softly. 'If she's— If I know my wife as I believe I do, she's already dying inside. Don't kill her.'

He left the Undetectables alone in the War Room.

Mallory stared at Cornelia, blue eyes wide with terror.

The jumble of whatever the fuck had just happened was starting to arrange itself into a coherent narrative in Cornelia's head, and she turned on Diana.

'Okay, so that wasn't my fault,' Cornelia started.

'I'd love to know your justification for this,' Diana burst out, and Cornelia realised she'd been pretending to be unbothered.

She was, uncharacteristically, *angry*-angry. This wasn't playful hex wars, ride-or-die 'oh Cornelia your impulsivity has got us into hot water again' best friend sparring they'd done for over a decade. She had surpassed the anger she'd expressed when Cornelia had let Beckett drink her blood that one (admittedly ill-advised) time – this was pure, unadulterated *rage*.

'You took the ghostlight,' Mallory said carefully. 'From the secret hiding place. The ghostlight containing a literal goddess of Occulture. One of the Ternion. And tried to… taunt the Reaper?'

'I think we were *all* trying to taunt the Reaper,' Cornelia said.

'No. No, this is bullshit. We are a *team*. The *team* hid the ghostlight in the safest place I know,' Diana snapped. 'And *you* took it out, overplayed your hand, and now you're… now we're…' She cut off, choking on whatever she was about to say.

'Fine, I made a judgement error. A big one. Mea culpa,' Cornelia said, knowing she'd have to do some serious, actual, genuine grovelling later. 'But if we're taking out subscriptions to *Blame Game Weekly*, *you* told me to speak.'

'Pardon?' Diana said, reeling back like Cornelia had hexed her.

'J'accuse! Back there. After the candles went out. You told me what to say. You were being so calm about it.'

'I didn't say anything. I *couldn't*. There was a wax seal over my mouth!'

'No, but I heard you so clearly, you told me…' Cornelia trailed off. It didn't take much for the extra horror to set in, but it did, pushing down on her and making her knees buckle. She hit the floor with a thump.

'Someone told me to open the ghostlight in the first place. A little voice in my head. I thought it was one of my usual impulsive thoughts, you know – I'd realised I've been letting everyone do everything, and that it was time to take action. Take back control, no matter how scared I was. My plan was to threaten to destroy the ghostlight, call the Reaper's bluff. But that voice...'

'What did it sound like?' Mallory asked.

Cornelia thought about it.

The cadence of it. Not her own voice, but a familiar one.

One she'd heard recently.

'I think... and this is going to sound weird... but I think I heard the Reaper tell me to open the ghostlight.'

'Whose voice was it?' Diana demanded.

Some of the anger had left her, so the demand was softer.

'I don't know. I don't know if I knew it wasn't – do we even know what kind of spell would do that? *Is* there a spell to do that?'

She closed her eyes, seeing the candles extinguished, the static, Elisabella standing among the witchlights, trying to *listen* to the memory, examine it with her eyes closed for irregularities.

She'd read once that the more you remembered a memory, the more you changed it.

She remembered the Lyrefly echoing Ethel's final words. *We understand.*

Her eyes snapped open.

'That's how the Wickermere Reaper is getting the victims to the burial sites,' Cornelia said. 'They're *convincing* them, through their own thoughts.'

'What, like demonic persuasion?' Diana demanded. 'We've already eliminated Harry—'

Cornelia shook her head. 'No. Not like that at all. That, we can feel as a prickle, a sense of someone *trying* to persuade.

This was as seamless as a thought. I could visualise myself opening the ghostlight like I was preparing to do it, but it was just… pictures.'

It reminded her of something else she couldn't put her finger on.

Diana and Mallory exchanged glances.

'That's an interesting hypothesis, and we can examine it in a bit. First, though – are you okay?' Mallory asked softly.

'I don't know.' It was honest, at least.

'Oh, so you answer *Mallory* nicely, but bite my head off? Charming,' Diana said.

'Not the time,' Mallory reminded her.

Diana flapped a hand. 'Yes, sorry. Just hard to know what to do now. We sat at the feet of an actual fucking goddess, just so we're caught up. The *real, not-alive Elisabella* stood in front of us. And tried to curse C— to curse her,' Diana said, catching herself. 'That's going to take some practice. I expect by the time I master not saying your name, we'll either be doomed forever, or the threat will have nicely passed us by. Nice to know the rules are so clear-cut, though.'

'What on Morrigan's green earth are you talking about?'

'Think about it. If you die, you might get turned into a giant bug. If you don't die by other means, but accidentally give consent to a ghost to take over your body, you will die. Other available methods include someone murdering you ritualistically to become a goddess, or murder you for… We don't know why the Wickermere Reaper is doing it, apart from to get their hands on Elisabella, but we could say material gain. And if all that doesn't wipe you out, if you die of natural causes, someone might dig up your bones for as yet undetermined reasons.' Diana rubbed at the skin beneath her ear. 'Maybe we're better off without the Ternion as physical beings.'

'Perhaps we should've left her in the lake,' Mallory said.

'Turns out the Ghoul Council really has a function, if they were actually right about something. It's a shocking Broadwick first,' Cornelia said. Neither of them laughed, and she felt a sinking desperation. 'Hey, come on. It's just a little curse, we can get through this. We've still got Elisabella – we didn't draw the Wickermere Reaper out, but we can keep trying? Switch to plan… what is it now, plan D?'

Her friends kept looking at her blankly, and the penny finally dropped.

They weren't just frightened; they were defeated.

'No,' Cornelia said fiercely. Something about their faces made the latest wave of terror threatening to drown her dissipate. The Reaper wanted her to give in to despair. In the face of everyone around her giving up, she refused. She had bugs to see, research to do, a life to live, a Mallory to—

'We are not giving up. What did you see around the table?'

Mallory and Diana looked at her for a long, long moment. If they'd exchanged glances, Cornelia thought something would've broken inside her – that they were not all three together, but two friends trying to contain her broken remains.

But they didn't. Without conferring, they took out their notebooks and phones in unison, and Cornelia had to bite down hard on her tongue to prevent herself from crying.

'Nova was drawing runes on the table as Elisabella broke free,' Diana said. 'The others were transfixed by her. If the

Wickermere Reaper could convince you to open the ghost-light – though we aren't blaming the Wickermere Reaper for bringing the dangerous goddess to the séance table in the first place – then it's possible they could've convinced Nova to break form.'

'I didn't recognise the runes, but I'll ask Kingston,' Mallory said, trying to draw them on the back page of her notebook from memory. 'I think they were something like this. It might be standard séance procedure—'

'Probably in the Ghoul Council rulebook they've all memorised,' Diana said.

Sending the photo to Kingston, Mallory said, 'Annie Warren confirmed the Reaper – *she* – was in the room. The Ghoul Council are now *obliged* to accept the Reaper has been among them this whole time.'

'And the candles flared in front of Olivia, Dot and Imogen, right?' Cornelia said.

Diana nodded. 'Yes. And me, for a second. I am obviously not the Wickermere Reaper,' she added. 'In case that wasn't clear.'

'Anything else?' Cornelia asked, even though she knew there wasn't. She hadn't been able to see what anyone was doing, and fragments were only starting to process.

'Everyone seemed frightened or awed,' Diana said. 'Transfixed.'

'Olivia just couldn't stop smiling for the first part of it,' Mallory said.

It was a little acidic, in Cornelia's opinion, and she longed to reach over and squeeze her hand, tell her *I get it now*, but

Mallory hadn't touched her since the lake. Now wasn't the time.

'Okay, so nobody gave us a reaction' – Mallory consulted her phone – 'and Kingston says that he doesn't know what the runes are for certain, but that they seem to be general Occulture protection symbols that have fallen out of use. He thinks they were around since the beginning of the… of the… oh for *fucksake*, the Vampire Wars.'

Mallory rubbed her eyes, trying to regroup.

'For the love of Blair, we *know* about the Vampire Wars, I wish I'd stop getting dizzy at the slightest mention of them. He says he thinks that most Occult folk got into the habit of salting their gateways and the front steps with runes of salt and iron filaments in an effort to protect their families from undue magic. So perfectly reasonable that Nova would, when confronted with a goddess who thinks we're still in Wars time, use something she'd recognise.'

'They weren't being influenced by the Reaper, that was all… you,' Diana said helpfully. Matching her energy, Cornelia *helpfully* didn't hex her about it. 'Anyway, we can come back to this when we aren't all trying to avoid being cursed for eternity and also watching time slipping away – focus. The Reaper hasn't given us next instructions, and now they know that we know they're on the Council, it's their move, as much as I hate it. Do we wait here and hope they'll reach out?'

'Or do we look to the person who brought us the letter?' Mallory's tone was light, but she had a point.

'Given that we've been caught out by that one before, surely at this point we would just need to go into a different line of work if we were fooled by someone being nice to us?' Cornelia asked.

Mallory raised her hands. 'We aren't infallible. It could happen.'

There was a note of defeat in her voice still that made Cornelia's heart constrict.

Mallory *never* gave up.

The Undetectables wouldn't exist without her. Cornelia would've probably succumbed to some sort of horrible Broadwick-driven life if Mallory hadn't made everything change by bringing them that letter eighteen months ago. As much as she hated Jacob, as much as she still lived in the shadow of his actions and as much as she wished the Undetectables didn't need to exist, she'd long come to believe that Jacob had been coming for her no matter what. He was determined to have someone to play his game with; it would've been them regardless.

The Wickermere Reaper had decided to take Agatha and Ethel without Cornelia playing at the table. She'd inserted herself into the game. They had to play until the end.

'Okay,' Diana said, sighing. 'We wait, then. Let's have a quick decontamination shower – sounds awful, by the way – grab our files and camp out here and just… wait.'

'What is wrong with both of you?' Cornelia shouted, feeling the absolute weight of everything crash down on her. 'We aren't going to be sitting ducks. If we're going to sit around and wait, we might as well make it count. For the love of *Blair*, Mallory and I *rescued a goddess from a murder lake*— Wait. Where's the ghostlight?'

Diana blinked, fluttering her eyelashes innocently. 'Everyone was pretty upset and confused, so I took advantage. Might be a while before the Council organise themselves and figure out one of them doesn't have it.'

Cornelia cracked a smile. 'At least one of us did something right. Can you hide it somewhere safe? Saf*er.* Tell Mallory where you've put it, just in case.'

Mallory's expression was unreadable and it made something painful snap inside Cornelia.

'What are you waiting for?'

The doors to Rowan House bolted shut with an efficiency that should've made Cornelia feel safe, but instead made her feel trapped. Stella, after a quick explanation, had been game to guard the entrance to Rowan House, and Diana had hidden the ghostlight somewhere safe. Ruby and Jo had insisted they were too busy to come, but wouldn't say why.

They were doing this now. Confronting the Wickermere Reaper.

The Ghoul Council were in the War Room, sitting at the table that was now lit by witchlight. Lucy had tidied the candles away, as if the Council was hoping to pretend the séance hadn't happened.

'Let's have a meeting,' Cornelia said. 'We have some time to kill, might as well use it.'

If the Reaper wouldn't talk, the Undetectables could wait them out. No twins, no ghostlight.

Cornelia was sure they'd crack. They'd offered more time –

even if Mallory was right and it was about maximum impact on the families of the victims, the Wickermere Reaper *wanted* Elisabella. Knew it was possible to have her. Had been within reach of her.

Knew the twins were worth more than Elisabella.

This could all be for nothing, and Cornelia was sure – gut-deep, bone-certain, absolutely *sure* – that no matter how much of a sadist the Wickermere Reaper was at heart, they would not be okay with being outsmarted.

'I'd like to start by claiming Chair of the meeting,' Cornelia said. 'And as you can't voice your objections to me by using my name, I will proceed.'

She stood at the head of the table, jumper sleeves rolled back, arms behind her back.

She felt strong.

She felt like herself.

'It perhaps has not escaped your notice that the Wickermere Reaper is in this room.'

'No,' Harry said. 'It has not.'

'Thank you, the speaker will take questions later and does not want to be interrupted,' Diana said. She grinned at Harry's furious expression, and held up his own copy of the Ghoul Council handbook. 'What? They're your own rules. All in here.'

Cornelia slammed a mechanical countdown timer she'd found in Agatha's room on the table, ticking down the remaining time.

'We are not leaving this room until we know who you are. Agatha and Ethel cannot die, so we are figuring out your identity by any means necessary. Everyone start talking.'

THIRTY

1:01:01

'We are not going to implicate ourselves for your amusement,' Imogen said, pressing a hand to her chest. 'That's what we have a lawyer for.'

'I don't think it's my job to implicate you, Imogen?' Harry said uncomfortably. 'Although I will admit that this' – he gestured – 'is not in the handbook, and therefore we must discuss it and raise a motion.'

'Motion to find the killer infesting your ranks and who is holding Agatha and Ethel ransom in order to obtain a goddess and do whatever the hell they want with it – all those in favour say aye,' Diana said, raising her hand.

Mallory, Diana, Cornelia, Dot, Nova, Lucy and, shakily, Olivia raised their hands.

'All those against?'

Nobody moved.

'The ayes have it,' Diana said, making a note on Dot's steno in front of her. Her range of incidental skills never ceased to amaze Cornelia, even if she'd never tell her that.

'For starters, let's look at the evidence,' Cornelia said. 'The Wickermere Reaper has been operating within the boundaries of Wickermere for the past few years. The alleged abduction of Agatha and Ethel Broadwick appeared to fit that pattern.'

'It made sense until we realised *someone* had gone to great lengths to make it appear the only boundaries affected were the Wickermere boundaries, and not the Rowan House ones. A *glitch*, the report says?' Diana said.

A whisper shot up between Imogen and Dot, and Cornelia turned sharply. 'No conferring!'

Dot blinked at her, but it turned to a smile quickly enough.

'I don't know what you're implying,' Imogen said.

'Lucy, where does the boundary line lie between the Wickermere wards and the Rowan House wards?'

'At the first entrance gate,' she said after a moment.

'Right! And where was the twins' car found? The car that was, allegedly, taken by Apparent police for testing, but is actually a burnt-out husk in Bonemarrow Lane?'

'At the first entrance gate,' Lucy said again.

'And who knows the exact start and end points of the Rowan House wards?'

'All of us, really,' Lucy said. 'The Broadwicks, Dot, Olivia, Harry… We'd all know, it's common knowledge. Or it is now, anyway.'

Cornelia had the wherewithal to feel bad about asking Lucy questions she couldn't lie in response to.

'I didn't know until recently,' Nova said, folding their hands. 'So suggesting Lucy's time in exile was as warranted as we believed.'

'I didn't do anything wrong! And if I did, *I didn't mean to*,' Lucy said, and promptly burst into tears.

'There, there,' Dot said, moving to comfort her. 'You weren't to know, were you?'

'She has a duty to the Ghoul Council,' Imogen said. 'She knew that, at least.'

'It begs the question, then – if it was common knowledge, how did the rest of the Council not notice? How, in all your collective wisdom, did you fail to see it was one of your own?'

'Well,' Harry began, 'there are rules about such things—'

'The Ternion cannot walk this earth,' Ezra said, looking at Imogen as he said it. 'What happened today was an abomination that should never have been possible. It is proof that Project TRIAD should be destroyed—'

'*Proof*? Our *youngest child* destroyed a TENET of our EXISTENCE,' Imogen shouted.

'So, Harry,' Cornelia said, cutting across the Broadwicks. 'We chose not to probe this at the time, but now that we're quite sure the Wickermere Reaper is a witch – did we mention that? It's one of four of you, and if we take Annie Warren's accusation seriously, it's only three of you. You were on a run at the time the twins were taken, isn't that right?'

'I appreciate the attempts, but this feels like a waste of time. I am a man of law, what you're doing is not right. We can't simply… accuse someone of being the Reaper.'

'Did anyone see you? Bearing in mind we already don't think you are the Reaper and your responses could have influence on who we look to next.'

'We were all out. Olivia was out, Ezra was gone. I came back to find Dot, and Olivia, Lucy, Nova and Imogen and later, Ezra, all mentally *stabbed* over what had just transpired here.'

Cornelia looked to Olivia, then Dot. 'Is that true?'

Olivia shook her head – not a *no*, more a *I can't believe this is happening*, and Dot hesitated just a fraction of a second too long.

'I... can't recall seeing Imogen *or* Olivia, if we're being honest. I'm sorry dear, I don't want to muddy your investigation—'

'Ezra, my so-called father. What do you remember, coming back to see Agatha and Ethel were taken? Where were you, anyway? We've seen dossiers – you were on "important Ghoul Council business"?'

He muttered something, and Diana held a hand to her ear. 'What was that? Didn't quite catch that.'

'I was driving to the next village to find some decent fucking coffee for myself and Imogen,' he said. 'As I told the Apparent police, so they could check my car for proof.'

'And did they? Mallory, what's in the police file on that?'

'They did a cursory check,' Mallory said. 'But I'm pretty sure if Ezra wanted to hide anything, he could've, especially given we know the police file is riddled with inaccuracies.'

Ezra looked a little bit like he wanted to strangle someone.

Cornelia chanced a glance at her countdown timer.

Agatha Ethel Agatha Ethel

'I'd like to know where you're getting any of this information,' Imogen said. 'The only dossiers you were permitted to see were the ones I gave you express permission to read. As the heads of the Ghoul Council, and as this is our premises, *and* as we've hired you to assist us, I'd rather you—'

'Don't interrupt,' Cornelia said. 'We don't have time.'

'Speaking of time,' Mallory said. 'Olivia, you were shunted off Project TRIAD to Project HAUNT, then to general duties. You told us that yourself – but in light of recent events, I can't help but wonder if it wasn't as amicable as you painted it.'

Olivia sat with her hands folded in her lap, and didn't respond.

'It must be so frustrating, to not get the recognition you deserved. I can imagine that was hard for you, wasn't it?'

She was, Cornelia noted, enjoying it a bit too much, to the point of it verging on un-Mallory-like.

'No,' she said shortly. 'It wasn't.'

'It's okay,' Mallory said. 'We're similar in lots of ways, I can imagine how tough it would be if *I* was denied the chance to finish something I'd started.'

'TRIAD wasn't working out,' Olivia said. 'I was happy to move to HAUNT, get to work with Dot for a while, and happy to move elsewhere. Enough of us have had a go at trying to make it successful. Enough have died. Besides, it's a project that likely has no real end.'

'And I was ready to retire,' Dot added. 'It was nice to have someone to show the HAUNT ropes to.'

'But Olivia, those HAUNT meetings – we read the minutes,' Diana said sweetly.

Cornelia blinked, taken aback.

'Yes, we did,' Mallory said, and Cornelia was delighted to realise it was a barely detectable lie. They really were getting better at being PIs. 'And all those denials of pay rises – strange, really, when you think about it, because the Broadwicks have nothing *but* money.'

'That's unfair,' Ezra said, then remembered himself. 'It's business, Mallory.'

'I'm sure it all makes perfect business sense. But what I've come to learn is that people aren't always made for business sense, are they?' Mallory crept closer, sitting beside Olivia.

If the aim was to freak her out – which Cornelia was reasonably sure it was – it was working.

'No. I didn't do this. I wouldn't. I didn't want any of this to happen, I didn't want to get involved. I wanted to help you if I could, I just feel so terrible. I feel so terrible,' she repeated, standing up, her fist closing around something.

Cornelia realised what it was a split second too late.

There was terror in Olivia's face that Cornelia knew was her doing – if not her, the Besiegement Curse itself.

A witchlight tumbled from Olivia's hand and she stepped into it, disappearing.

Before anyone could react, Dot stood.

'Don't worry, I know where she's going. This isn't my first time dealing with a panicking witch, and it won't be my last,' she said, and disappeared too, a second witchlight clutched in her hand.

'That was my witchlight,' Lucy said sadly. 'From my desk.'

Mallory met Cornelia's gaze.

'I have a bad feeling about this,' Mallory said.

'Well, we won't be letting anyone else have one of these,' Diana said, pushing the witchlights away.

'Stop it, Diana,' Harry said, and Cornelia saw Diana hesitate, her own scalp prickling.

'This is ridiculous,' Ezra said. 'We could—'

The door crashed open, swallowing the end of his sentence, and Stella stood on the other side, looking elated.

She signed faster than Cornelia could keep up with.

It took her spelling it out four times before Cornelia got what she was saying.

L - Y - R - E - F - L - I - E -S ARE READY

WHAT? Cornelia signed, scarcely daring to believe it.

Stella pointed out to the foyer urgently and Cornelia followed.

Lock the door behind us, don't let anyone leave, Cornelia signed. *And don't let any of them touch the witchlights!*

She took off the second Stella nodded her assent. Jo and Ruby were outside in the misting rain, little wooden boxes clutched in their hands.

'They're ready,' Ruby said breathlessly.

A flush of excitement had crossed Ruby's face, and a genuine smile creased her dark features. Jo looked elated and Cornelia could hardly believe it. 'The Lyreflies. Enough of them hatched that they'll produce an echo. You'll get the twins back.'

'Don't say her name!' Diana yelped, running up behind Cornelia, Mallory several steps behind.

'We know,' Ruby said, sadness crossing her face for possibly the first time in Cornelia's entire time of knowing her. 'We know all about it.'

Cornelia didn't have time to question this, her attention on the boxes. The impossible boxes Ruby and Jo had thrust into her hands.

She sank to her knees, trying to peer in through the airholes. They were clicking and buzzing away inside atop helleborine flowers.

'They'll need something of each of the twins' to smell,' Jo instructed. 'Preferably something biological, like hair or nails.'

Cornelia was taking the stairs two at a time before Jo had even finished the sentence, returning with hairbrushes helpfully emblazoned with each twin's monogram.

'Here.'

'Carefully put it in here.' She turned the box, uncapping a little opening. 'Do not let them out.'

Cornelia stuffed the hairs through and heard a melodic buzzing inside, a sound she never thought she'd get to hear in real life.

Certainly not this week.

'Once you let them go, you'll need to be quick. They move like lightning if they've got a scent on them.'

'Now?'

'It's not like you're on a time crunch,' Jo said sourly. 'Yes, *now*.'

'Don't mind her. In your own time. Let us know when you've found them,' Ruby said.

'Thank you,' Cornelia said, rushing forward and grabbing them both in a hug.

They spluttered, but it was for show. The Witches of Bonemarrow Lake were pleased with her.

It was another first.

'Get the girls back here to irritate us once again. I never thought I'd miss it,' Jo said.

Cornelia signed *thank you* to her and Jo winked.

Cornelia opened the box and they all watched as the *Celyphidae lyrescua* took to the sky, their blue bodies glinting in the sunlight. She held one back as it whined and droned, trying to follow the rest of the swarm.

'Quickly,' Ruby urged. 'They'll swarm when they find them, and this one will echo back what they're hearing, but best to try to keep up. You don't have long.'

They'd tried to cheat the Reaper, and were cheating them again.

The Undetectables took off, Mallory trying her absolute valiant best to keep up. She waved them on, pain overtaking her.

'Go, I'll catch up,' she said, dropping to a fast walk, her jaw clenched. 'I'll text Stella to notify the Apparent police that we're on the move, see if we can finally get feet on the ground to help retrieve the twins.'

Cornelia looked back at her once and then sped off, her jumper billowing in the wind as she moved. After a few seconds of sweating, she pulled it over her head as she ran, dropping it on the ground.

She was going to find Agatha and Ethel. She could feel it in her bones, in her heart. Insects didn't lie, and she'd spent enough time studying their hypothetical and theoretical behaviours to know this was going to work.

They covered the first mile with no swarm in sight, the Lyrefly in her hand still angry and determined to escape her gentle-but-firm grasp. Cornelia leaned on her knees, gasping for breath.

'If we double back, we can cover about half a mile in that direction, so if the twins—' Diana broke off with a hiss, pressing her hand to her side.

'Stitch?'

'No, I get this stabbing pain in my side that my brain is

convinced can only be alleviated if I say your name,' she said, her teeth gritted.

Cornelia swallowed. The curse was so close at all times, following them, stalking them as they ran.

The Lyrefly clunked and Cornelia skidded to a halt.

'What?' Diana asked, but Cornelia shushed her.

Thunk. Thunk. Thunk. The Lyrefly buzzed mechanically, then fizzed.

'LAKESIDE,' Cornelia shouted, taking off. 'SOMEWERE YOU CAN HEAR THE COTTAGE FACTORY!'

The *thunks* got louder and louder, both from the Lyrefly and from the actual factory itself, until they skidded down a narrow pathway beside the lake, opposite to where Stella had been buried. Cornelia focused on the path as she put one foot in front of the other, a line of witchlights on their left, trees reaching for them on their right, roots and broken branches threatening to push them off-course into Lake Wickermere itself.

As though they were at the edge of a horror forest, but where the horror was human inability to run and not fall over small obstacles.

'THERE!' Cornelia could hear what sounded like a violin string being plucked repeatedly, and she and Diana stumbled towards a dirt clearing among the trees, finding the promised swarm of shiny blue Lyreflies steadily eating their way through the dirt, singing amid repeating *thunks* as they went.

Cornelia could've walked over this section of ground repeatedly and never known it had been disturbed. Nothing out of place, nothing trampled except where she and Diana had walked seconds prior.

The Wickermere Reaper was someone who knew how to clean up, someone who knew how to slip in and out unseen. Someone who knew the rules and how to bend them.

Cornelia dropped to her knees beside the Lyreflies, letting go of the one she'd held captive, and started digging with her hands just as Mallory caught up to them, raising her phone as an explanation when Diana looked at her askance. 'This app really does let you find your pals,' she said weakly, sinking to the ground beside where Diana and Cornelia and the Lyreflies were digging enthusiastically.

'AGATHA,' Cornelia called. 'ETHEL!'

'NO,' Mallory said, reaching to grab her arm but stopping herself, her hand outstretched in warning. 'They can't risk saying your name, they don't know what's happening!'

She was, as always, absolutely right, and Cornelia felt a swoop of terror hit her stomach.

'AGATHA? ETHEL?' Diana tried. 'IT'S DIANA. YOU LIKE MY CLOTHES BUT YOU HATE ME AND YET I'M HERE TO RESCUE YOU!'

Cornelia kept scooping back handfuls of Lyrefly-softened earth even against their buzzing protestations.

'I'm not threatening your food source, I am helping,' she lied.

'Stella texted, police and the Broadwicks are on the way.' Mallory threw her phone down and joined in the digging.

'AGATHA! ETHEL!'

There was a distant sound, so small Cornelia wasn't sure she wasn't just hearing things.

'ETHEL! AGATHA!' Diana shouted. Her hands connected

with something. 'It's a box. They're here. They're here,' she said, pulling the earth away with more urgency.

'Where are they? Are they alive?' Imogen jogged up, a shovel in her hand. She didn't look like she knew how to use it. Ezra was close behind her.

'I think I heard something but I can't be certain,' Diana said. 'AGATHA!'

'AGATHA!' Imogen shouted, handing Diana the shovel.

If ever there was a moment to delegate, it probably wasn't now.

'ETHEL!'

The sound again, small, far away, but a voice.

Cornelia wrenched the shovel away from Diana and dug.

THIRTY-ONE

0:22:12

The Lyreflies, feeling threatened, dug with renewed fervour as Cornelia attacked the earth, sweat pouring down her face.

She glanced up and Mallory was staring at something across the water, her head turned so Cornelia couldn't see her expression. The sunlight had burned away most of the ever-present fog and she could see across the lake for the first time since they'd arrived in Wickermere. Imogen had wrapped her arms around herself and Ezra stood with his arm around her, too worried to even begin to try to bark orders the way he normally would.

She wrenched her attention back to the ground in front of her, the Lyreflies rolling earth away in efficient movements like dung beetles. Cornelia wanted more than anything to stop and watch them in action, but kept going until her shovel made contact with something solid.

The edge of a wooden crate.

'ETHEL! AGATHA!' Imogen shouted. 'MOTHER IS HERE.'

Cornelia wanted to hit her with her shovel, but she kept going.

She scraped at the layers of dirt until it revealed the lid, covered in pulsating red algae. Like it was breathing.

Diana shouted an unintelligible spell to lift the lid off the box and they moved it aside, sliding in the loose earth as they fought to get a grip on it, revealing the Bonemarrow Lake shipping crate beneath. Inside was painted grey, with two small beds shoved inside, and the wan faces of Agatha and Ethel looking up at them.

Agatha's nails were bloody. There were claw marks on the walls, on her arms, on Ethel. Ethel's eyes were dark, her skin yellowed and pinched. She raised a hand to protect her eyes, but not before she'd seen who her rescuers were.

'C—' she started, but Diana screamed.

'DON'T SAY YOUR SIBLING'S NAME OR WE ALL DIE,' Diana shouted, as the twins blinked up at them. 'Maybe. Ghosts don't play by any rules we understand. But let's not risk it!'

'Are they alive? AGATHA? ETHEL?' Imogen rushed forward and Diana caught her, Ezra trying to pry her hands off his wife.

'Wait, you'll just fall in, just wait a second!' she said, and to her credit, the Broadwicks did.

'Help me,' Cornelia said, and Diana helped her toss the lid back. The Lyreflies circled Ethel with interest, but upon seeing their underground find was living, lifted upwards in an angry swarm, reaching a particularly uncomfortable crescendo as they disappeared.

'Oh. Elisabella, thank you. Thank you,' Imogen whispered, clambering in.

Even though it was categorically not Elisabella who had made this happen.

'Why the fuck can't I say her name? She's my sister,' Ethel said.

'Sibling,' Cornelia corrected. 'And because if you do, a goddess and her known and unknown associates get to take our bodies away to live in them. Some sort of ethereal ancient contract.'

She put a hand down to help Agatha climb out, but Agatha pulled her down into the crate in a fierce hug. The others crowded around, staring down at them. Ezra looked stunned, wiping his glasses on his shirt methodically.

'Thank you,' Ethel said, extricating herself from Imogen's hug. 'We were starting to think we were going to die in here. It reminded us of those frightful stories the papers kept running, about someone in the area burying people alive?'

Cornelia didn't dignify that with a response. It was probably for the best that they hadn't quite managed to put two and two together.

Ezra seemed to snap into reality; he pushed Diana out of the way and pulled Ethel and Imogen out of the box, holding a hand out for Agatha, leaving Cornelia to help herself out. Imogen clung to Mallory and sobbed while Ezra gathered his daughters to him.

'You're safe now. We've got you. You're safe now,' Ezra was saying.

Mallory motioned for Cornelia to come up and Imogen joined the Broadwick hug, relinquishing her hold on Mallory.

'Mum,' Agatha sobbed. 'I thought we were going to die.'

'We would never let that happen. We would never ever let anything happen to you. Oh, my girls,' Imogen said. 'Always my girls, no matter how old you get.'

Those words had never comforted Cornelia as a child, didn't comfort her now. She wished it was possible to live in the same world Agatha and Ethel inhabited, where no matter how old they were, or how clueless, or how much danger they were in, the Broadwick name would be enough to protect them.

Looking at them now, standing so close and yet so far from the centre of the family, she could see the path she'd been making for herself was the right one. Her parents were people. They were mortal. They were fallible. No amount of money or prestige or connections would change that. They were so caught up in the Ghoul Council – living and breathing the Ghoul Council values, *really* believing they were doing what was right – that they *were* the Ghoul Council. Their fates had been set out by Grandad Cornelius. Imogen had chosen this life the day she met Ezra. They had moulded their entire existence around the Broadwick name in search of something bigger, something less tangible: the safety of Occulture as they believed it should be. Sacrificing the few for the good of the many. Even if those few were their daughters.

It had hurt them to do it, she could see that. But she could see they believed so steadfastly in what they did – had wanted, so badly, to keep the Wickermere Reaper from getting their hands on Elisabella – that they were willing to suffer for the rest of their lives as a consequence.

It was so noble it bordered on cowardly.

It wasn't a world Cornelia wanted to live in. Perhaps cutting her off had been the best thing her family could've done.

'Look,' Mallory said, holding out a hand but not touching her, which made Cornelia's heart ache, a panicked thump that made being in the lake seem even more of a dream than it had before.

'Something's wrong.' Mallory pointed across Lake Wickermere to Bonemarrow Cottage, where bright light lit up the windows – brighter than they should've been, cutting through the haze of static over the water.

She turned to Imogen and Ezra. 'Did Dot or Olivia make a reappearance before you came here?' she asked, though Cornelia knew Stella would've texted if that was the case.

'No,' Ezra said, still hugging Agatha and Ethel to him. The whole thing was a bit nauseating, even amid the relief Cornelia could feel washing over her. One part of their ordeal completely over.

Just the Wickermere Reaper to find.

'Where did you put Elisabella?' Mallory whispered to Diana, who hooked an arm around Cornelia's waist and sagged forward.

'Safely away. I thought Bonemarrow Cottage was the best— Oh,' she said, squinting across the lake.

'I have a terrible feeling about this. Is there a witchlight—?'

Diana pulled one out of her pocket, and Mallory took a deep breath before stepping into it, disappearing.

Cornelia let her family continue their reunion, trying to find the happiness within her. She was relieved to have them back. Relieved to see they were mostly unharmed, but could not bear to think about how much panic Agatha must've been feeling to bloody her nails.

She could feel the Jacob in her head reminding her she knew what it was like to wait for someone to come and find her. To sit with the fear that they wouldn't. Images flashed through her head, plunging her back into a sense memory where she sat in bloodied darkness like a nightmare that wouldn't die, chased by the shame at making her sisters' abduction about herself, even if she'd never express it aloud.

'Where *is* that ambulance? Lucy was meant to be clearing them for Wickermere entry,' Imogen said.

'I can see lights,' Diana said, pointing over the water to the other side of the lake, where flashing blue lights crawled closer and closer.

'We need to talk to you,' Cornelia said urgently, trying to get the twins' attention. 'We need you to tell us anything you can about what happened when you got put in here.'

'Leave them be, they've just survived a dreadful ordeal,' Imogen admonished.

'There's still a serial killer on the loose. I'm quite sure it's one of your colleagues,' Cornelia said. 'Even if you don't want that to be the case.'

'We were in the car, having just come back from seeing Poppy,' Agatha said. 'She's had the baby and we wanted to bring her presents.'

'Where does Poppy live?'

'In Grasmere, in the cutest little townhouse. Like it's *one* townhouse, if you can imagine that,' Agatha said.

'I was driving,' Ethel said. 'Poppy's on some sort of dreadful feeding schedule – Poppy Junior, I should say – so we had to time it around whatever worked for our Poppy. We were on our way back – darling little thing, but very…'

'Vomit-y,' Agatha supplied. 'And then someone ran out in front of the car, or so I thought, so I stopped inside the gates.'

'Then what?' Diana asked.

'It was like darkness closed in around me,' Agatha said.

'Like someone had put a bag over my head,' Ethel added.

Cornelia waited for them to elaborate, but they continued blinking owlishly at her and she had to remind herself that they'd clearly had a shock.

'*Then* what?'

'I was walking somewhere. Couldn't see anything, just knew I had to.'

'Was it like a compulsion? Like someone told you to do it?' *Like demon magic*, she wanted to say, but needed to not lead them into an answer.

'No, no… I don't fully remember now…' Ethel said. 'It was…'

'A threat, I think.' Agatha looked thoughtful, her beautiful face furrowed with troubled confusion. 'If I cooperated, it wouldn't happen.'

'What wouldn't happen?'

'Something awful.'

'And then it was dark, but we were safe. I could see Agatha, and there were beds, and water. No windows. I had this sense something was happening outside of me, like there was something I'd just forgotten…'

It was starting to sound like some kind of amnesia, or mind-wiping spell, but as far as Cornelia knew, the latter didn't exist.

'Don't bother them with this now,' Ezra chided. 'They're tired, they can answer all your questions in a few days, when our other ordeal has concluded.'

'The killer is still out there,' Cornelia said sharply. 'We found the twins by sheer luck!'

'And the killer will be found,' Imogen said, cradling Agatha's face to hers. 'Thank you. And you,' she said, looking to Diana. 'But your job is done now.'

Ezra nodded in agreement.

Cornelia took another step back, Diana coming with her, observing the family unit as they went through the motions of reuniting. Although Agatha and Ethel were crying and expressing relief, she'd learned they were not stupid. Agatha's eyes darted suspiciously between Ezra and Imogen and back to Cornelia, full of questions she may never ask, full of a worry that it was not her family's name that had rescued her from a certain fate, but something else.

Cornelia would never know what it had really been like for them in there. Maybe it would be a story the twins would tell each other at night, to check it was real.

And maybe Cornelia could be the one to try to break that barrier down, to tell Ethel and Agatha she knew what it felt like to be taken by someone. To be betrayed. To be held somewhere and threatened with death.

To believe nobody was coming to save you.

She remembered now, in a sudden flood, what she'd said to the twins the day they'd threatened to bury her alive all those years ago. She'd been eight. Grandad Cornelius had just died. She remembered the anger shaking through her limbs, how ferocious she'd felt. How unfazed they were by it. How quickly they forgot on the drive up here.

But she hoped they hadn't recalled it. Either of them. In the dark.

The Broadwicks would perhaps no longer be as united a

front as they'd pretended.

Cornelia no longer felt like she was part of it. She had her own family now. Her own life. She owed them nothing else.

Diana's arm was still wrapped firmly around Cornelia's middle. At this point, Cornelia was sure this was the only thing still holding her upright. Relief sagged through her and she wanted to lie down for a few days, not face down a killer. She didn't know how many more facing-downs she had in her.

Lights flashed closer and an ambulance arrived, and for once Cornelia and Diana got to shrug them off, directing them to take care of Agatha and Ethel.

Cornelia was anxious as they were checked over – mostly afraid there was some extra curse, one more hex that would kill them anyway when the time ran out – but the medics were satisfied that Agatha needed bandages and Ethel needed a drip, and the Broadwicks negotiated to allow their family doctor – who was really a surgeon friend of theirs – to set up a hospital room for them at Rowan House, rather than taking them to an Apparent hospital an hour away. Cornelia resolutely avoided looking at Diana during this exchange; the infrastructure had remained from when her grandfather was dying and was not as ludicrous as it sounded.

'We'd better go check in on Mallory,' she said, both as a glad distraction, and because she didn't want to be party to the scene in front of her anymore. She wasn't part of this.

'Do you think it's her?'

'Who?'

'Olivia,' Diana said.

'I don't know.'

'Mallory said it wasn't rational, how Olivia reacted, and she was right.'

'When did she say this?'

'While you were distracted. She's worried. Either Olivia is the culprit and Dot's in danger, or someone sent Olivia out there. What the twins just said… I don't know what we're up against.'

'But it's time to find out,' Cornelia said, pulling out another witchlight.

'Wait!' a voice said, looming out of the fog. 'Wait! Help me! She's after me!'

THIRTY-TWO

??:??:?? (ad infinitum)

The light burning brightly in the front windows of Bone-marrow Cottage swelled and broke the glass in a sudden whoosh, engulfing everything in hot navy smoke.

Every bit of the building, from the factory to the cottage, up in flames.

Including the room Mallory had the misfortune of witch-lighting right into.

Fire ran up the walls to the ceiling. It tracked steadily across the window frame, the kitchen cabinets, leaving Mallory in the centre of the room, only the door behind her free, the front door swinging open but the frame burning, burning, burning.

Screams ripped from her throat before it had even really registered, screaming for Ruby and Jo, terrified Stella was inside somewhere and unable to hear her. The button panel she'd seen Ruby press before was alight.

Diana's hiding place for Elisabella's ghostlight – the oddments drawer of the Witches' kitchen table – was smashed to pieces on the ground, and flames caressed the edges of the table, ready to claim it. The air was too thick to breathe, her vision blurring.

Self-preservation kicked in as the front door swung towards her, and she ran towards it.

'RUBY!' Mallory screamed, safely outside as the fire roared.

Gasping, she watched as the upper windows blew out, then ran around the side of the cottage, stumbling in the dark through the gardens as she tried to get close enough to see in the windows, the heat pushing her back and making her eyes water.

She turned the corner, and saw the first body.

'RUBY!' Mallory wheezed, scrambling over.

She lay motionless in the garden beneath the apple tree. Her arms were outstretched, a dark, oozing injury on her temple, as though she'd been struck by something.

'Ruby?' Mallory checked for a pulse, but there was none.

She tried not to touch the body – always, even in her darkest hours, thinking of the practical options. Ruby's eyes were open, reaching. They'd just seen her at Rowan House. In the time it took for them to find the twins, someone had killed her.

It wasn't looking good for either Olivia or Dot.

Mallory sank back on the ground, coughing, her eyes stinging. Flames licked up the trees closest to the cottage walls, fire spreading from the roof of the cottage to anything within shivering distance of it. The top-most window of the factory blew out, flames licking through it, and Mallory scrambled backwards, coughs wracking her lungs as she scanned for signs of life.

Then she saw it, a wave of defeat spreading over her.

A foot, encased in a familiar green velvet shoe, stretching over the back door threshold.

Swearing under her breath, Mallory tried to crawl closer to Jo, but the fire roared, as if in warning. Summoning every scrap of energy she had, she tried extinguishing the flames with magic – desperate, whispered spells that did nothing but make her lungs spasm and her body shake – until a scream of pain up her arms told her to stop.

There was nothing she could do but watch as Bonemarrow Cottage burned to the ground, the factory and the Witches' work with it.

In the midst of it all – the horror, the heat, the terror that rose up within her – she also felt… cheated. Like the Reaper had made her play a game by their rules, and then switched it up at the last second. Killing the Witches was cruel.

Unless that wasn't the Wickermere Reaper's intention. Unless something went horribly wrong.

Unless the Lyreflies had foiled the Reaper once, and they weren't prepared to let it happen again.

Mallory sent a text, and got a response that made her fold in on herself in partial relief, partial devastation that she would have to break terrible news soon.

> *Stella*
> still at rowan house
> did you find the twins??

The cottage burned, acrid smoke rising into foggy night sky, and Mallory tried her best to think. Olivia ran, Dot followed.

Imogen and Ezra were resistant to giving in to the Wickermere Reaper's demands, but their relief, Imogen's lack of interest in anything to do with retrieving Elisabella…

No one was that good an actor.

Her earlier instinct was correct. It had to be Olivia or Dot.

Mallory felt a pulse in her chest, sharp across her sternum, that made her gasp. Her mouth formed a word she could not say, but desperately wanted to. Her mind tried to convince her it was okay to say it, when she wasn't here in front of her. That saying it would be a relief.

The Besiegement Curse ticked over in the background, trying to make her end it. End the pain.

And it hurt.

The fire raged on, the tree fully alight but not close enough to the rest of the garden to pose a risk. Mallory moved further away and pulled her t-shirt up over her mouth, trying to breathe normally.

She wanted to get the bodies out before it became too difficult for a third party to identify them, then hated herself for thinking that. They weren't *bodies.* They were the barely cold corpses of two Witches who had done nothing but help them.

Helping to save Agatha and Ethel was probably the last thing they'd done with their lives.

The Undetectables had brought that danger to them. She and Diana had been sure nobody would look in the Witches' house for Elisabella. This was entirely their fault.

She'd underestimated the Reaper. In their efforts to get ahead of her – that much Mallory was sure of – she'd looked away from the facts. Imogen kept dossiers, but others had access to them. If Diana could steal them, so too could the Reaper. If the Broadwicks could watch them, so could the Reaper. If anything, they'd made it easier for her.

The Wickermere Reaper knew the way they thought, the way they acted. They were no strangers to killers making things personal, to killers being cleverer, but Mallory had really thought that in the last year, their little PI agency had flourished into something unstoppable.

There had been a time when Mallory was sure she and her friends were smarter than most killers. That they could use wit and skills and tools to win any fight. But bodies kept dropping around them and cases kept spiralling out of control.

With difficulty, Mallory pulled herself to her feet, calling the fire services and an ambulance, trying to put distance between herself and the smoke. It had to have been visible from where Cornelia and Diana were now.

She stumbled back a few steps as another tree in the garden burst into flames with a *whoosh*, burning leaves raining down on the path below.

That's when she saw it.

Or rather, that's when she fell over it.

She crunched over pieces of shattered witchlight and knocked against something solid and animal.

An arm. A hand, red and bloody and mottled, pieces of witchlight crystal embedded in the skin as if the owner had tried to catch it as it shattered. Mallory fumbled in her pocket for her own witchlight, holding it up, fearing the worst: that Stella had come back in the minutes where Mallory hadn't replied and died somehow, dark tousled hair over the face so she had to turn the body and see, to know for sure.

But it wasn't Stella, and it wasn't a body.

She was still alive.

Mallory found a pulse, soft but strong, and tried shaking her, whispering her name, but she wouldn't wake, her eyes closed, her skin pale.

Shaking, Mallory pulled on gloves and reached into the body's – the *living* body's – pockets, but did not find what she was looking for, even when she held the witchlight high, forcing her streaming eyes to focus. There was no mistaking it. Empty pockets.

The body's eyes flew open and her hand reached for Mallory.

'Help,' she whispered. 'Help them.'

'There's an ambulance coming,' she said. 'There's someone coming.'

Mallory felt a shiver race through her as she scrambled to her feet.

She knew who had taken Elisabella.

And she knew who the Wickermere Reaper was.

THIRTY-THREE

Covered in ash and soot, her face twisted in concern, and limping along the path they'd taken through the trees, was Dot.

Cornelia and Diana rushed forward, grabbing Dot under her arms, and she slumped forward with gratitude.

'—we can get Lucy to order us a nice takeaway when we get in,' Imogen was saying, oblivious. 'I think we can afford to live a little for one night, don't you think, darling?'

'She doesn't work for us anymore, remember? We brought her back for the séance as a kindness – one she evidently won't repay, as she was making noises about quitting,' Ezra said. 'We'll get back to the house—'

'Ezra,' Cornelia said sharply.

Surprised, her father looked up at her, finally noticed what was going on, and ran to Dot.

'What happened? Where's that medic?'

But the ambulance was gone, the lights barely visible on the other side of the lake as the fog rolled in, thicker than ever, and it was just the Broadwicks, Cornelia, Diana and a possibly injured, terrified Dot.

'Get her some water,' Cornelia urged.

Ethel held up a water bottle, and Imogen passed it to Ezra while Diana and Cornelia tried to sit Dot up against a tree.

'Dot? Can you hear us? *Dorothy*,' Diana said firmly, patting her on the face.

It wasn't quite a slap, but it startled Dot enough that her eyes shot open and a spasm of coughing forced her forward onto her hands, fingers gripping the ground covered in damp, shimmering ferns.

'Who's after you?' Cornelia asked after she finished, easing her back into a sitting position.

'Olivia,' she said, her face grave.

Cornelia's stomach plummeted, and the fear gave way to a mix of nausea and shame.

Mallory had tried to warn her, but Cornelia had been so convinced that she wouldn't be fooled again so easily by someone bringing her a letter, or being helpful, or smiling at her in a way she liked.

'I didn't… I really didn't think…' Dot said, struggling to get the words out.

Cornelia made her take another drink. Imogen stooped over Dot with her hands folded between her knees, watching her face. 'She's skittish – has been the whole time I worked with her. She'd call it caution, but you know, Imogen, I've told you…'

Diana frowned and Cornelia bit back the immediate question of why that hadn't appeared in the dossiers, but Imogen nodded uncertainly. 'I wouldn't have said *skittish*, my dear. We only employ the best, and we screen for that kind of thing, but you did mention it, yes.'

Dot swallowed, coughing again. 'I knew she'd go to the Witches for help, try to manipulate them, but I got there and… oh. She had set that place on fire. It's gone.'

Cornelia shot an alarmed glance across the lake. *Mallory.*

'All of Bonemarrow Cottage, the factory too, I suspect, gone. Their work. Stella…'

'What happened to Stella?' Diana asked urgently.

'She'll be all alone in the world,' Dot said, pressing a hand to her head. 'Help me up, I don't think we have much time—'

'We won't let her near you,' Imogen promised. 'We got the girls back, she won't hurt us again. There are measures in place. Rules.'

'No, no, you need to listen to me,' Dorothy said, gasping again. 'She's coming. She's coming for you,' she said to Cornelia. 'She wants to say your name, enact the Besiegement, so she can take Elisabella and bargain with her to lift the curse. She wants you all to die. She wants the Broadwicks to perish, so she can take control of the Ghoul Council.'

'How do you know all this?' Diana asked. 'Did we miss the villain speech?'

'We don't have time,' Dot said again. 'Where's the ghostlight?'

'Somewhere safe,' Diana said, looking out over the lake again.

The light from Bonemarrow Cottage was starting to dim – hopefully that was the fire going out – and Cornelia's stomach twisted in discomfort, torn between wanting to go after Mallory and wanting to not condemn all of them to a life of being dead.

'Give her to me. Go get her, give her to me. I can bargain with her. She can have my life in exchange for it. That's all she cares about.'

'No,' Cornelia said sharply. 'No. You're not doing that.'

'Love,' Dot said fondly. 'I'm old. I'm retired, I'm disposable. I've made my decision. This is how you get out of it.'

'We need to go back to Rowan House,' Diana said. 'That's where Elisabella is.'

Cornelia shot her a look, confused, but Diana met her gaze.

It said, unmistakably, *trust me*.

Cornelia nodded. 'Back to Rowan House. We can remove Olivia's access, stop her getting in, and we can regroup. Make a decision,' she said uncertainly.

'Let's go, then,' Ezra said, but Diana's witchlight flared and Mallory stumbled out, arms wrapped around herself.

'I know who—' she said, but stopped dead, breathing ragged. She pushed her shoulder against a tree and focused on breathing, her eyes taking in the scene as she slid down to the ferns below.

'What happened? Someone get Mallory a blanket, she's shivering,' Dot said, struggling to her feet even as Diana caught her.

'I'm fine,' Mallory said, in the manner of someone who was not, in fact, fine at all.

'We thought you'd been caught by Olivia,' Diana said urgently. 'Did you see her?'

Mallory took a steadying breath. She was always so calm in the face of something awful.

'We need to go back now,' Imogen said, her anxiety palpable.

'I am ready for a shower,' Agatha announced. 'And to receive my much-needed medical attention. Is Dr Curtis coming, Mother?'

'Did anyone water my plants while I was gone?' Ethel croaked.

Cornelia ignored all of this. Mallory's face was set, serious.

'Someone fill me in,' Mallory said finally.

'Dot's come here from Bonemarrow Cottage, she said it's in ruins. That Jo and Ruby…'

'Are dead, yes,' Mallory said. 'I know.'

'We need to move now,' Ezra said. 'I don't like us being out in the open like this. Can someone call Harry, let him know we're coming and that we've got the culprit?'

Mallory straightened. 'You know, what's really interesting about all of this is how *determined* we were not to be caught out again.'

Cornelia felt shame flare in her stomach. 'I know, I shouldn't—'

'Let her cook,' Diana said.

Something in her expression told Cornelia to shut up and listen, so she did.

'The Wickermere Reaper is quite a fascinating figure,' Mallory said quietly. 'Starting with Apparents, moving closer and closer to the Broadwicks. Careful not to make mistakes. Not to leave traces – except one. The reminder spell. We had to resort to scrappier methods to confirm it – I'm not sure our more sophisticated methods would've picked up on it, they certainly had our beetles confused. Every step of the method was evasive of our current measures – but then, the Broadwicks had been watching us all this time, so anything we could do, the Reaper would know about.'

'I don't think—' Imogen started, but Diana shushed her.

'We saw the dossier, you literally have no defence,' Diana said.

'Besides, our methods are fast becoming standard now, though there are limitations. You either need to know *where* a crime happened and if there was something worth finding there, or you need to find ways to determine how that crime happened, and both would hopefully lead you to the answer of *who*. In the case of the Reaper, there wasn't time to establish new methods. We barely knew *where*, and when we did, we didn't have the facilities or the luxury of establishing extensive facts. We had to go on face value.'

Dot coughed again.

'Mallory, please,' Agatha said. 'Ethel and Dot need medical help. You can do your little speech back at the house.'

'This won't take long,' she promised.

She curled in on herself for a moment, coughing, and Cornelia wanted to stop her, get her on oxygen, make sure she didn't have lung damage. Make sure she was okay.

'At face value, it was someone within the Ghoul Council,' Mallory said, recovering. 'Someone smart, with access to internal information that would lead them to know that Elisabella was *here*, or at least have reasonable belief that Elisabella was here and not in Wrackton. Who would know that there was a way to get her from the bottom of the lake.'

'That could be anyone who worked on Project TRIAD,' Ezra said.

'Speak for yourself and your pet project, darling. I would *never*,' Imogen said, scandalised.

'But the Ghoul Council doesn't look at the big picture. They look at the trees, and miss the forest,' Mallory said. 'We proved that, by finding the ghostlight ourselves. Among you, only the Reaper was capable of believing it was possible. Only the Reaper could know how to manipulate the Broadwicks – I am sorry to say that you *were* manipulated, even in your attempts to not be – and could be still trying to do it as we speak. It all rests on Project TRIAD.'

'That's how she knew,' Dot whispered. 'That's how Olivia knew.'

'It is,' Mallory agreed. 'That's how Olivia knew the Wickermere Reaper was you, Dot.'

THIRTY-FOUR

Someone screamed; Cornelia had to check it wasn't her.

'Me?' Dot said, her brow furrowed. 'Mallory, did she hurt you? Did she make you say that?'

'I found Olivia unconscious outside Bonemarrow Cottage,' Mallory said. 'She'd been hit in the head.'

'I confronted her, when I found her there,' Dot said. 'She was trying to hurt me, I had to defend myself.'

'With what?'

'Mallory, is this *necessary*?' Imogen asked.

'With what?' she asked again.

'A branch nearby, I don't quite remember,' Dot said, holding a hand to her temple.

'I found pieces of witchlight beside her. Looks like someone clocked her one, a big welt on her forehead,' Mallory said.

'It all happened so fast,' Dot said, wincing. 'I… didn't think I hit her that hard. Elisabella help me, I was just desperate to get out of there. She was coming for me and I ran. Thank Blair I stumbled upon you here, I don't know what I would've done if I hadn't.'

Mallory nodded. 'Self-defence makes sense. And how did you kill Ruby and Jo?'

'*What?*' Diana stepped forward, but Cornelia stopped her.

She was floating out of her body, watching Mallory, watching this unfold.

It had always been a possibility that it was Dot – she'd suffered the betrayal of her parents murdering or being involved in the murder of Theodore, had looked into the faces of Harry and Dot and the rest of the Ghoul Council and had been *ready* for it to be any of them, but preparation couldn't save her from the gut-punch that accepting the truth served her.

She'd wanted it to be Imogen, she realised belatedly. Wanted it to be neat and tidy. Wanted to be right.

'I didn't!' Dot's brow furrowed.

'Well, if you're not going to tell the truth, someone may as well,' Mallory said. It was almost sarcastic – but only almost. 'Ruby and Jo were on the way to Rowan House when you witch-lighted after Olivia, so she had to have been hit first. Ruby and Jo must've returned while you were tossing the place. Ruby had the same type of wound on her forehead. I couldn't get properly close to Jo, but I'm willing to bet our dwindling agency money that she'd been hit too. It was Lucy's witchlight – we watched you take it from the table in Rowan House to follow Olivia out to the cottage. The pieces are all still out there, I think it'll be easy to determine if that same witchlight we saw you take, the one you admit to hitting Olivia with, is the murder weapon. Or attempted, in Olivia's case.'

'I don't know what to say. Imogen, Ezra, you're not… you're not entertaining this, are you?' Dot said, incredulous.

'No, and that's quite enough, Mallory,' Ezra said firmly. A sheen of sweat covered his forehead, and it was hard to tell if that was the Besiegement Curse, or if he was genuinely distressed by the accusations.

'You've had a terrible ordeal, darling,' Imogen said to Mallory. The Broadwick mask firmly in place once again. 'Let's get you back, get you rested. We'll have folk out looking for Olivia, I'll let Harry know to tell the paramedics she's over by Bonemarrow Lane.'

They gathered up their daughters and Ezra took Dot's arm as they started walking towards Rowan House, leaving Cornelia, Diana and Mallory looking after them, aghast.

'Let me check her pockets,' Mallory said desperately. 'You can't bring her back—'

'One more step, and I'll say her name,' Dot said.

The Broadwicks froze and Dot worked herself free of Ezra's grasp.

Dot smiled at Cornelia, her face crinkling with pure joy.

'Thought that'd get your attention,' she said. 'Mallory, look in my pockets. Go on. I know you don't want it to be Olivia, and I can't say I blame you.'

Diana took a step towards her, but Dot shook her head. 'No, let Mallory do it.'

'What's going on?' Ezra asked.

'I think you should be quiet,' Diana said.

To his credit, he seemed to agree.

Mallory reached into Dot's pockets, methodically searching, patting around the lining of her coat until she pulled something out of the inside pocket and held it up.

A folded piece of creamy-white paper, the same size and shape as the ransom notes.

Dot's face blanched.

'I've got you,' Mallory said quietly.

'I'll say her name,' Dot said cheerfully. 'I'll say it, and that'll be that.'

'MALLORY,' Imogen exclaimed.

Dot held up a hand. 'I suggest you all go stand over there,' she said, pointing into the clearing they'd just left. 'All together now, that's the one.'

She reached down into the top of her cheerful little boots and pulled out Elisabella's ghostlight.

Imogen gasped, but did as she was told.

'All of you,' Dot said, pointing to the Undetectables.

'Auntie Dot, you can't be—'

'Hush, hush. This won't take long,' Dot said to Agatha or Ethel or whichever one had spoken.

She balanced the ghostlight on her palm. 'A ghostlight's not like a witchlight. If I shatter this now, she's free for good. A design flaw. Bad engineering, one might call it. I don't know what I'd call it. Lucky, perhaps, especially as she's not just going to pop back to Wrackton now. Wasn't that an *interesting* development? That's the kind of intellectual stimulation that might've kept me in the job a bit longer.'

'You?' Ezra said, finally catching on.

'Me,' Dot said, shimmying her shoulders. 'Surprise.' It was as playful as if she'd announced she'd drunk the last of the wine at dinner.

'But...'

'But what? I'm too… old? Too… nice? Too… familiar?'

Yes. As much as Cornelia wouldn't want to admit it, all of that had passed through her head. In a family of alleged murderers and all-out idiots, she'd wanted to think at least one of them was good, even if she wasn't Broadwick by blood.

'You'd think any of that would matter, but it doesn't. One thing I learned in my life, C— Ooh, can't make that mistake now, can we dear? The best lesson I've learned is that you cannot let other people tell you who you are. Remember I taught you that? And you girls, too?'

Agatha and Ethel nodded slowly.

'You cannot let yourself be defined by others' expectations of you. Your family expected me to be loyal, expected me to be a bit doddery as time wore on, gave me less and less to do – managing my stress, I think you called it, Ezra?'

'Yes.' He was staring at her, unblinking, like she had a bomb on her person and there was no way to talk her down.

Technically, she had two bombs, but Cornelia didn't want to digress.

'So, no promotion for steady old Dorothy when things really kicked into gear with the Mayoral Offices two years ago. Everyone was busy writing manuals and giving the UML rules and staying very, very far away from the Offices themselves. Official, permanent retirement, I think you suggested. Take a load off, a promise to come back as a consultant instead, with no scope for rehiring.'

'Are you saying you did all this,' Cornelia gestured, 'because you didn't get a promotion?'

Dot smiled at her. 'Oh, my dear. It's baffling how you're the brightest of them and the most oblivious of them all at once. A walking paradox, and they've never seen you for who you are. No, Ezra, don't argue, it is fruitless and you know it. No, what I'm saying is that choice actually freed me up to do a bit of thinking. A bit of designing my own fun, dedicating myself to my own projects.'

'That's better, isn't it? Time to yourself?' Imogen tried.

'That's what I thought too! That retirement would suit me. Would let me pick and choose what I did in my own free time. It made me feel so much *lighter*, to only have to worry about my own whims. The last time I felt this good was when Cornelius was around— aha, you all thought I was about to make a mistake there, didn't you?' she laughed, as the unwilling audience gasped. 'You noticed, didn't you Imogen? You kept saying how I was glowing.'

Cornelia felt sick to her stomach.

Dot straightened her blouse, clearly enjoying herself. 'I'd like you all to kneel. I heard my friend Lyle liked that one, Hexana help him. Not the brightest spoon in the drawer, but I do admit it is a nice touch. I write to him a bit, you know. Pen pals are hard to come by these days and he's got nothing better to do. Anyway, sorry, Diana and Mallory,' she added. 'I'd really hoped for this to just be the Broadwicks, but you're here now. We have to adapt where required!'

'I'm not kneeling,' Imogen protested. 'Nor are the girls, or my other child, or my husband.'

It was the first time she hadn't included Cornelia in 'the girls', and Cornelia felt strangely validated.

'You will,' Dot said. 'Or I will say her name right now and

unleash Elisabella on this town. Wouldn't that be fun!' she said cheerfully.

They knelt, reluctantly, facing this woman they'd trusted – that Cornelia had known her whole, entire life – who was using threats and not much else, and feeling powerless nonetheless.

Cornelia ran through magic they could use on her, ways to incapacitate her, but drew a blank.

And then Mallory moved. She was quick, and Dot was small, and in seconds she was on her, one hand clamped over Dot's mouth, the other gripped tightly around the hand with Elisabella in it.

'Don't struggle,' Mallory said, panting. 'Just drop it.'

Dorothy became perfectly still, her face reddening as she raised her fingers to her ruby pendant.

Ezra, apparently growing something of a spine, climbed to his feet and went to help Mallory. A static crackle made Mallory cry out, and then Mallory was thrown off Dot, hitting the ground like a rag doll.

THIRTY-FIVE

Mallory lay motionless, her arms cradled close to her chest where she'd tried to break her fall. Cornelia darted towards her, but Dot shook her head.

'No no nooo,' she said, sing-song, as though Cornelia had just reached for a cake she wasn't finished cutting. 'Little thing, actually. I rather think you've been labouring under the illusion that there was one killer, one person doing all this, one person behind all of this. And while it's true, you didn't consider possibilities outside of the box. Or rather, possibilities that were uniquely available to me all this time. I wanted to ask you if you were ever really scientists – though I suppose there's a reason you're in government jobs instead.'

Sweat trickled down Cornelia's forehead, and she realised for the first time that it wasn't fear. It was warm. Warm like the lab, warm like the lake.

Static crackled in the air around her and the pieces started to slot together, too slowly, too late.

The logistics of someone Dot's size and strength digging.

How one – arguably tiny – woman could do all this with no help.

'Haven't you ever wondered how witchlights were powered? Why they were ghost-safe?' Dot asked.

Or why Cornelia had been able to store a spell in a crystal necklace for Mallory. Why magic could be stored at all. Why they'd only been able to pull a single magic trace with the beetles.

The magic had been contaminated in the first place, because it hadn't been any one person's magic – it had been lots of different scraps of magic jumbled together.

'They're powered by ghosts,' Cornelia said, everything slotting together at once. 'Non-corporeal ghosts. There's a high concentration in the lake, but you figured out a way to get them to help you.'

'Ahh. There's a reason you've always been my favourite,' Dot said, clapping her hands together. 'What else?'

'You used it to help you dig the burial sites, you used the magic to confuse your victims. Convince them to go with you. Wipe their memories afterwards, somehow.' Cornelia was, at this point, guessing, but a hunch told her she was right.

She remembered the voice in her head telling her to open the ghostlight.

'You used the ghost magic on me. During the séance, you made me open the ghostlight.'

'Very good.' Dot beamed at her. 'I'd get you an ice cream for that. See, Ezra, you're never too old for ice cream.'

He was expressionless. Cornelia wanted to kick him into action. There was a panic in her chest at the idea of the heads of the literal fucking Ghoul Council being incapable of taking action when the time required it.

'Why?'

'Why not?' Dot shrugged. 'Why does anyone do anything?'

'But why did *you* do it?' Diana asked. 'We're not interested in anyone, we're interested in you.'

'That's flattering,' Dot said, grinning softly. 'You're great with words, I'll give you that, dear.'

'I know why,' Cornelia said. She felt the truth, greater than a hunch, greater than anything else she was feeling.

'Do tell,' Dot said, peering at her over her glasses.

Cornelia adjusted her own, trying to ignore the fingerprint she'd just smeared over the lens.

'This isn't a ritual, or rooted in anything. You wanted to do it because you *could*. You made a monster – someone who would bury people alive, someone with endless power, a spectre in the night, because you *could*. Right under the noses of the Broadwicks. You wanted Agatha and Ethel to die, but that's not the fun bit for you, is it? It's not about the victims, it's about us. Us panicking, and spinning, and worrying, while you get to gleefully watch it unfold the way you'd planned. You don't want Elisabella for anything in particular – you're threatening to release her with no care for the consequences, because you *don't* care what happens. You've had access to every single file the Ghoul Council have – you could've had Lucy bring you anything you couldn't get your hands on – and if you had a grand plan anyone could possibly theorise in advance, you'd be doing it now. But you don't have one.

'You hung around the Council instead of fully retiring

because they wanted you to. They kept saying they'd arrange a full handover, but they weren't handing your role over to anyone else. They relied on you as a font of knowledge, but didn't respect you.'

'Well, that's not—' Ezra started.

'It is true, don't insult me,' Dot said lightly. Her stance had relaxed, interested in what Cornelia had to say. 'She's right, you know. What's the other part?'

'So you could keep an eye on them if they got close. Misdirect, help bury them in meetings and rules. I doubt Harry needs the encouragement, but you were enthusiastic about wasting time.'

Her mind whirred, feeling how Mallory must've felt most of the time, her mouth struggling to keep up.

'Do keep going, I am enjoying this. I love a good peer review.'

'You killed the first Apparent victim not long after you retired. So you must've had this idea for a while.'

'It wasn't even my idea, you know,' she said conspiratorially. 'The Wickermere Reaper's main MO came from a book I stumbled upon. It was an old torture concept. Blocking folk up in walls and letting the oxygen run out slowly – they did a load of that before the Vampire Wars started. It tickled me, I'll admit. I wondered who was suffering most – the buried, or the people outside, knowing they could do something about it and choosing not to. Or worse, realising too late that they *could've* done something. Fascinating concept, guilt. Suffer once, then suffer again from your own feelings. Then I remembered the time you told me the twins had put you in that bunker – do you remember that? Everything clicked together. I'd bury them underground! I had an oxygen source from the algae – easy to leave a reminder spell with the victim to set off the mechanism to burn it off. The timeline was my idea, of course – added a bit of danger to it – but the spellwork existed already. I was simply conducting further research by adding to the framework. Keep going!'

Cornelia swallowed. Letting Dot see how horrified she was wasn't an option.

'You were testing things out, with the first Apparent victim. That was a straight-up killing, you wanted to see what would happen if they discovered the body. If they could link it back to you. The ransoms – they were to see how much responsibility the family took, weren't they?'

'Oh, very good! Yes, they were too preoccupied with arguing that they couldn't have seen them, instead of viewing it as a missed opportunity. I had to have a think about avoiding further confounding variables, and realised the only way was to deliver a note to them directly. Fascinating outcomes from that – there was *still* blame on external forces. I asked for money, I asked for artefacts I *knew* they could get their little Apparent paws on if they really tried. Alternative hypothesis accepted *every single time*,' Dot said.

'So you did another, and another,' Cornelia said, afraid if she stopped speaking, she'd start crying. 'And when you were satisfied you knew what you were doing, you started on Occult folk.'

'Very good. I waited a little between each experiment, really honed my analyses. I was going to wait longer – to be perfectly honest, I was content to keep building the Wickermere Reaper up and up into a monster until the day I died. But then the

Ghoul Council got *very* preoccupied with Wrackton and the exploded Mayoral Offices, and all the things you were getting up to there. Van Doren's death really affected those in the UML who benefited from his presence. So many meetings and so much red tape, things I wasn't even involved in but made to hear for *months*. Have you ever wanted to blow your own brains out rather than listen to a single word more on a topic?'

'That was my entire formal schooling state of mind,' Cornelia said.

'It's always been boring here, and I have always been looking for ways to make it more exciting. I had other ways to amuse myself before this. Preliminary research, let's call it, but your grandfather put a stop to that – not even on purpose, sadly. He really believed Apparents were just wandering in here and falling into the lake, the old fool. I couldn't tell him what I was up to, not without him wanting to requisition the base assumptions for some silly Project TRIAD nonsense – he'd have frowned on my methods, of course, but that's to be expected. He was soft-hearted, your grandfather.

'Anyway, base assumptions – I was measuring the electromagnetic charge of the lake, how new souls changed it. Not only *changed* but made it more powerful, more volatile, which was an incredibly exciting finding to have to keep to myself. Live subjects were out of the question once he shut the village down and put the wards in place, but I took my lumps and behaved. Did everything right for years, kept wondering about the electromagnetic power of the lake and how that could be used, until I realised there was no point in behaving. I had discovered something *huge* in letting those Apparents die, and I'd never get Imogen and Ezra on board with a little bit of discriminate killing.

'I suppose that's how it started. I wondered how I'd make things exciting for myself, how I was going to get any freedom working under all these stuffy rules, and I realised how *bored* I was. I needed to spice things up. So I made a monster. But I'll tell you a secret. The conclusion nobody wants to draw, though it would save them a lot of heartache: *monsters are just people.*'

Dot looked at Imogen, who had drained of colour and was now a particularly corpsely shade of grey. 'Took you a *surprising* amount of time to look into it, Imogen. Remember all those times I told you to worry, and you told me no need? This was why. I really needed you to look in the right direction. The papers were full of the stories of the so-called Wickermere Reaper. Trending on the internet, even! That's what Lucy told me. She was worried, as was young Olivia. Even Harry, at one point, had "some concerns". But Ezra and Imogen knew better, didn't you? Nothing worth looking into, I think you said at first. Laser-focused on your own projects, you didn't think there was anything to concern yourself with here. It was just fine by me.'

'So you took Annie, and Ali, and then you went for Stella. But you made a mistake,' Cornelia said.

'I really didn't think there was a way to find her,' Dot said. 'I misjudged how much of a relationship you had with the Witches when you were here last, talking non-stop about the Lyreflies and what have you. I'd all but forgotten it. Sometimes you think you know everything, and then something comes along and shows you how to put the world to rights. But Stella didn't seem to remember a thing, so it was okay in the end. It was the closest I'd come to getting caught. Going over to the Witches every week for tea and a natter, knowing they'd kill me if they knew. Hexana help me, the fear I felt… I'd have done anything to feel that alive again.'

'So you did,' Cornelia said.

Dot nodded, eyes sparkling.

'You took the twins, and you asked for the one thing you knew the Broadwicks wouldn't give you. But instead of being coy, like you were with the Witches, you outright asked for the impossible – except you knew it wasn't. Difficult, sure, but not *impossible*.'

'I thought they'd drag the lake, send in a team, do *something*. And then you brought Elisabella to me! I was utterly astounded when you whipped out that ghostlight – it was very exciting to work on the fly, but I had all those ghosts, the witchlight was right in front of me… It was easy to convince you to open it. I really thought this would tie them up in knots – the big no-no of the Ghoul Council, happening on their watch. Oh, Cornelius must've been rolling in his grave. We all know Nova made calls to the UML as soon as they left the table. But up to that point, I was having such *fun*, dear. Letting the time run out while the Council spun their wheels, then swooping in at the end with a little note for you…' She shivered dramatically. 'I can't tell you how delicious it all was. I could only hope you'd rise to the challenge, but of course I should've known you would. None of this is what you wanted to hear, I'm sure – with the Besiegement and so forth, the rest of you have probably been expecting some sort of ritual killing. But that's boring, you understand? Everything that little fool Whitlock did, young Van Doren – or Gabbott, is it? Terribly dull, to repeat history, when you can do something new and exciting. I've read your files. The Undetectables. Exciting cases, all of them. But no.' Dot clasped her hands behind her back. 'The truth, the barest truth to all of this, is that I just wanted to. I wanted to kill and torment the living in the process, so I did. Any more questions, or…?'

'Yeah, I've one – what did Mallory find in your pocket?' Cornelia asked.

Dot's face crinkled into a pleased smile.

'Ask her. When she wakes. She's clever, that one.'

'You got what you wanted,' Imogen said stiffly. 'Can't you let us go now? We'll go easy in our report. We'll make sure the UML are lenient, on our recommendation. You've been under immense strain for so many years—'

Dot laughed. 'Oh, she's not getting it, is she?' She winked at Diana. 'You do, though, the pair of you. And now's the part where you try asking me to stop. "Let me go! I'll do anything you ask!"' she cried, hands clasped in front of her, a mocking plea. 'It doesn't matter, my dears. None of it matters.'

Cornelia tried to stand up again, but Dot waved a hand. 'No, no. Stay on your knees for now. This won't take too much longer.'

Cornelia didn't like that one bit.

'You have Elisabella. What could you possibly want to do now?' Diana asked.

'What's amazing about that question is that the world is my oyster,' Dot said thoughtfully. 'I could go anywhere, do anything, be anyone, and you can't stop me. Only the Curse could stop me, but that'll wear off soon. Say, I joined the Ghoul Council thinking it held the answers for me – I was always just a bit sharper than my peers, always willing to ask the tough questions. I had the interest, the ambition, the *drive* to really make a change in the world. And for a short while, it was satisfying enough to be challenged every day. Then I got older, and my brilliant colleagues were replaced by ostensibly younger and brighter ones, and I realised quickly that the Ghoul Council, *my* Ghoul Council, was a special group. Ezra and Imogen came into Cornelius's power and tried to make a change, but they never got as close as I imagine they'd have liked to. And then I realised they relished the red tape, the rules, the bureaucracy that keeps the Occult world ticking over. If we're all wrapped up in what's wrong, we can't do anything right. The Ternion had the right idea.'

'What idea?'

Dot pursed her lips, raising her eyebrows playfully. 'I guess you'll never know.'

'Dot,' Cornelia pleaded. 'You've known me my whole life. You used to help me build my vivariums. You can tell me anything. You're right, the world is your oyster now. What's the harm in telling us what we want to hear?'

'*That's* the harm, dear. Giving you answers, leaving you satisfied.' She turned the ghostlight in her hands and examined the clasp.

The fear of seeing Elisabella uncontained roiled through Cornelia's stomach.

Dot's fingers tightened around the ghostlight. She shrugged

her jacket off, folding it and dropping it on the ground with a flourish. She stepped out of her sensible boots and stood on the grass bank of the lake in her stockings, inside the witchlight line. She took a step backwards. And another, and another, until her heels were right at the water's edge.

There was a hiss of static.

'Don't,' Cornelia said, realising what she was about to do.

'Don't what?'

'Don't kill another person.'

'But it's so much more fun this way,' Dot said earnestly.

'No, it's not. Don't you want to see what happens? Don't you want to see your legacy?'

Dot laughed, a hearty cackle. Cornelia had always liked it; it used to make her feel safe. Now it made her nauseated, like she'd been living a lie and was only just waking up to it.

'This wasn't about *legacy.* It was about you people knowing, for once, that I was behind things. But more than that, it was about breaking rules. Making my own decisions! Before my little experiments, I'd had a sewn-up life. Exactly the sort of life my parents had mapped out for me. My father wanted me to either be a rich man's wife or go into some sort of government. Inspired by Apparent wars, I imagine, but he only had daughters and he had visions for us all. I was never the marrying kind, so I chose the second path. Getting into science was my little rebellion, but all roads led to a governmental role. I could always tell this is what he really wanted for me – let the prettier daughters marry, let me work in solitude.'

'Tell me about it,' Cornelia said.

'I am,' she said.

'No, that's an aphorism,' Cornelia said. 'Because my father had similar attitudes to his children. I'm relating to you, by way of aphorism.'

'I am right here,' Ezra cut in.

'Oh shut up, Ezra. You know you are a lousy father,' Dot snapped, then rearranged her features. 'I've always wanted to say that to you. Imogen, your crab puff cakes are atrocious. Agatha and Ethel, you have a single brain cell between you and I am sick of your nonsense. If the others were here I'd tell Nova they're too loud, Harry he's a pompous twat, Olivia that she's too goody-goody, Lucy to stop snivelling in the toilets because if everyone can hear you, you're not having a "secret cry". If I could dig up the old Night Mayor of Wrackton, I would do that just to bash him over the head with a shovel and send him down again. I do wish the Ternion had envisioned a pit to put the worst of us in, because you'd all be in it.'

She looked back over her shoulder, contemplating.

'Although we made our own pit, didn't we? Instead of solving our problems, or making the world a better place. We just made a pit and tossed everything inside, then pretended it wasn't a pit whenever we were asked about it.'

Cornelia let her monologue, inching closer to Mallory. She was fully awake now, but lying in the same position she'd fallen in. Their eyes met, and something passed between them. Cornelia could almost hear what Mallory was saying, could almost hear the suggestion as though it was spoken aloud.

She shook her head, but Mallory's hand inched closer to hers. Still not touching, but a sign.

'Do it,' she whispered.

'—and really, we should be ready to deal with our own filth. So no, I don't care for legacy, but I do care for cleaning up after myself. The world would be heaps better without the existence of the Broadwicks. I can't do *everything*, but I can certainly take care of this one thing.'

She closed her eyes for a moment.

'Oh! One last thing – should Harry survive this, wherever he is, he'll have fewer successful in-meeting suggestions on account of not being able to lay claim to my ideas. He didn't come up with sequestering Lucy in squalor on his own, no matter what he'd like to tell you.'

Her eyes twinkled as she closed them again.

'Wait!' Cornelia said. 'What about Elisabella?'

'What about her?'

'You can't put her back in there again,' Cornelia said.

'Why?'

'Because… of a reason we haven't thought of yet, but I don't like that idea,' Diana said.

Cornelia wished there was a way to communicate what she was about to do.

But it had to be done. There was no other way. She'd been thinking it from the moment Dot threw Mallory off her, there really was only one way out of this.

'You were going to create havoc with her. Folk will know she's down there – the burning of the Witches will bring more folk to Wickermere, if anything.'

The smoke was still blowing across the lake. There was no sign of fire trucks, or anyone else that had been in Rowan House, and Cornelia wondered briefly if this was, somehow, another lake nightmare. If being with Mallory felt absolutely real, there was every chance this could, too.

'That's not a bad point,' Dot said. 'I'll give you that. I always liked the sound of you, Diana.'

'I had never heard of you before in my life until we got here, so I can't say the feeling is mutual.'

'Why don't we just go back to the house,' Imogen tried. She was teary-eyed, the twins huddled close to her even though they towered over her.

'Yes! We can make you a nice cup of tea. We'll even forget all about this business of burying us alive,' Agatha said.

'Will we?' Ethel asked, sotto voce.

'Yes,' Agatha hissed, hitting her in the side. 'We can do some therapy, it'll be fine.'

It was unlikely to be fine, but Cornelia had to admire their unflappable optimism.

'I'm not going back. I've been planning this too long, and this was always the ending. Us, here, and me doing what I'm about to do. I'd like to go out knowing how it ends,' Dot said. 'There'll be an epilogue, and the bit where you try to put me on trial, and the bit where I'll be remembered or whatever those true crime folk do with their killers and their artists and their mavericks. I'll be remembered as a monster, and that is just fine with me. I don't need to see that ending. No, I want to go out knowing it'll kill you, too. I'm holding a bomb and standing on the edge of another one.'

And holding one over their heads, too.

'It's exciting, you have to admit. I fall back in there alone and I take you with me. The ghosts are so *hungry*. They've been hungry for years, decades, centuries. They want a last meal, and I'm happy to hand it over.'

She closed her eyes.

'But—' Diana tried again.

Dot opened one eye a crack, then tossed the ghostlight straight up into the air.

'Catch,' she said, crossing her arms over her body and throwing herself back into the water.

There was a splash and the water rose up as Cornelia moved to catch Elisabella, grateful when Diana slid under it and caught it in her proffered skirt.

'Worth you seeing my knickers,' Diana said, holding the ghostlight tightly. 'I know asking earlier if I missed the villain speech sounded like I was upset, but just *once* I'd love if we could bypass the Villainous Monologue Unskippable Cut Scene.'

'Diana—'

The water had not gone back into the lake. Rather, it was suspended above the surface, which was now outright bubbling like a volcano.

'We need to move, we need to get out of here, get the witch-light—' Cornelia said, but then the lake burst like a geyser and flowed out towards them.

On the bank, the TV stack burst into life, blue light glowing. More TVs, green with rust and algal bloom, rolled out of the water and burst into life, antennae quivering.

Cornelia scrambled as one landed next to her feet, the screen alight with a face pressed against the inside of the screen, mouth moving, eyes frantically searching. The channel flipped and a hand slapped against the inside of the glass, static bursting, a voice screaming.

She was now starting to understand why she was meant to leave the TVs alone as a kid.

'Don't let the water or anything in it touch you!' Diana shouted, scrambling back. She and Cornelia grabbed Mallory by the arms and pulled her to her feet. She was barely able to stand as they half dragged, half carried her away from the water and whatever thing the TV had going on.

'The witchlight, we need the witchlight,' Imogen was saying over and over.

'Diana,' Cornelia said urgently.

'What?'

'I have to.'

'Have to…?'

'I'm so sorry.' She took a deep breath, and said, in the clearest voice she could: 'CORNELIA BROADWICK.'

THIRTY-SIX

Of course, nothing happened, because magic does not work like that. An ancient curse could only continue to function as a viable threat if the stakes were high enough, and if it was to the maximum benefit to the curser. Self-sacrifice wasn't allowed.

In fact, it was frowned upon.

The lake seemed to agree.

'Fuck,' Cornelia said, continuing to move back towards the treeline at a steady pace as hot, staticky water advanced towards them, flowing up and over the TVs and the ghosts trapped within like arms desperate to grasp them.

The water swallowed Dot whole, making ghoul dinner of her. She grinned the whole time.

Diana held her hand out and shouted 'COME ON!' and the witchlight flew into her hand, where she promptly dropped it, hissing as her skin sizzled. It smashed where it hit the ground, like an overcharged bulb.

Cornelia kept pulling her back by the arm as the crackling

water swallowed the pieces of witchlight like a tide rolling in rapidly.

'RUN,' Diana shouted.

Cornelia wished for one eternal second that so many of their denouements didn't end in absolute chaos.

Her boots tangled over ferns and moss as she tried to keep one foot in front of the other, unable to tell what was static and what was general glasses-filth as her vision blurred.

'There's a salt line and iron in the land here,' Ezra shouted, holding his hand out. They'd made it far into the trees, but the water kept coming, pushing the TVs forward like flotsam on a tide. The water seemed to hesitate – if water was capable of such a thing – as it reached the salt line, but continued moving, slowed, but undeterred. The TV closest to them screamed, a mouth filling the screen.

The channel flipped again, back to the hand. Cracks appeared in the glass as the hand flexed and pushed against the screen.

Mallory cleared her throat.

Mallory, who always did the right thing.

Mallory, who was doing what Cornelia could not.

'Cornelia,' she said, so quiet it was a whisper. 'Cornelia Broadwick.'

The water receded like the words had pulled a plug, a gurgling sound echoing through the space. The TVs went dark.

A wind picked up as it had during the séance, and Cornelia had that sense again of being out of her body. She felt sick. She felt defeated.

Three bombs held over their heads – Agatha and Ethel,

Elisabella, the Besiegement. Only one with a long fuse. The water would've kept spreading, probably put Wickermere and everyone in it underwater. Elisabella would've destroyed everything in her path.

Tears tracked down her cheeks, knowing Mallory was the only one brave enough to do what she'd done, and brave enough to suffer the consequences of knowing she'd just condemned them all to a later death.

It was a stay of execution, and it would be temporary.

This was still better.

This was okay.

Cornelia had always imagined making the most of her life, doing good, studying things that interested her. She'd kept up a careful facade and had only just figured out how to express what it was she wanted.

She wanted Mallory.

She wanted a life with Mallory.

She wanted to keep working together, build their PI business, and figure out a way to live a life free of fear. To make the world a better place by constantly learning about it and doing what she could.

The wind whipped up stronger, whispers all around her, both in her head and outside it, pressing hard on her head, trying to make her listen.

'CORNELIA BROADWICK, WE CLAIM YOU. MALLORY HAWTHORNE, WE CLAIM YOU. DIANA CHEUNG-MERRIWEATHER, WE CLAIM YOU. EZRA IMOGEN AGATHA ETHEL, WE CLAIM YOU. SHOULD DOROTHY EARLY SURVIVE THIS, WE CLAIM HER TOO. YOU HAVE ONE...

HUNDRED... AND SIXTY-SIX... DAYS AND THEN YOU ARE OURS. GET YOUR AFFAIRS IN ORDER. WE DO NOT WANT TO DEAL WITH THEM.'

The wind disappeared and Cornelia felt a sting on her skin. A star appeared on the back of her hand, in the soft space between her thumb and index finger – not a pentagram, but a curved four-point star, stark black, beneath the skin like it was permanent.

Or as permanent as something could be, in one hundred and sixty-six days of remaining life.

The faces of everyone around her told her they'd received a similar fate.

Cornelia didn't have to count the days properly to know where the countdown left them, because they should've known from the start. The deadline was Samhain. Where it all started eighteen months ago, so too was where it would end.

Ezra and Imogen and the twins screamed for the ghosts to come back, offering anything else in exchange for their lives, and Cornelia did her best to tune them out. There was no point. Either they'd find a way, or they wouldn't.

'Hexana,' Mallory croaked.

'I know. It'll be okay,' Cornelia said.

'No, I mean this is Hexana,' Mallory said. 'Hexana's star. She must've… I dunno.' She trailed off, words leaving her. 'I'm sorry.'

'Don't be. There was no other choice.'

'Die now or die later. I know what I'd choose every time,' Diana said.

Cornelia had to believe that to be true. Otherwise they'd never make it through the next few months.

Rowan House was in disarray when they got in. Stella was curled on a two-seater in the hallway with Lucy sitting beside her, painstakingly finger-spelling out words. Stella was, understandably, monosyllabic.

Are you okay? Cornelia asked.

No, Stella signed.

But she will be, Lucy signed fiercely – emphatically, if a little unclear. *I'm going to make it okay. We'll rebuild the business together.*

Cornelia took it to mean that Lucy was leaving the Ghoul Council for good, but now wasn't the time to ask. She felt dazed, exhausted.

Nova and Harry hastened – as much as someone like Nova could stand to hasten – to calm the Broadwicks, offering decontamination showers. Diana managed to cajole Mallory into at least being checked over after breathing in so much smoke, after which the gang sat in the foyer for hours watching Council members run to and fro as Lucy made them tea, steadfastly reminding them she was doing it as a kindness and not as an employee.

Cornelia overheard just enough of a conversation to learn that Olivia was alive and had been brought to the Rowan House hospital wing, as Cornelia often thought of it. She was concussed and vomiting and had a broken hand, but fundamentally otherwise unharmed.

Cornelia imagined she probably felt guilty.

'I didn't think you had it in you,' Nova said, upon hearing

Mallory was the one to enact the Besiegement. 'I'm impressed. Honestly, has anyone ever told you three that you're too much? Because they shouldn't.'

'We don't really care for the approval of others,' Diana said, cracking a not-entirely-genuine smile.

'And I can't help but be marginally grateful that the rest of us were spared. I had not expected the curse would be so incidentally lenient, but there are always loopholes amid the red tape, especially with the older curses and such. The unaffected members of the Ghoul Council will repay that gratitude with every effort to prevent your deaths before Samhain.'

Cornelia had an insult on the tip of her tongue, but swallowed it. The Council would do their best, and it wouldn't be good enough, but there was no use in pointing it out. They'd have to live with the guilt when they all died.

'We'll all have to stay here,' Imogen said, sniffling. 'The Ghoul Council will need to take charge of this case. Nova, how soon do you think we can begin the testing?'

'We need to call a meeting,' they said languidly. 'But I expect in the next day or so, I can perform preliminary tests.'

'No,' Cornelia said.

'What?'

'No, I'm not staying here. You can have my blood or whatever, but I'm not spending the literal rest of my life trapped in this place.'

'*Trapped?*' Ezra asked incredulously. 'You've always had the run of the place. I'm surprised you wouldn't want to be here, with us, in this time of… sorrow. Your friends are more than welcome to stay too, though I imagine they'll want to be with their own families.'

Diana's face fell, and Cornelia knew she was thinking about Taylor. Having to tell Taylor that after all they'd been through, she was going to die anyway.

'I need some air,' Cornelia said, despite having spent a great deal of time outside recently.

Without waiting for anyone to respond, she pushed open the doors of Rowan House and ran out into the cool night air and across to the lake.

One piece of advice she'd read online in her endless attempts to put away the nightmares was to not let places where bad things happened become symbolic of the fear. As much as she'd like to never see the lake again, she needed to be brave. To face it down, even if the next time she saw it – if there was a next time – she reacted with fear, she needed to know a part of her could keep the terror under control. That she was safe sometimes, even if she couldn't guarantee it forever. Or even for the rest of her life.

Diana and Mallory followed, despite Diana trying to convince Mallory to stay where Dr Curtis could keep an eye on her and, at the very least, give her a muscle relaxant. Mallory's responding cough didn't help her case, but Diana gave up. Cornelia had to admire Diana's restraint in not commenting on the Broadwicks having their own family physician – except for when she'd asked him if he kept leeches in one of the pockets of his briefcase.

Cornelia strode to the pier and sat down in the middle of the boardwalk, legs crossed, staring at the fizzing water visible through the slats, lost in thought.

'I bet it won't, though,' Cornelia said out loud.

'What won't?' Mallory asked, coming to sit near her.

Still maintaining distance.

'Sorry, started the sentence in my head,' Cornelia said. 'I was just thinking that Occulture will probably never really know what happened here. I expect we'll be dragged in to sign NDAs any minute now and that'll be the end of it. We'll meet an untimely end that will be spoken of in years to come with confusion.'

'Or on a true crime podcast,' Diana said, shivering. 'Surely not, though? To the NDA part. I know who we're dealing with, but they're *involved*. They recovered the twins, the Wickermere Reaper is dead, and all those crimes are solved – what more is it there now but tying it off with a neat bow?'

'That bow can't be neat if the Wickermere Reaper was one of their own,' Mallory said softly. 'They can't be seen to be that mortal, or that susceptible to mistakes. It's classic pride before the fall. To miss the obvious would be a death knell for the Council's power, for the respect and trust others have in them. That's what you think, isn't it?'

'Yeah,' Cornelia said. 'That's exactly what I think. They'll be too embarrassed by this, and by the explanation for the Apparents dying during Grandad Cornelius's time. It has all the makings of a ruinous scandal.'

Diana took the ghostlight containing Elisabella out of her pocket and passed it to Mallory, who held it up to Cornelia. 'Should we throw her back? I don't want to hand her over to the Ghoul Council.'

'Let's keep the empty one as an "I got Besieged by the ghosts of Wickermere and all I got was this stupid rock" souvenir. You can do the honours, as a little treat,' Diana added.

'See you on the thirty-first of never.' Cornelia took the ghost-light and hurled it as hard as she could, hoping for a geyser-like reaction from the lake. Instead it hissed briefly, accepting the return of the Ternion ghost. A goddess returned to her grave.

It was underwhelming, but Cornelia felt something lift off her chest. Something akin to freedom lifted her above the mess and the certainty of her imminent death.

She wondered if Dot really was dead. If the lake ghosts had eaten her whole, or if she was somewhere down there, dreaming out loud and caught in an endless loop. If she'd die from dehydration or starvation before she died of ghosts in her blood, or whatever the technical explanation for death-by-spirit was.

She thought about all the things Dot had said. About expectations, and falling in line.

She'd never thought of fighting the Broadwick expectations placed on her as a valiant effort, or rebellion. They were anathema to her existence, so she'd refuted them one by one, until she was the co-founder of a mildly successful PI agency. The last vestiges of those expectations had been unfettered access to the Broadwicks' money, and her own refusal to rock the proverbial family boat too hard.

Cornelia looked up at Mallory and Diana, who were watching her, their faces concerned. Diana had made Mallory take the fluffy coat. She looked really cute, like a worried owl.

There was maybe no point in what Cornelia was about to say next, but for the remaining few months of their lives, it would make everything more bearable.

'I think it's probably time I accepted I am, in all likelihood, non-binary,' Cornelia said, carefully watching the water.

'Sounds right to me,' Diana said, almost immediately. 'Good work, detective.'

'Thank you for telling us,' Mallory said, her voice warm. 'We're so proud of you, always.'

'Do you want to change what you go by?' Diana asked.

Cornelia shook her head. 'Nah. My name is my name. I've threatened to change it so many times, but none fit like my name does. I've grown into it, made it my own. I think I'd need longer than one hundred and sixty-six days to get used to going by different pronouns – but we'll see how I feel in the morning. But hi. I'm Cornelia Broadwick, and I've never, ever been a girl in my life.'

'It's nice to meet you,' Mallory said, and Cornelia looked at her then, saw the way Mallory was smiling at her. So ready to accept Cornelia's truth.

She let her gaze track to the sky, rubbing a hand over the indelible star on her hand.

The fog had covered the stars above, but she knew they were there.

'We're all going to die soon,' Cornelia said. 'Might as well live as myself a little.'

THIRTY-SEVEN

The Undetectables stayed overnight in the Laurels after permitting Nova to take blood and force them into the decontamination shower – 'Olivia can work with any of the particulates we get from your clothing' was the reason they were given – and allowing Dr Curtis to give them the all-clear. He'd prescribed Mallory muscle relaxants, and all of them rest.

Cornelia slept on the couch. Their argument was both that they wanted to be alone and didn't want to disturb Mallory, but really, they couldn't face the thought of Mallory not remembering what happened in Lake Wickermere.

Or of Mallory telling them in the dark that it never happened at all.

Diana woke Cornelia up by loudly packing her suitcase and planning lunch, swinging her wet hair around and extolling the virtues of showering, which she was sad she would only get to experience a hundred or so times more in her life. Mallory dragged herself into the sitting room to help, her movements slow and stiff and clearly painful, but better than they had been the night before.

Cornelia took this opportunity to announce that, from this point on, they'd prefer if they and their multitudes were referred to as a single gender-neutral entity. Diana called them a pretentious idiot, asked them how long they'd spent thinking up that particular statement, and both she and Mallory promptly altered how they referred to Cornelia, as though the other Undetectables had been independently practising it for some time. It felt as natural to hear as Cornelia had hoped it would.

Between them, the Undetectables hadn't brought much, but packing it all back up felt like a ritual that needed to be punctuated with biscuits and a near-continuous round of tea. Diana suggested fancy sandwiches, and a potential pub dinner in the evening, both of which were gratefully received suggestions after several days without proper meals.

'You only live once,' Diana said, and Cornelia hexed her. 'Hey!'

'Too soon,' Mallory said. 'I'm still really sorry about it. I knew it hadn't worked when you tried, Cornelia, but part of me was terrified I was somehow imagining you'd said your name, like the curse was trying to make me do it.'

'Dot was going to kill everyone in Wickermere, *or* possibly all of Occulture,' Diana said, taking a bite of her sandwich. 'It's not my fault she found the genius hiding place—'

'I really thought it was a better hiding place than your diorama,' Mallory said.

'We can't all be motherfucking geniuses all the time. Anyway, we were going to die, you just let us choose to go later, and on our own terms. Sort of.'

'You had no choice,' Cornelia affirmed, focusing on pouring

tea into cups. 'None of us did. You did what I couldn't do.'

They stirred the tea carefully. Part of the problem, Cornelia had mused when they'd woken for the umpteenth time, seeing faces in the darkness that weren't there, was that they hadn't done the reality test they and Mallory had – allegedly – discussed in the boat.

With shaking hands, they poured a single spoonful of sugar into Mallory's tea and stirred it.

Mallory had enthusiastically eaten the largest club sandwich Cornelia had ever seen and seemed to be regaining some of the life that had drained out of her yesterday, to the point that she'd pulled out her lavender agency notebook and was leafing through it with a puzzled expression on her face.

'I am saying this with nothing but love and affection, but what the *fuck* are you doing?' Diana asked.

'If we only have one hundred and sixty-five days left on this earth, we have some loose ends to tie up,' Mallory said, as though it was the most natural fact in the world.

It occurred to Cornelia that Mallory might be intellectualising her feelings too close to the sun.

'We have the Wrackton Digger case to finish off when we get back and I probably need to apologise to Theodore – I wasn't particularly kind about his body being taken, and—' She cut herself off, chewing her lip. 'And, I was refamiliarising myself with the details, except I think I've taken the wrong notebook, as half of this seems to be a story. "The Curious Case of the Dead King",' she said, smiling as she read. 'Theodore's actually quite good at this. Once we've sorted out the Digger, we should encourage him to write in his spare time.'

'You need to go to *bed* when you get home, remember?' Diana said.

'Plus, Theodore's probably solved it in the time we've been gone,' Cornelia said, passing out the cups.

Their hands shook as they placed Mallory's down, barely acknowledging the appreciative smile Mallory beamed in their direction. Cornelia took their cup to the window, taking a sip and staring out at the lake, tapping their shoe off the waiting row of haphazardly packed suitcases. Watching her drink was too much to bear.

'These are his Digger notes,' Mallory said, turning yet another dog-eared, torn page, like Theodore had been worrying the edges excessively. 'He's been really diligent. I know that shouldn't be that surprising, the Mayoral Offices kept him around for long enough that he's clearly always been competent. I think I've been really unfair about what value he brings to the Undetectables as a whole – he could be a good PI in his own right. Maybe he can take over for us in a few months.'

'I was going to make a joke about you burying us before we'd actually died, but in light of the last day and a half I don't think that's appropriate,' Diana said dryly.

'Think of how useful he'd have been in the Caine case if he'd been there to simply walk right through the wall,' Cornelia said, turning around just in time to see Mallory grimace, her hand on her mug.

Cornelia felt their heart fall through their stomach and further down to somewhere around their ankles.

The lake had felt so real. It had *been* real. But it had also been an elaborate dream made up by angry ghosts in a living, angry prison. Cornelia would've probably done the same if someone had splashed in on top of them after years of peaceful cohabiting with other ghosts.

They would never be a ghost, Samhain or otherwise. A ghost would take their body over and they – all the Besieged – would cease to exist. The remaining members of the Ghoul Council would order them killed, or they'd be locked up in Rowan House forever, subjected to testing, and Cornelia would be none the wiser.

The idea panicked them more than it brought any kind of comfort.

In the meantime, Cornelia wasn't going to have even a taste of the life they wanted, because they couldn't tell Mallory how they felt. Couldn't put it into words.

How they felt around her was real, even if the rest of it wasn't. Calm, like the answers to the world around them could be solved by listening to Mallory talk. Delighted, watching Mallory get excited about something. Seen, by Mallory listening patiently whenever Cornelia got a particularly new and exciting insect for the bug room. Comforted, by looking at her whenever she walked into a room and feeling their heart constrict with something that could only be love.

Cornelia had felt all that for years, and hadn't known there was a name for it.

Now they could add a constant sense of falling, like they'd put the pieces together only to be obliterated in a matter of hours.

The tea was wrong. They'd never kissed. It wasn't real.

'You okay over there?' Diana asked. 'You're unnaturally quiet, it's freaking me out.'

'I'm thinking about death,' Cornelia said.

'Never mind, I regret asking.'

Cornelia flicked their fingers and Diana's tea splashed over the rim, making her swear.

Mallory's expression hadn't changed. She pushed the teacup away and smoothed the notebook down.

'His notes get a bit wild,' Mallory said, still reading. 'And the dates are all messed up – this entry is from a couple of weeks ago. He's written "dog-ears" over and over, and then "dog-eared books", whatever that means. This is about the mausoleum, but… that didn't happen,' Mallory said, frowning. 'It has a name, and a description of a witness, but he told me there wasn't one. Someone "tall, dark haired, definitely not a ghost, maybe straight? Too obvious".'

'You know Theodore,' Cornelia said, reaching for a biscuit despite feeling as though they were dying – which they were, and was therefore not an entirely dramatic response.

'Yes, but I thought we'd put all the strangeness behind us last year. It's been well over a year since he's done anything odd – basically since Jacob's body was found in the Mayoral Offices, he's been entirely normal. This is… strange, even for him,' Mallory said, her brow furrowed.

She looked up suddenly. 'Theodore!'

'What about him?' Diana asked.

'How's he going to feel about all of it?'

'Being told his notes are weird is not the worst thing that's ever happened to him,' Cornelia said.

'No,' Mallory said patiently. 'Everyone he loves is in this room. Everyone who loves *him* is in this room – Taylor, Felix and Kingston are fond of him, but even with the practical stuff sorted out – him taking over the agency, that kind of thing – we're all going to die, and then...'

Diana burst into tears.

'Taylor,' she explained, wiping her eyes aggressively. 'Pretend that didn't happen. I haven't been able to tell her yet, I need to tell her in person.'

'And we'll need to tell Felix and Kingston and Langdon and Cloud and Sully, and Honourable Dr Night Mayor Ray, and my parents and Diana's parents and...' Mallory inhaled shakily.

'What if we just don't?' Cornelia suggested.

They moved to the door to answer a timid knock on the other side, both glad of the distraction and dreading whatever bullshit they were about to be subjected to.

'What now—' They stopped at the sight of Olivia, wearing sunglasses and a brand-new cast. 'What are you doing out of bed?'

At Cornelia's behest, Olivia came in and sat beside Mallory, who smiled at her, but it didn't reach her eyes. Cornelia felt something foolishly hopeful rise in their chest again.

'I wanted to see you. To thank you, Mallory, for saving my life.'

'I actually didn't,' Mallory said. 'I checked you were alive, and then checked your pockets to make sure you weren't the Wickermere Reaper.'

'How did you know I wasn't?'

Mallory swallowed. 'Two – no, three – things. One was the forehead shot – Ruby had also been bashed in the head, and it was unlikely the Reaper would be attacked the exact same way they'd attacked others. The second was that you didn't have a ghostlight in your pocket, and the third was a case of absence of evidence not being evidence of absence.'

'The paper,' Diana said, catching on.

'I want to just remind you that I am a little bit concussed, and if you could keep brainteasers to a minimum, that would be much appreciated,' Olivia said wryly, though there was an air of vomitus about it that made Cornelia nod at Mallory to continue, as much for Olivia's benefit as it was for their own.

'The Wickermere Reaper hadn't yet had anyone actually make good on their ransom. The Witches quite literally burned for it—'

'Entirely my fault,' Diana said. 'I thought the ghostlight would be safe with them.'

'You cannot think that way,' Olivia said firmly. 'I suspect she wanted a way to get rid of the Witches, especially after they helped you, too.'

'—and it stood to reason that Dot intended to actually give us a physical clue, which meant it had to be on her person.'

'You thought it was me, when I brought the letter, didn't you?' Olivia said.

'Yep,' Diana said. 'But don't feel bad, our whole job is to suspect everyone and trust no one. Plus, we'd literally been caught out by that one before. Fool us once, and all that.'

'She handed it to me. Dot. Told me it came in for you, when we were sorting out Lucy's desk. I believed her; I shouldn't have. I just didn't see the signs. Afterwards I wondered why it felt so *urgent* that I brought it to you, with so little time to find the twins. Honestly, I thought the Wickermere Reaper was Harry, especially after how he treated Lucy – we agreed to sequester her, but I hadn't realised what that actually meant until Lucy told me where she'd been. She resigned this morning, did you hear? Says she's going to help Stella rebuild the Witches of Bonemarrow Lake brand, take it global.'

'And may I say, good for them,' Diana said, raising her mug. 'That was a clever deduction, though, Mallory.'

Mallory allowed herself to smile. 'I read it when I found it – the clue she was going to give us in exchange for Elisabella's ghostlight was cruel. It said "look to the shore". If we hadn't already narrowed things down, or hadn't got the Lyreflies, we'd have spent the last few hours of the twins' lives flailing trying to figure it all out. But part of her wanted to play fair, I think.'

'She said she was bored,' Cornelia said, mildly concerned that Olivia hadn't been fully briefed, but she nodded.

'Nova filled me in this morning. I know she was behind the Apparent deaths that lead Cornelius to shut this place down. Might be a reason to open it again. The Broadwicks… I'm so sorry,' she said, faltering. 'It's just so easy to forget that everyone will be…'

'We know,' Cornelia said.

'Apologies if this is a grim question, but did we ever figure out how she was supplying oxygen?' Olivia asked.

'I had a hypothesis that she mostly confirmed,' Mallory said, and Cornelia smiled at her despite themself as Mallory explained the algae. 'She rigged the chamber to burn off the algae, then flood the chamber with carbon monoxide. Victims wouldn't have known they were dying when it came to it.'

Olivia nodded slowly. 'That's… horrifying to contemplate, but a solid hypothesis. I think that's testable, too. Without a living subject,' she added hurriedly.

'Thanks for coming round,' Cornelia said after a silence had elapsed. 'We need to get back to Wrackton, though. Cases won't solve themselves.'

'They'll have to, in about five months' time,' Diana said.

'But until then, we're still needed back home,' Mallory said, something softening within her.

Olivia hesitated. 'Mallory, if things work out differently, and you… all find a way out of this, I am absolutely sure the Ghoul Council could use someone like you. I'd vouch for you. We need more scientists with a genuine desire to learn.'

'I'll let you know,' Mallory said, and Cornelia stood to let Olivia out.

Olivia surprised them by pulling them into a hug that they were sure a day ago would've made them blush to the point of death, but being embarrassed or flustered didn't seem worthwhile anymore.

Instead, they let Olivia waltz out on a cloud of gratitude, where she almost barrelled into Agatha and Ethel who were shuffling towards the Laurels, holding a bakery-style box between them that categorically did not need two people holding it.

'Here's our little saviours,' Agatha sang, stepping past Cornelia without being invited in. 'Just a little token of our appreciation.'

Cornelia looked at them blankly, but it was Diana who said, 'You do know we saved you from suffocating to death, but that we immediately undid that by condemning you to a life of having your body claimed by a ghost?'

'Oh she's so funny, Cornelia,' Agatha said, laughing. Ethel managed a raised eyebrow.

'Funny, yes, I guess, in an ironic way. Correct, though?' Cornelia said, already exasperated. Their sisters took up so much space just by being there.

'Obviously the Ghoul Council aren't going to let it happen,' Ethel said, when nobody else spoke. 'It's a temporary bump in the road that'll be sorted in no time – there's been a special meeting called. Honestly, what's the point in being a Broadwick if the rules have to apply to you?'

'You're welcome,' Mallory said, after a beat.

It did seem like the best possible reply, all things considered. No point in bursting their idiot bubble. If being abducted, almost dying and potentially learning that the Broadwicks had no intention of saving them hadn't made them wise up to the reality they inhabited, nothing would.

'We brought you a cookie,' Ethel said. 'Baked it earlier.'

Agatha opened the lid with a flourish. It said *THANK YOU!* in perfect bubbly script across what was, undoubtedly and somewhat disappointingly, a giant cookie.

'What a thoughtful and yet simultaneously baffling gift,' Diana said, reaching over to break off a corner. 'What's in it?'

'Chocolate chips, peanut butter chunks… secret ingredients,' Ethel said.

'And our heartfelt gratitude,' Agatha added. 'Ethel and I are thinking of opening our own bakery soon, right here in the village. When all this business is over with the Besiegement. It's our calling.'

'Does the village know?'

'We'd be doing speciality baking. Thank-you cookies, that sort of thing.'

Cornelia broke off a bit and sniffed it suspiciously before taking a bite. It was surprisingly delicious.

'Why'd you write letters to Lyle Whitlock?' she asked bluntly, chewing.

'Who?' Ethel asked.

'The Dollhouse Murderer.'

'Oh, him,' Ethel said, straightening up a pile of Mallory's papers on the table.

'We can't tell you,' Agatha said.

'What the fuck are you talking about? This is a *murderer*,' Diana said.

'Is it some kind of sex thing?' Mallory asked suddenly.

Cornelia choked on their bit of cookie.

'I'm serious, are you engaging in some sort of psychosexual, parasocial connection with a known serial killer for some reason?'

'No,' Agatha said coolly. 'But we can't tell you.'

'You never stopped being infuriating. I half wish I'd left you in that box,' Cornelia snapped.

'Charming,' Ethel said. 'We just can't tell you, as we said.'

Cornelia saw something in Ethel's face that made the penny drop.

'Oh. You *can't* tell me. Some sort of hex, or prevention spell?' Cornelia guessed.

'I feel like there are ghosts in my brain at all times,' Agatha said quietly. 'Like we're in some sort of nightmare. Our lives were supposed to be normal. Not like Cornelia's. You were always going to be weird. You used to play murder games and regularly climbed into illogically small places to look at worms or whatever. That wasn't for us. And now I feel…'

'Broken,' Ethel finished.

'You're not broken,' Mallory said firmly. 'There are no rules for how one *should* react to being abducted by a known serial killer. But if there is a hex or something stopping you from talking, we need to get through it, so excuse us while we continue prodding you with questions.'

'Was it Dot? Did she make you contact him?'

There was a flicker of something akin to recognition, then an emphatic headshake from both of them.

'Did she compel you, like a demon spell?'

No reaction.

'Did she direct someone to do it for her? A ghost, perhaps?'

Another glimmer, an almost-nod from Agatha whose eyes had begun to sparkle with tears.

'Do you know why?'

'No,' Ethel said, with difficulty. 'But it was important that we— What was I talking about?'

The Undetectables exchanged glances. Now wasn't the time to deal with this, the twins needed more time to heal.

'If you think of anything that might help us figure out what she was up to, please let us know,' Mallory said, rummaging through the back of her notebook for an agency card.

'Of course,' Agatha said sweetly, pocketing it. 'Anything you need. We really are *so* grateful.'

'We'll leave you to your… meeting,' Ethel said, glancing around the room with obvious distaste. 'We've got a debrief meeting with the Ghoul Council, and then an appointment to view a potential bakery space before Nova wants to run more tests.'

'Best of luck with it,' Diana said, showing them the door. 'Perhaps you'll leave the agency an anonymous review? A positive, anonymous review.'

Agatha and Ethel laughed like Diana had said something funny, and then the Undetectables were finally alone enough to finish lunch.

Mallory continued flicking through Theodore's notes as she ate, an expression on her face that made Cornelia feel a bit sick. They'd last seen it when Katherine had shown them who'd murdered Theodore, and had hoped never to be in a situation where they'd need to see it again.

'I have this horrible little hunch that all our cases are connected in some way. Jacob' – she was proud of herself for not stumbling over his name – 'and Whitlock – they both said the "monsters of mavericks" line, and some of Dot's speech reminded me of that too. Maybe it's just general serial killer thematic villain speech content, but I'm not sure. Plus the twins talking to Whitlock, it's just too weird.'

'What Cornelia said,' Diana said.

'Speaking of… I need to tell you something. Both of you.' Mallory looked up. 'It was a Directorial decision not to say it earlier, but when I went back to Theodore – when he was upset because the Wrackton Digger had taken his body – Jacob's body was also gone. I still don't know what to make of it.'

Cornelia expected to feel clawing terror, but there was nothing. They'd been waiting for the other shoe to drop.

'My only comment is that it took so fucking long to bury him, it's annoying we have to care about him all over again,' Diana said.

Mallory glanced at Cornelia, who shrugged. Where there should've been panic lay spreading numbness.

'You're probably right that we need to tie this particular loose end off,' Cornelia offered. 'Wrackton would want to get its shit together. We aren't going to be around to fix all its problems forever.'

After a moment's hesitation – there was a chance they were collectively laying it on too thick with the morbid flippancy – Mallory resumed turning pages of Theodore's notebook, frowning deeper. 'It's all very strange. I kept expecting that we'd be able to link the Wickermere Reaper with the Wrackton Digger somehow, especially when we were talking about finding Elisabella's remains, but that's a moot hypothesis. If I'm being totally honest, I'm worried about Theodore again. It's like he doesn't know what day it is. Some of these entries are compiled like he's been consumed with this case for weeks—'

She turned another dog-eared page, where a corner had been torn out, and something fell to the floor.

'I'll get it.' Cornelia bent beneath the chair.

They paused, staring in horror at what was in their hand.

'Turn another page,' they said quietly, and Mallory did.

Another one fell onto their sleeve and Cornelia got to their feet.

'We need to go back now,' Cornelia said. 'To Wrackton.'

'At least let Mallory finish her tea,' Diana protested, still working her way through the twins' cookie.

'It's cold now,' Mallory said, standing with difficulty. She had several heat patches on and looked on the verge of crying, but she was looking at Cornelia with nothing but trust. 'Let's go.'

THIRTY-EIGHT

'I expect you all know why I gathered you here today,' Theodore said, putting his hands on his hips with a flourish. 'No, that's not the right intonation. You have to give them the ol' razzle-dazzle, Teddy. Ahem. I expect you *all* know why I've gathered you here today. Better, still needs work.'

He stopped mid-pacing and looked up from a handful of notes, his face lighting up at the sight of the rest of the Undetectables as they emerged from the witchlight. Mallory had to bite her tongue to avoid crying out in pain.

'You're here!' he exclaimed happily, before stopping short, his face creased with concern. 'Are the twins…?'

'Alive,' Cornelia said shortly, before Mallory could say anything.

They had not been forthcoming with the reason for their abrupt return, and Mallory's stomach had not stopped twisting in anxiety.

'As are we, for now.'

'Because all of life is so fleeting, yes! Good, good, I am

thrilled to hear it. May we all be tormented by a Broadwick twin or two once more.'

'And Evil Miss Marple has been defeated,' Diana added.

'What's going on here?' Mallory asked, hearing what sounded suspiciously like a small crowd gathered outside Undetectables HQ.

'Not too close! They'll see you!' Theodore said quickly as she hobbled closer to the basement window to see a queue of folk standing on the stairs, impatiently shuffling from foot to foot. The early morning sun was just starting to burn through the clouds, but in true Wrackton fashion, nobody was dressed for sunshine.

'What Mallory said,' Diana said.

'Ah. Well. You see. You put me in charge of the case, and in your absence I took some liberties – really moving into the PI aspect of my role, as it were. I tried to take the old-school approach, but some witnesses and, well, suspects, were not that receptive to the suggestion that you were not contactable by phone *or* by email for the duration of your absence, so even with Taylor and Kingston and Felix – Felix who, by the way, left this message,' Theodore said, holding up a piece of paper.

Mallory took it and read: *I FUCKING TRIED HAD TO GO ON TOUR SORRY LOVE YOU ALL X*. She managed a soft laugh.

'Anyway, with all their valiant efforts to help me coordinate my meetings, some things got… lost in the ether. And unfortunately, all my meetings and interviews and interrogations and what-have-you got scheduled to… now. Diana, you will make a dreadful curtain-twitcher in your old age,' Theodore said haughtily.

Diana dropped the curtain. 'Want me to go out and tell them all to get lost?'

'You know, I *had* considered giving them the old heave-ho, but that would've involved a pipe and a can-do attitude, so I devised a better plan.'

'Can you walk us through what the plan is?' Mallory kept her tone patient.

'Yeah, *Teddy*,' Cornelia said.

It was uncharacteristically mean to the point that even Diana looked ready to reproach them.

'I have no idea what gave you the idea that was an appropriate diminutive, but never call me that. I shall not respond to it,' Theodore said primly. 'The plan is simple: I was going to bring in the suspects and the witnesses, and rather than overplay my hand, make them believe I was going to reveal the real Wrackton Digger.'

'Did you not think perhaps we might want to be present for this?' Mallory asked gently.

'Ah. You're right, I suppose I got a bit carried away.' He dropped his notes, entitled *The Speech 2.0: The Speechening*.

Mallory's heart swooped sadly.

'I should send them away, shouldn't I? Say we've got emergency agency business, can't be avoided, but don't leave the town. Mostly because I cannot follow them, but also because it sounds a little more serious, I think, than *not* saying it. Weird how what you say aloud can have an impact on reality.'

'Let them in,' Cornelia said.

'What?' Diana and Mallory said in unison.

'Let them in, let's see the denouement,' Cornelia said. 'He's worked hard on it, we should see the fruits of his labour.'

'Cornelia—' Mallory started, but they'd been through hell and Mallory didn't want to press them too hard.

It was all unlike Cornelia, looming death aside.

Cornelia wrenched the door open. 'Everyone! Wipe your shoes, come in, don't touch anything, take an iron bag to protect your electronics if you value them.'

Diana hurried to cover the murder board and quietly lamented not having enough tea.

In filed the family of Freya Evans, Mrs Blackburn – who made sure to shoot them an eviscerating glare – the owner of the wine bar near the cemetery, Observer Johnson, the two gravedigger boys, and, to Mallory's horror, Delilah Gabbott. Diana got her a seat wordlessly, moving over so Mallory also had a place to sit down. She sank onto the sofa gratefully, her muscles begging her to go to bed. Diana settled back against the wall, her good ear turned towards Theodore so she could hear him, her eyes darting around the room.

'Start,' Cornelia said, gesturing to Theodore.

'Ah. What my young friend would like me to say is: hello. *I* bet you're all *wondering* why I've *gathered* you here today,' Theodore said, wincing.

Mallory had to admit that the second practised inflection had been the correct one, but he ploughed on valiantly.

'As you know, for the past few days I've been looking into the case of the Wrackton Digger. We have all been, I should say. The rest of the agency wasn't meant to be here, so I was going to take more credit.' He paused.

Observer Johnson scratched his face and looked away, his

expression one of absolute defeat and, perhaps, second-hand embarrassment.

'Tough crowd,' Theodore said. 'Gotcha.' He fumbled with the pages in front of him, then began pacing in the limited space, static pinging off coats and jackets. 'At first, I thought the culprit was someone who desired chaos. Who wanted to cause upset, and ructions. Whose sole purpose in life was to disrupt those at rest. Someone smart, with a clear goal of something dastardly. Of course that means, Observer Johnson, that I was looking at you first.'

'Supremely hope you looked the other way after some deliberation,' Observer Johnson said.

'Haha! We've a jokester in our midst,' Theodore said.

Mallory managed a weak smile. The only thing holding her up was the chair beneath her, and even then she was ready to lie down forever. Cornelia was utterly focused on Theodore, an expression on their face that Mallory didn't recognise.

She wished she'd been brave enough to take a sip of the tea Cornelia had made her earlier. Then she'd know if any of it had been real, or a cruel trick of the lake.

'But, of course, it wasn't Observer Johnson. The true culprit is someone who had an *extrinsic* goal. Someone motivated by outside forces, perhaps against their will. Which is why I looked to *you*, Mrs Blackburn, as the face behind the Wrackton Digger.'

'Me?' Mrs Blackburn said. 'Utterly preposterous. I'm an injured party, Theodore. I want my husband at rest.'

'And that is precisely why you are *not* the Wrackton Digger,' Theodore said. 'The evidence led me in a different direction.

Someone who had been injured by the Wrackton Digger, but who maybe was only injured to detract from the real victims. That led me to—'

'This is ridiculous,' Freya Evans's brother said.

'Right? We're all grieving, we didn't sign up for being randomly accused by a cat-eared *hack*,' Freya Evans's father said.

The volume in the room rose with protestations, and the gravediggers tried to walk out. Diana closed the door with a spell.

'Just hold on a second,' she said.

'Yes, let's hold on, let me re-find my place,' Theodore mumbled, frantically flipping through his note cards. The static energy in the room was building, and Mallory really wanted to leave herself.

'Why don't we discuss the concrete evidence?' Cornelia cut in, climbing onto their desk. 'Hi, Cornelia Broadwick, founding member of the Undetectables. My colleague is correct on all fronts. It's someone intelligent, someone who had something to gain from this. Someone motivated by outside forces, *perhaps* against their will, but perhaps not. I can't speak on that without further evidence. Theodore's suggestion that it's someone who *appeared* injured by the proceedings is absolutely correct.'

Delilah Gabbott watched, her expression set with defiance.

Cornelia gestured for Diana to kick their bag closer, and they fished in the bottom of it. This was the most serious Mallory had ever seen them in an Undetectables context, and it made her heart swell painfully with pride, despite her confusion.

'We didn't have many clues in this case. Our usual methods

of magical detection were unresponsive, to say the least. We were left with something undetectable, unfathomable, *unprecedented* for what was otherwise such a simple case. Admittedly, we were sidetracked by something more pressing – all cases taken on by the Undetectables are of equal importance to us, et cetera, but this was of mission-critical status and took our attention away for a couple of days. So all we were left with was an inconclusive piece of evidence that suggested magical interference, a plant pot that got destroyed—'

'You little *bastard*,' Mrs Blackburn hissed at Theodore. 'I'll sue for this, don't think I won't!'

'—and little pieces of paper,' Cornelia continued, ignoring her. 'We had no true motives, no true leads, bar the ones that led us to questioning all of you lovely folk' – Mallory couldn't help but interpret that as sarcasm – 'and brought you to this room. Our lead investigator fed information back to us, but we happened upon a piece of evidence that the Wrackton Digger could never have foreseen we'd get our hands on.'

Cornelia opened Theodore's notebook, turning to the back pages.

'Often when PI cases follow a format that makes sense, the culprit or target will have some kind of tic. The cheating husband exhibiting the same patterns of behaviour. The thief hitting up the same kind of marks. The killer wanting attention, wanting to be caught. A wise ghost once told us that absence of evidence is not evidence of absence—'

'What the fuck are you on about?' Freya Evans's husband asked.

'If you'd let me finish, perhaps you'd actually find out,' Cornelia said.

He dipped his head in acquiescence.

'Which just means that sometimes when something looks like it makes no sense, you either don't have the full picture, or you're putting it together wrong. One of our clues was quite literally paper, recovered at two of the scenes. Tiny little pieces of paper, like someone had shredded them by hand.'

They held up Theodore's open notebook where, unmistakably, there were little torn circles taken from the edge of the paper, leaving a jagged edge. They had tiny pieces of paper cupped in their other hand, much like the ones Mallory had bagged and tagged at the cemeteries what felt like a lifetime ago.

Mallory was in too much pain to move, could do nothing but stare at Cornelia, the blood draining from her face.

'Diana, if you would,' Cornelia said, and Diana brought them the original evidence bag and a glove.

Theodore had fallen utterly still, his face stony. Static crackled around his ears, the trail of tears on his face more stark than usual.

'As you can see, the paper matches perfectly. Oddly enough, we noted the contents of this notebook contained details that hadn't occurred yet. Our early hypothesis had been that someone was influencing the gravediggers to do the Wrackton Digger's bidding, perhaps forcing them under compulsion or some sort of magical interference. Our early soil samples were contaminated here in the lab, in what we thought was a show of uncharacteristic incompetence, but was rather a shoddy attempt to keep the ruse up longer.'

'No,' Mallory said.

She refused to believe it. Refused to accept that after all this time, after rebuilding her trust in him, after finally putting to bed her guilt at bringing Theodore back—

'Yes,' Theodore said quietly.

He pulled his shoulders back, standing tall but seeming smaller and younger than Mallory had ever seen him.

'That is what needs to be said, in the face of all the evidence. I am the Wrackton Digger.'

THIRTY-NINE

'What the fuck did you drag us all here for, then?' Freya Evans's brother demanded.

'Okay, you know what? You can go,' Diana said. 'Case closed, thanks for coming, leave us a review, take a card. We're the Undetectables, private investigators, and we've just helped you detect the undetectable.'

Delilah Gabbott hadn't moved, hand on her cane, her gaze still giving nothing away, but Cornelia thought they saw tears gathering in her eyes as Diana helped her to her feet.

'Good luck with that,' Lee the gravedigger snorted, then he yelped, holding the crown of his head. Diana's gaze wandered innocently.

Cornelia climbed down from the table as the room emptied out, leaving Mallory, Diana and Theodore standing in a small circle in the centre of the room. At Cornelia's gesture, Mallory sank down into a chair Diana dragged closer.

'Talk to us,' Mallory said plainly. 'Explain.'

'The evidence tells you all you need to know,' Theodore said, still subdued. 'I am the Wrackton Digger. You figured it out.'

'No.' Cornelia knew they were being harsh, but anger burned through them. 'You made us take on this case. Ordered us around. You knew why we had to go to Wickermere, and you kept trying to stop Mallory coming to help. You dug *yourself* up, to try to force her to stay, didn't you? All of this, and you were the one behind it. Start talking, now.'

'I didn't dig *myself* up, technically. Or any of the bodies. I used a suitable proxy, unbeknownst to them. Two, in fact, who I've taken to – lovingly – referring to as the Brothers Dim.'

'We are getting sick of reapers and killers and diggers and insert-target-heres who keep wasting our time,' Diana said. 'AND who steal my jokes.'

Usually the quickest to anger, Diana seemed unnaturally cool about the whole thing, which just made Cornelia more incandescent. They'd been relying on Diana to want to set the lab on fire.

'Okay. I'll talk,' he said quietly. 'Mallory, I owe this to you most. Remember when Jacob… when Jacob killed me?'

'Vividly,' Cornelia said, when Mallory didn't answer.

'Right. Well. Remember I came back?'

Mallory nodded once, guilt passing over her face. She'd been the one to bring him back, and had long harboured the fear she'd done it wrong.

'Good, we're on the same page there. Excellent news. Okay. So. I did not come back correctly.'

'We sort of knew that.'

'To whit I will say, I was not meant to come back at all. The spell you did, Mallory, did not work. I came back via other means, and I am incomplete. I've known it since the moment I returned here, to this very basement, and I've known it every waking moment since. Which has been every moment, on account of the fact I don't sleep.'

He hunched his shoulders, the tears on his face taking on a particularly shimmery sheen that made Cornelia illogically want to punch him. The betrayal swam too strongly in their blood to make sense of any thoughts.

'And that wasn't my fault?' Mallory leaned forward. 'All this time, I thought I'd ruined your life. That I'd been selfish in bringing you back. That I broke you! Every time I brought it up, or said I brought you back, you—'

'Let you think that, but didn't actually confirm it. One of many points of subterfuge I unlive to regret on a daily basis.'

'So why dig up the bodies? Is this just what you think a bad ghost should do, something chaotic?' Diana asked.

'Why dig up your *own* body? Why call me back here, when we were in the middle of trying to save—' Mallory started, her hands pressed to her face.

'Did you think we didn't have enough to worry about?' Cornelia spat.

He looked strained. 'Anything I thought would harm you, I… tried. Mallory, I need you to believe me. I tried.'

Mallory shook her head; whether it was disbelief or anger, Cornelia couldn't tell.

'Mallory, I know you have no reason to trust me. I couldn't find the notebook and assumed I'd left it somewhere. I had no idea you'd… I really thought I…'

'Why did you leave the clues?'

'I didn't mean to. The shredding paper… that's a tic I've developed of late. Any time I want to stall on instructions—'

'Instructions from *who*?'

Theodore snapped his mouth shut. He flickered once, twice, and closed his eyes.

'Can't say.'

'I'm getting really sick of that excuse,' Cornelia said.

'I've only used it once,' Theodore protested. 'You're hardly being fair.'

'Fair?' Diana rose from her seat. 'FAIR? You think any of this is FAIR, Theodore? You don't even know where we've been. You don't even know what we've been *through* the last few days, because you've been spinning your own bullshit here!'

'Well, that's not quite accurate, Diana, but I suppose we should not let accuracy get in the way of a good story.'

'Oh FUCK OFF,' Diana said.

There it was. Cornelia wanted to hug her.

'Language, Diana,' Theodore said, and there was a moment where Cornelia was sure Diana was going to swing for him, ineffectual as that would be.

He'd backed against the iron-and-glass partition that led to the lab, sparks flying from where his hands pressed against it.

'Was it Katherine? Is she making you do this?'

Theodore shook his head once.

'I just want you to understand I didn't want to do any of it. I had no choice. I had *less* than no choice. In fact, I'm pretty sure I wanted to be caught, this time.'

'What the hell do you mean, *this time*?' Mallory asked.

'Great question! Anyway, I tried to think of ways to show

you the truth. I wish I'd thought of paper, that would've been much cleverer. I always wondered how that Apparent story of the children who got lost in the woods and left a trail behind them would work in real life, and it turns out in real life you just create trails whether you mean to or not.'

'I don't understand why you made me come back. The twins could've died, Theodore, and you made me come look at your grave that you disturbed *yourself.* You dug Jacob up, and he was just put in the ground, and you cried and made Felix get me back here, and for what?' Mallory said. 'And the showdown – what was the plan? Were you going to tell a roomful of people that you were the Wrackton Digger?'

Diana's phone rang and she silenced it, and it rang again and again, buzzing constantly, as a slew of emails and Hexana-knows-what-else came through.

'I was going to make up a guy for them to all get mad at – craft the Wrackton Digger as a mysterious figure, and then tell them that guy was gone for good. That the Undetectables drove him out of town. I got scared while you were gone, and wanted… I'm terribly sorry, Mallory. I made an error in judgement, I thought for sure if you could put the pieces together we'd have a sensible— But alas, it wasn't to be. I was determined to wrap this all up, move it away from me – from us – so you'd continue to like me.' His head dropped, cat ears sparkling in the air. 'Do you still like me? Please say you do. You're all I have left in the world.'

'Is someone making you do this?' Mallory's eyes were filled with tears.

'I serve no one,' Theodore said, straightening up, but it

was not his usual voice. It was familiar in a disquieting way Cornelia couldn't focus on. 'I serve nothing. I simply right the wrongs.'

'Why did you dig up those bodies?'

'I can't say.'

'What are the bodies being used for?'

'I don't know.'

'Where are the bodies right now?'

'I can't say.'

'Did you have anything to do with their deaths?'

He hesitated, mouth working, shaping something terrible. 'I can't say.'

'Theodore,' Diana whispered. 'No.'

'It's not what it sounds like!'

'It is.' Mallory struggled to her feet. Tears dripped off her chin, but her voice was steady. 'It *is* what it sounds like. We can't let you continue like this. We've ignored and explained away so much in the last year and a bit, but we know there's so much you aren't telling us. That you haven't told us. I don't trust you anymore. I *can't* trust you.'

She reached into her pocket and pulled out the empty ghostlight, the one that came free with Elisabella.

'Mallory,' Theodore pleaded. 'Don't do this.'

'I'm sorry, Theo,' she whispered.

'Mallory, *no*—'

He threw himself to the side as the ghostlight glowed from within.

'Theodore Wyatt, I seal you away,' Mallory said.

'No. No, no, no. No!'

He pushed back on her and Mallory staggered, a static pulse destabilising her.

Diana took her free hand, and Cornelia took Diana's, forming a chain of witches against the ghost that had been their friend, their mentor, their colleague, for so many years.

Cornelia reached into their pocket for the salt packets they'd carried around since the day Theodore had come back wrong.

It felt horrible to think it, but there it was. Cornelia cursed the way they'd let it slide, the way they'd accepted his return to old form as though the period where he'd acted strangely hadn't happened.

They weren't sure they could take much more betrayal.

Cornelia threw the salt in an arc and it rained down on top of Theodore. Instead of dampening his power, he writhed at the contact, his features changing and morphing into something else. Into *someone* else.

Gone was the sweet-faced man they'd known for the better part of a decade, in his place something twisted and wrong.

'What's happening to his face?' Cornelia asked, taking a step back.

'Now's not the fucking *time* for insults,' Theodore snarled.

A crackle of static flashed in the air, sparking, and Cornelia waved a hand to block it, glad their boots had rubber soles.

Mallory stepped forward.

'No, Mallory, we have to—' Cornelia started, but Theodore had gone blue with effort.

Sparks rained down on his head as he edged away. It was done by the time Cornelia realised what he was doing – he entered the witchlight crystal in his microscope, and vanished.

Around them, glass shattered. Every witchlight in the basement exploded as soon as he disappeared, the static he'd been holding back discharging at once. The ghostlight in Mallory's hand shattered too, and Cornelia, Diana and Mallory huddled together instinctively for what felt like hours until the crackling quieted, and there were no more sounds of glass falling.

'I sure hope there's insurance on this place,' Cornelia said, pulling away.

The windows on the basement had blown out too, and the glass in the iron partition between the research room and the lab.

Mallory had beads of blood dotted on her arms where she'd tried to protect her face, and she frowned at Cornelia's forehead until they checked. Their hand came away soaked in blood.

'Shit. Do we know where there's a first aid kit? I know you insisted we get one, Mal, I just don't know where...' They trailed off.

Mallory and Diana were staring at them, mouths hanging open.

'What? It's just a surface wound, heads bleed a lot. I'm fine.'

'No,' Mallory said, pointing. 'Behind you.'

FORTY

There were few words in the English language that could elicit as much horror as 'behind you'.

Cornelia turned slowly, trepidation seizing them.

It occurred to them that the air hadn't cooled in Theodore's absence, that there was still a soft crackle of static, and so they were somewhat prepared for what they were about to see.

A short woman with a round, pleasant face stood with her hands folded in front of her. Her clothing was elaborate – Diana probably knew what era it was from, all full skirts and frills and heavy fabrics, her flame-red hair half-loose but neatly pinned. She looked as though she had stepped through time to be there, glancing around her politely as a means of situating herself, avoiding staring.

All Cornelia could think was how much Agatha and Ethel would've loved her.

The only indication that she was dead was the gaping wound in her chest, blood staining the expensive material.

That, and the crackle of static that indicated she was semi-corporeal.

'Hello,' she said politely, realising their attention had shifted to her. She had, evidently, been waiting politely for them to finish being glassed. 'What day is it?'

'Sunday,' Diana said, checking her watch. The glass on it was cracked, the hands frozen. 'Better question, who are you?'

'And where did you come from?' Cornelia added, not sure why they were trying to placate an already placid Samhain ghost. They were already dying soon, this could hardly be worse.

'Rose,' the ghost henceforth known as Rose said. 'My name is Rose.'

'Are you from Wrackton?' Mallory asked.

It was a valid question that wouldn't have been quite as clever had they not seen Elisabella stay in Wickermere. Their collective lack of knowledge about Samhain ghosts was starting to show.

'It was my home.' She folded her arms around herself, her eyes distant. Her fingers, encased in soft satin gloves, traced the edge of her chest wound. 'I've been elsewhere, for some time now. Tell me, where am I? Only, I am not familiar with the custom of shattered glass. Perhaps there is some festival I am unaware of?'

'You're in Wrackton. We had a mishap, don't worry about it,' Diana said, her voice forcefully bright. 'Say, what year do you think it is?'

'I'm not sure, though it can't be much longer than when… It is summer, that is for sure. Perhaps the fifth Bealtaine has just occurred?' Rose looked expectantly between them, but there was a flicker of uncertainty. She knew, based on their outfits and their watches and their horrified faces, that she was not in her own time.

'Translation?' Cornelia whispered.

'I think she's from Ternion time,' Mallory clarified.

'I didn't want a war,' Rose said softly. 'I *didn't* want a war. Is this all that remains of the war? Shattered glass? We had too many moments where we could've turned back, could've stopped it all. But we didn't, and that is my burden to bear. I bore it. I went to the pit and I suffered for it.'

'Do you mean the lake?' Mallory asked, creeping closer.

She had always been the bravest of them when it came to ghosts, though Cornelia supposed they should stop caring about mortality at all. Die now or die later, it was all going to shit no matter what.

'We got you out of the lake yesterday – not on purpose, but you hitched a ride with another ghostlight and… well, here you are.' Mallory splayed her hands, a weak smile on her face. 'Anything you can tell us about yourself would be really helpful at this point. We're private investigators – a sort of detective?'

Rose continued looking at her blankly.

'Police,' she said finally. 'We're like police.'

'I cannot believe you just said that,' Cornelia hissed, scandalised.

Diana elbowed them to be quiet.

Rose's face relaxed in recognition, though her eyes kept darting over their clothes, their hair, their surroundings.

'The lake was meant to be a last resort,' Rose said. 'She fucked us all over. Said this was the way to go about it, and we followed. But her plans… we had no idea. I promise you we had no idea.'

Cornelia looked to the other two for confirmation that they had no idea what Rose was talking about.

'Why don't we back up, try to establish what you remember. Just to be clear, as we have experience in this before – you are aware that you are dead?' Mallory said delicately.

'Yes,' Rose said, an unhappy laugh escaping her. 'I know.'

Her hand fluttered to the gaping wound on her chest. Her heart was missing.

'Okay, good! So you are what we would refer to as a Samhain ghost.'

'Samhain ghost,' she repeated. 'Oh, the Hallowed Ones?'

'Yes, but as they're – *you're* – usually formed on Samhain, we kept the name around,' Cornelia explained.

'I see,' Rose said.

'And you said you were from Wrackton?'

She nodded.

'Are you Occult?'

She laughed then. 'Yes. I'm a witch. Mother Morrigan, I haven't heard that question in a long time. To be anything else in Wrackton of all places, with the… with the War… Oh, but I didn't want there to be… They're all dead. They're all dead. They're ALL DEAD,' she screamed.

The Undetectables took both a collective and an involuntary step back.

'Okay, you're a witch, you're from Wrackton,' Mallory said, her voice steady and soothing. 'What else can you tell—'

'She's a rotten, DECEIVING little BITCH,' Rose shouted. She pointed at them. 'One of you will betray the others. That's what happens. You cannot have three. You cannot have trust. You cannot have anything other than DECEIT.'

'We do have a tried-and-tested system of worship that

suggests that's not really the case,' Cornelia started, but Mallory silenced them with a look.

'And this betrayer, what can you remember about them? We're asking as we can probably find out some things about you, maybe find out if you have any ancestors in the area, that kind of thing,' Mallory said.

Rose raised her hands to her hair and pulled hard on the curls that cascaded over her shoulders, her face crumpled with despair.

'She was my best friend. It was all her idea. Stay the course. Be the best. Make it go away. End it all. We didn't start it, but we planned to finish it. She wanted glory, I didn't. We didn't want anything like it. She made us… Oh.' Rose sobbed. 'My sister. I don't think she knows. I think she died not knowing it wasn't her fault. Help me tell her it wasn't my fault. KATIE,' she howled.

She sank to her knees, sobbing, as a static charge built around her. Cornelia's hand tightened around their last salt packet, unwilling to take their eyes off Rose.

It seemed beyond belief that this was the third time the Undetectables had to talk down a devastated semi-corporeal person who was – understandably – emotionally volatile and could potentially blow the roof off Broadwick Mansion, but what Theodore had said about coincidences still rang true – three was a pattern.

Cornelia was also not morally opposed to the roof being blown off, but they'd have to immediately find a new place to sleep, and Cornelia didn't think any of them were up for that after the last few days.

'Right. You have a sister, you were betrayed by someone you thought was a friend, you've been dead a long time, what else can you tell us? Your family name, perhaps?'

Rose thought for an impossibly long time.

'Vane,' she said.

'Wait,' Mallory said. 'Rosemary Vane?'

'Oh, Goddess,' Diana breathed.

'Yes,' Rose said. 'That's me.'

'We know your sister. She's been looking for you a long time,' Mallory said.

'Good. I didn't think anyone would remember me as Rosemary,' Rose said. There was a dreamy look in her eyes, one that made Cornelia feel apprehensive.

'What would they remember you as?'

'I was Rosemary, or Rose, for the longest time, until the War started. But perhaps I am better known as Blair.'

PERIMORTEM V

????

She was one of those people who carried herself with poise, with elegance. It was admirable, anyone could say that about her and be right. Detective Inspector Alyssa O'Sullivan would never let anyone see her rattled. But there were tears in her eyes as she stood over the body, her heart pounding. That was the best part, when the nightmare refuses to end.

Even better: when it restarts as though it never really ended – the point where she's realised it never *would* end. That nightmares are nightmares because they hang onto you, clutching your ribcage, hitching a ride to consume your soul.

The body lay on the ground in front of her, eyes open, staring ahead. She was alone and she touched the body almost reflexively. Funny how training can go out the window when the situation calls for it. She lifted the hem of the body's shirt to reveal a pattern too sickening to look at directly, circles and lines that made the viewer nauseated, that made them feel as though they were looking at something more horrific than the murder before them.

There was no blood, save a little dribble on the body's chin.

DI O'Sullivan swallowed, and reached for her phone. She was not an expressive crier, she kept her wails and her exclamations close to her chest.

But she could not stop the hiss that escaped her when her eyes alighted on it, tucked beneath the body's hand.

The witchlight, still warm, clutched under stiffening fingers.

ACKNOWLEDGEMENTS

This is always the easiest part to write of any book. TU3 has been an enormous undertaking for me in so many ways, and so my thanks:

To my agent Zoë Plant, for everything. To George 'Spreadsheet' Sandison – time almost broke us, but at least we kept our sense of humour 'til the end. (I think). To Julia Lloyd for smashing it out of the park once again with another cracker of a cover. To Kabriya and Charlotte, for conversations with no statutes of limitation. To the Titan sales teams, and especially to Jacq and the Gill Hess team, for getting my books into eager hands, and to everyone in Titan who played a part, from typesetting to copyediting and beyond – thank you.

To Amy (especially for all your help with Diana's hearing), Deirdre, Fran, Meg and Robin – thank you for holding me together in the ways that you do. A massive thank you to Darcey, for all your help with Stella and for being so lovely! Any mistakes I've made are entirely my own. To Nik, for being the number one TU series fan, and for helping me with a

Cornelia question that bordered on spoiler (we made the right call). To Axel, who showed me the way almost a decade ago. (I'm forever delighted to be your nonbinary child.)

I've known Cornelia was nonbinary from the moment they walked into my head, but I didn't know when, exactly, we'd get to the point of saying it, or how they'd feel about it. We live in a time of trans scapegoating and of transness being treated as something to fear, when that couldn't be further from the truth. The world I live in is populated with trans and nonbinary people and it is beautiful because of it. I believe it is worthwhile to be yourself in whatever way it is safe to do so. Cornelia is for you, they are for me, and they are for everyone who came before us and who is yet to embrace themselves in future. Thank you, all of you, for existing.

To all the booksellers and bookshops and book clubs around the world who have championed The Undetectables series and shoved them into the hands of readers, you are, as always, a huge part of why I get to keep writing. To my readers, and everyone who has written me a message or said a kind word about my books. And to you, holding this. Thank you.

Finally, to Michael. There aren't adequate words to thank you, except for this: up top, Big Dog.

ABOUT THE AUTHOR

Courtney Smyth is a caffeine fiend, one web search away from their newest fixation, and, most relevantly, a writer of stories. Their work has also appeared in anthologies *Into Chaos* and *The Last Five Minutes of a Storm*, and in *Paper Lanterns Literary Journal*. They have been writing about ghosts, demons and murders since they were ten and have no plans to stop. They are from Dublin, currently living and writing in the West of Ireland with their partner and their pet corn snake, Steve.

@cswritesbooks
courtneysmythwrites.com